WHO ATTACKED THE BABYSITTER?

Why had the intruder come after Marissa? Was it something to do with Teddy Ryerson, or the Ryerson family as a whole? Was it something to do with there being a baby-sitter? That made no sense at all, but these two bookended crimes over twenty years couldn't be completely random, could they?

No. They were too similar. A knife wielded against a babysitter at the very same house. There had to be a connection. But what? Why?

Emma . . . Jamie had wrestled all night with whether she should alert her sister to what had happened. Emma had already mentioned that she didn't like the Ryersons. She still seemed slightly bemused by the fact that Teddy and Serena were grown and that Teddy had twins of his own.

Her gut told her not to tell Emma anything that had happened last night. But on the other hand, if Emma found out from some other source, someone who might not know her full history . . . Jamie had a vision of Emma yelling, *"It's his eyes . . . his eyes!"* and inwardly shuddered. . . .

Books by Nancy Bush

Published by Kensington Publishing Corp.

THE
BABYSITTER

NANCY
BUSH

ZEBRA BOOKS
KENSINGTON PUBLISHING CORP.
www.kensingtonbooks.com

ZEBRA BOOKS are published by

Kensington Publishing Corp.
119 West 40th Street
New York, NY 10018

All Kensington titles, imprints, and distributed lines are available at special quantity discounts for bulk purchases for sales promotion, premiums, fund-raising, educational, or institutional use.

Special book excerpts or customized printings can also be created to fit specific needs. For details, write or phone the office of the Kensington Sales Manager: Attn.: Sales Department. Kensington Publishing Corp., 119 West 40th Street, New York, NY 10018. Phone: 1-800-221-2647.

Zebra and the Z logo Reg. U.S. Pat. & TM Off.

First Printing: July 2020
ISBN-13: 978-1-4201-5075-9
ISBN-10: 1-4201-5075-8

ISBN-13: 978-1-4201-5076-6 (eBook)
ISBN-10: 1-4201-5076-6 (eBook)

10 9 8 7 6 5 4 3 2 1

Printed in the United States of America

Chapter One

Then . . .

Jamie stuck her head under the coffee table, with its deep sides that made it damn near impossible to reach the tossed cards from the Memory Game she'd been playing with Serena and Teddy, the Ryerson twins. They were in bed for good now, God willing. The seven-year-olds had had their last drink of water, their last story, their last *everything*. Jamie was honestly sick of them. She'd been babysitting them for *eons* and she was supposed to be at the Stillwell party tonight. She'd been invited by Cooper Haynes himself. Coolest guy in school. He'd smiled at her this afternoon and asked if she was going to be there. And she was only a sophomore and wouldn't be able to drive until the summer, but he'd specifically asked *her* even though he was in her sister Emma's class.

Emma was supposed to babysit the twins tonight. Jamie had begged and begged her older sister to take over for her. She'd promised her *anything*. Emma had wanted to know what the big deal was. To her, the party at the Stillwells' was just another senior get-together for her class, of which she'd been to *kazillions*.

But Cooper Haynes had invited her, Jamie Whelan, specifically!

"Please, please, please," she'd begged Emma, dramatically prostrating herself on her sister's bedroom carpet.

"Jesus, what's the big deal? There'll be another one," Emma said.

Jamie would rather cut out her tongue than admit that Cooper had asked her to go. Emma would laugh or make fun of her. Emma and Cooper were friends, had once even gone together for a short time when they were in junior high. If Emma knew of Jamie's secret, secret crush, it would be all over the school.

"I want to go to this one," Jamie said, rising into a squat, her hands in front of her in prayer. "Just, *please*, Emma. Take over for me."

"Mom won't let you go to a senior party anyway."

"She doesn't have to know. And I'll get there somehow."

"Oh, you will?" A smile played on Emma's lips. She was the rebel and Jamie was the good girl, as far as their mother knew. And it was true, up to a point. Jamie worked on her grades and stayed in and babysat for extra cash because the Whelan family was damn near dirt-poor since Dad had his midlife crisis and took up with that bitch with the fake boobs and big hair and houseboat on the Columbia River. Jamie and Emma had visited him exactly once and it had been an epic fail.

"What do you need from me to make this happen, Emma?" Jamie asked, rising to her feet and shifting into business mode.

"Fifty dollars."

"*What?*"

"I've got some things to buy." She lifted a shoulder and started to walk away.

Jamie swore a blue streak in her mind, then said quickly, "Twenty. It's all I've got."

"You've got scads in your savings account."

"I'm saving for college. I've got thirty. Please, Emma."

"I've got things to do and wouldn't be there till nine at the earliest, so . . ."

"I'll babysit them till nine, and you can take over."

"I don't know . . ." She made a face.

"Fine. I'll get you fifty!"

"This must be really important," Emma said, turning back to give Jamie a long look.

"I can't be the total nerd any longer," Jamie said, the truth popping out. Emma's popularity was legendary and Jamie, who'd finally gotten her braces off—which had taken for-effing-ever, thank you, God—had grown her hair out from the short bob Mom had given her since she was three, and was working on matching a little bit of that popularity. "Take my place at nine and I'll give you the fifty and all the money from tonight's babysitting, too."

"Seriously?"

"Seriously."

It had taken Emma a few more agonizing moments to consider, but then she'd finally agreed. "But if I get killed, it's on you," she said.

"Yeah, yeah."

She was referring to the two babysitters who'd been attacked that summer, one in Vancouver, apparently the victim of a masked robber who'd stabbed her during his getaway, and the other falling from a rooftop deck in Gresham, where she'd supposedly been trying to meet her boyfriend. Neither of those places was close to their River Glen neighborhood, a suburb of Portland's westside.

Now it was eight forty-six. Jamie had checked the Ryersons' mantel clock before ducking under the table. About fifteen minutes to go. She had a brush in her purse to fix her hair and some lipstick and mascara. The Stillwell house, really an estate, was only about twenty blocks north of the Ryersons', down a long, hedged driveway so the neighbors, noise, and cops wouldn't be aware of the party, fingers crossed.

As Jamie started to slide out from under the table, a shadowy figure standing to one side caused her to shriek and smack her head on the table's underside.

"Shii—ouch!" She just managed to stop herself from swearing a blue streak when she saw it was Serena standing there in a pale nightgown. "Serena. What are you doing up?"

Jamie shimmied out from under the table and stood up, rubbing her head. Irked, she frowned down at the little girl.

"I had a dream that I was dying."

"Oh, honey." Jamie's annoyance dissipated, and she gently put her hands on the girl's shoulders, turned her around, and slowly marched her back to bed. "You're fine. Your mom and dad are going to be back soon. Just try to sleep."

"Is your friend coming?" Her voice wavered.

Jamie had told the twins that Emma might spell her and not to be scared if they woke up to find her there instead of Jamie. "My sister. You've had her babysit you before."

"I want Mommy," she sobbed, clinging to Jamie's leg.

"Don't be a baby." Teddy's voice rang from down the hallway to his sister's room, which made Serena cry even harder.

It took Jamie till after nine to calm Serena down and get Teddy, who hadn't wanted to give up chastising Serena, back to bed. Their mother had assured Jamie that the twins would sleep soundly because they'd been to the Oaks Park amusement center for the day and ridden on all the rides. Nadine Ryerson had said, "Don't worry, they'll sleep like the dead."

Ha.

Jamie half-expected one or the other or both of the twins to get up again, but they seemed to have finally settled down for good. But then, where was Emma? She was late. And because neither Jamie nor Emma owned a cell phone—they were too expensive and Mom didn't trust that they wouldn't lose them—Jamie was stuck waiting for her sister to show up. She paced the living room floor, her eyes on the clock above the stone mantel. It felt like the minute hand wasn't moving at all.

Where the hell was she?

At nine-thirty Emma finally appeared, knocking on the door so loudly, Jamie flew to answer it in a panic. "Don't wake the kids!" she shushed angrily.

Emma just pushed her way inside. "You're lucky I'm here at all," she declared, nearly running into Jamie in the process.

"Are you drunk?" Jamie demanded, panicked.

"No. God, no. I'm just . . . pissed."

"What happened?"

"Nothing. Go on to your party. I had to walk from there and it's a long, long way. You owe me. More than what you said."

"Whatever." Jamie was out the door in a flash.

It turned out Emma was right. The twenty blocks or so, half of them up Stillwell Hill, to reach the entrance to the Stillwell estate, felt like forever. Her steps slowed as she climbed to the crest, her steps slowing even further as she headed across the last few yards to the wrought-iron gate set between towering laurel hedges. The gate was open, but now that she was here, she was reluctant to step foot on the ribbon of tarmac that led to the house. She could see lights at the end of that long drive, but suddenly she felt naked and alone. She desperately needed a girlfriend to be with her, Camryn or Rosie, but their parents would never let them attend an unsupervised senior party either. Maybe Gwen, whose Mom and Dad were like hippies or something and not as concerned with keeping tabs on their daughter's every move, but Gwen was a weirdo and not a real friend anyway.

Jamie hovered by the main road, loathe to walk between the hedges. Now that she was here, she felt like the uninvited. Cooper was the only one who'd really asked her to come, and what if he wasn't here? She should have asked Emma about him, but that would have given the game away, and Emma would know and tease her mercilessly and probably tell Cooper to boot, so that was a no-go.

What to do . . . ?

The answer was taken away from her when she heard the roar of a sparking engine and saw car taillights flash red far ahead. A car was backing out and turning toward her. Moments later, a dark blue Mustang, Race Stillwell's car, came right at her, headlights blinding. She would have melted into the hedges if she'd been able, but as it was, she was pinned in the twin beams, frozen like a deer.

The Mustang's engine rumbled beside her. The passenger window rolled down, and Dug Douglas threw out a cigarette butt. It was late October, dry as a bone, and Jamie immediately stamped out the ember even though it had landed on the asphalt.

"What're yer doin'?" Dug slurred.

A million excuses raced across Jamie's brain, but in the moment, she just said, "Walking."

"Go on up to the party," Race said, leaning past Dug to get a hard look at her. "Who're you?"

"Emma's sister. Jamie."

"Well, there's booze up there. Help yourself. We gotta little thing to do," Race said. "Later."

And then they pulled onto the street and roared away.

Jamie trudged the rest of the way toward the house. SUVs, sedans, and one or two minivans that had to be parents' cars were parked along the drive. She heard the thump of music from outside, the bass resonating inside her, as she let herself in the front door. Kids were standing around holding red Solo cups full of drinks. They eyed her as she walked by, into the kitchen. All her desire to attend, the raging torrent that had been building inside her ever since Cooper asked if she was going, was leaching away, and she was almost embarrassed to be there. For hours, all she'd thought about was being at this party. Now all she wanted to do was turn tail and leave.

But not before finding out where Cooper was.

"Beer?" a guy in the class ahead of her, Ken somebody, asked. He was standing by the keg, leaning an elbow on the counter.

"Sure."

It was a relief to be treated as if she had a right to be there.

He straightened to pour her a foamy capped cup of beer. She accepted it and stood to one side for a few moments. Icky Vicky, one of the girls in Emma's friend group, was making out with her boyfriend in the corner by the back windows. His hands were running all over her and she was riding his thigh. There was a lot of heavy breathing, smacking noises, and moaning.

Half-embarrassed, Jamie sidled out of the kitchen and up some back stairs, hoping Vicky wouldn't notice her. If Vicky recognized Jamie, she'd probably make a big deal of it, because she was fierce about keeping the line separated between grades. She'd pretty much slept with all the senior guys when she was a sophomore and had been excoriated by all the senior girls for poaching, so she wasn't about to let any underclassmen get away with what she already had.

Jamie wandered the second floor, looking for Cooper, then went back downstairs and checked out all the rooms down there as well.

"Looking for something?" It was Race's younger brother, Deon. He was a junior, one year behind Race. And he was smaller and meaner and looking at Jamie with cold suspicion.

"I was hoping Gwen was here. Gwen Winkelman?"

"Don't know her."

Of course he did. Everybody knew Gwen. She'd made a name for herself by reading fortunes and selling crystals. Normally, Jamie steered clear of her one-time grade school friend because she was so odd, but now she was desperate to make a connection.

"I don't see her," Jamie said, moving away. She yelped in surprise when his hand shot out and he dragged her to him. His other hand went right to her crotch. "Hey!" she snapped, immediately grabbing that hand and flinging it away from herself.

"Babe, you asked for it." He leered, white teeth gleaming.

She wrenched herself out of his grasp and practically ran out the front door, shaken. No Cooper. She stood at the front of the house, drew several deep breaths, then looked up at the white, three-quarter moon. October 21, or maybe 22 by now, and all she wanted to do was be home in bed.

And then Gwen suddenly appeared. Running up the driveway, laughing, her long, brown braid swinging behind her, a guy chasing her whom Jamie didn't immediately recognize. "Hey, Jamie!" she said in surprise and delight. "What're you doing here?"

Now she saw the guy was their classmate, Nathan Farland, and he said, "Where are your books? There must be some test to study for."

"Shut up," Gwen said good-naturedly. "Jamie doesn't study all the time." She grabbed Jamie's arm to propel her back inside. "What're you having? Beer? Nah. Let's have some vodka. Nate's got some."

"Sure," he said.

Jamie really didn't want to go back inside with them, but she didn't have a ride home, and it would feel like a lot longer to get to her house alone in the dark than the trek she'd just made to get here. She'd had some hazy idea about cadging a ride, but that hadn't been looking so good until

Nate appeared. He had a driver's license and an older Toyota Celica.

Back in the foyer, Jamie made certain to steer clear of Deon Stillwell. She hung close to Nate and Gwen, who was really being nice, which made Jamie feel kind of bad for thinking she was such a weirdo.

Hours slid by. At one o'clock, Race Stillwell returned alone, his Mustang roaring back up the drive just as Jamie, Gwen, and Nate were getting ready to leave. No Cooper. Jamie had consumed one beer and two glasses of vodka and Sprite, but the slight buzz she'd gotten had already worn off.

Race was wild-eyed as he burst into the room.

"What the fuck?" Deon muttered. He was waaaayyy loaded and staggering by then.

"Shit. The cops. Get everybody out. *Everybody out!*!" His bellow reached to the upper floor. The smart kids, the ones still sober enough and aware, didn't wait to be asked again. They trampled down the stairs and out of the house, running for their cars. Jamie, Gwen, and Nate did the same. All of them tore down the driveway, nearly rear-ending each other in their haste. Only when he was well away and driving out of town did Nate heave a sigh of relief. "Think we're okay. If the cops come, they won't find us."

"You know where my house is?" Jamie asked. Now she was anxious to be home. Her mom worked graveyard at the hospital, but anything could happen time-wise and she could come home early.

Nate grunted an assent. He dropped Gwen off first at her family's sprawling ranch with the trees adorned with fake Spanish moss and the birdhouses and the whole crazy garden thing. Jamie's house was a two-story Craftsman style with a wide porch and a mostly trimmed yard. Mom was death on weeds. After their father's defection, she'd gotten out the edger and beaten back the crabgrass and dandelions and thistles as if her life depended on it. Gardening seemed to be her way to get out her frustrations and put her life in order, and she spent most afternoons working on their grounds before heading to her job.

Jamie lightly ran down the driveway to the back of the house and jogged to the right in front of the detached garage toward the back steps. She was pretty sure Mom was still out, but she didn't want to explain herself just in case. She picked up the gnome near the bottom stair, the only whimsical piece to the yard, saved by Emma when Mom had tried to throw it out in her never-ending need to put things right in the yard. She shook the gnome and the key fell into her hand. Quickly, she tiptoed up the outdoor steps, turned the key in the lock, and let herself inside, grimacing at the soft creak the door made. She paused. Nothing but the familiar tick of the clock on the wall.

Hurrying upstairs, she passed her sister's room. Emma's clothes were tossed about, some hanging on the chair, others on the bed, a pair of jeans on the floor. Mom's door was closed, but it always was.

Jamie's room was next to Emma's, which was at the end of the hall. She let herself inside, slipped off her shoes, ripped off her clothes, and slid into an oversize T-shirt with a picture of the Hollywood sign on the front before climbing beneath the covers. She was wide awake. Unsettled. She'd given up her babysitting job to find Cooper Haynes and he hadn't even been at Race Stillwell's party. She recalled Deon's hand on her crotch and her blood boiled. She punched the pillow several times, furious with herself and the world as a whole.

Emma was the one who'd scored tonight, which really pissed Jamie off. The Ryersons always stayed out late, which made for good babysitting money, and Emma was reaping the benefits.

Jamie was still awake when she heard the distant sirens.

An auto accident? Her mom was an ER nurse. Saw all kinds of bloody, mangled victims. Ugh.

She covered her head with her pillow.

Brrrinnnggg!

Jamie jumped when the landline down the hall started ringing. Middle of the night. Mom?

Reluctantly, she climbed out of her warm bed and scurried down the hall to her mom's bedroom and the phone. She opened the door and nearly ran into her mother, who was standing by the side of the bed, nearly right in front of her.

"Oh, God!" Jamie gasped, surprised, as Mom, who was still fully dressed apart from her shoes, was reaching for the phone.

"Hello . . ." she answered, hitching her chin to let her know she was handling things and Jamie could go back to bed.

Jamie, who'd hoped she wouldn't have to explain why she was home and Emma wasn't, turned back toward her room.

"Oh, God . . . oh my God!" Mom gasped.

"What? What?" Jamie stopped cold, her hand to her throat.

"Okay, I'm . . . on my way. Right now. Right now!"

Mom slammed down the phone, reeling.

"What is it?" Jamie cried.

"It's Emma. She's been hurt. Attacked. The police are there." She whirled around, staring at the floor, searching for her shoes, grabbing her coat.

"At the Ryersons'?" Jamie's voice was a squeak, but she was shrieking inside.

"Yes. Emma's at the hospital."

Stumbling into her shoes, Mom was heading out, but Jamie said, "I'm going with you," and ran for her clothes.

"I'm not waiting," Mom said, halfway down the stairs.

"Wait! Wait! Please!"

"What are you doing here?" Mom suddenly demanded. "You were babysitting them. What happened?"

"I–I've got on my jacket and jeans." She'd thrown the jacket over her sleeping T-shirt and was hopping on one foot, the other inside her jeans. She grabbed her forgotten socks and sneakers and ran into the hall.

Mom led the way downstairs and Jamie stumbled after her. They raced to the car. Jamie shivered in the passenger seat.

"Is she okay?" she asked in a small voice.

"I don't know. Why weren't you there?" Mom demanded.

"I . . . we traded."

Twenty minutes later, they pulled into River Glen General, Glen Gen to the locals. Jamie was told to stay in the ER waiting room while Mom went through the double doors to the inner cubicles. All Jamie could do was shiver. She'd gone to bed without taking off her makeup, and now, after waiting a few minutes, she found the restroom outside the ER and looked at herself in the mirror. Her makeup had turned to dark smudges below her eyes and she was white-faced. She tried to clean herself up a bit with the end of her little finger and water. When she returned to the ER waiting room, Mom was there, pale and stern.

"You were fixing your makeup?" she demanded in a flinty voice.

"Well, just . . ."

"Your sister's been stabbed in the back and she has a head injury."

"What?" Jamie whispered. Did she mean literally stabbed in the back? "With like . . . a knife?"

"Yes. Someone came into the house and stabbed her."

"Oh . . . God . . . Oh my God. She's gonna be all right, though?" Jamie quavered.

"She's unconscious. They think she hit her head on the mantel as she fell. They've stitched her wound."

"But she's okay?"

"I don't know, Jamie! She hasn't woken up! I just don't understand what happened. Tell me what happened tonight. Tell me everything!"

"Okay . . ." Haltingly, feeling sick with worry, Jamie told her mother about wanting to go to the senior party, bargaining with her sister, leaving the kids with Emma.

Mom's face, already grim, grew grimmer still. "Did you tell the Ryersons?"

"Well, they kind of rushed out and I . . . no, I told Serena and Teddy, and they know Emma."

"You shouldn't have done that."

"I know."

"By the grace of God it wasn't you."

Jamie felt stabbed herself. Right in the heart. She knew Mom was scared. She knew she probably didn't mean it. But it felt like the wrong daughter had been attacked.

They waited in silence. Mom pressed the button on the wall to release the locked doors and went back and forth from the waiting room to the examining cubicles several times. She was with Jamie about an hour later when a doctor she knew came out to see them again. "We've moved her to a room," he said.

"She's still unconscious?" Mom asked.

He nodded.

Mom looked at the floor for a moment. "Okay, I'm taking my daughter home and I'll be right back."

"I want to stay with you," Jamie said, but Mom wasn't listening to her, and they drove home in silence. "Are you mad at me?" Jamie asked weakly when she was getting out of the car.

"I'm not happy with you," Mom said.

"I . . . why weren't you at work?" Jamie deflected. Her mother never got home much before seven a.m.

"Half shift tonight. It was my night off, but they needed me."

Jamie watched her turn the car around and head back toward the hospital, then walked heavily up the stairs to her room and to bed. She lay awake a long time, unable to stop the all-over quivering that afflicted her. Emma's words, that she didn't want to be killed, came back to her. *But it's not my fault,* Jamie thought. *It's not!*

What had happened? Was it that same robber from Vancouver? The one in the ski mask they never caught?

When her mother came back late the following day, Jamie was in the kitchen. She'd made tuna sandwiches and offered one up, but her mother sank onto a chair at the table in silence.

"Mom?" Jamie quavered.

"She came to. She's having trouble speaking. Can't focus very well."

"Ohhh . . ." Jamie felt tears gather behind her eyes, and her nose got hot. "But she's going to be okay. . . ."

Mom said tightly, "Yes," in a way that made Jamie's blood run cold. She'd seen that determined resolution in her mother once before, when she'd nodded that yes, the marriage was going to last, almost as if her mother was going to make it so by sheer determination.

But it hadn't happened for her marriage . . . and it didn't happen for Emma either.

She came home three days later, walking with a shuffle, as if she'd forgotten how it was done, silent as a tomb, lost in a distant world outside of reality. Mom took care of her during the day while Jamie was at school, and Jamie was in charge of her at night.

Emma Whelan, one of the most popular girls in school, Jamie's outgoing older sister, was gone. In her place was the special-needs woman with the dark memory that would rise up almost every night into shouting screams that Jamie would try to soothe away.

"I see his eyes!" she would cry. "I see his eyes!"

And she would say it and say it and say it until she fell back into exhaustion.

After three years of it, Jamie eloped with the first guy she met at community college. She rode on the back of his motorcycle to her new life in Los Angeles, leaving Emma in her mom's care. Even though Emma's nightly fits had subsided by that time, she still was childlike enough to need some supervision. Jamie came to realize that her mother expected her to help out indefinitely, but when Emma was well enough to dress and feed herself and work part-time at Theo's Thrift Shop, Jamie left.

Irene Whelan never forgave her youngest daughter, and Jamie never forgave herself.

Chapter Two

Now . . .

Come home.

Jamie sat straight up in bed, heart pounding, half awake, fumbling for the light switch.

She'd heard the words plain as day. In her mother's voice.

The light switched on, flooding her bedroom with warm, yellow illumination. She could see the worn, marred chest of drawers at the end of her bed, with its untidy array of makeup items, ones she'd used, ones she'd set aside to throw away.

No one there. The room was empty.

Her pulse still rocketing, she sank back against the pillows, eyes wide open. She was no stranger to fear. She'd lived with it ever since the babysitting attack eighteen years earlier.

Five a.m. Too early to call Mom to make sure everything was all right with her.

Maybe it had something to do with Emma.

Jamie was swept once more by her age-old guilt. More than half her life had passed since her sister had been changed forever. Closing her eyes, she drew in a shuddering breath and blocked out the memory, but it was etched into the curves and whorls of her brain, never to be forgotten or even diminished. She could push it away, but it was never gone. Just out of reach every time she sought to kill it entirely.

Throwing back the covers, she jumped out of bed, grabbing up the robe she'd tossed over the end bedstead. She walked to the window and stared out. Beneath the yellowish streetlights, she could see the roofs of other apartment buildings and the cluster of other residences, houses, and condos, all jammed together in this part of Los Angeles. Wires overhead. The beat of helicopter rotors seemingly a daily occurrence. The roads and alleyways crammed with parked cars. She had a designated parking spot for her aging Toyota Camry, but more times than she liked to admit she had to shoo somebody out of her spot. The only positive was that the school where she mainly substitute taught was a quick drive away. She'd been trying to get on full-time, but it was almost fall and she'd yet to be called. Over the summer, she'd been working at a nearby Vietnamese restaurant, serving up banh mi sandwiches and hearty bowls of Pho to make ends meet. She was trying not to dip too far into her meager savings. It was barely enough to get by, and her daughter, Harley, was doing her part by babysitting as well.

Babysitting . . .

Everything came back to the night of Emma's attack. Sometimes Jamie felt a spurt of pure fury. Why hadn't the police caught the guy? There'd been three attacks that summer and fall. One in Vancouver, one in Gresham, and one in River Glen. Maybe they were connected. Maybe they weren't. But why didn't somebody know? Emma's attack was a cold case, but damn it, whoever did it was still out there.

"Emma deserved better," she muttered, fully aware that she'd run away from the problem.

After a few moments, she crawled back in bed, still in her robe. She drew the lapels up to her chin and watched the digital clock work its way to six. Her cell phone was on the nightstand. She unhooked the charger and picked it up, scrolled through her favorites list. Her mother's number was fourth, just below the two school districts she worked for most often. After that, she had the number for CPK, California Pizza Kitchen, Harley's favorite restaurant, which made great salads along with pizza, one with easy pickups.

She put a call in to her mother and braced herself for the icy reception she was sure to receive. Mom loved Harley and was always eager to see her, whenever Jamie returned to River Glen, which wasn't often. But Jamie's relationship with her mother was fraught. It had been ever since Emma's attack.

The phone went to voice mail. As soon as it clicked on, she cleared her throat and said, "Hey, Mom. It's Jamie. Just wanted to see how things were going." She cringed at the sound of her voice. So light and careful. "I'll call back later."

She hung up and got out of bed again. Shrugging out of her robe, she pulled off her sleep shirt and headed for the shower. She let the hot water stream down her face. In her mind, she pictured how Emma had looked that last year of high school. A cheerleader with a bright smile, glinting blue eyes, and long, lustrous, light brown hair. Her attacker had carved a jagged line down her shoulder blade that looked like a jack-o'-lantern's mouth. The scar had faded, but it was still easy to see. Had he meant to kill her? A murder gone wrong? Emma was running from him and likely slipped and—

A dark, shadowy figure appeared on the other side of the frosted glass.

Jamie shrieked and dropped the soap.

"God, Mom, it's just me," Harley said, half-annoyed. "Sorry."

"It's all right." Her pulse raced.

"Your phone's ringing. It's probably the school."

Harley didn't like it much when Jamie substituted at her school. But then, Harley didn't like much of anything when it came to school. She'd asked to be homeschooled by Jamie. Ha. There was no way Jamie was going to put herself through that living hell. Harley was smart, capable, and tough as nails. Like her father. She just wasn't good at taking directions.

But then, neither was Jamie at her age.

Harley left and Jamie toweled off and hurriedly found her phone, on the bed where she'd tossed it.

It was indeed the school district, and she quickly called back and said she would take the job. It was at Harley's school, of course. Well, too bad. Jamie needed to put food on the table. Paul Woodward might have been Harley's father, but he was more of a teenager than his daughter could ever think of being.

"Her name'll be Harley," he'd insisted, christening her after the motorcycle company, Harley-Davidson. Paul had been a motorcycle freak from the get-go, who'd moved Jamie and his young daughter from place to place around Los Angeles, where he'd attempted to be a stuntman. Jamie had worked as a waitress and finished up her aborted college career with night classes, finishing her fifth year literally weeks before Paul's death on the 405 freeway. Paul had pooh-poohed her outrage at the motorcycles that would drive between the cars during traffic tangles, maniacally changing lanes, careless of when the stalled cars would start moving again. "It's legal," he kept saying.

And then he'd become a victim of that very same thing. Clipping a car as it suddenly slowed, unable to stop himself from flipping end over end to his death.

Spooky Karma.

Jamie quickly dressed and called to her daughter as she headed out the door to her car. When Harley climbed in and learned Jamie was subbing at her school, she groaned. "Tell me you're not in my classroom."

"I'm not in your classroom."

"Good."

Jamie squeezed the Camry into a spot in the school lot. She only had five more payments on it. That would help.

Briefly, she thought of the house she'd grown up in, the one Mom had won in the divorce. It had been in her father's family for years, but her dad lost it when he drifted away with his girlfriend. He'd been a ghost in Jamie's life ever since Emma's attack. His perfect Emma was broken, and he'd gone so far as saying they were all cursed. At least he hadn't blamed just Jamie.

Harley was silent as they climbed out of the car. Fifteen years old and moody as hell. She and Jamie had always had a bit of a push-and-pull relationship, but the last few years had been a living nightmare. Jamie, aware of how difficult those years were, was giving her daughter lots of space. She loved her fiercely, but the ingratitude of youth sometimes caused words to fail her.

Jamie purposely let Harley walk ahead of her so her daughter wouldn't be seen entering with her mother. But today Harley decided to hang back, her steps slowing, almost as if she were waiting for Jamie to catch up.

They reached the double doors together. Harley made no move to open them, so Jamie, aware that students were coming up the steps behind them, clasped a handle.

"Mom," Harley said, in that tone that bodes serious stuff is about to be revealed.

Jamie's pulse sped up again. She looked into the anxious face of her daughter. Her heart clutched. "Yeah?"

"I had a weird nightmare. Grandma was standing at the door to her house and saying something I couldn't hear."

"My mom?" The hairs on the back of Jamie's arms lifted.

"I think it was . . . 'come home.'"

Jamie's ears buzzed. She felt faint. She could see the same image of her mother, as if Harley had planted it in front of her eyes.

"Mom! You okay? Mom?"

"Yeah, yeah." Jamie drew a breath. "I'm fine. I gotta . . . make a call. You go ahead."

"Jesus. You're freaking me out!"

"Just . . . give me a minute."

Harley threw her an angry, frightened look as Jamie stumbled back down the stairs, breaking through a clutch of girls who called hello to Harley. She shoved her hand into the purse slung over her shoulder, scrabbling for her cell. Pulled out the phone.

One missed call.

Mom.

How hadn't she heard it?

She punched in the number and it rang and rang and finally went to voice mail. She clicked off, feeling like she was having an out-of-body experience.

There was a message, she realized belatedly.

Heart beating heavily, she pushed the button. She was oblivious to the noise surrounding her, the students parting around her as she stood on the grass by the flagpole, the sea of faces blurring as if in an impressionistic landscape.

"Hi, Jamie. You should come home. Mom's dead," Emma's voice said matter-of-factly. "You'd better come home. The po-po's here. Mom's dead. And I'm gonna need help."

Chapter Three

It took two weeks for Jamie to put things together, sell her already secondhand furniture, ship necessary items to River Glen, and generally wrap up her life in Los Angeles. When she was finished, she was surprised at how little there really was to do to effect the move. She'd thought Harley might object to being yanked out of school when the school year had barely begun, but she was completely sanguine and almost eager for the move, if you could even use the word "eager" when describing the teenager. Resistant, recalcitrant, suspicious, and reluctant were better adjectives.

However, Jamie had overheard a snippet of conversation between Harley and a friend, and it appeared that a boy Harley had been interested in had been seen with one of Harley's friends. "It doesn't matter, I'm leaving," Harley had told the person on the other end of the call. "They can do whatever the hell they want."

So maybe that was the reason Jamie hadn't heard one word of flak. As soon as she'd announced that they were moving back to Oregon, Harley had started packing up, as if she'd just been waiting for her mother to make that decision.

They stuffed the Camry to the gills and drove straight through, almost sixteen hours from Los Angeles to River

Glen, taking a few bathroom stops and two turnoffs for fast food drive-throughs. Harley, who was flirting with vegetarianism, had fallen on her Big Mac like a ravenous wolf, and Jamie had hidden a faint smile and done the same. They were in crisis, of a sort. They could get back to being their better selves once they were home.

Home.

As the miles passed beneath the Camry's balding tires, Jamie's thoughts hovered around her mother and Emma and the events of eighteen years earlier. The guilt she'd felt upon leaving, which had been a constant companion, was magnified a thousand times. Though she knew none of it was her fault, like always, she couldn't quite make herself believe it. If she hadn't wanted to go to the Stillwell party so badly, if she hadn't switched her babysitting job with Emma, if she hadn't raced off to her new life with Paul so eagerly, almost maniacally, maybe all their lives would have been substantially better.

Except now Mom was dead. She'd died on the very night Jamie—and Harley, apparently—had received those eerily creepy messages of her death. Irene Whelan was a victim of heart failure, according to Emma, who was very short on serious information. Jamie managed to connect with Theo Reskett, from the Thrift Shop, but she, too, had been kept in the dark about Mom's deteriorating health.

"Emma never said a word," Theo revealed. "You'd think she would have told me, but she never said a word about your mother."

No one had told Jamie either that Mom was ailing from heart disease and had been for a while.

But then, you didn't ask, did you? You didn't want to know.

That wasn't exactly true . . . she *had* wanted to know. She just hadn't wanted to be sucked into a conversation with

Mom, or even Emma, that would go round and round and only serve to exacerbate her guilt, which it invariably did.

Theo owned and managed Theo's Thrift Shop, Emma's place of employment ever since she'd recovered from the attack that nearly killed her. Since Mom's death, Theo had stepped in and stayed with Emma, though Emma had insisted that she was fully capable of taking care of herself, which was almost true, except it wasn't. Emma left alone was a little like leaving a teenager in charge of a house while the parents were away. Most things might be taken care of, maybe all, but there was also the chance of serious problems erupting, bad choices being made. Emma, nearing forty, had the mind of a twelve-year-old . . . maybe. She'd regressed after the attack and had never fully moved forward developmentally since.

"I see his eyes!" she still cried whenever she was stressed. Mom had told Jamie that much. When she was still living with her sister and mother, Jamie had tried and tried to learn what that meant, but pressing Emma had only increased her fear and distress, and Mom had angrily told Jamie to back off. Though Emma's hysteria had diminished in the years after the attack, her attacks of fear almost gone by the time Jamie left with Paul, they'd never completely disappeared.

Now, as she and Harley reached the outskirts of River Glen, Jamie drew a calming breath. She hadn't seen Emma in nearly two years and was anxious about meeting her again and the living arrangements that would need to be made. Emma needed a caretaker, and that caretaker had been Mom. Now it was going to be Jamie, at least for the time being. It was hard to know what to expect next, impossible to plan. Jamie was going to have to take things day by day.

But one thing was for certain, at least in Jamie's mind, and that was that she was going to fulfill all requirements needed for her to get her teaching license in Oregon. She was duty bound to be in the state at least for a while, and though substituting was fine, Jamie really needed a full-time job. She'd made a point of lamming out all those years ago, but she felt almost glad to "come home" as her mother had requested in her dream . . . and Harley's. . . .

Jamie shook that off. She and Harley had left for Oregon in the early hours of the morning and now, as they reached the outskirts of River Glen, it was about six p.m. Harley, who'd been half-sleeping most of the trip, suddenly straightened in the passenger seat. Her long, dark hair was tangled and she brushed it away from her face. A soft smattering of freckles crossed the bridge of her nose and her blue eyes were intense, a gift from Paul as Jamie's eyes were brown. Paul had called her his "Little Doe" or sometimes, "my brown-eyed girl," other times "Raggedy Bitch," or even more often, "What the fuck, Jamie?" which was how she most often remembered him and their relationship. A sad truth.

"That's the Stillwell place," Jamie said as they drove past the entrance to the long drive that led to Race and Deon Stillwell's home. She'd learned from her friend, Camryn, whose contact with Jamie was mostly through Christmas cards, that both of the Stillwell parents were gone and the two sons had apparently inherited Stillwell Seed and Feed and still lived in the family home.

Harley peered down the long, passing drive that wound through the hedges and out of sight. Only the roof of the house could be glimpsed from the road. "That's where you were the night Emma was stabbed."

"Yes," Jamie said soberly. She always felt that same stab of guilt. Maybe she deserved it. Mom had never hidden her feelings about how she felt about Jamie's switch with Emma, and she'd never been afraid to talk about that night in front of Harley, even when Jamie had protested.

"It's really too bad," said Harley.

Jamie silently agreed.

"But if things hadn't happened that way, I wouldn't be here. You would have never run off with Dad."

Jamie wasn't sure whether that was an olive branch or a jab of some kind. Or maybe it was neither. Just Harley relating what was on her mind. "Hard to say."

They drove into River Glen proper. The downtown area was made up of restored storefronts and a central square. It looked better now, Jamie decided. Fresh paint on the buildings and crosswalks. A new set of traffic lights. Modern city meters that allowed for credit card payments. A row of Kelly-green motorbikes, which she saw were rentals, the kind you could take around town and exchange for another.

"Wow," Harley said in surprise, staring at the bikes.

"I know, right? I thought those were only in large cities, like Portland."

"How old do you have to be?"

"Sixteen, I'm sure, at least. With a license."

"Damn."

Jamie would have berated her for swearing, as she automatically did as a matter of course, but they were turning onto Clifford Street, the street she'd grown up on, and she could see the outlines of her mother's house. She glided to a stop on the opposite side of the street, taking her measure of it. The maple trees lining the street had grown, and the dogwood in the center of the front yard still had a few green leaves. Autumn hadn't gained its harshest grip yet.

An older, green Chrysler minivan was parked on the street in front of the house, its side stenciled with Theo's Thrift Shop and a phone number. Theo was eager to pass off her increased caretaker responsibilities to Jamie.

"Aren't you going to pull in?" Harley's blue eyes regarded Jamie critically.

"Yeah . . ."

"What's wrong?"

"It's just kind of . . . strange."

"'Cause Grandma's gone." She said it with a nod, as if she understood completely, though there was no way for Harley to grasp the intricacies of Jamie's relationship with her mother. Jamie had trouble grasping those complexities herself sometime. She'd resented her mother, especially for blaming her, but she'd loved her, too. Fiercely. Which had made Mom's anger at her all the harder to accept.

"All right," Jamie said now, and cranked the wheel, aiming the Camry toward the driveway. They bumped along the cracked asphalt, and Jamie pulled up in front of the garage door. "Leave everything for now. Let's just go inside."

Harley followed Jamie up the back steps. Jamie wondered if the keys to the house were still in the backyard gnome. One of these days she was going to have to find out, but for now, she just banged on the door.

She heard a dog barking, small, excited yips, and she and Harley exchanged a glance. While Irene Whelan had been alive, there had been no pets.

"Dogs dig up gardens," Mom had said.

"We don't have to have a dog," Jamie had argued. "How about a cat?"

"No."

Even Emma had tried to persuade their mother. "A small dog. I'll make sure it doesn't get into the garden."

"No." Mom had been adamant. Emma had started wheedling, but for once, Mom was proof against Jamie's older sister's tactics. No dog. No cat. No pets.

Emma came to the back door, throwing the lock and yanking it inward. "Hi, Jamie. Hi, Harley," she said in her monotone way.

Emma's hair had grown out to her shoulders, the light brown tresses darker and streaked with gray. She blinked at the bangs hanging in her eyes, but didn't brush them aside. Her shirt was light-and-darker-gray-striped, the tails hanging over a pair of black sweatpants. Her feet were in once-white sneakers that had seen better days.

"Good to see you, Emma," Jamie said, sounding somewhat stiff, not how she wanted to come off.

Harley said, "Hello, I—" just as a black-and-white streak of fluff shot from the front of the house and swarmed their feet, nearly tumbling down the back steps in its haste to greet them. A small dog of indiscriminate breed, Jamie determined, its bright, beady eyes nearly obscured by a thatch of white-and-black fur that fell forward, much like Emma's bangs.

"How cute!" Harley cried, reaching for the animal. It lithely sidestepped her attempts to catch it and started barking madly, as if it suddenly decided it was a watchdog pointing out an intruder.

"That's Dummy," said Emma.

"Dummy?" Jamie repeated.

"He has a stupid name, so I call him Dummy," she explained as they entered the house. "He's Theo's."

"I saw her van outside," said Jamie. Harley was still trying to corral the speeding dog.

"It's the Thrift Shop van," corrected Emma.

"Yes . . . well . . ." Jamie was reminded how everything had to be precise with her sister.

They followed Emma inside, with "Dummy" squirreling after them, squeezing between their legs, nearly tripping them, then shooting forward like a dart when Theo, who'd been in the living room, ducked her head around the corner so they could see her.

"Oh, we've been waiting for you!" she declared, unable to hide her relief. She'd called Jamie several times, urging her to hurry home, but Jamie had been unable to get here any sooner than she had.

Theo's hair was a mop of gray curls and she wore a pair

of half-glasses at the tip of her nose. She was in jeans and a red plaid flannel shirt open over a black T-shirt.

"I saw the van outside," said Jamie.

"That thing is on its last legs. Truly. I don't know what I'm gonna do when it's gone, but that day is coming."

"I'll get you a new one," said Emma.

"I know, doll." Theo smiled indulgently at her.

With what money? Jamie almost asked, but she knew that would be a waste of time. Emma's reality was Emma's reality.

Harley asked, "What's the dog's name?"

"Bartholomew," Theo said. "He charged to the back door before I could catch him."

"Dummy," Emma said with a nod, as if her point were proved.

"He's so cute!" said Harley.

"Yes, well. He's a charmer." Theo made eye contact with the dog and shook her head, which caused "Dummy" to dance around on his hind legs and bark some more. "Oh, stop it," Theo said with a wave of her hand, but she was smiling indulgently all the same. "I've got to go. I laid out some dinner for you. Nothing much. Just wanted you to have something when you got here. That's quite a drive, isn't it? I'm no good in a car that long."

"I'm no good in a car that long," repeated Emma.

Bartholomew had started growling, but Jamie thought it might be a good-natured, playful kind of noise. At least she hoped it was.

"Come here, you," Theo said, swiftly moving to grasp the dog's collar before he could shoot away, which he'd definitely gathered himself to do. She dragged him forward until she could get her arms around him. "Okay, now. Stop wiggling, you little beast." Over her shoulder as she headed toward the front door she said, "I'm going to leave and give you all some peace."

"You're going to leave us?" Emma asked, alarmed.

"Your sister's here now, Emma." Theo regarded Emma soberly, making eye contact. "I'll see you at the store."

"But you're coming back?"

"No . . . not here, to your house. Jamie and her daughter are here. I'm sorry, I've forgotten your name." She peered at Harley, who was still enamored with the dog.

"Harley," said Jamie.

"Oh, yeah. Hi," said Harley.

"Harley. How could I forget? I won't forget again. It's memorable. I gave the lawyer your number. I told you that, right? I have his number on my desk and I'll text it to you."

"He called me," Jamie assured her. "I'm meeting with him on Monday."

"Oh, good." She hesitated, holding the dog close to her side as he was wont to wriggle free. "You need anything else . . . ?"

"I think we're okay. Thanks, Theo," Jamie said, meaning it.

She gave Jamie a sad smile. "It's been a hard month," she admitted. "Take care."

When she was gone, there was a moment of silence. Harley was looking through the front windows wistfully, her eyes on the dog. Emma seemed kind of shell-shocked. Clearly she hadn't expected Theo to leave her with, well, a family that were mostly strangers to her.

She swiped at her bangs, said, "Mom always cut my hair."

"I'll get you to a stylist," Jamie said.

"I can do it," said Harley. "I can cut your bangs and trim up your hair."

"Since when?" asked Jamie.

"Since . . . about now. I've cut some girls' hair at school."

"I don't think—"

"Okay," said Emma, and walked toward the small dining set off the kitchen.

"Right now?" Harley was surprised.

"No time like the present," Emma said succinctly. Another Mom-ism.

Harley looked happy. "Okay."

"Wait. Maybe we should just try the bangs first?" Jamie suggested, seeing this was going to happen.

"I can do it," Harley said again, a bit more belligerently, following after Emma.

Jamie couldn't help glancing at the tabletop, unerringly finding the place where she'd carved her initials, JW, into the maple top. Mom had tried to sand them off, but even with her ministrations they were still visible. A stupid, childish whim that had caused one of their huge fights.

Emma said now, "It's still there," and Jamie looked up to realize her sister's eyes had followed her gaze. "You should talk to Mom about it. It will make you feel better."

Jamie's pulse jumped, and she wasn't quite sure how to take that. "Well, Mom isn't here. . . ."

"Oh, yeah, she is." She flung out an arm and pointed to the mantel. "There."

A plain wooden box sat in center place.

"Are those . . . ?" Harley's lips pressed into a grimace.

"Ashes." Emma nodded importantly. "Mom went to the funeral place and signed up for it, so that she would be with us when we got together. She paid for it herself. The man told me."

"The man?" Jamie asked.

"At the funeral place. He said she was in good hands. Theo agreed. She took me and Mom home and put Mom there. You should talk to her. It will make you feel better," she said again.

"Well, that's creepy," said Harley, definitely put off.

"It's not creepy," said Jamie.

"Yes, it is!" her daughter disagreed. "Really creepy. I can't even look that way. Where are your scissors? Do you have some?" she asked Emma, turning a cold shoulder toward the fireplace.

"I'm not supposed to use them. Mom said."

"Could you just show me where they are?" Harley asked.

"Okay."

Emma led Harley down the hallway to the downstairs bathroom. Jamie could hear the medicine cabinet open and shut, and then several drawers pulled out and slammed closed again. She wandered toward the wooden box, reaching a hand up, then closing her fist before she could touch its smooth sides. It wasn't her mother. Her mother was gone. What remained were only ashes.

"I don't know if this is such a good idea," said Jamie when Harley had Emma seated in one of the kitchen chairs, scissors in hand.

"Could you get that out of my sight?" Harley asked, half-turning away as Emma was facing the mantel with a full-on view of the box.

"We are supposed to spread her in the garden," Emma said. "Theo said that's what you're supposed to do. Spread her out. Mom loved the garden, so we need to spread her out there. I was waiting for you."

"Sooner the better," muttered Harley. "And I think I'll pass."

"No. You come, too," stated Emma.

Jamie could see her daughter's expression even if Emma couldn't, and she had to smother a smile, the first moment of levity she'd felt in a long time. Harley was horrified, but didn't find it as easy to put off Emma as she could her mother.

"I'll start getting things from the car." Jamie headed away from the makeshift beauty shop.

"Can we get a dog, Mom?" Harley's voice floated after her.

"No dog. Mom won't allow it," said Emma.

"We'll see," Jamie called back.

"Mom won't allow it!" Emma stated more emphatically. *Well, Mom's not here.*

Jamie stepped into the cool October evening. She stood outside for a minute, inhaling the sweet, heady scent of the roses that lined the side of the detached garage and bobbed their heads toward the yard. They were almost over, the leaves nearly gone, the petals growing limp. She recognized the brilliant red of Mr. Lincolns, her mother's favorite.

This experiment of stepping in and taking care of Emma was going to be . . . different. A challenge, for sure, but maybe also a taste of family for Harley in a way she'd never had before. Paul had been gone too long for Harley to remember him as anything but a dim figure, more lore than reality. Jamie wasn't sure how long she planned to stay, but it didn't look like Emma could really live by herself. She was compromised and always would be.

Heart heavy, Jamie hefted out several boxes and set them on the driveway, which was spiderwebbed with cracks. For all the beauty of the garden, the house and garage, the drive and walkways, all looked like they could really use a good handyman. A good handyman and a cheap one. Jamie wasn't entirely sure what her mother's finances were, but she'd been contacted by one Elgin DeGuerre, the lawyer Theo had mentioned, and undoubtedly he'd be able to clear things up.

Before she'd left LA, Jamie had gone online and learned what her requirements for teaching would be in Oregon, and was planning to get started right away. Tomorrow morning, she was registering Harley in school. That was priority one. Preliminary information had been filed, but the school needed to see both Jamie and Harley to admit her.

Paperwork and more paperwork. A lot to be done to re-settle. Just thinking about it made Jamie tired and dispirited. What she could really use was a nice glass of wine, some-thing crisp, clean, and dry. A glass of rosé, or Pinot Gris.

But not yet. There was still too much to do.

"Ta da!" Harley said, tossing her hands in Emma's direction as Jamie came downstairs after her second trip to the car.

Emma's bangs looked all right, good even, but one side of her shoulder-length hair was noticeably higher than the other. Jamie debated on what to say and decided to hell with the truth. "Looks good," she stated brightly.

Harley regarded her suspiciously, then looked at Emma. Her face clouded. "It's shitty."

"Don't swear," Jamie and Emma said together, with Emma adding, "Why is it shitty?"

"It's uneven. I might have to make it a little shorter on this side." She pointed to the longer sweep of hair.

"Okay." Emma sat back down.

Jamie spent the next hour finishing unloading the car and putting their things in their respective bedrooms. Emma, looking better after Harley's corrections—Jamie had to admit the cut was not too bad—was still ensconced in her old room, and Harley had pounced on Jamie's one-time room next to it. Jamie found herself placing her belongings in her mother's room, though she made up the fold-out couch in the tiny office-cum-storage closet-cum-guest room next to Emma's. She could dress in Mom's bedroom, but she couldn't sleep in her bed just yet. Maybe never. It seemed sacrilegious in an indefinable way. It was Mom's bed. No one else's. She'd bought it new when Dad lammed out. Jamie would figure out what to do over time.

In the back of her head, she was seeing this move home as temporary. Maybe she and Harley would stick around the Portland area. Maybe not. Being in the house she grew up in felt like going backward. She didn't want it. Didn't even know if there was enough money to keep it. If she and Harley did stay in the area, they would need to find their own place.

But what about Emma?

An inner part of Jamie was already rebelling. Emma was capable of taking care of herself on a day-to-day basis, at least domestically. She could dress herself, take a shower, brush her teeth, even put on makeup, pretty much the full-on toilette of anyone else her age. But she had difficulty in so many other areas. Socially, for sure, but also the comment their mother had made about her inability with scissors. She'd never been able to cook because she struggled with processes. She was forgetful, yet sometimes frighteningly insightful. There was no accounting for what she was thinking at any given time.

Traitorously, Jamie wondered if Dad would be willing to take care of Emma. At least some of the time. And maybe there could be a helper, an aide of some kind.

She's your responsibility.

Jamie looked at her mother's clothes, hanging in the closet. She was going to have to gather them up and donate them. She was going to have to do a lot of donating and cleaning up . . . and organizing . . . and figuring out what to do.

Chapter Four

Jamie went downstairs to find Emma watching a cooking show and Harley checking out YouTube on the laptop she and Jamie shared.

"What's that?" Jamie asked Harley softly, nodding her head toward the television. Emma was seated on the couch directly in front of it, rapt.

"Emma's favorite show. They're making risotto. She watches it every day, along with a whole bunch of other episodes on the DVR."

"Did you set it up for her?" They were both whispering.

"Uh-uh. She's good at it. She told me not to DVR anything because it takes up her space. She said Grandma was terrible at it."

"My mom thought TV was a brain drain. She never watched anything but the news."

Harley made a disgruntled sound. "She was wrong."

"Yeah, well . . ."

Into the pause that followed, Harley said, "Should we tell her that Grandma contacted us?"

"She didn't contact us," Jamie denied.

Harley didn't say anything, just looked at her, silently calling her a liar.

Jamie turned away and opened the refrigerator door. "Looks like we're going to have to go out to dinner."

"I already ate," said Emma, never turning from the television set.

Had she heard them? Jamie wasn't sure. "Harley and I need to get something. Is Deno's Pizzeria still at the end of the street?"

"Uh-huh."

"Can you stay here alone while we go eat . . . ?"

"Uh-huh. But I want to go with you."

"Oh, okay."

They all found their coats and climbed in the Camry with Emma in the back seat. "It's safer," Emma told them, which tickled Harley, who claimed shotgun with no qualms about usurping her aunt's position.

Friday morning dawned dark and gray, and before Jamie could get to the school, huge raindrops fell, turning into a rattling storm of hail.

"Whoa," Emma said from the back seat, staring out at the white balls of hail bouncing on the rain-drenched street all around them.

Harley said, "Holy hell."

Jamie and Emma said together, "Don't swear," and Emma added, "Mom said it costs a quarter every time you swear."

"My mom'd be broke if we lived here," said Harley. "She swears all the time."

"That's not true," Jamie said, but thought, *Okay, maybe it is.* But she'd starve for a month rather than admit it. "We won't be long," she added as they pulled into one of the few spots and waited while hail continued to pelt them.

"Mom should be in the garden. She would like this," said Emma, peering through the fogged windows.

"You mean her ashes," Jamie said carefully.

"'Ashes to ashes, dust to dust . . .'" Emma quoted flatly. "She should be in the garden."

"I was thinking about a memorial service, small," Jamie said. "A few people over to the house and then we could spread Mom's ashes."

"I am not doing that." Harley slid a glance into the back seat to Emma, who was still trying to peer past the steamy window.

"She will haunt you," said Emma, which drew a gasp from Harley.

"Grandma liked me. Loved me," she shot back. "She would never do anything to hurt me!"

"Now, wait, let's keep it real. She's not going to—" Jamie began.

"She wants you to be with her when she's put to rest." Emma was adamant. "In the garden."

"We'll spread her ashes this afternoon," Jamie said quickly. "After Harley's back from school and you're home from the Thrift Shop. We'll have people over later." Harley said nothing, just stared through the windshield. Emma looked perturbed, her expression darkening. "Mom wants to be in the garden," Jamie riffed. "I get that. We want her to be happy. We'll make sure she's happy today, okay? Okay, Emma?"

"Harley needs to be there, too," she said stubbornly.

At the school Jamie slid a look toward her daughter, whose face was tight and white. Feeling the weight of her gaze, Harley flicked her a look back.

"Okay," she agreed reluctantly.

"Emma, we'll be right back," Jamie said. She'd wanted to leave Emma at home to drive her to work after she saw Harley off, but Emma refused to be alone.

"I'm coming," Emma said.

"Would you mind waiting?" asked Jamie. "I'd like to take Harley by myself. It's her first day and all."

Emma scowled and looked as if she were about to argue. "Don't be long," she said.

"I won't."

Though the hail had abated, the rain continued, and Harley flipped up the hood of her coat and ran ahead of Jamie into the school. The office was the first door on the left and it was open. There was a din of voices and scuffling footsteps and slamming lockers as Jamie opened the door. She tried to get Harley to go in ahead of her, but she stayed right behind her.

At the counter, Jamie was conscious of the water dripping from the hem of her raincoat onto the tile floor. She explained who she was, and the administrative receptionist clicked some keys on her computer and pulled up Harley's paperwork. There was some question over her address. They wanted proof that Harley lived in the school district and Jamie had nothing in her name to support that fact. With a dark look, she handed Harley a packet and said there was a map of the school in there, among other helpful items. After promising her that she would get the school all the pieces of information needed ASAP, Jamie turned to Harley, who looked aghast when she offered to walk with her to her first class.

"Don't worry. I can find it," Harley told her. "They all know I'm coming, right?" She glanced at the administrator.

"Your teachers, yes. If you would like another student to show you around, I can—"

"Nope. Got it. I'm good." Harley hitched her backpack onto her shoulder. She wore a denim jacket over a cream-colored T-shirt, a pair of ripped jeans, and sneakers that looked as if someone had tumbled them through the dryer with rocks.

"See you this afternoon."

"Yeah, for the ashes. Great. Can't wait."

And she pushed through the door and disappeared into the hall, heading in the general direction of the noisy students.

Jamie made sure her name and correct phone number were on the list for substitutes. She was impressed by Harley's fortitude, yet fully aware it was because her daughter would rather face a pool of sharks than be seen being escorted by her mother.

She headed back outside. The hail and rain had stopped and there was a watery sun playing tag with some fast-moving clouds. A woman in a blue suit and white blouse, her blond hair swept into a chignon, was hurrying up the walk. She and Jamie made eye contact at the same moment and the woman stumbled a bit.

"It's . . . Jamie, right?" she said on a surprised intake of breath. "Jamie Whelan?"

Jamie took a half beat before saying, "Yes. Uh . . ."

"Victoria Stapleton. Victoria Barnes Stapleton. It's good to see you! What a surprise. Do you have a student in high school? My son's a junior."

Icky Vicky.

"Um, my daughter. Harley. She's starting today, actually. She's a sophomore."

"Harley. Huh. My, my, you got going about as fast as I did on the parent track." She laughed. "Did you just get into town?"

"Last night."

"Are you staying?"

There was a navy Kate Spade purse slung over her shoulder and her blue pumps were the same shade. The ring on her left hand was big and sparkly and ornate, a ribbon of diamonds sweeping across her finger.

"For the time being. My mother just died."

"Oh. I heard that. I'm so sorry. How's Emma doing?"

Though Icky Vicky and Emma had been friends and classmates, Jamie felt a swelling of protective instinct and anger . . . anger that Icky Vicky had clearly prospered since high school, whereas every day was, in its way, a struggle for Emma. The anger melted almost as soon as it formed, however, and guilt took its place. Guilt. Her old friend.

"She's doing all right."

"Are you . . . well, I know your mom was taking care of her . . . so are you now . . . ?"

"That's the current plan."

She brightened. "Well, your daughter will love it at River Glen High. My son's on the football team, and River Glen has a real chance of winning district this year, maybe even taking state!"

"Wonderful."

She shot Jamie a quick look, clearly uncertain if there was sarcasm behind the word. There was, but Jamie had carefully kept it from being heard.

"Well, I'm kind of in a rush. I'm in real estate, you know," she said, slipping a hand into the purse and magically producing a red card with gold lettering. "If you need anything, anything at all, just call. I would love to personally reacquaint you with the town and all our friends."

In her peripheral vision, Jamie saw Emma getting out of her car. "Thanks, Vicky," Jamie said, accepting the card. If there was room in Harley's shark tank, Jamie would plunge right in rather than be trotted out in front of anyone she'd known from her River Glen days.

"It's Victoria. And that's my cell phone," she said, pointing a navy-blue lacquered nail at the number on the card. Do you have a number, or email?"

Jamie had no interest in handing out her cell number yet. Emma was standing outside the car, looking at both women. Jamie worried that she would come over and prolong the

conversation with Vicky, so she rattled off her email and
Vicky whipped her hand back inside her purse to grab a
small notepad with a pen attached to write it down.

"Your phone?" she asked.

"Not set up yet," Jamie lied.

"There's a new Verizon store where Barnaby's used to
be," she said helpfully.

"Oh. No more Barnaby's, huh?" Barnaby's had been a
kind of tired-looking diner that Mom had long felt should be
shuttered.

"Nope. But the Waystation is still in business, if you can
believe it."

The Waystation was a dive bar where, once upon a time,
kids from high school had been able to pay some of the
regulars a little extra cash for them to buy them beer.

"Okay. I'll see you later, then, huh?" she said with a brilliant smile. Icky Vicky had had some dental work done over
the years, it appeared.

Jamie hurried over to where Emma was still just standing
by the car.

"I saw him," Emma said.

"Who?"

"The guy who did this to me."

"What?" Jamie froze in the act of pulling out her keys.
"Who did what?"

"Why I have trouble."

"Who are you talking about?"

She pointed up the street. "He just drove by. Going to the
police station. That's where he works."

Jamie's mouth formed the word, "Who?" but she never
said it. She only knew one guy from high school who'd gone
into the police force.

"Cooper." Emma's mouth quirked. Maybe a smile. "You
had a big crush on him."

Jamie fleetingly felt surprise that Emma had known, but

there was too much else to unpack in her statement right now. "What do you mean, he did this to you?"

"He was there. You know he was there."

"The night you babysat for the Ryerson twins?"

Emma nodded.

"A bunch of the guys from your class were there, trying to scare you," Jamie pointed out. That had been established long ago, though none of the boys had been at the scene when Emma was attacked.

Emma cocked her head, frowning.

"They all came forward to the police," Jamie reminded her. "You saw them. They admitted to it, and you said so, too. But that was before you were . . . hurt."

"But he came back?" She asked it as a question, clearly confused.

"I never heard that. You never said that before. He's a police officer now."

"They came back," she said, looking past Jamie as if to the long-ago past.

Jamie waited. She realized her heart was pounding triple time, like she'd just run a blisteringly fast race. Emma had never said as much about the night she was attacked, at least not to Jamie's knowledge.

And there was no way Cooper Haynes had attacked her. No way. As she'd said, the man was a police officer now, and he'd been a decent guy in high school, too. After Emma's attack, a group of her male classmates had come forward and told the authorities that they knew she was babysitting and had decided to scare her. Emma was a popular girl they all liked. Halloween had been less than a month away that night, so they'd decided to spook Emma and therefore tapped on the Ryersons' windows, rattled the garbage cans, found one unlatched window that would *creeaaakkkk* when they see-sawed it back and forth. It was teenage high jinks; nothing sinister. According to them, Emma had come out on the porch and good-naturedly told them all to go back to fourth grade where they belonged. Two of the guys, Race Stillwell and Dug, who was really Patrick "Dug" Douglas, had been on their way to "haunt" Emma when Jamie ran into them leaving the Stillwell party just as she was arriving to it that night. In fact, they were the two boys Emma had yelled to as she stood on the porch, but there had been a number of others there, too, Cooper Haynes among them.

Jamie, like almost everyone else, had learned this information when it was reported in the paper. She could still recall Mom swearing softly beneath her breath after reading it, crumpling up that newspaper into a myriad of tight, little balls, her face a cold, stone mask. Jamie had gathered the pieces of newspaper surreptitiously from the trash and unwrapped all the little balls till she found the offending piece of print about Emma's classmates. She, too, had felt a wave of fury at them. How could they? *How could they?* And yet, it was clear that whatever had happened to Emma was after they'd all left.

Now she looked at her sister and asked cautiously, "Who came back?"

Emma, who'd been gazing in the direction she'd said she'd seen Cooper go, jerked as if goosed. "Who?"

"The night you were hurt at the Ryersons'? You just said 'they came back.' You mean the guys from your class." She swallowed and added, "Cooper."

"Cooper Haynes. You had a crush on him. That's why you wanted to go to the party."

"Yes," Jamie admitted. Clearly, Emma had that information, so it was no good denying it. "But was he one who came back?"

"He liked me." She sounded wistful. "They all did."

"They did," Jamie agreed. "You said they came back," she reminded her, opening her driver's door. Emma remained outside, staring down the road, almost as if she were waiting for something. "You'd better get in before it starts raining again."

"It won't rain." She turned her face to the sky.

"Or hailing."

Emma took a few more minutes and then finally climbed into the back seat again.

Jamie drove away from the school and in the direction of the Thrift Shop, a route that took her past the police station.

"No one ever said they came back," Jamie said, hoping for even the slightest bit of further information.

"No one ever said they didn't," said Emma wisely.

"Who came back?" Jamie was tired of this pussyfooting game.

Emma's eyes were glued to the police station as they went by. Jamie flicked a look at the unimposing, one-story, tan brick building, but her gaze came right back to Emma in the rearview mirror.

"We should tell Dad that Mom died," Emma said, meeting Jamie's eyes in the rearview mirror. "That's the right thing to do. You always need to do the right thing."

"Dad knows," Jamie told her.

Emma nodded gravely. "He's an asshole, but Mom still loved him. He should be with us, too."

Jamie clamped down her frustration. It felt like there was something very important in Emma's revelations about "they all came back," but maybe it was blither-blather. A lot of what Emma said was. Sometimes she repeated things she'd heard on television . . . even from commercials . . . that she incorporated into her own reality.

But still . . .

"We're going to spread Mom's ashes today, and I doubt our father can make it," said Jamie.

"All you can do is ask," Emma said in an eerily on-point mimicry of their mother's words and tone.

"You're right about that."

Ten minutes later, Jamie watched her sister mount the rear steps to Theo's Thrift Shop's back door and disappear inside. She drove home slowly, reviewing their conversation. Talking to Emma was like starting ten different conversations and never finishing even one. Was her comment about her guy classmates even true? The boys' statements had been vetted by the police, and Cooper had even gone on to become part of law enforcement himself.

You really, really don't want him to have any part of it.

"Let it be Race, or Dug, or any of the others," she said aloud.

If it was even true.

Which was unlikely.

Most people had initially believed it was the Babysitter Stalker who'd attacked Emma that night. Jamie had wanted to be in that camp. But further information on those other attacks had poked holes in that theory, and it didn't appear to be so. Jamie had wanted that version to be the truth so she wouldn't have to look at anyone close to Emma: her friends, her boyfriends, anyone.

How did she know how you felt about Cooper?

Was it more obvious than you believed?

The thought made Jamie cringe inside even now, decades . . . a lifetime . . . later.

She spent the rest of the day on her laptop, researching her next moves. She could get an Oregon Reciprocal Teaching License, which was good for a year, while finalizing other requirements. The school year had already started, so it was unlikely she would get a full-time job somewhere, but currently, substitute teaching was all she could probably handle anyway.

She drove back to the school at three to pick up Harley, who was standing outside the front doors with a group of girls, huddled under the front overhang, though the rain and hail had been replaced by fretted clouds. This was promising, Jamie thought. Harley made friends fairly easily when she wanted to. It was the wanting to that was hard to define.

She got out of the car and started heading Harley's way. Maybe the fact that school had only been going a few weeks was working in her daughter's favor. Relationships hadn't gotten cemented in concrete yet.

It didn't bode well, however, when she realized Harley was a few steps away from the group of about six girls, with others coming outside and joining in, their voices growing louder as more kids exited the school. Jamie felt oddly exposed as she walked across the parking lot and toward the steps, wondering if she'd be heard over all the excited voices if she yelled to get Harley's attention.

"Hey! There you are!" a voice cried above the rest. "Jamie!"

It was coming from behind her. Reluctantly, she turned around, recognizing Icky Vicky's voice. In her navy suit and shoes, she was hurrying toward Jamie. Her blond hair had fallen out, or been taken out, of its chignon and fell around her shoulders. Jamie remembered her at the Stillwell party, riding a guy's leg while his hands groped her familiarly with a lot of moaning and hard breathing. Jamie had enjoyed sex with Paul . . . for a while . . . but it had never been so eager and overt. She'd always been a little embarrassed and would have died a thousand deaths to have people *walking by* when she was with someone. Yet Vicky hadn't seemed to mind, and clearly didn't think much of it anymore.

"I want to meet your daughter. Tyler would be heading right to football practice, but we have a dental appointment. Is she out here yet?" Vicky looked toward the front steps.

Harley was actually engaged in talking to another girl and

was *smiling*. Jamie marveled a bit. How long had it been since she'd actually enjoyed something?

"She's the tall one with brown hair talking to the dark-haired girl in the blue sweater," Jamie said, the weight on her heart lifting a bit. She hadn't even known it was there until now. If Harley could make this work, maybe things wouldn't be so bad in River Glen.

"Oh, with Marissa Haynes, well, Dalworth. Marissa's a really nice girl. I keep hoping Tyler picks someone like her instead of Dara Volker." She barked out a short laugh. "Dara's a slut, unfortunately, and Tyler thinks she's a hottie, which she is. I should know, right?"

This was an unexpected nod to her high school reputation and there was no right way to answer it. Besides, she'd said something that had definitely caught Jamie's attention.

"Marissa Haynes?" Jamie asked carefully.

"Oh, I know. She's Cooper Haynes's stepdaughter. Her real last name is Dalworth, but she took Cooper's. You remember him from high school?"

Chapter Five

Jamie didn't have a chance to answer as Vicky went on. "He and your sister were an item once, like in junior high . . . maybe high school. I'm not sure Cooper ever got over Emma. All the guys liked her, but after what happened, you know . . ." She shrugged lightly. "Anyway, Marissa is great, and so's her mom, Laura."

Jamie was just digesting that Cooper was married when Vicky added, "I don't know if he was the cause of the divorce, but Laura's been seeing someone else for a while. David Musgrave. He and Laura are looking to buy on the west side of River Glen, but Marissa stays with Cooper a lot, too, because he lives in the old Haynes house."

East side of town. Like Jamie's mother's house.

"You know a lot about them," observed Jamie lightly.

Vicky pretended to look rueful. "I shouldn't have said all that. It's just . . . you and I are such old friends!"

That was probably stretching it a bit, as Vicky knew Emma, not her little sister. However, recognizing she might have inadvertently stopped a font of information, Jamie put on a false smile and said, "Oh, I know exactly what you mean. It's really been like old home week for me."

Vicky beamed. "We were all so jealous of Laura when

she landed Cooper. Who was this girl from Portland, moving into River Glen, snagging one of our most eligible, you know? But she's really lovely. I'll have to introduce you."

"Uh . . ."

"Oh, is this your daughter? She's so pretty!"

Harley had finally noticed Jamie and she hitched up her chin and gave her a nod, but didn't immediately come her way.

"She's gonna be a heartbreaker," Vicky predicted.

Jamie was beginning to see Vicky could be a great connection, even if her motives for approaching Jamie were unclear. They weren't "old friends" by anyone's standards. Vicky likely perceived Jamie as a curiosity. But that didn't mean she couldn't use their association to her advantage. "Cooper's with the police force?"

"Yesiree. He's like a detective or something. He's only gotten more handsome with age. Dara's mom, Meghan, made a play for him when she and her husband were separated, but he wasn't interested. Good thing, too, because Meghan's husband was not okay. They're divorced now. But the rumor is, he knocked her around a bit first. I don't know. Who can tell what's true and what's just a good story? In any case, I wouldn't let Tyler go anywhere near that house while he was still there, but it's hard to keep horny teenagers away from each other, right? Wow, your daughter is all leg. She looks a lot like you. Your brown hair and the way you both walk. Is she going to the mixer tonight?"

"I don't know about any mixer. This is Harley's first day."

"Normally, they do them closer to Halloween, but some of the moms in the PTA got a rod up their butt. Afraid of drinking and vaping, smoking dope and sex, just everything. So, no Halloween. It's Autumn Daze, or something stupid like that, but the kids have fun. I've gotta run and find Tyler.

He's taking long enough. Don't be a stranger. Like I said, if you need anything . . ."

"Let me give you my cell number," Jamie suddenly decided.

"Oh? You got hooked up?"

"Went to Verizon today," she lied.

Vicky whipped out her notebook and pen, and Jamie gave her the number. "We'll get together soon and I'll introduce you to some of the other moms," she promised.

"Thanks, Vicky."

"Victoria." She gave her a quick smile, then hurried up the steps and into the school.

"Who was that?" Harley asked. She'd hung back while witnessing her mother talking with Vicky.

"A friend of Emma's from high school."

"She looked like she was talking your ear off."

"She sort of was, but I'll take any information I can get. How was school? Like any of your classes?"

"No."

"That's what I like about you, Harley. Consistency."

Her daughter rolled her eyes. "You're just always so funny, aren't you?"

"Not always. Sometimes."

Harley almost smiled but stopped herself. She shrugged and said, "It was okay. Some of the kids are pretty nice."

"Like Marissa?"

Harley turned swiftly her way. "You know Marissa? How do you know Marissa?"

"I just heard about her from Ick . . . from someone I know."

"That lady?" She jerked her head in the direction Vicky had gone.

Jamie nodded. "Her son's named Tyler and on the football team, I believe. She said Marissa was a nice girl."

Harley squinted. "Tyler."

"Did you meet him?"

"I met a lot of people." She brushed it off, clearly done with the conversation. She hiked her backpack over her shoulder. "Are we going home or what?"

The *tone*. It made Jamie want to scream at her, but she'd learned that approach did no good. Ignoring it wasn't really an answer either, but she let it go for now because it was Harley's first day. Tomorrow would be a different story.

They were walking back toward Jamie's car when they heard footsteps behind them and Marissa came flying up. "Hey, give me your phone number," she said to Harley. "We could go tonight to the mixer? You want to?" She glanced up at Jamie and said, "Hi, I'm Marissa."

"I'm Jamie."

Harley looked at Jamie and said in an accusing voice, "I don't have a phone."

"I could give you my number," Jamie suggested.

"Okay." Marissa swept her phone from her back pocket.

They exchanged numbers while Harley remained silent, maybe seething, as Jamie entered Marissa Haynes into her contact list, feeling slightly weird. *You're too old for this,* she told herself.

"Oh, there's my dad." Marissa waved, and Jamie turned her head as if pulled by a string.

Cooper Haynes. Vicky was right. He was downright handsome. Looked even better than in high school. Broad shoulders. Fit. His dark hair, tossed a bit by the breeze, was a little longer than the clipped cut she remembered. He wore jeans and a white shirt and a black windbreaker. His eyes were blue, she knew from memory, and his long strides ate up the ground between them as he approached Marissa, who was waving madly.

"That's your dad?" Harley asked.

"Well, my stepdad, but I call him my dad. I took his name."

"You can do that?" asked Harley.

"I just use it. It's not in my permanent record."

Jamie was only half-listening as she watched Cooper approach. She looked at him, and looked away, and looked at him again, feeling like she was the one in high school.

"Hi," Cooper said as he neared.

"Hi," Jamie said as recognition slipped across his expression.

"Jessie . . . ?" he asked.

"Jamie. Whelan."

"Sorry, yes. Emma's sister, right?" He held out his hand. She offered hers and felt him squeeze her fingers. A surf roared in her ears.

Jesus Christ, Jamie. Get a grip!

"I'm Cooper Haynes. Don't know if you remember me." He smiled, and laugh lines formed at the corners of his eyes.

"You know each other?" Marissa asked, delighted.

"We went to school together," Jamie said. Her voice sounded strange to her own ears.

"You know Aunt Emma?" Harley asked him curiously.

"We were classmates." The smile slowly disappeared.

"I'm Harley Woodward," she said, thrusting out her hand. Cooper shook her hand, too.

"My daughter," said Jamie, desperately trying to act nonchalant. "Emma's niece."

"Harley and I are going to the mixer together tonight, right?" Marissa turned to Harley, who nodded and shrugged, like, why not?

"Want us to pick you up?" Marissa asked, and then the conversation went on around Jamie, plans being discussed, decisions made, a flurry of information that ended with Harley looking at Jamie for their address. Jamie gave it woodenly. She felt like she was having an out-of-body experience.

Fifteen minutes later, they were pulling into the drive and

Harley was suddenly bright-eyed and eager about the evening ahead. She chattered on about her day without being prompted. Clearly, Marissa had eased her fears about being the new girl by inviting her into their group of friends, who appeared to be welcoming. Harley mentioned a girl named Lena and another called Katie. "I don't think it's the most popular group," Harley revealed. "For the seniors I think that's Tyler and some other guys, and a girl named Dara and another, Michaela, and a few more."

"Oh, good."

"Marissa's great."

"I'm glad. I hear Dara's dating Tyler," Jamie said.

She got the reaction she'd expected when Harley whipped around in the passenger seat to gaze at her in surprise. "How do you know that?"

"Oh, it's all over the school."

"But how do *you* know that?"

"I'm clairvoyant?"

"Mom! Oh. Tyler's mom told you."

"Alas, my powers of detection have been found out," Jamie said on an exaggerated sigh as they pulled into the driveway.

Harley shook her head, as if she didn't know what to do with Jamie. They climbed out of their respective doors and Harley glanced back at the garage door. "Are you ever going to park in the garage?"

"Mom's car's in there. We'll have to figure that out, too, I suppose. Her Outback might be newer than the Camry."

"When I turn sixteen, I'll take the Camry, you take the Outback."

"We'll jump off that bridge when we come to it," Jamie said as she bent down and grabbed the key from under the gnome where it still was kept, opened the door, then put the key back. "I've gotta get some keys made and find a better hiding place." She'd left the key beneath the gnome because it was where Emma could find it.

Baby steps, she reminded herself.

Harley asked as they pushed inside, "So, what's our plan? I mean . . . am I going to be at this school for a while, or are we going back to LA?"

"I don't have any idea. Emma needs care . . . she's really not independent . . ."

"You don't want to take care of her, do you?"

Jamie gave Harley a hard look as her daughter dumped her backpack on the kitchen table and automatically opened the refrigerator. Harley didn't notice as she gazed over the meager offerings—Jamie had stopped at the store for basics: milk, cereal, bananas, and coffee—finally choosing a yogurt. "It's past the pull date," she said, pulling out the small carton and eyeing it suspiciously.

"How far?"

"Two days."

"Up to you," Jamie said.

"Can we go to the store and get something else? Something good?"

"Yes . . ."

"Well, let's go, then. Marissa's going to call you, and I want to be ready. And I need a phone. I know, they're too expensive, but now that we're at Grandma's, isn't that cheaper? Like we don't have to pay rent?"

"For now, we use my phone."

"Jesus, I'm the only one without a phone!"

"Oh, you are not. I'd venture to say there's somebody else at the school without a phone."

"They *all* have phones."

"No, they don't."

Harley was heading through the back door again. "I haven't met anyone without a phone yet."

"Well, look harder. And don't swear."

Chapter Six

Cooper dropped Marissa off at her mother's house, the house he'd once shared with Laura before their split, the house less than a mile from his parents', now his own.

He watched as she walked up to the garage, hitching up her backpack as she pressed the numbers on the pin pad to open the door. She lifted a hand to him without turning around. He watched the door lumber upward with a few squeaks and groans—*gonna have to check those springs, Haynes, make sure it's still functioning right*—then back down again before he reversed out of the drive.

He and Laura had determined to keep their split as amicable as possible for Marissa's sake, even though there had been huge fights between them toward the end of their three-year marriage. He'd married Laura for all the wrong reasons, chief among them that it was the time when all the guys he knew were taking that trip down the aisle and Laura was eager to take the same steps. There were other reasons, too . . . chief among them being he'd liked her looks. Then a buddy of his at work, a guy about ten years older than Cooper who'd also graduated from River Glen High, Howie Eversgard, had pointed out to him, "She kinda looks like that girl from the Thrift Shop." This observation had come about a year into Cooper's marriage. Howie's father haunted

Theo's Thrift Shop, as many grandparents did, buying up the gently used discards from some of River Glen's wealthier families, who gave away their belongings rather than sell them on craigslist or other similar sites.

"The hell she does," Cooper had growled, trying to cover up that he'd been knocked sideways a bit. But as soon as he'd heard it, he'd recognized its truth: Laura had a passing resemblance to Emma Whelan.

Howie had been undeterred. "No, man. Check it out sometime. Go to the Thrift Shop for a look-see."

Though Cooper had attempted to shrug off Howie's words, he'd gone to the Thrift Shop in his off hours to see the real Emma Whelan to compare. He'd learned Emma looked remarkably the same as in high school, though her face had lost its expressiveness. "Hi, Cooper," she'd greeted him, as if there hadn't been years in between since they'd seen each other. Her voice was flat, as smooth and uninflected as her mien, not a ripple in the water. It hurt his heart, as it had when it had happened.

That trip to the shop had also made him hyperaware of his marriage, the chinks in the armor, the little rips in the fabric. Laura looked like Emma, but she wasn't Emma as Emma had once been. Laura was careful and a little sensitive, where Emma had been self-confident. Laura wanted to be with him twenty-four seven, where Emma had always made it clear she liked him just fine, but maybe she had better things to do. Their relationship, such as it had been, in junior high and, briefly, in high school, hadn't really gotten off the ground. All the guys had wanted Emma, and maybe he'd gotten a little closer than most, but it hadn't been a real relationship. He could admit that now.

Her aloofness was one of the reasons they'd all gone to scare her at her babysitting job the night of the Stillwell party.

"I'm taking over for my sister," Emma had said breezily

when Tim Merchel, whose parents had bought him a cell phone, had called her on her home phone.

"Ah, c'mon, Emma. Stillwell's having a party."

"Have fun," she'd told them, hanging up.

She'd relented later, actually stopping by the party briefly before going on to her babysitting job. Race had asked her what took her so long to show up, but she'd refused to say before taking off. Her departure left Race in a bad mood and then . . . plans were made.

They all knew she babysat for the Ryerson twins.

Cooper shook the memories away as he drove back to the station. Whenever Marissa called and he was around, he tended to take off work for a few minutes to pick her up from school and drop her off. Laura expected her to walk home, though she lived over a mile from the school, but with iffy weather and a heavy backpack, Cooper kinda thought Marissa needed a little extra help sometimes. Which pissed Laura off.

"She's my daughter," she told him crisply time and again, usually on a phone call after she'd worked up a head of steam.

"She's a fifteen-year-old girl with a backpack three times as heavy as it ought to be."

"She's not your problem anymore."

"I'm saving her from future back surgery."

Which was when she invariably hung up on him. Laura was angry that he'd never been committed to the marriage in the same way she had. He'd tried, but she was a "ruleser." Everything had to be just so, and well, he didn't fit into the mold. He'd found himself heading home from work later and later, and finally recognized he didn't want to go home at all. Laura was a nice, friendly person in front of others, but she was quick to drop that facade in the privacy of her own home and became tyrannical when things didn't go her way.

They'd gone to a psychologist, at Laura's insistence,

who'd said they both needed to try harder, which hadn't been what Laura wanted to hear. She wanted complete vindication. So, no more trips to see Gwen Winkelman, which was fine with Cooper; Gwen was another River Glen alum and the less gossip about his failing marriage around town, the better, and though he trusted she wouldn't blab about all their problems, just seeing a psychologist was enough to start a few tongues wagging.

And then they'd divorced and everyone had gasped, how had that happened? Cooper and Laura? They had the perfect marriage! How can that be?

During the split, Laura was good about not giving too much away and so was he. Irreconcilable differences. That was it. Nothing more to say. And then Cooper's father had a stroke and his attention was diverted, completely taken up with his father through his illness and until his death a few months later. By that time, Cooper had moved out of the house he and Laura had purchased together and into the home he'd grown up in. His mother had died years earlier from breast cancer. He had no other siblings and now no wife or children. Work was all that mattered and he attacked it as if his life depended on it, which in a way, it did.

Eventually, the gossip had died down. Laura moved on and was currently dating David Musgrave, who seemed a decent-enough guy. He'd heard talk that the two of them might even move in together. They were shopping for a house in Staffordshire Estates, River Glen's chichiest area, a development that adjoined the Stillwell property, a parcel sold to home builders by Race and Deon Stillwell's parents before their deaths in a small plane accident.

Now Cooper pulled into the back lot of the station. Several black Ford Escapes with the River Glen Police Department's gold ribbon sat idle. Cooper parked his own SUV, a black Ford Explorer that looked a lot like it belonged in the River Glen PD fleet, and took the short flight of steps in two bounds.

Inside, he walked down a short hall that held the break room, restrooms and a storage closet to an open area that held six desks in three groups of two, front to front. His was one of the two closest to the window and faced Howie's. Only three of the others were ever used. Today, they were all empty. Howie and Elena Verbena were on a case, a domestic fight between a man and his wife, both of whom were currently in the hospital from the injuries they'd inflicted upon each other. Cooper had been unavailable at the call out, and the department sent whoever was closest to the incident.

The River Glen PD chief, a man who'd been appointed by the mayor, knew less than nothing about law enforcement from experience but was smart enough to stay out of the way of those who did. Hugh Bennihof had an office at the end of the squad room. The door was a glass pane, so it was possible to see when he was at his desk, except for the few times he pulled down the blinds.

Cooper had just finished writing up his notes on an investigation he'd done for a case that was going to court: a messy custody case. He was glad to be done with it. He hadn't been impressed by either parent of the six-year-old boy.

He was now a little bit at loose ends, which made him restless. He walked to his desk but kept standing, looking out the window to the street. Seeing Jamie Whelan again had broken something loose. Something he'd thought he had under tight lock and key. Not Whelan, he realized, she'd said her last name was . . . ?

I'm Harley Woodward.

The daughter's name was Woodward, so Jamie's was likely to be, too. Jamie looked a lot like Emma, and yet she didn't. He remembered her from high school. She'd been skinnier, but not by much. Her hair had been blonder, he thought. Now it was a light brown. She'd had a quirky smile back then, like she was embarrassed, or a fish out of water. He hadn't noticed that today. She'd been poised and . . . careful.

She was supposed to babysit that night.

Cooper had given the attack on Emma a lot of thought over the years. It was the event that had spurred him to go into law enforcement. He'd had an uncle who was a River Glen cop, now long retired, and he'd harangued the man for answers, begged him, damn near threatened him, to find out what had happened, but there were no clues that went anywhere. If Emma could help, then maybe, his uncle had told Cooper over and over again, but it became clear that was never going to happen.

His cell phone rang and he clicked on. "Yeah," he answered Marissa.

"Mom won't let me go to the mixer tonight! I can't believe it!" she cried, practically in tears. "I have plans! I have friends!"

"The mixer?"

"At the school. It's like music and stuff, and it's the Halloween one early because *already* the school won't let us do Halloween. It's so *unfair*! It's just so *unfair*!"

"Why won't your mom let you go?"

"*I don't know.* Can you talk to her?"

He knew better than to try to get between Laura and her daughter. Boy, did he know better. "Find out what her reasons are, and maybe then you can work it out with her."

"You won't help me?" She moaned, as if her life were destroyed.

"Find out," said Cooper.

She moaned again and hung up. Ten minutes later, Laura's number popped up on his cell.

"I don't want her to go alone," Laura said without preamble in a hard tone when Cooper clicked on. "There are drugs at the school. I don't want her to be a part of it."

"Drugs? This is something you heard?"

"Yes! There are drugs."

Knowing he was putting too fine a point on it based on the tone of her voice, Cooper nevertheless waded in. "Do you mean kids are using during the day? Or just this evening?"

"Does it matter?" Her ire was rising.

It wasn't that he was purposely making light of the issue. He didn't doubt that a certain percentage of kids were experimenting with drugs. It was what happened at every school. What he was objecting to was Laura's capacity to come up with excuses to win an argument or have her way, whether she believed what he was saying or not.

And he didn't believe Marissa and her friends were users.

He said, "Marissa goes to school during the day, so the drugs are there when she's there . . . ? But she can't go to the school tonight because the drugs will be there?"

"I don't think tonight will be chaperoned the same way," she delivered through her teeth. "Unless you want to go there? Be the policeman for all those teens? You want to do that?"

Hell no.

"Sure," he said. "Just let me know when I should pick Marissa up."

She hung up on him.

"We're not going to spread Mom's ashes tonight," Jamie said as she threw together a peanut butter sandwich for Harley and slid it onto the table.

"Good," Harley expelled with relief.

"I've got to pick up Emma at five and then you're going to that party. . . ."

"Mixer." Harley fell on the sandwich like a ravenous

wolf. "I didn't eat lunch," she admitted around a huge bite that was obviously sticking to the roof of her mouth.

"I gave you money," Jamie reminded her, pouring her daughter a glass of tap water. That was one thing about Oregon. The water was good.

"I just didn't like what they had."

Jamie held back further comment. She'd been the same way. Starving herself all day for similar reasons. But why couldn't growing up, school, be better for Harley? That was all she wanted.

Harley rolled an eye at her. "Maybe you and Emma can just spread the ashes without me."

"No. I called my father. We changed the date. He and Debra are coming over Sunday afternoon."

Harley put down the glass of water and stared at Jamie. "I thought you hated him."

"Hate's a pretty strong word."

"Yeah? Well . . . ?"

"Emma and I blamed him for leaving Mom, yes. It was a tough time and he didn't handle it well. We all thought Debra was a passing thing, but she wasn't. I wasn't sure Dad knew Mom died, so I called him this afternoon and left a message on his phone, and he called me back."

She'd worked up the courage to even phone her father, calling herself all kinds of a coward for making something that should be so easy, so hard. She'd been relieved to leave a message, and when he'd phoned back she'd been in her bedroom and had answered with trepidation.

"Hey . . . Dad," she'd said diffidently.

"Hi, honey," he answered with false warmth.

His tone. She remembered that tone so well. He just couldn't pull off sincerity. It had spurred her to bluntly give him the news about Mom, which he had somehow already heard, but when she'd explained that they were spreading her ashes in lieu of a memorial service, he'd been eager to drop the whole thing.

"We're doing it this Sunday," Jamie had decided that moment. She didn't really care if he was there or not, but it had pissed her off how relieved he'd sounded that he couldn't make the event.

Apparently picking up on her anger, he'd finally said, "Well, maybe Debra and I can come. What time?"

She almost asked him not to bring Debra. Nobody liked her. Nobody wanted her there. But Debra had been with her father for so many years that it seemed churlish and pointless to say no.

Now, Harley said, "I don't even know what he looks like."

"You're not alone. None of us have seen him in years."

"Has . . . uh, Marissa texted yet?" Harley tried to disguise the hopeful tone in her voice, but wasn't completely successful. Jamie found herself praying Marissa was as nice as everyone was saying. She hoped to God Harley wasn't left in the lurch on her first day of school.

"Not yet."

Her cell gave off its incoming text tone at that moment. Harley jumped up and demanded, "Where's your cell?"

"I've got it right here." Jamie plucked it from her purse and placed it on the counter. She gave her daughter a look that said, *Hold your horses*.

"Is it Marissa?"

"No, it's Ick . . . it's the lady I was talking with at the school . . . Tyler's mom." She fished Vicky's card out of the side pocket of her purse. "Vicky Barnes, uh, Stapleton."

"Wha'd she say?"

"Well, I'm going out with her tonight, while you're at the mixer."

Harley frowned. "Really? Why? What about Emma?"

"She can stay by herself. My mom worked nights, pretty much always."

"You don't want to take care of her, do you?"

Jamie drew a breath. "It's all a change. For you, too. And I'm glad, and surprised, that you're so okay with the move."

Harley physically pulled back, as if Jamie had trod into her space. "You're not both coming to the mixer, right?"

"Not on your life."

Twenty minutes later, Marissa texted: will pick Harley up at 6, k?

Harley practically yanked the phone out of Jamie's hands and sent back a thumb's-up emoji. "When am I getting a phone?" she demanded for about the billionth time.

"I don't know," answered Jamie. Again. "Keep asking and it might not happen at all."

"So, you are thinking about it?" Harley perked up, hearing what she wanted to hear.

"A day hardly goes by that it's not brought up about six times."

Harley narrowed her eyes, as she often did at her mother's sarcasm, but then she raced upstairs to her room to get ready.

I need to go back, to remember how it started. I need to recall every detail. To think through each piece. It's important. It keeps the path I walk on straight.

I sit in the full dark. I have been sitting here a long time. Days . . . maybe a week?

I don't want to hurt anyone, but these women . . .

They shouldn't do the things they do. They need to back off, or be made to.

The newspaper clippings are on my computer, which sits on the table in front of me. If I open the file I'll read about what was reported, but not what happened.

I didn't hurt the babysitter, but she needed to be hurt, needed to be stopped.

For some reason my mind is full of images of dolls.

They're enhanced like Barbie but they're not her. They're sluts. Zeroed in on men. Any man. Whether married or not. An army of vicious, self-gratifying females.

I breathe hard, pulling my energy inward, needing to calm myself. Not now, I warn myself. Not ever, if I can help it.

But can I help it?

The doll images slowly coalesce into one face. One I knew all along. The one that started it all . . .

Emma . . .

Chapter Seven

River Glen High's media room was festooned with autumnal banners made by every class, basically declaring why their class was the best. Lots of stars and exclamation points and #1 signs in green and gold, the school colors, along with pictures of pumpkins, cornstalks, and scarecrows. There was a DJ setup at one end whose playlist was thumping so hard you could feel it in your chest. Harley walked in behind Marissa, who was trying to fight off a deep fury at her mother and doing a half-assed job.

"My dad has to be here. He has to! She made it a prerequisite. So now he's over there by the door, and I know he hates it. He says he doesn't, but he's just being nice. He hates it. He'd rather be home."

Mr. Haynes, the cop, had picked Harley up, and she and Marissa had taken the back seat, leaving him to be like a butler, driving them to the school. He'd let them out and then gone to park. They'd entered without him, but Marissa had said he always listened to what her mom wanted because, well, she was the real parent.

"It pisses me off," she said now.

Harley knew how she felt. She hated being blindsided by parents, and they always, always seemed to want to do it. Like they were incapable of not screwing their kids up. She'd said as much to her mom in the heat of an argument once, and her mom had thought about it for a moment and said, "I guess you're right," which had annoyed Harley, probably way more than Marissa was annoyed, because she'd really kind of wanted Mom to go ballistic and have a parent fit, but Mom generally just looked faintly amused, like Harley was reacting just the way she expected.

It sucked.

"Let's go over by the DJ." Marissa was already threading her way there.

Harley wasn't sure her ears could take it, but she didn't want to appear to wimp out. God no. At her old school, she had a reputation as one of the bold ones. She was the friend her friends turned to. A leader, one of the teachers had said, which made Harley secretly proud.

She'd tried to explain that to Mom, but Mom had typically shot her down with, "Be careful. Sometimes being in the vanguard boomerangs."

Being in the vanguard? Harley had had to look that one up. Basically, it meant being on the front lines, first, ahead of the pack. She liked that, but not the comment that it could boomerang.

Beyond the thumping noise, she had butterflies in her stomach. They'd been there all day. She would rather die of a million paper cuts than admit that to Mom, though. She'd been purposely blasé about the whole move and change of schools. She'd almost welcomed it in the beginning, because things had gotten weird with her friends or, more accurately, her boyfriend. Only he hadn't really been her boyfriend. He'd made out with her on Rich Renley's porch swing and had tried to feel her up, which she'd kind of gone with for a second or two before she pushed his hand away, which had only emboldened him, and then . . .

She squinted her eyes closed at the memory of his crowing and bragging to all his friends about things that had not really happened. Things had gotten really bad after that. Rather than fight and try to explain herself, she'd just ignored it all, but her reputation had tanked. Bold? A leader? She'd cried herself to sleep and had jumped at the chance to move.

"Too loud?" Marissa said near her ear.

Harley's eyes popped open. "Nah. It's all right."

"C'mon, there's Lena and Katie." And with that, she grabbed Harley's arm and dragged her toward her friends.

Jamie walked into Leander's Wine Bar, her inner eye still seeing Cooper Haynes's black Explorer and the lifting of his hand behind the windshield as Harley ran out of the house to meet Marissa and the girls both slammed inside the vehicle. She'd raised a hand in return and then gone back inside as the black SUV pulled out of the drive.

Leander's was a tiny, long, and narrow place with a gray, leather banquet against one long wall, and small, square tables dotted the length of it, where Vicky and a couple of friends were already seated. Vicky had grabbed two of the tables and a number of loose chairs and was seated talking to two women who looked vaguely familiar, but whom Jamie didn't know. Vicky scooted over and Jamie took a seat on the banquette. The women were mostly friends from high school, too, and they knew Emma, having been in her grade.

"God, you look just like your sister," the one named Jill declared.

"You do," another, Alicia, agreed. She was not a River Glen alum but almost acted like one.

"Except Emma has those big, blue eyes," Vicky said. "You have . . . ?"

"Brown," said Jamie.

"It's such a terrible shame about her," said Jill. "Was

it that Babysitter Stalker killer? I mean, I never knew. We never heard."

"The guys were all in such trouble for scaring her. It like scared them straight," Alicia agreed.

Vicky lifted an arm to signal to the woman in black pants, blouse, and apron behind the bar. "When you have a chance?" she called loudly, wagging a finger at Jamie. "We need another glass." She turned to Jamie. "You okay with red?"

"Yes," Jamie said. The bottle on the table was almost empty. She hoped it wasn't too expensive; she thought she might be expected to order another.

You should have said you wanted a glass of white.

She could feel tension building inside her. She had a small amount in savings, but there wasn't a ton of money for extravagances. She wasn't even sure how much Vicky and her cohorts would become her friends. She almost wished she'd stayed home.

Home. She was still bothered by the fit Emma had thrown when she'd learned they were not spreading Mom's ashes till Sunday.

"She needs to be in the garden!" Emma had yelled on the way home from Jamie picking her up at the Thrift Shop.

"Sunday's only a day and a half away," Jamie had tried to explain. "Dad and Debra will come over and—"

"She's waited and waited for you, and now you're here. She needs to be in the garden *today*. You promised!"

"Would you prefer Dad and Debra not come over?"

"Mom didn't like them!"

"And she had good reason," Jamie agreed quickly. "But he is our father, and Hayley's grandfather, and I invited him in the thought that . . ." She sighed, losing steam herself. "That this could be a starting point for us with him."

Emma's face was a hard mask. She wrapped her arms

around herself. "When Mom doesn't like someone, she takes care of things."

"Meaning what?"

"Meaning, you should take care of things, too. Be like Mom."

Come home. Jamie remembered her dream and shivered a little bit. "Our mother's dead, and I want to spread her ashes in the garden as much as you do."

"Not as much as I do!"

"Okay, not as much as you do. But I do want that. We're going to do that. I just would like to wait till Sunday. Can you do that? Can you wait, Emma?"

She sat stonily for a full minute. Jamie was just taking a breath to try to convince her some more when she suddenly capitulated with a flat, "Okay."

After that, when they got home, Jamie explained that both she and Harley would be gone for the evening. Jamie had been drying the glassware that she'd quickly washed in the sink as the dishwasher was DOA. She'd hung the damp dish towel over the dishwasher handle beside a matching one, both of them light green with colorful flowers embroidered on them. Emma walked over and refolded the towel Jamie had just used and then straightened them both so they were dead even with each other.

"She has to have order in her life," she recalled Mom saying. "Don't try to reason with her when she lines up your perfume bottles. Don't tell her to mind her own things. It won't do any good and will just upset her."

Jamie hadn't noticed that particular behavioral quirk in her sister since she'd returned until the dish towels. She wondered if Emma's need for control manifested more when she was feeling under duress.

As the proprietress brought over another stemmed glass, the door to the wine bar suddenly blew open on a cold, shivery breeze.

"Bette!" Vicky waved furiously. "Brrr. Come on over!"

Jamie glanced at the petite brunette with boobs that wouldn't quit. The one who'd made a play for Cooper, undoubtedly.

Bette sank down across from Jamie at the second small table but turned her attention to the other three. "Oh my God. I hate Kearns. He's a prick."

"Phil Kearns is Bette's husband," Jill explained for Jamie's benefit, though Jamie thought she recalled the name from high school and was trying to place him.

Bette turned angry eyes Jamie's way. The anger dissipated some as she looked at Jamie, perplexed. "Who are you again?"

"Jamie Whelan," said Vicky. "She's the little sister of a classmate of ours. Emma. The one who was attacked?"

"Oh." She blinked several times. "I'm sorry. I didn't know your sister."

"It's okay." Jamie was really thinking she should skedaddle tout de suite.

"Bette and Alicia married into our little group," said Jill. "Do you remember Phil Kearns? He was a couple of years older than us?"

"I think I've heard the name."

"Well, I married the asshole," Bette said. "Stupid me. We met at UDub. I'm going to move back to Seattle."

"No, you're not," Vicky said. She'd poured the rest of the bottle into Jamie's glass and now signaled the proprietress for another bottle. "Bette's thinking about divorce."

"I met with an attorney. It's more than thinking."

"Her son's a friend of Tyler. Both seniors," Vicky added. To Bette, she said, "You won't leave till he graduates."

"I've got Joy, too."

"Joy's a seventh grader. She'll be fine," Vicky stated firmly.

"Neither one of them sides with me. Kearns has 'em both convinced I'm the devil."

"Oh, that's not true," said Alicia.

No one else said anything. Another bottle appeared and glasses were refilled. Jamie sipped at hers, plucking her phone from her purse and surreptitiously checking the time.

The conversation went right back to Emma's tragedy and speculation on the babysitter killer.

"There was no serial stalker or killer," said Jill. She was rail thin and had a way of lifting her chin and tossing her dark-brown, shoulder-length hair whenever she laid down an edict. "The Vancouver one was a burglary, and the other one fell off a roof fighting with her boyfriend."

"Why do we ever put up with men?" Bette complained, draining her glass so fast, it made Jamie wonder where she put it. "They're terrible, terrible human beings."

"Half the population," Alicia reminded. She was a paler blond than Vicky, with a wan complexion and a small frame that made it look as if a strong wind could blow her over.

"Maybe the girl who fell off the balcony wasn't because of a serial killer, but I think the murder in Vancouver, and what happened here, too, definitely was," said Vicky. "The guy who stabbed her was wearing a mask. Just like . . . what happened to Emma."

"We don't know Emma's attacker was masked," Jamie corrected. No one had seen him.

"Why did he stop?" Jill demanded, nose in the air. "This said killer? There's never been a babysitter attack since in this area."

"Maybe he hasn't. We just don't know it. He's still out there. He attacked Emma and then he disappeared." Vicky shrugged.

Jamie could tell she was slightly miffed at having her theory questioned.

"What do you think?" Alicia asked Jamie.

"Me? Well . . ." When they all just looked at her, as if

waiting for more, she added, "I always thought the police
should've tried harder."

Bette snorted. "Don't expect a man to do anything."

"You didn't feel that way about Cooper when you went
after him," Vicky reminded her.

"Cooper Haynes was in our grade and he's a detective
now," Jill explained for Jamie's benefit.

"She knows Cooper." Vicky waved a dismissive hand.
She was very big into gestures. "Her daughter's friends with
Marissa."

There followed a lively discussion about the kids in the
school and who was friends with whom, which ones were in
the popular crowd—both Vicky and Alicia's sons, for sure—
and what they were going to do about the drug problem.

"Drug problem?" Jamie asked.

"Alleged drug problem. None of our kids have been
caught with drugs. It's just rumors. Drink up, honey. I'm
buying." Vicky flapped a hand at her. "My husband is cheap,
but I keep him from being a total skinflint."

"I can buy," Jamie tried to protest.

"God, no. Let Lawrence Stapleton pay for it." Jill tossed
her dark locks. "He's loaded."

"I thought Kearns was," Bette said with a sniff.

"I thought Deon was," said Alicia somewhat sorrowfully.

"He was. He is." Vicky gave her a kind look. "He's just an
asshole. Alicia got pregnant by Deon Stillwell, not sure if
you knew him?" Vicky said to Jamie. "Younger brother
of Race Stillwell. Good-looking and inherited big-time,
like Race, when their parents died, but neither of 'em
amounted to anything. Pardon me. I should be nicer, but I
got screwed by them on a deal. I did all the work on that
property outside of town, and he turned it over to—"

"That Portland real estate bitch, Tricia something. We
know, Victoria," Jill said, long-suffering.

Jamie was still processing hearing Deon Stillwell's name. The quick revulsion she felt again, remembering his hand on her crotch.

"Yes. Her. That would have been a big commission. A really big one." Vicky drained her glass.

"You have a husband. I barely get child support," bemoaned Alicia.

"Cooper Haynes is a stand-up guy," said Bette, on her own track. "When I'm divorced, I'm going there. I'm letting you all know now."

Vicky snorted. "Don't let Bette fool you. She's not waiting for the divorce!"

Alicia warned, "Cooper better look out."

Bette shrugged them both away.

Jill looked down her nose and said to her, "You just said men weren't human beings."

"Some of them are. Cooper's a decent guy. We all agree on that."

"And Jill and I have decent guys," said Vicky. "Even if Lawrence is cheap."

"Jim has his moments," Jill agreed. "Although we don't have kids, and I think a lot of men epically fail as soon as they're fathers."

"No kidding," Vicky said, heartfelt.

Bette said, "I gotta go tinkle," to which Jill snorted and said, "Why is that word so annoying?"

"'Cause it's babyish." Vicky's gaze followed Bette as she headed for the restroom.

"What about you, Jamie?" asked Alicia. "Any guy in your world, now that you've heard about the miserable creatures in ours?"

"Nope." Jamie drained her glass. Well, if Vicky was buying . . .

"You divorced?" Vicky asked.

"Widowed."

"Really? What happened?" asked Alicia while the others all made surprised noises as well.

"Motorcycle accident."

"Oh. No. Sorry . . ." Vicky lifted a glass to her and made a face to show she felt she'd stuck her foot in her mouth.

"It was a long time ago. Harley was a baby."

"Harley is her daughter," Vicky said. "Gorgeous girl. A sophomore. Fifteen?"

Jamie nodded.

"Tell us about him," urged Alicia.

"There's not much to tell. . . ." They were all looking at her expectantly, so she told them how she'd met Paul and eloped with him. She didn't mention that she'd basically run away from her responsibilities, though the thought crossed her mind, as it always did.

Bette returned and caught the tail end of her story. "We all had 'em young, didn't we?" She sighed.

"Sure did." Alicia gave a sad smile. "Troy's seventeen now. Just one more year and split custody's over."

Vicky leaned into Jamie. "She doesn't like him being at that house."

"Animal House." Jill made a face.

Alicia immediately protested, "It's not that bad. It's just that there's no woman there. Just Race and Deon."

"Too much money, too little blood to the brain," Jill declared.

"Oh, they have brains," said Vicky. "They're just lying, conniving bastards."

"All the blood goes to the prick, not the head," said Bette.

"Except Cooper," Vicky said dryly.

"Except Cooper," Bette agreed.

Except Cooper.

* * *

Harley listened to Marissa and her friends as much as the loud music would allow. Normally, she would jump in and dance like a maniac, but she was overcome with unnatural shyness. The girls were all dancing with each other and the guys were hanging around in groups. Everyone was looking at everyone else. Harley tried not to look at Tyler Stapleton and his group of seniors, but they were the center of attention. One of them, Greer Somebody, had broken free and was talking to some of the senior girls, Dara, Michaela, and such, who were clearly trying to figure out a way to break into the guys' group.

Marissa's group had wandered away from the DJ and were standing nearer the refreshments, cans of soda, chips, salsa, cookies, and Rice Krispies Treats dyed orange and black. Harley picked up a black one.

"Watch out, it'll turn your lips black," Marissa warned.

"Good." Harley took a big bite.

"Hey," Greer said, almost as soon as her mouth was full. He'd left Dara's group to come to the refreshment table. "You're new. I saw you today."

"Mmm-hmm." Harley nodded. It felt like a piece of puffed rice was caught in her throat.

"Where'd you come from?"

"LA," she managed to squeak out. That piece would not go down!

She finally smiled, and Greer laughed.

"Your teeth are all black," he said. "Here. Gimme some of that." He picked up another black Treat and bit into it, then grinned like a jack-o-'lantern.

Harley grinned back.

Marissa was hovering nearby. She grabbed Harley's arm and dragged her away.

"Hey," Harley protested.

"Greer's not somebody to hang with."

"Why not?" Harley demanded.

"Because he's a senior. The senior girls'll get you."

Harley let that sink in as Greer left their group and headed back toward the upperclassmen, where he grabbed Dara from behind, scaring her. She turned around and shoved him hard, at which he just laughed.

"Dara and her friends live to make our lives miserable." Marissa pulled Harley back toward the DJ. Harley let herself be moved, recognizing the wisdom of Marissa's advice. She saw Tyler Stapleton put a hand on Greer's chest and push him away; not aggressively so, just to get him out of earshot of the others as he leaned down and said something in his ear. Greer said something back that caused them both to grin like devils.

"Something's up," Harley said.

"What?" Marissa followed her gaze.

"I don't know. But something."

"Whatever it is, we're out of it. My dad's here and I don't want to get into any trouble or my mom'll go batshit crazy and ground me, or worse."

Harley looked toward the main door, where Marissa's stepdad was talking to one of the women who was looking up at him in that way that older women did sometimes. Kind of eager and disgusting.

"Okay?" Marissa asked, a little tense.

"Okay," Harley agreed.

The wine and superficial talk had given Jamie a headache. She finished her glass, tried to pay, was waved off, and Vicky poured her another before she could escape.

Jill lifted her nose and said, "I loved Emma. She was so smart. Sassy. I don't know who could have it in for her."

"I don't know that they 'had it in for her,'" Jamie responded. "She was just in the wrong place, the wrong time."

She wasn't certain she really believed that, but she never liked anyone saying anything about Emma.

"Maybe they were after you?" Vicky suggested with lifted brows.

"Victoria." Jill looked scandalized.

"We all heard that Jamie was supposed to be babysitting that night." Vicky turned her attention on Jamie. "All I'm saying is, maybe they thought Emma was you."

"You think I haven't thought of that?" Jamie questioned. She tried to say it lightly, but her guilt was so deep that she couldn't stop the catch in her voice.

"Oh, no." Alicia, the sensitive one, shot Vicky a dark look. "Come on, guys."

"Oh, shit. I'm sorry. Shoot me. I didn't mean to make you feel bad." Vicky looked chastened.

"It's fine, it's fine," assured Jamie. "I don't really think it had to do with me. I agree that it could have been a burglary gone wrong. Maybe they didn't know Emma was there. It didn't seem like it at the time—it seemed so personal—but maybe that's what it was. It's just that the police have never figured out anything, and it stole Emma's future."

"Let's not talk about it anymore," said Alicia. "It's . . . how long ago?"

"Twenty years, about." Jamie could've told them to the day if she'd wanted to.

Bette said, "Can we get back to me for a minute? If I divorce Kearns—"

"*When* you divorce Kearns," Jill interrupted.

"*If* I divorce Kearns, I'm going to take a terrible hit to my lifestyle. I don't know what I'll end up with. The house has a mortgage I can't afford, and the kids are expensive. And he's turned them against me anyway, so maybe I should just spend some money now . . . take a trip to Hawaii, or Bora Bora. I'd really like to go there."

"Expensive," Vicky pointed out.

"Kearns would never take me," she said, her lower lip protruding. She was clearly feeling sorry for herself.

Alicia said, "Maybe you can work things out."

Jill and Vicky both gave short, aborted laughs. "Sorry, Bette," said Vicky when Bette turned hurt eyes on her. "But when Kearns finds out about . . . stuff . . ."

"Your extracurricular activities," Jill said.

"It's just not going to work," finished Vicky.

Jamie finally remembered Phil Kearns from high school. Studious. Maybe a tad humorless. Was he the guy Emma had labeled "repressed"? "What does your husband do for a living?" she asked.

Bette sniffed. "Whines about his job. He's in commercial real estate. He's never happy. He says I'm never happy, so we're never happy."

"For God's sake, get a fucking divorce," Jill said.

Alicia asked, "What can we do to help?"

Bette managed to pull herself out of her pity party. "More wine?" she suggested.

And Vicky started waving for the proprietress again.

Chapter Eight

Cooper stood just outside the doors to the media room, recognizing most of the songs on the DJ's playlist, and for that he had Marissa to thank. He didn't feel old, but he was cruising toward forty, only a few years left. His stepdaughter was keeping him teen relevant.

The administrators at the school and the volunteers, mostly women, had taken him up on his offer to help chaperone, as if he were sent from heaven. They posted him outside the main door, while others kept vigil on the other exits, just in case some enterprising teen decided to escape. Kids were clustered in groups all over the main floor and on the stage above. Two of the volunteers were on the stage as well, a man and a woman, though they seemed more interested in talking to each other than watching their charges.

He looked down the empty hallway that led to the main doors of the school, the length of a basketball court away. There was another chaperone outside the media room's second door to the hallway, which also was the nearest exit to the bathrooms. A couple of kids had told him they wanted to use the facilities and he'd turned them back in and said to use the other door, to which they'd groaned and muttered comments about being jailed.

He smiled to himself. Laura had wanted to exert her

parental superiority, which was an ongoing need of hers; she believed he and Marissa were somehow plotting against her. She was therefore constantly making sure they knew who the real boss was. Tonight, he'd thwarted her by simply going along with her suggestion to chaperone. He'd learned early in their marriage that it was the best way to blunt her need to turn everything into a fight wherein he was always at fault. His seemingly easygoing attitude had won him major teasing at the station. Howie tried to make out that he was "pussy-whipped," a completely politically incorrect term that was also spectacularly inaccurate. Cooper hadn't explained his tactics to Howie. He didn't much care what anyone thought. What he cared about was working for the department and solving crimes and being there for Marissa. That was his life, and he was satisfied with it.

But then his thoughts turned traitorously to Jamie Whelan again. She'd hovered on his mind all day, no doubt about it. He'd wanted to reach out and hug her when they were standing in the parking lot.

Like that would make better what had happened to Emma. Emma.

"She was here for like ten minutes," Race Stillwell had told him in disgust the night of the attack. "Did you have something to do with it?"

They'd been standing outside the house after Emma left.

"Me?" Cooper had held himself back from shoving Race up against his car. Race had always been pugnacious; his younger brother was even worse.

"Well, what the fuck. She's *babysitting.* Took over for her sister for the Ryersons."

Cooper had a quick mental image of Dr. and Mrs. Ryerson. Nadine Ryerson oozed a certain sex appeal, while her husband seemed uptight and quiet. A MILF, one of his friends, Mark Norquist, had said of her, but then Mark was always saying stuff like that.

Cooper shrugged. He'd been thinking of blowing off the Stillwell party himself, had only gone because Emma might be there. Had spontaneously asked her sister at school that day to come because she looked like Emma.

"Let's spook her," Dug Douglas said. "It's almost Halloween. We know where the Ryersons live."

"She should still be here," Stillwell growled.

They were standing by their cars. Race's words burned Cooper. He knew it was a bit crazy, but he thought of Emma as his. They'd shared a few kisses, but Emma had made it clear she wasn't interested in anything further. Race was practically obsessed with her, however. Anything Emma did, any tiny little thing that seemed to show interest in him, he blew up into a major deal. Patrick "Dug" Douglas, his eternal sidekick, was always trying to help Race in his quest for Emma Whelan.

"Let's do it," said Robbie Padilla.

"I'm in," Mark Norquist agreed, and Tim Merchel, Cooper's closest friend, said the same.

It was decided that fast. Race said he had to get things settled at the party and then they would all coordinate at the Ryersons'. Dug, as ever, stayed with Race, and the rest of them were supposed to catch up with them later.

Cooper tried to talk Tim out of it. "Let's not go. Video games at my house," he tried to entice his friend.

"Are you kidding? It's almost Halloween. Let's get some pumpkins. Line 'em all up at the house. Ring the bell. Give her a scare."

"She's babysitting. There are kids there."

"They're probably already in bed. What's the matter? You still hung up on her?"

"It was never like that between us."

Tim smirked. "Race wants it to be that way with them. He's planning to pop her cherry."

Rarely had Cooper ever even noticed that kind of crude

talk among his friends, but when it was directed toward Emma, it made him uncomfortable. "Well, he's not gonna do it."

"Why? You got there first?"

"Shut up, man."

Tim cackled. "Oh, that's right. She's moved on to college guys. We're all too immature for her."

"Why're you getting on Emma?"

"Chill, dude. I'm just yanking your chain."

Cooper'd let it go then. Clearly, Tim, and probably all the guys, knew of his feelings, whether he thought he was hiding them or not.

Tim drove Cooper, Mark, and Robbie, and soon enough they met up with Race and Dug about three blocks from the Ryerson home.

"Have you seen Emma's sister?" Robbie asked. He was the shortest guy in the group, but he worked out and had strong biceps he loved to show off. He also was proud of the facial hair he could grow and was currently sporting a dark, Fu Manchu mustache. "She's just as pretty."

"And younger. Maybe you have a chance with her, Haynes." Tim grinned at him. Tim had sandy blond hair he wore long.

Cooper smiled and said, "Maybe." It had been a bold move to invite her to the party but cute girls were always welcome and Jamie Whelan was definitely cute.

"I'd do her," said Mark, but then, he could hardly keep from showing how horny he was all the time. Hugging and touching girls was all he wanted to do. Race had told him to knock it off, going so far as to suggest he step up his masturbation and give the girls at River Glen a break. Robbie had confided to Cooper that all Mark did was watch porn, which had made Cooper wonder if advising more masturbation was really the answer.

The six boys got to the Ryerson house and started tapping on the windows, sawing one that was partially open back and forth, which made wonderful, creaking sounds. They rolled the plastic garbage can at the side of the house along a rough stone path, and Tim made a low, moaning sound that could almost have been the wind had there been any that night. Robbie had a Michael Myers mask from the film *Halloween* that he jammed over his head before running onto the porch with a couple of pumpkins, which he set down in front of the door before ringing the doorbell. He was jumping down the porch stairs, planning to stand at the end of the front walk and stare back at Emma in a menacing way while Dug, who'd left the rest of them hiding behind a laurel hedge, was tapping on the front windows. But Emma, true to form, boldly threw open the door and stepped onto the front porch, not giving Dug time to hide as he half-stumbled, half-fell off the porch.

"Okay, Race. Dug. Time to go back to fourth grade where you belong!" Emma's voice rang out.

"Shit," Tim whispered beneath his breath from their hiding place.

"Shhh," said Robbie.

"Man, she's got boobs," said Mark.

Dug and Race, who'd both stumbled and run out of Emma's sight in opposite directions, circled around to meet the others behind the laurel hedge.

Once together again, Robbie said, "We should go."

"Don't be a pussy," said Dug. Though he was speaking to Robbie, he threw a look toward Race, trying to read his friend's mood.

"I'm not a pussy," Robbie declared.

"Shut up." Race was glaring intently at the Ryersons' front door. "It's still cracked open."

"Did she forget to close it?" Cooper asked.

"Nah. . . . She's waiting for us to come back." Race's face was set.

"You think she's got one of those water bazookas that really shoot out?" Tim asked. "She could be lying in wait."

"We should've thought of that!" Mark moved closer, seeking a better view of the door. "I'd like to see her in a wet T-shirt."

"Fucking pervert," Race snapped, and Mark shrugged and pulled back.

After a whispered consultation, they decided to try a few more things. They even went so far as to throw pebbles at the house, but Cooper told them to cut it out. He didn't want to break a window. He'd gone along with them because he'd hoped to see Emma, but the whole thing had grown dumber by the minute, and now she was on to them. When they realized the front door was fully shut, they realized Emma had given up the game. Everyone decided to leave except Dug, who never knew when to give up. Cooper tried to talk Dug into coming in his car, but Dug wouldn't listen. Irked, Race assured Cooper that he'd get Dug to leave before Emma did something stupid like call the police. Cooper ended up dropping Tim, Mark, and Robbie back at the party, then went back into town, cruising past the Ryersons' again to see if Race really had picked up Dug like he'd said he would. The street was entirely quiet as he drove by the house. The living room light was still on, the bedrooms dark. He turned around at the end of the block and took one more pass by. No sign of Emma, and no sign of Dug. He went home, never dreaming what was about to come down.

As soon as they learned about the attack, Cooper and all his friends had admitted to what they'd done at the time, pranking Emma, but none of them had seen anything. They'd left before the attack happened. They were all, to a one, full of rage over what had befallen Emma, and had expected quick answers and justice. Some sick, pervert needed to be caught and thrown behind bars.

But then the investigation had stalled.

And then it became clear that Emma wasn't going to recover completely.

Cooper was consumed with guilt. His friends, not so much. They were all just relieved they weren't considered persons of interest. For his part, Cooper haunted the police department. It killed him, what had happened to Emma. That her attacker had gotten away was a travesty. Somebody needed to *do* something. But there was no evidence, he learned much later, when he was in a position to view the case from a professional angle. No weapon. No witnesses. Nothing. If not for the knife wound, the case could have been ruled a complete accident.

No one at River Glen PD believed Emma's attack had anything to do with the two babysitters' deaths in Vancouver and Gresham. The prevailing theory was that it was a burglar or druggie looking for items to steal. That Emma, after the boys finished their scaring, had settled down and turned off the lights, that maybe she hadn't quite closed the front door, because there was no sign of forced entry, even though the boys assured the authorities she had, or maybe it had been the creaking window that had allowed access . . . that whoever had come in had been surprised at finding Emma, who might have believed it was one of her classmates and foolishly decided to confront them . . .

His uncomfortable thoughts brought him back to the present and where he was and what had precipitated that uncomfortable trip down memory lane. Jamie Whelan. Emma's sister. She looked a lot more like Emma than his ex-wife did. It annoyed him that Howie could be right: he clearly had a type.

"What's wrong?" a girl's voice asked. She walked through the media room door to stand beside him in the hallway.

He was about to tell her that once she left, she couldn't go back in—the rules were specific and strict—when he saw it was Jamie's daughter, Harley. He started to warn her not to venture into the hall through his door when the vice principal, Adam Wellesley, was suddenly there. "Miss? Miss? Are you leaving?"

Harley turned to give Wellesley a hard look. Something about her, too, reminded him of Emma. Not the Emma of the past, who was bold but polite to adults, but the Emma of today, at least the last time he'd seen her, with her lack of affect and inability to pick up social cues.

"I was talking to Mr. Haynes, who brought me to this event," Harley said in a careful tone.

There was a warning in there, which Wellesley chose to ignore, or was too obtuse himself to give it any credit. "Well, get back inside. Otherwise you have to go," Wellesley sniped.

Harley looked at Cooper. "What's wrong?" she asked again.

"Why do you think something's wrong?"

"You're glowering. Or you were. Did something happen?"

"Miss?" Wellesley wasn't giving up.

"Let's step back in," Cooper said, and Harley looked at Wellesley and jumped back inside while Cooper stepped into the semidarkened room lit only with the current DJ's black lights.

The rumor that the school had a drug problem was one shared by more parents than just Laura. The teachers and administrators were on high alert as well. Cooper had been told to watch all the students carefully. Cooper didn't doubt that drugs were around, but so far, he hadn't seen any blatant users, nor had he smelled the skunky scent of marijuana. If anyone asked him, his guess would be alcohol as the substance of choice of the high schoolers, though he hadn't seen anyone in particular he thought might be inebriated. It was just more his own history that clued him in. When he was in school, it was damn near a rite of passage.

As if belatedly realizing her friend wasn't with her, Marissa came charging over. "What happened?" she asked Harley. "Come on. We're all still talking with . . . uh . . . well, just come on."

"I thought it might be better to . . . y'know . . . stay out of the line of fire."

Marissa half-laughed. "Maybe he just likes you," she said, jerking her head to get Harley to come back into the center of the crowd.

Harley followed after her a bit reluctantly. Cooper wondered exactly what had happened, but then one of the parent volunteers, a woman named Caroline, hovered by him, initiating conversation. She'd been hovering all night, as a matter of fact. Cooper wasn't dense. She was interested.

You should ask her out. Forget your unhealthy obsession with Emma Whelan and her sister, which is based on fantasy. Get out there. Make a move.

He made a point of making direct eye contact while he smiled. Caroline's own smile widened into joy and disbelief.

Cooper looked over the crowd of heads, trying to pick out Harley and Marissa, and then saw that they were on the stage.

"Want a popcorn ball?" Caroline asked him, holding out an orange one.

"No, I—"

A collective shriek suddenly ripped through the crowd, so loud it drowned out the music.

Cooper glanced over to see Harley teetering at the edge the stage, arms pinwheeling, a guy in a Michael Myers mask with his hands around her neck.

Before Cooper could move, she was falling backward off the stage.

Chapter Nine

Cooper was halfway to the stage, running like a madman, when Harley landed on a sea of hands of students who held her up. Everyone was shrieking in delight. Once down, Harley crossed her arms over her chest as the students passed her across the top of the crowd, while Marissa, face to the ceiling, her hands already folded across her chest, was pushed backward off the stage by a guy in a Grim Reaper outfit onto the now freed and waiting hands below.

"Déjà-fucking-vu," Robbie Padilla said under his breath to Cooper, his gaze on the Michael Myers masked figure who had threatened and then pushed Harley, when Vice Principal Wellesley's booming voice over the loudspeaker caught everyone's attention: "Stop what you're doing right now!"

The lights came up in a flood and the boys were caught before they could scramble around enough to hide their masks. There were others in "killer" masks on the stage as well. Jason from *Friday the 13th* in his hockey mask. Freddy Krueger from *A Nightmare on Elm Street*. Dracula. Varying and assorted zombies, and even Chucky, the vicious "doll" from the series with his name. Senior boys, mostly, Cooper thought, recognizing some of them. Apparently, they'd decided to make Autumn Daze a Halloween party all on their own.

"Call the police!" one of the parents yelled, and others

echoed that sentiment. It took close to twenty minutes for the crowd to realize that Cooper, who was already there, *was* the police. Wellesley and several other chaperones took the miscreants into a back room, where the vice principal could be heard giving them the lecture of a lifetime.

The scare effectively ended the mixer. While Cooper became in charge of crowd control, the DJ was asked to pack up his gear and, when he was convinced that he would be paid in full, did so. By that time there was still an hour or so to go before some of the kids' parents were due to pick them up. Cooper's offer to stay on the premises rather than call all the parents was gratefully accepted by the harried chaperones and staff. Some students were picked up, mostly from the younger classes, and left, but almost all the upper-classmen stayed on.

As soon as they were safely on their feet, Cooper had immediately checked with Harley and Marissa, both of whom shrugged off his concern. Marissa, in fact, appeared to be on cloud nine. She was all a-bubble about having been singled out by the seniors, though from what Cooper had seen, it was Harley who'd been the chosen "victim." Had it been an honor? Marissa was definitely treating it as such, and Harley was being a pretty good sport about it, especially considering it was her first day. But maybe she'd been in on the prank? Still, there were twin spots of color high on her cheeks and her eyes were wide.

"They picked you because you're new!" Marissa crowed. "I was so scared! Those guys can be harsh . . . well, the girls for sure."

"They didn't mean it as a bad thing," Harley finally spoke up.

"Scary, though, huh? If the kids hadn't caught you, I would have grabbed Troy by the hair before I let him push me off!"

"Troy Stillwell?" Cooper asked.

"Yeah. He's a senior."

"I know who he is." Cooper was short. "That was dangerous," he added.

"Yeah, but the administration is so overprotective. They had to do something." Marissa frowned. "Maybe they'll be expelled," she said in dawning horror.

"They'd have to expel half the senior class," Cooper remarked, looking around at the remaining kids standing beneath the glaring overhead lights. They stood in defiant groups, shooting angry glances toward the adults, especially the ones who were the most righteously offended, Caroline being one of them, who swore the boys in the masks should all be arrested.

"They're little short of terrorists!" he heard her declare from across the room. Her daughter looked like a freshman. She was caught in her mother's arms. Two other mothers were hovering nearby, gripping their own daughters tightly. All three girls' expressions were long-suffering as the moms chattered over their heads in collective outrage.

"You sure you're all right?" Cooper asked Harley again. "I can call your mother."

"Don't call her. Don't tell her, okay? I don't want her to know."

Marissa shot a quick look at Harley and said, in a non sequitur, "Maybe he likes you."

Harley didn't respond to that.

Cooper said, "Your mom's going to find out about what happened, and—"

"Just don't tell her tonight. *Please?*" Harley cut him off.

Cooper had no wish to tell Jamie about what had transpired, especially regarding the Michael Myers mask. In Race Stillwell's account to the police after Emma's attack, he'd copped to the fact that he'd worn that mask, and that detail had made it into the paper. Jamie would likely remember.

"I don't want my mom to know about the *Halloween* mask," Harley said, which pretty well explained that she knew about it, too.

It deeply embarrassed Cooper that he'd been part of the group who'd played those tricks on Emma. Robbie Padilla came up at the end of their conversation with his son, Marcus, in tow, one of Marissa and Harley's classmates. He gave Cooper a look that said he was feeling much the same way. Marcus had been named for Mark Norquist, their horn-dog friend, who'd died serving in the army in Afghanistan.

"What a way to start the school year, huh?" Robbie said when Harley, Marissa, and Marcus had wandered back to the punch bowl.

"Yeah."

"I keep thinking about that night. You?"

Cooper nodded slowly.

"And that new girl is Emma's . . . niece?"

"Jamie's daughter. Yes."

"Right." Robbie nodded. "I remember Jamie."

"I saw her today."

"Yeah?"

"She looks a lot like Emma."

Robbie exhaled heavily. "What a way to start the school year," he repeated.

"Well, thank you, all. It was great fun," Jamie said, grabbing her purse and getting up. She'd barely touched her second glass of wine, and when the women had protested, she'd said, "I've got driving in my future. Can't drink anymore."

"You can't leave yet." This was from Bette, who'd decided not only to include Jamie, but to make her her new best friend. Bette, however, was half-sloshed.

"I've really got to go. My daughter's been texting me. She's ready to leave."

"The kids are all going out afterward," said Vicky. "I'll text Tyler to make sure he takes care of Harley."

"*No*." All four women's heads turned at Jamie's emphatic response. "Please. It'll only embarrass her. Again, thank you. Really. It was so much fun. Another time . . ."

She sketched them all a bright wave, then hurried out the door. She felt weird. Exhausted. Like she'd just escaped some dire fate by the skin of her teeth. Gulping air, she emitted a half-hysterical laugh. She'd been without friends for so long, it was like learning a foreign language to be accepted by a tight group. It was damn hard work.

She drove back to the house, knowing Harley would never want to come home even a minute early. Sitting outside in her car, she rolled down a window and let the cool, almost cold, October air inside. A smashed pumpkin on the sidewalk and the earthy scent of a pile of red and gold and brown leaves slipped inside as well. A faint breeze sent leaves on the trees whispering.

Jamie lay her head back against the headrest and closed her eyes. She didn't want to go in yet. Emma would likely be in bed. She'd told Jamie she liked to be in bed by eight-thirty, no later. Mom's shift was from seven to seven. She'd generally worked three-and-a-half, twelve-hour days a week, and she was back in the morning to take Emma to work. There was also just enough time to pick her up in the evening before starting another shift. It had worked well for both of them, and Mom and Theo scheduled it so that if Mom had to work a Saturday, Emma would be at the Thrift Shop that day as well, so that she wasn't alone for hour upon hour. Even so, there were those times that Mom was sleeping and Emma was home, but Emma, understanding, was notably scrupulous about keeping the house quiet.

Jamie knew all this from the brief communications she'd

received from her mother over the years, along with the somewhat rambling accounts Emma would sometimes relate.

Now, though, she didn't want to go inside. She didn't want to go to her bed in the storage closet. Instead she switched on her cell and scrolled through her contact list. Before she could chicken out, she phoned her old friend, Camryn. She hadn't talked to her in a couple of years, maybe more. The last time Jamie had come home had been two Christmases ago. She and Harley had driven up, but it had been so tense with Mom that Jamie had cut the trip short, and they'd driven home with snow drifting down in the Siskiyous. They'd just gotten out ahead of a major snow-storm.

"Jamie?" Camryn answered warmly. "I heard you were in town! I've been meaning to call you, but it's crazy with work. You've got your daughter with you, right? What is she, a freshman? Oh, God. Is she at River Glen High?"

"Sophomore. Yes," Jamie said. She started to say some-thing more, but was stopped by a thickness in her throat and a sudden sting of tears.

Luckily, Camryn didn't notice. "Wow. I should've had kids. I never found the right guy, though, and the thought of a sperm bank . . . I don't know. Not for me."

Jamie, recovered enough to respond, said, "Harley started at River Glen today, and she's at the fall mixer tonight."

"Oh my God! They still have those? Where are you? At your mom's place?"

"For now. I don't really know what my long-term plans are."

"I mean *right now*. Are you free? Come over here! You know where my condo is? Off Fernwood?"

"Well, yeah."

"Do you have time? When do you pick up Harley?"

"She getting a ride back with . . . Cooper Haynes. He's got a daughter, a stepdaughter, in Harley's grade."

"Ah, Cooper, yes. He still looks good. Have you seen him?"

"He and Marissa picked up Harley, too, and . . . I saw him earlier, at the school."

"He's a cop. Can you believe it? And Robbie Padilla's the phys ed teacher at the high school. God, get over here and let's talk. What do you drink? Wine? I have some vodka . . . or coffee?"

"Coffee," Jamie said firmly.

"Do you have a cold? You sound kind of stuffed up."

"Allergies," she lied, swallowing back the tears that were damn near impossible to hold back.

"They're a bitch, aren't they?" Camryn said knowingly.

"Maybe I should come in and tell your mom what happened," Cooper said again as they drove into Harley's driveway.

"*No.* Please! No. I'll tell her." Harley had one hand on the door handle and was opening it the moment Cooper got the vehicle into Park.

Marissa said, "Dad, don't do that," the same time Harley protested.

Harley was already out of the car and dashing toward the back of the house. She'd said she knew where the key was, which alarmed Cooper some more. Was Jamie not home?

"The lights are on," Marissa said. She was seated in the front seat beside him. "Let's go."

The truth was, Cooper was heading to the station to meet with, and hopefully pacify, some of the parents, Caroline being one of them. They wanted some sort of police action, pointing out that at least one of the boys had been "brandishing a weapon." He'd been the one wearing the long, evil-looking Freddy Krueger finger knives, and though they were blunted metal, part of a costume, these parents wanted him arrested for terrorism. Cooper had tried to suggest letting the school take action first. The school had strict rules of their own. But he'd seen that wasn't going to cut it, so he'd agreed to meet the angry parent posse at the department.

"You're not going to arrest Tyler, are you?" Marissa asked now. "You're not going to listen to those crazies."

"They're concerned parents and there are school rules," he began.

"It was just a joke!"

Marissa had come a long way from being sanguine about the senior boys being expelled to out-and-out alarm. She'd fully adopted the general feeling of all her classmates: that the parents were crazy freak-outers just looking to jump off the deep end. Also, she had been particularly interested in several of the perpetrators: Tyler Stapleton, Troy Stillwell, and the kid who'd pushed Harley, Greer Douglas, Dug Douglas's son.

Earlier, Robbie had said of Greer, "Branch of the same tree."

Cooper didn't know the boy himself, but he knew Dug, who'd taken over his dad's auto and home insurance business, with satellite offices in River Glen and several other Portland bedroom communities. Dug and his wife, who lived in a sprawling home in Staffordshire Estates, had twice been reported for disturbances by the neighbors; they had a tendency to have screaming fights when they'd had too much to drink.

Cooper took Marissa home, and Laura was already waiting outside. He could tell she wanted to talk, but he waved her off and went to the station. There was limited administrative staff after-hours, while two officers worked nights with others on call, if need be, so he was alone except for Howie and the small group of assembled upset parents looking for police action.

Howie was on his feet as Cooper entered, ready to bolt. "You got this?" he said, and Cooper nodded somewhat tiredly. The posse of parents were furious that the boys had been released to their parents' custody at the school.

"They should all be in jail," one woman declared. Edina Something. This had been her mantra from the beginning.

He spent the next hour listening to Edina, Caroline, and a woman named Marty, and her husband, Hal, complain vociferously about the boys involved in the incident, the school's lack of discipline, the deplorable state of the country's youth, and the problem with lack of respect in the world as a whole. He wrote down notes about the boys and tried to look attentive. He didn't offer any advice, and as the four of them wound down, Edina, short, sturdy, with a fierce look in her eye, who seemed to be the self-appointed head of their group, asked suspiciously, "You're not going to do anything, are you?"

Cooper pretended to think that over. It occurred to him that a fair amount of his job was acting. "They're minors. The 'weapon' they brought onto school property is a prop for a costume."

"They pushed that girl off the stage!" Marty reminded on a gasp.

Cooper nodded. "She was caught by a number of kids who had their hands up, ready to catch her. It was planned. I'm not saying it's—"

"It's a conspiracy!" Twin flags of color rode high in Edina's cheeks.

Hal, a voice of reason Cooper learned, reminded his wife, "One of those kids was ours."

Marty burst into tears and Edina sucked in her lips, as if she'd tasted something bad. "So, you'll do nothing?"

"I'm going to let the school make the decisions," said Cooper, which satisfied none of them, but at least he got a nod of agreement from Hal.

"You've got my formal complaint," Edina said, pointing at the form she'd filled out.

Cooper nodded.

Caroline, who'd taken in the whole debate, but had said nothing, lingered after the other three trooped out the door. While Hal looking back dolefully at Cooper as he pushed through the exit door, clearly already over the whole debacle, Caroline asked Cooper, "Do you have a number where I can reach you, just in case I need to?"

Cooper flashed on how he'd shown himself to be receptive to her earlier. He could have kicked himself now. What had he been trying to prove? That he wasn't interested in Jamie? That he just needed to meet other women? He saw that Caroline may have used this excuse to keep their earlier connection alive. Somewhat reluctantly, he gave out his cell phone number, though he tried to press upon her that it was best to reach him at the station. He could have denied her, but that felt like it would be inordinately rude, especially after he'd acted interested earlier.

After she'd gone, Cooper picked up said cell phone and scrolled through it for Jamie's number, which he'd gotten from Marissa before he'd dropped her off. She'd made him swear on her life that he wouldn't call Jamie and tell her about Harley and her being pushed off the stage, so he wouldn't, but he was going to follow up later to make sure Jamie eventually got the straight story.

Jamie sat at the small kitchen table in Camryn's condo, feeling tensions slip away as her old friend regaled her with stories about friends of theirs from high school. Camryn, whose hair was cut in a short, blondish bob and who always seemed to wear a smile, was an aide at the grade school and was in contact with lots of their schoolmates through their kids. Only a few of them had high school kids like Jamie.

Camryn said, "Dug Douglas, Icky Vicky, and, well, Cooper, sort of. Some others, I think, but mostly the parents have grade-schoolers or no children at all, like me."

Camryn had moved to Portland after college and married an older man with kids who'd been in high school. They'd divorced about four years earlier, and she'd ended up with enough money to buy her condo outright with enough left over to make it easy for her to support herself. "I should do like you and become a teacher. I like it. I like being around the kids. I probably should have had children when I could."

"It's not too late, is it?" Jamie asked. Camryn tried to refill her cup of decaf coffee, but Jamie waved her off. She'd laid out a plate of assorted crackers and cheese, and Jamie, who'd managed half a peanut butter sandwich at home with Emma and Harley, dug in, famished.

"It's way too late. For me anyway. I just don't see it happening. If I'd started when you did and had one already in high school, that would be okay. I think maybe I'm too lazy. I like just taking care of me, and I volunteer at Luv-Ahh-Pet Animal Shelter, a great place. It's just outside the River Glen city limits." She pointed northeast.

Jamie thought of her own responsibilities. The uncertainty of her life was enough to make her yearn for what Camryn had.

"Oh, by the way. You know whose twins are in one of my classes? Teddy Ryerson's."

Jamie moved sharply in surprise and knocked into her mug, sloshing coffee. Apologizing profusely, she jumped up to help, but Camryn told her not to worry, she'd find a sponge. Luckily, only a little liquid had spilled onto the table and Camryn easily swiped it up.

"His wife died. Leukemia, I think. So, he's in charge of the twins, Oliver and Anika. They're seven now. Second-graders. And Teddy's some kind of investment guy. He lives at his parents' old house. You know they divorced. Of course you do."

"Yes."

Dr. William and Nadine Ryerson had split not long after the terrible attack on Emma, citing irreconcilable differences. Teddy and Serena had stayed with Nadine in River Glen, while William moved on to a new relationship and a new life in a new area.

Palm Desert, maybe? Jamie wasn't sure. As soon as Teddy and Serena were of age, Nadine left River Glen as well and had also chosen to live somewhere in the Southwest.

"She gave the house to Teddy and Serena, right?" Jamie asked. Anything that touched on Emma's attack made her feel like she was gossiping about her sister.

"Yes. Serena lives in Portland. She's a nurse. I think she worked at Glen Gen for a while. Oh, right. Your mom knew her."

Jamie nodded. Mom had been very circumspect and careful about Serena Ryerson. She couldn't look at any of the Ryersons, or their house, without thinking about Emma's attack. She had made a few remarks about Serena to Harley, whom she spoke with more often than Jamie, but in the long run, she'd grudgingly admitted Serena worked hard and did a good job. Somewhere in the last few years, Serena had moved on to a Portland hospital, and Jamie had heard she worked in the cardiac unit.

She knew next to nothing about Teddy Ryerson.

"So, Teddy has twins," she said now.

"Yep. They're cute as buttons. Oliver's fairly outgoing, but Anika's shy."

"A lot like Teddy and Serena."

"Ah, yes. You babysat for them."

Jamie nodded slowly.

"It's still hard, isn't it? Especially with Emma, the way

she is." Camryn sighed. "I still wish I knew what happened that night. We all do, I guess."

"Yeah."

They talked for a while more, but Jamie was starting to feel tired and worn out. It had been a stressful day. "I'd better go," she said, putting her empty mug by the sink. "Harley's probably back by now. I'm kind of surprised she hasn't called me already. And I want to check on Emma."

"If you need anything? Any extra help, or anything, anything at all, I'm around, with a lot of time on my hands since I broke up with my last boyfriend. More like a friend really. It never got out of the gate, truth be told."

"I've had a few of those," Jamie admitted. Friendships that couldn't seem to turn the corner to romance, although she suspected it was more her fault than theirs.

"I was dating this guy for a while . . ." She seemed to want to continue, then said, "Well, it was never going to go anywhere." She made a face, then changed the subject. "No one in your life either?" she asked curiously.

"Nope."

"You know who I was dating? Nate."

"Nate Farland?"

"He lives in Seattle, so it was kind of whenever he was in the Portland area. His job's something in tech. He used to live here. We connected on the tail end of that, but then he moved. He made a half-hearted attempt to get me to move to Seattle, but I'm stuck in River Glen. By choice," she added.

"Nate . . ." Jamie smiled and shook her head. He'd been a sometime buddy of theirs in high school, never anything more.

"I know, right? I kind of thought, hey, maybe this'll turn into something now that we're mature adults. . . . Ha! I kept thinking about how he was such a goofball. Couldn't get past it!"

They both laughed. It felt good.

Jamie said, "I'm glad you're here. It's nice to have a real friend."

"Me too. Did you know Gwen Winkelman's a psychologist in town? You were good friends with her."

"Once upon a time. We don't really keep in touch." Jamie felt that same twinge of guilt she always did that she hadn't been quite fair to Gwen as a friend.

"Her parents left her the house, too. A lot of that going around in River Glen."

"Did she get rid of all the weird tchotchkes and fake Spanish moss and other decorations around the outside of the house?"

"God no. I think she likes being 'mystical.' It's worse than ever. I talked to Rosie, too, about a month ago. She lives in Florida now. I keep telling myself I should go visit her, maybe in January when the weather's cold and wet. We should go together."

"Yeah." Jamie knew that was never going to happen with her current responsibilities.

Jamie hadn't mentioned that she'd met with Icky Vicky and her crowd for drinks earlier. Hadn't wanted to. She'd enjoyed just listening to Camryn and not having to add much input. But now she let her friend know about meeting them for wine, admitting she felt she was invited because she was a curiosity to them.

"Because of Emma," Camryn said, and Jamie nodded. "Well, they're nice enough, I suppose. Very protective of their boys, Vicky, Jill, and I don't know Bette well, but she's right in there. I remember Phil Kearns. Kind of supercilious."

Jamie remembered that about Bette's husband, too. "People change."

"Not that much."

Later, as Jamie was driving home, she got a call from the house phone. Harley.

"Hey, finally. I was getting worried," she answered before Harley could say anything. "I didn't call because I didn't want to wake Emma. How was the mixer?"

A pause. "You didn't wake me," her sister said. "Harley did. She's in bed crying."

Jamie broke the speed limit driving home and screeched into the driveway. She ran to the back door to find it locked. Of course. She banged on it with the flat of her hand, then whirled around and went for the gnome that held the key. Not. There.

She just managed to keep from screaming before Emma appeared at the door. "Be quiet. You'll wake the dead," she said in her flat voice.

"Where's the key?" Jamie demanded as she brushed past her and racewalked for the stairs.

"Harley forgot to put it back. Tsk-tsk."

Jamie ran up the stairs and took a moment at the top landing to pull herself together. Her heart was pounding. It would do no good to scare her daughter. Maybe it was nothing. Maybe everything was okay. It was just that Harley never cried.

She walked down the hall with measured steps, forcing herself not to race. She hesitated outside Harley's door. There was no sound.

She heard Emma come up the stairs and stop at the top, like Jamie had. Jamie looked back at her sister. Emma wore sweatpants and a loose, white T-shirt with "River Glen General" stitched across the breast pocket.

"Are you going in?" asked Emma.

Jamie nodded, then tapped softly on the door. "Harley?"

When there was no answer, she twisted the knob and cracked the door about two inches. "Harley?"

Harley was lying on her stomach, deathly still. Jamie knew her daughter well enough to suspect she was feigning sleep. "Can I come in?"

Still no response.

Jamie's pulse sped up in spite of herself. She swiftly moved inside and laid a hand on her daughter's arm.

Harley snatched her arm beneath her and lifted her head enough to growl, "What are you doing?"

"Just checking on you."

"Well, I'm fine. Just fine. Trying to sleep, if anybody'd let me." She flopped back down.

Except she wasn't just fine. Her voice was strained and she was hiding her face.

"How was the mixer?"

No response.

"Emma heard you crying."

"I wasn't crying!" Muffled. Into her pillow.

"What happened?"

"Nothing!"

"Did something happen to you? Or your friend . . . Marissa?"

A long, long pause. Knowing she was probably pushing it, Jamie placed her hand on Harley's head and stroked her hair. They were both quiet for long minutes.

Jamie had closed the door when she'd ducked inside, but now it cracked open and Emma looked in.

"We're okay here," Jamie told her.

"I put the key back. Harley left it on the counter. I'm going to bed." Emma closed the door and Jamie heard her shuffling down the hall, then the muffled sound of a closing door.

Harley slowly edged herself in a sitting position, her back

to the headboard. Her bed was a twin and she'd clearly been crying. "I'm not crying. I'm angry!" she declared.

Jamie nodded, though she didn't believe it for a second.

And then it all came pouring out. A boy. An older boy, Greer, had shown Harley some attention. He'd seemed kind of nice at first, but Marissa had warned her to be careful. And then . . . and then . . . it turned out Marissa liked him! That she had for a long time. Either him or Tyler Stapleton . . . or maybe Troy something or other. The coolest guys in the senior class, even though Marissa said the senior boys were off-limits because of the senior girls. But this guy liked Harley. He'd called her up on stage, and Marissa, too, but then all the boys ran back to where they'd hidden stuff earlier and came out in these masks and costumes. Greer put on a Halloween mask and then pretended to come at Harley like a zombie. She knew it was Greer by his shoes. And then he put his hands around her neck and *pushed* her over the edge of the stage.

"What?" Jamie asked on a swift intake of breath.

"No, no . . . it was fine. He whispered in my ear before it happened. It was a mosh pit. The other kids all knew to catch me. Everyone was pissed about the school canceling the Halloween mixer, so they decided to make this one like it."

Harley's animated face collapsed, and it looked like she was about to cry again.

"Well, then, what was it?"

"It was kinda scary . . . and . . ."

Jamie kept very still and waited. Harley confided in her so rarely that she didn't want to blow this moment by being too eager.

"They found out that I was Emma's niece and one of 'em talked about her like she was . . ." Harley's voice had gotten softer and softer and Jamie could scarcely hear her.

"What did he say?" Jamie asked again, her voice like steel.

Harley shook her head. "You know."

"Which boy?"

"Just one of 'em."

She clearly didn't want to reveal his name. Jamie understood the teenage code, but she could well imagine the kind of thoughtless, cruel slurs that could come out of a teenager's mouth. Her blood boiled, but she clamped her jaw shut even though she wanted to rage against the injustice of it all.

"But . . ." Harley pressed her fingers to her eyes in a fruitless attempt to stop more tears. "I did kind of like him. But I really like Marissa. She's the only one I know."

Jamie knew very little about what had transpired between Harley and her boyfriend from her last school and was tempted to brush off the importance of liking some new guy she'd just met, but this connection with Harley was too fragile to trample over.

"Maybe it'll work itself out. Maybe Marissa'll get with Tyler," she said lightly.

Harley suddenly glared at Jamie as if she'd lost her mind. "Tyler Stapleton? Not a chance. Jesus, Mom. He's the coolest guy in school. That won't happen!"

"All right."

"She might as well get with a rock star! She'd have about the same chance!"

"Fine." Jamie rose to her feet.

"I have a way better chance of getting with Greer than Marissa ever will with Tyler!"

"Well, it looks like you've clearly figured out the cliques at school after just one day." Jamie eased toward the door. Cease-fire was over. Harley was again throwing slings and arrows.

"It's just such a pisser! And Greer'll probably be thrown out of school. He didn't even wear the metal claws. That was Troy. And Tyler's in trouble, too. He had on the hockey mask."

Goose bumps rose on Jamie's skin. Halloween mask . . . "What mask was Greer wearing?"

"The one from the movies."

Jamie had never told Harley the particulars about how the boys from Emma's class had scared her with a Michael Myers mask. Harley knew about the attack, but not all the ins and outs, unless someone told her or she read about it. Clearly that hadn't happened as yet, or she would know how that particular mask would affect Jamie and, more importantly, Emma.

She was feeling anxious inside, both from Harley's take and from something else, too, that she couldn't quite define.

Harley sighed and settled into the bed. Now that she'd passed on her fears to Jamie, she was more relaxed. Realizing it was her cue to leave, Jamie headed into the hall. "Thanks, Mom," she thought she heard Harley say as she was shutting the door behind her.

She went back downstairs. Found the key on the kitchen counter, as Emma had said. Hurrying outside to put it back into place, she felt a shiver slip down her spine from the stiff breeze rattling the maple leaves and heard the soft *ding, ding, ding* of the garden wind chime.

Back inside, she double-checked the door was locked, then went through the first floor checking windows and the front door. Upstairs, she walked through her mom's room to stand by the window and look over the garden and the side of the garage for long moments before she undressed for bed and made her way to her closet bedroom.

Chapter Ten

It was a trick getting Emma to wait until Sunday evening to scatter Mom's ashes in the garden. The waiting made her anxious, and beside making sure all the dish towels were lined up, she couldn't help herself from going into both Harley's and Jamie's bedrooms and doing the same to their bath towels, not to mention organizing their personal beauty supplies. Jamie had come back to find her rather meager supply of facial creams and nail polish and hair supplies lined up by descending height. Harley got the same treatment, but Emma also organized her eye makeup, laying each piece on the counter in neat rows by width, fattest to skinniest. Jamie talked it over with Harley, expecting her to have a conniption fit, like she would if Jamie touched anything of hers, but Emma got a pass.

"If it makes her feel better, fine." Harley shrugged.

"Okay."

"But if she touches my backpack . . ."

Harley's backpack apparently held her most prized possessions. Jamie had unapologetically sneaked through it a time or two, afraid there might be secrets within that could cause harm, but had only discovered doodles in the margins of her notebooks with different boys' names, one surrounded by a heart . . . only to be scratched out the next time Jamie had peeked. These forays into Harley's life were few and far between; her daughter was very careful. Jamie hadn't been able to check in a while. Now, she said, "You'll have to give her a pass on that, too. You can ask her not to look again, and she might respect your wishes, but getting Emma to alter behavior is a trick I haven't learned yet."

Jamie had gone to the store and purchased a variety of crackers, several cheeses, and some fruit. She was really low on funds and was trying to stretch the budget until she could earn some income. It broke her heart a bit when Emma, who'd been with Jamie at the store and apparently understood why Jamie was carefully adding the items in her cart, pulled out a hundred dollars in twenties. "I didn't give it to Mom because she was dead," Emma explained. "You can have it."

"I don't want to take your money," Jamie had told her, but Emma shook the bills at her.

"I want you to make bucatini carbonara."

"What?" Jamie had asked faintly.

"It's pasta," Emma explained, and when Jamie took a moment to think that through, she clarified, "noodles."

"I think it's on one of her saved Food Network episodes," Harley told Jamie later. "She likes pasta."

Jamie had dutifully found a recipe online and bought all the ingredients, but she was planning on attempting the dish sometime in the future. She wasn't taking that on on the same day they were scattering Mom's ashes. Jamie had invited Theo to join them, but she already had plans, and then Harley had begged, begged, *begged* her to let her have Marissa come over, too.

"Marissa doesn't need to be spreading Mom's ashes," Jamie had told her a bit heatedly. In truth, she just wanted it over herself.

"Pleeeeeaaassseeee . . ." Harley had pressed her palms

together and gazed at her beseechingly. "I'll be the only kid and I don't even want to do it."

Emma had overheard this ongoing battle and had kept out of it. But on Sunday morning, Harley turned to her aunt and asked, "Don't you think I should have someone here?"

Jamie opened her mouth to protest, then shut it, waiting. Emma walked across the room to the urn that held their mother's ashes. She touched her forehead against it and closed her eyes, which made Harley and Jamie slide a look to each other. After a full minute, Emma lifted her head and walked away from them.

"What . . . did Grandma say?" Harley asked her.

Emma stopped on her way down the hall and gave Harley a queer look. "Mom can't talk anymore," she said, then headed on her way to the downstairs bathroom.

The perplexed look on Harley's face nearly brought Jamie to laughter.

"'Mom can't talk,'" Jamie repeated, fighting a grin, though it took everything she had.

"Please, Mom. Please can I ask Marissa?" begged Harley, back to what she really wanted.

"You're wearing me down." Jamie sighed and finally nodded, but as Harley ran to the landline, she added, "Tell her what we're doing. Make sure she knows what kind of weird invitation this is."

It turned out that Marissa was more than eager to come. "She and her mom are still in a kind of fight over what happened at the mixer and she just wants out of the house," Harley admitted.

"Wouldn't she rather go to Cooper—her stepdad's, er, dad's place?"

"Just call him her dad. She does. I think he's busy, too," said Harley.

Jamie thought about that while she finished preparing for the evening's event. Was he busy with work, or was it something in his personal life? Though Bette had said she was after him, Vicky hadn't acted like he was hooked up with anyone new, but it probably was only a matter of time. Cooper was the kind of guy women naturally flocked to. Even she, who'd convinced herself she was long over her high school crush, found her mind snagging on his name whenever it came up.

But even as Jamie got ready for her father and Debra and Marissa to come over for their five p.m. event, the doorbell rang. Jamie was in the kitchen, laying out the cheese and fruit plates, and the sound of the bell caused her to momentarily freeze.

She wiped her hands on one of the dish towels, then walked to the front door. It was too early for her dad and Debra, so who?

When she opened the door she didn't recognize the tallish man and woman on the front porch. The man was holding an orange-wrapped package in his hands. Lifting her brows, Jamie smiled at the strangers, who looked to be somewhere in their twenties.

"Jamie," the man said on a relieved sigh, as if he'd been looking for her and finally found her. He was fairly tall, with blond-brown hair, blue eyes. His mouth twitched as if it wanted to smile but couldn't quite figure out how. The young woman wore her blond hair in a low bun at her nape and, despite her height, had a delicate facial structure. She looked at Jamie, and then at her companion, who said, half a beat later, "I'm Ted Ryerson."

Jamie inhaled in surprise. "Teddy . . . ?"

"I know. It's been a long time. This is Serena. You remember my sister . . . ?"

"Yes, yes, of course," Jamie said, smiling at the quiet, slender woman beside him, thinking of the scared little girl in the nightgown. She opened the door wider. "Can you come in for a bit?"

"No. My kids . . . the twins are in the car. Oliver and Anika."

Jamie looked past him to the Mercedes SUV. She could see one towhead, bent over something, in the back seat; the other person was obscured by a headrest.

"They're on their iPads," Teddy admitted.

"Well, you can all come in," Jamie invited, doing a quick inventory in her head about how much each person would be able to take from her appetizer tray.

"We'd better not," said Serena. "We just wanted to stop by."

"You look just like her," Teddy said, staring at Jamie. Serena's head whipped around to stare at him, then back at Jamie.

"Uh . . . you mean . . . ?" Jamie asked, fading out.

"Emma," he clarified. "Except you have brown eyes. I remember that."

There was an awkward pause. Serena really looked at Jamie, but by her frown, Jamie guessed she didn't feel quite the same way as her brother. To fill the gap, Jamie said to Teddy, "Well, you look quite different."

"Everyone says I look just like my father." He handed her the package. "This is for you."

"Thank you," said Jamie as she tried to recall what William Ryerson looked like. Her memory was from twenty years earlier and wasn't all that clear. She remembered he was tall, though. Both he and Nadine had been above average height and Teddy and Serena were, too.

Serena said, "I don't really see the resemblance. I know Emma. I've seen her at the Thrift Shop." She spoke a bit woodenly, it seemed, but then she added in a more natural voice, "I'm sorry about your mom. We worked together at the hospital."

"Yes, she told me. Should I open this now?"

"Ah, no. It's just chocolates and some of my business information." Teddy waved her off.

"You sure you won't come in?" Jamie asked. "I have some hors d'oeuvres. My father's coming by and we're . . . saying goodbye to my mother."

"Oh, no. We're on our way," Teddy assured her hurriedly, clearly thinking he'd stepped into a family affair that didn't involve him.

Serena, however, looked like she had been about to change her mind about leaving. She smiled and opened her mouth, but with Teddy's words, she closed it again, her face shutting down. She glanced back toward the car. Jamie could see a blondish boy's face for a second before he bent back to his iPad. Oliver, who Camryn had said was about seven years old.

Jamie hadn't bought any wine, but she had purchased some sparkling water, which she invited them again to come in and enjoy. But Teddy demurred. "Just wanted to stop by and say welcome back. Good to see you, Jamie."

Serena said something similar and Jamie responded with, "You too," just as a car pulled in behind Teddy's Mercedes SUV. She realized it was Marissa as the girl jumped out of the car. She braced herself for another meeting with Cooper, or possibly Laura, Marissa's mother, but the car backed out of the drive without further incident.

Marissa waved enthusiastically to the kids in Teddy's car, then bounced up to the front door. She smiled at Teddy. "Hello, Mr. Ryerson."

"Hi, Marissa," he said.

Marissa looked at Serena. "Oh, hi, Miss . . . Ms. . . . ." Marissa stumbled on her greeting to Serena. "You're Mr. Ryerson's sister."

"I'm Serena," she said with a bit of a bite.

"That's right. You told me to call you by your first name.

Serena." She dazzled both the Ryersons with a smile, though it landed on Teddy with a little more wattage.

"Marissa babysits for me," Teddy explained.

"We live in the same neighborhood," said Marissa. "Well, until Mom makes us leave. Ugh. I hate looking at houses. It's really boring."

"You babysit for Teddy?"

Jamie turned back at the sound of Harley's voice. She'd come down the stairs and heard Marissa's voice.

"Oh, yeah." Marissa said as Jamie stepped back and she entered the foyer. "Mr. Ryerson's a great tipper!" She giggled back at him, and then the two girls raced up the stairs together, thundering like a herd of elephants, laughing wildly.

"They look like they've become fast friends," Teddy observed as he and Serena turned away, back toward their SUV.

"Yes. It's great for Harley."

Jamie closed the door. Almost immediately, Harley and Marissa raced back down the stairs and into the kitchen, where Harley threw open the refrigerator door. "There's nothing to eat!" she declared. Then, "Can we have some of these?" as she spied the trays of hors d'oeuvres.

"Wait till Grandpa gets here."

"It's okay. I'm not really hungry," said Marissa.

Jamie looked at her. She had thick, dark hair and a killer body. She was shorter than Harley, and her eyes were hazelish, whereas Harley's were blue. "Did your . . . Mom think it was odd you were invited to our . . . ash spreading?"

"Oh, I didn't tell her. She probably would freak out. She's like that," Marissa said matter-of-factly.

"Well . . ." Jamie was nonplussed. "I don't want to be the weird parent who—"

"Don't worry about it. I don't tell her lots of stuff."

This was hardly the answer Jamie was looking for.

"Mom," Harley said in a warning voice, recognizing

Jamie's discomfort. She apparently was worried Jamie might ruin her burgeoning friendship with Marissa. "What's in the box?"

"Chocolates, Teddy said."

"Great!" Harley unwrapped the box with the zeal of a Christmas present. She pounced on the small box of chocolates, and she and Marissa bounded back upstairs. Jamie picked up the business card still inside the box with Teddy's name and number. He'd labeled himself as an investment adviser.

Emma suddenly appeared in the kitchen as if by magic, causing Jamie to jump and gasp a bit.

"I saw them," Emma said. "I was watching from the hall."

"Teddy and Serena, or Marissa . . . ?" Jamie set the card on the counter.

"It was their house."

"Their . . . ?" Jamie didn't expand as Emma's tight expression answered the question before it was fully asked: the Ryersons. It was no surprise that Emma had focused on the Ryerson twins. "You could have said hello."

She shook her head. "I don't think I like them. They killed me."

"They were in bed, Emma. They didn't . . . You were babysitting them, and someone came in. It wasn't anything to do with them."

Emma's breathing grew in tempo. She spied the dish towel Jamie had used and quickly yanked it back into perfect line with its partner. "He came in . . ."

"Let's not talk about it," Jamie said, realizing Emma was growing upset.

But she was glancing wildly around, her blue eyes wide, the pupils dilating. "He came in!"

"Emma." Jamie was stern.

"What's going on?" Harley called from the upper landing.

"Emma . . ." Jamie warned. She knew the signs from

those years living with her sister in high school, and now they flooded back. Emma was ratcheting up to a full-blown fit.

"I see . . . his eyes!" It was a whisper, but her voice was full of terror.

"Whoa," said Harley.

Jamie glanced up the stairs to her daughter. Harley was mesmerized. She'd never seen Emma in full panic. Jamie immediately went into combat mode to mitigate the attack. "You're safe, Emma. He's not here." Stern voice. Warning tone. Harsh words if necessary. Whatever it took to break the rising tension.

"I see *his eyes!*"

"Stop! You're fine. We're fine. We're at our house. We're together. You're safe. *You're safe!*"

"*I see his eyes!*"

Emma's hands flew to her face. For a moment, Jamie thought she was going to burst into tears, but she stood stock-still.

"Mom . . ." Harley murmured, scared, as Marissa came out of the bedroom and joined her, looking down at them, then at Harley, clearly confused.

"It's okay," Jamie soothed. "It's all okay."

Emma turned blindly down the hall toward the back door, her hands still over her face.

Jamie waved Harley off. "Go back to your room. It's fine."

Once they were gone, Jamie followed after her sister. Emma was standing at the back door, her hands still covering her eyes. She couldn't decide whether to touch her sister or not. They'd never been touchy-feely before the accident, and that had only worsened afterward. Only Mom had been able to put a comforting hand on her shoulder.

"Emma," Jamie said. She was glad her sister had only repeated her line a few times. That was an improvement over the days when Emma would cry, "I see his eyes!" twenty times or more.

"Mom needs to be in the garden," Emma said now in a tremulous voice.

"Yes, she does. We can do it right now, if you want. We don't need to wait for anybody. Dad and Debra can come whenever, and we'll just show them where Mom is."

Emma bent her head. "Harley needs to come."

"Yes. And she will, with her friend, Marissa, who's a really nice girl and will help Harley get over her misgivings about . . . spreading Mom's ashes. Dad and Debra are on their way."

"I don't like Debra either," Emma said.

"None of us do."

That finally got Emma to drop the hands that were covering her eyes. "Okay," she said.

"Okay," agreed Jamie, relieved.

A full-on fit had been averted, at least for the moment.

Cooper scrolled through old newspaper clippings on his home desktop. He often brought work home and could log on to his department account remotely. He scoured around for phone numbers and addresses pertaining to whatever case he was working on, drudge work that sucked up time on the job, but killed hours when he was home alone. His sister, who lived in Toronto, was bent on having him get a pet. A dog. He'd managed to put her off so far, but one day he imagined she would bully him into a rescue animal, as Jeannie's burning mission was to save every animal on the planet. Like Cooper, she'd never had children. Unlike Cooper, she professed a dislike for them. Only animals held her heart.

Today he had a beer, which was growing warm as he web surfed, looking up files from the summer and fall when

Emma Whelan was attacked. Jamie's appearance in town had flickered through his thoughts off and on since he'd seen her in the flesh on Friday, and encountering her again had in turn reminded him of the events of that year.

Emma's was the third of the three infamous "Babysitter Stalker" attacks. The first girl was killed in Vancouver, an apparent botched robbery attempt that had left Tyra DeProspero dead. The second was in Gresham, where the babysitter, Muriel Carrell-Wendt, fell from the second-story balcony to her death. Initially, it was thought she'd been chased by a would-be killer, but then it was concluded that she was actually trying to hide her boyfriend from the returning parents. She'd helped him onto the roof and he'd crab-walked to the front of the house, where it was only one story above the ground. He'd gotten himself down and taken off. Unfortunately, Muriel lost her balance and tumbled two and a half stories to the cliff side. The boyfriend had eventually come forward and told the truth, but the urban myth that she was the second victim of the "Babysitter Stalker" still persisted in some circles.

And then there was Emma, who had escaped death, but had been mentally compromised ever since. Nothing appeared to have been stolen from the Ryerson house, except for the knife that was used in the attack, so the prevailing theory was that Emma had thwarted a burglary.

Was any of it true? Were the attacks connected in some way, as unlikely as that seemed? At least the one in Vancouver and Emma's, as they were both home invasions? It was more credible that they were three separate incidents that occurred coincidentally within a couple of months of one another when each time the victim was a babysitter. The first was a burglary, the second a tragic accident, and Emma's attack? Again, a burglary? Unless it was something more personal, where Emma was the target . . . or Jamie.

A lesser-explored theory was that Emma's attack was

because the would-be thief was searching for drugs because Dr. William Ryerson had been rumored to be a bit of a "pill doctor." The reason this scenario was discounted was because, whether Ryerson's label was deserved or not, it was unlikely he would have the "stash" at his residence . . . though a desperate addict might not logically come to that conclusion.

Cooper leaned back in his chair. He thought about the guys he'd gone with to the Ryerson house to spook Emma. He could still see her standing on the porch, calling them out as "fourth-graders," her chin held high, her posture defiant, her tone more dismissive than scared. *Yeah, yeah, yeah. You guys are scaring me. I'm really, really scared.*

He wished one of them had stayed that night. With almost religious fervor, he wished he'd been there, looking out for her, when her attacker had stabbed her in the back.

If wishes were horses, beggars would ride.

The girl he knew was gone. Seeing Jamie, so much like the Emma he remembered, had gotten to him in ways he hadn't believed still possible.

He got up and prowled around the room. He felt, probably unjustifiably so, that he was partially to blame for what had happened to her. He'd been the one to invite Jamie to the Stillwell party that night. He'd seen her in the halls, a freshman or sophomore maybe, while he'd been a senior, in his last year and happy to be getting the hell out of River Glen. That had been his mantra in those days. *Gotta get outta this hole.* All his friends sang the same tune, like they had any clue at all what life had in store for them. High school had been some of the best years of their lives. They just hadn't known it then, maybe didn't still. But if he hadn't invited Emma's younger sister, she wouldn't have been in harm's way babysitting for the Ryersons.

But Jamie would've . . . maybe, if the attack was as random as everyone seemed to believe.

Cooper shook his head, physically putting that thought aside. There was no reason to heap further blame on himself and his friends, more than he already did.

He thought about those friends now. More acquaintances today than friends. Mark Norquist was dead, and Robbie was the phys ed teacher at River Glen High. Tim Merchel lived in Sacramento. Had gone into law and worked at the California state capitol. Race Stillwell, and his younger brother, Deon, were living in their parents' home, like Cooper was in his. The Stillwell parents had died in a small plane crash, leaving their home and business to their sons. Deon had fathered a child with a woman named Alicia, who'd moved from Portland to River Glen. She apparently had lived with Deon and the child at the Stillwell estate for a number of years before she'd either left or been forced out. Whatever the case, she now shared split custody with Deon, but had her own residence. Dug Douglas, his wife, Teri, and their son, Greer, lived at the new Staffordshire Estates, on the westside of the city. Greer had already had a couple of minor brushes with the law running with Troy Stillwell, but Dug, with the money from his insurance business, had hired some of the best, and therefore expensive, lawyers, and Greer had so far gotten off with mere slaps on the wrist. Dug frequented a number of the town's best restaurants, but still low-browed it at the Waystation. Cooper had run into him warming a stool at the bar there more than once. Though he and Dug had run with the same crowd in high school, they'd never been bosom buddies in any sense of the word. With Cooper now a lawman, Dug gave him an especially wide berth. He still hung with Race Stillwell, but it seemed to Cooper that Race had gotten over having Dug as his acolyte. Their friendship, like all of the guys from their high school group, had turned fairly tepid.

Cooper started with the archives on the babysitter killing in Vancouver. He had a number of files on his computer that

he'd downloaded over the years, and he referred to them now
after he found nothing online that wasn't years old. As of
five years earlier, the family was still looking for closure for
their daughter, Tyra's, death. They were infuriated that the
Vancouver police hadn't done "enough," though Cooper felt,
from what he read, that the local police had worked hard
with what they'd been given from the crime scene. He in-
serted everything he deemed pertinent to the girl's death into
his own cell phone notes.

The death of the Gresham girl from the balcony had
been settled once the boyfriend had come forward and confessed that the girl had helped him onto the roof and must've
fallen to her death. There was nothing suspicious about her
death after he filled in the blanks, but still Cooper plugged
all the information he had on the families into his cell phone
as well.

And then there was Emma. There'd been a lot of play
about the Ryerson home invasion in the beginning as another by the "Babysitter Stalker." Jamie's mother, Irene, had
spoken to the police, the media, anyone who would listen.
She'd been angry in her grief, and had intimated that she
would find whoever was to blame and take care of things
herself if the authorities couldn't. Partly on her adamancy,
the police detective on the case at the time, Mike Corliss,
had doubled and redoubled his efforts. Cooper and his
friends were dragged in time and time again. Initially scared,
they'd gushed out the truth about scaring Emma, but about
the third time they were deposed, some of them grew sulky
and silent. Cooper was one who became more vocal. Like
Emma's mother, he demanded more than was being done.
His Uncle Rodney, who was with the Portland PD, told
Cooper to take it easy, explaining that sometimes when an
investigation didn't seem to be moving forward, it actually
was. Cooper had subsequently learned through his uncle that

the police were looking into the Ryersons themselves, but in the end there had been "no there there."

Now, Cooper picked up his beer, which had gone flat. It was Sunday evening and he'd been alone all weekend, tinkering around the house, doing a whole lot of nothing, mostly. Laura had been silent after the fiasco at the high school. He'd left a message on Marissa's phone about wanting to talk to her more about the mixer, and she'd texted back, ignoring his ask and then saying she was over at the Whelan house and could he pick her up afterward? He'd texted back: Sure. Just let me know when. But then, apparently, Marissa had relayed that information to her mother, because Laura had sent him a terse: I'll pick Marissa up.

So, okay, he was free again.

His mind moved to Jamie. He was attracted to her in a way he hadn't felt in years, yet it made his heart ache a little to see her, too, because of the terrible tragedy that had happened to Emma.

He looked out the kitchen window, which faced west. The sun was beginning to set. He watched it for a few minutes, then walked back to his desk, then back toward the kitchen. Feeling like a caged lion, he decided to break free. To that end, he headed out to his SUV and a trip to the Waystation. Dive it may be, but it was still the most comfortable bar in town.

Chapter Eleven

"Is that it?" Debra Whelan asked, hugging her sweater close to her body as she leaned in to Jamie's father. The two of them were standing at the back of the house, watching as Emma spread the ashes over the last of the Mr. Lincoln roses and some orange and yellow dahlias.

Donald Whelan's face was set in a kind of earnest stoniness. It was as if he felt if he displayed any emotion at all, it would somehow show weakness, or maybe allegiance to Irene in a way Debra wouldn't maybe like.

Emma now clutched the urn close to her breast. She'd drifted the ashes over the remains of the vegetable garden, which was looking kind of ragged, a few zucchini and pumpkins and some leftover cucumbers, since Mom's death.

Jamie, too, could feel the cold as the temperature dipped, almost as soon as they all stepped outside. From a watery sun to a coolish evening, the six of them had trooped into the backyard after mowing through the appetizers and suffering through stilted conversation. Jamie had steeled herself to utter a few words. She'd thought hard and long about what she wanted to say, but Emma had put her finger to her lips when she started to speak, and so Jamie had waited.

After a moment, Emma intoned gravely, "Mom knew."

They'd all waited for her to say more, but when it hadn't

happened, Jamie had looked over at Harley and Marissa, whose eyes were both rounded as they'd apparently felt the solemnity of the occasion.

Jamie had been about to take up her speech again, about motherhood, love, and hard choices, when Donald suddenly spoke up.

"She's still watching out for all of you," he said. "That's what she did. Watch out for people. Take care of them."

"Take care of things," Emma agreed.

And before Jamie could recover from her surprise at her father's words, Emma suddenly turned around and marched up the back steps and into the house, clearly feeling the rite was concluded. Harley and Marissa needed no invitation. They ran after her. Jamie looked at Debra and her father, then spread her arm to indicate that they should precede her into the house.

At the top of the back steps, Jamie looked over her shoulder. She half-expected some other word from her mother, something more besides "*come home*," but apart from a gust of wind soughing through the backyard oak tree, all was silent.

The Waystation had opted for a train motif once upon a time. There were rails painted onto the beaten plank wood floor. A blue-and-white-ticked engineer's cap was hung on a hook behind the bar next to crossed red-and-white trestle arms, but the decor had the patina of age, and not in a good way. The trestle arms were dulled and yellowed. The engineer's cap looked as if it would disintegrate in the wash, and the railroad tracks' paint was chipped and cracked and wholly missing in spots.

The rest of the rooms were made of beat-up wooden furniture: tables, chairs, barstools, and booths. Cooper seated himself on an end stool with one leg shorter than the rest, so he rocked back and forth while he waited to catch the bartender's eye: a young guy with a full beard and a shaved head Cooper had never seen before. The man sauntered over after serving a guy on the opposite end of the bar who was shelling peanuts from a bowl, dropping the shells to the floor, his eyes zeroed in on his iPhone screen.

"What're you lookin' for?" the bartender asked.

"A beer. Light beer."

"You don't look like the light beer type," he observed, heading back to the taps and pulling one that said Coors.

"He's a cop," the guy at the opposite end of the bar said as the bartender handed Cooper his beer.

"That so?" The bartender gave him a longer look.

"That's so," Cooper agreed.

"Huh."

Cooper sipped his beer, thinking the place was pretty dead. It was a Sunday night, and River Glen had a tendency to roll up the carpets early. There was a pool table in an adjacent room that no one was currently using. The only other people in the place were a young couple sitting across from each other, deep into a discussion while they rubbed each other's arms across the tabletop, and an old guy with uncombed gray hair who desultorily ate some of the peanuts, eyes glued to the overhead TV monitor that was showing a cupcake competition. Go figure.

When the bartender slid him a bowl of peanuts without being asked, Cooper asked him, "Can we change to a sports channel?"

"Have to ask Otis. He picks the channels when he's here, which is damn near all the time."

"That all right by you, Otis?" Cooper called to the old guy.

"Competition's almost over. Lady with the gluten-free seems to really know what she's doing."

Cooper watched as well. Otis's prediction proved right as the gluten-free cupcakes won the day. As soon as the baker was crowned the winner, Otis made a motion that he was through, and the bartender turned to an NFL game. Cooper tried to get interested, but he found his mind wandering back to the cupcake competition, which, in turn made him think of Emma and her obsession with cooking shows. She liked pasta, Jamie had said, almost to the exclusion of all other foods. Just another of the mysteries that made up Emma Whelan.

Jamie was feeling warmer toward her father after his supportive words about her mother until he showed his true colors almost immediately after both he and Debra had mowed through the hors d'oeuvres by checking his watch and declaring they had to be somewhere else. Debra looked relieved, and they scooted out to the porch. Emma was upstairs, having declared it was time for bed, even though it was barely seven o'clock, and Harley and Marissa had disappeared to Harley's bedroom as well.

Jamie followed her father and Debra out to their car even though she could tell they wanted to bolt. "Can I talk to you a minute?" Jamie asked.

"I'm really busy, honey. Can it wait?" He didn't even look at her. She could tell he was already gone.

"It's cold, too. Brrrr!" said Debra, hunching her shoulders.

"I want to talk about Emma," Jamie persevered. "Harley's a sophomore and though she's in school here, I'm not sure how long we'll be staying."

"You're kidding. Emma needs you," Debra said, giving Jamie a look that said she was appalled that Jamie could even hint that she might be leaving her sister.

"Emma needs someone," Jamie said evenly, looking at her father, not his wife.

"You won't do it?" Donald challenged.

"I'm not saying that. I'm only saying, this is a big change

for us. I'm not sure how it will end, and that maybe we should work together to figure it out."

"Your father and I live on a small houseboat," Debra put in. "We don't have a spare room. There's nowhere she could be, and we all know it would be best for her to stay in River Glen, where she's comfortable."

"All I know is, I could use some help."

Donald sighed. "I'm sorry, but Debra's right. Emma needs to stay here. And frankly, Jamie, I can't do it. I can maybe offer a little bit of money for her upkeep, but that's it. I'm not a caregiver. That's all."

And I am? Jamie wanted to yell at him, but she could already hear his argument to that: *You're taking care of your daughter already. You can take care of your sister.*

"Let's go," Debra said, and they both hustled into their car.

Back inside the house, Jamie was seething as she cleared up the meager remains of the hors d'oeuvres when Harley and Marissa cruised back into the kitchen.

"That whole thing was freaky," said Harley. "Weird, thinking Grandma's out in the garden."

"Weirder than having her on the mantel?" Jamie muttered.

Harley shrugged and made a face.

"I thought it would be . . . different, I guess," said Marissa. "Creepier."

"It was good." Jamie's tone said the matter was closed as she plunged her arms into soapy water and began washing the dishes. "It was good for Emma. Mom is now where she would want to be. Emma was right."

"Did you tell . . . Grandpa . . . about being 'called'?" Harley asked.

"No." Jamie was abrupt She dared a glance at Marissa, who was tuned into her phone. She shot a second look at Harley, who shook her head, indicating she hadn't told her friend about their similar dreams.

Marissa groaned. "My mom's coming to get me. I'm not going to tell her what we did."

Jamie said, "Spreading the ashes? You didn't tell her?"

Marissa blinked.

"I don't think you should keep it from her," Jamie went on more firmly. "This was never a secret. She should know that."

"Maybe," Marissa muttered. After some thought, she added, "It was weird, but it was cool. I'm glad I came."

"Don't keep it from her," Jamie warned. "That makes it seem like we're . . ."

"Hiding it?" Harley suggested.

"Something like that."

"Oh, it'll be okay," Marissa said.

Jamie'd heard that before.

Emma appeared at that moment in her pajamas, blue flannel pants and a long-sleeved top with a pattern of black Scottie dogs. "I heard what you said to Dad," she informed Jamie.

Jamie tried to think what exactly that was. "Um . . . ?"

"I can take care of myself," Emma declared.

"Oh."

"I can!"

Sensing a fight brewing, Harley grabbed Marissa's arm. "We're going outside to wait for her mom."

Marissa protested, "It's cold out there."

"We're still going there." Harley steered her friend away.

When the door shut behind them, Jamie turned back to Emma. "I know you can take care of yourself, but you do need some help."

"Nope."

"Yes," Jamie said tiredly. She rinsed off the dishes and began stacking them on the counter rack. She was going to have to get the dishwasher fixed ASAP.

"Well, you don't have to do it," her sister answered a touch belligerently.

"Emma, I'm going to do what I need to do to make sure you're safe, Harley's safe, and I'm safe. That's what I'm going to do."

"I'm not a burden!"

"Oh, Emma." Jamie felt her chest swell with emotion. She wanted to break down and cry. She didn't know how to explain that caring for Emma was just part of all the changes that had hit her like a freight train.

After a long, silent minute, Emma walked around Jamie and straightened the dish towels one more time. "I don't like Debra," she said. "And I don't think I like Dad either."

Jamie managed a faint smile, nodding.

Harley burst back in at that moment, followed by a swirl of cold air. She slammed the door shut and said, "Shit, it's like negative degrees out there! Marissa's mom picked her up. She looked kind of pissed off. No wonder Marissa doesn't want to tell her about spreading Grandma around." She cocked her head as she looked at them. "You two . . . okay?"

"We're fine," Jamie said.

"We're sisters," Emma added, as if that explained it all. "And don't swear."

"You're with River Glen PD?" the bartender asked Cooper as he brought him his second beer.

"Off duty," Cooper said, eyeing the man who, after delivering the beer, was now leaning over the bar next to him.

"I think you were in here once, when I was here. Yeah, I think you got pointed out to me one time by a friend of mine, but not of yours. He said you were . . . well . . . it wasn't polite."

Cooper occasionally patronized the Waystation and had come to the bar tonight thinking, in the back of his mind, that he might run into someone he knew, so he wasn't surprised that the bartender had connected him with some-one else.

"One of my old classmates, likely," he said with a thin smile.

"Don't know, man. Could be, I guess."

Cooper didn't have to work hard to make a guess. Dug Douglas. Dug had had a serious problem with Cooper's oc-cupation and had made no bones about it. "Patrick Douglas. Goes by Dug."

"Ah, you know." The bartender shrugged and moved away. "Maybe 'friend' is the wrong term," he added, as if he'd decided maybe he shouldn't pick sides between Doug-las and "the cop."

Cooper ordered a burger and fries. No one he knew came in while he was working his way through them, and soon enough he was ready to leave. He checked the notes on his phone and thought some more about the attack on Emma. Seeing Jamie had stirred up all the uncomfortable edges of a crime he felt had never been adequately explained. Seemed like a good time to do something about that, if he could.

Throwing money on the counter, he left, stepping out into a coolish night with a stiffening breeze. The person he needed to contact first was Mike Corliss, the detective, now retired, who'd overseen the investigation into Emma's attack.

He had the guy's email address, and maybe even a phone number, if he dug into the official files. He would contact him tonight.

His phone rang as he climbed into his Explorer. He glanced at the screen. Marissa. "Hello, there," he answered, happy to hear from her.

"I need to live with you," she said abruptly. "I told Mom

why I went to Harley's place and she freaked out, like I knew she would. I don't know why I told her! I wasn't going to, but I just did and . . ." She sounded like she was holding back tears. "I need to live with you. Tell her that. Tell her, *please*!"

"Okay, but you know your mom's not going to go for that."

"I don't care! I *don't care*! She's like a *jailor*! Thinks there's drugs at the school and now she hates Harley!"

"What do you mean?" he asked sharply. "What happened? She doesn't hate your friend."

"I just went over there for the ceremony. The grandma's ashes, because Harley was freaked out and so I was there for her. And Emma? The aunt? Who's kind of messed up but really nice? She was very serious about it, and so we were there and it was . . . *cool*. And I'm glad I went, but I should never have told *her*!"

Cooper asked a few more questions until he understood fully what she was saying. He tried to calm Marissa down, with limited success, until he said he would talk to Laura himself, although what he could possibly say that would cut any ice with her was anyone's guess. Laura was strung a bit tightly, and Marissa attending a ceremony whereby Jamie and Emma spread their mother's ashes would be way too strange for a lot of people, doubly so for Laura.

He called Laura as soon as he got back to his house. She answered on the first ring, but upon hearing that Marissa had called him, hoping for a savior, she gave him a blistering piece of her mind, told him to "butt out of our lives," and hung up.

Never, he thought. He and Marissa had bonded as much as if she were his own child. But he didn't need to antagonize Laura, even though her attitude pissed him off. Instead, he pored over the events that took place before and after the attack on Emma. He went to bed late and dreamed of Jamie.

* * *

Monday morning, Jamie got Harley off to school and Emma to the Thrift Shop and then hurried back to the house and got ready for her meeting with her mother's lawyer, Elgin DeGuerre. His office was in River Glen's downtown area, a square lined with maple trees that had already lost most of their leaves, on the second floor of a red-brick, renovated building. A set of double glass doors led to the building's lobby. Jamie pushed through and saw the signs that indicated the DeGuerre Law Firm was up the stairs, or there was an elevator down the hall. Jamie peered down the short hallway and saw doors on either side with an elevator bank on the left. There was a sharp corner at the end, but she could see through a glass window into an anteroom with an abundance of ferns.

She climbed the stairs, and directly in front of her was the entrance to DeGuerre's office. Faux marble columns flanked a windowed door with a pane with pebbled glass that displayed Elgin DeGuerre's name in scripted, gold paint.

Jamie let herself into a small anteroom with four chairs. There was a reception desk, but no one seated behind it. Several doors marched along the left side of the room, also with pebbled glass, running alongside the reception desk and disappearing down the hall. As Jamie considered ringing the bell on the desk, she saw a figure move behind the obscured glass of the nearest door. The door opened, and a man in his midforties appeared. Jamie didn't think this could be Elgin DeGuerre, who'd been her mother's lawyer for many years, but she looked at him expectantly, nevertheless.

He smiled and came toward her, hand outstretched. "Hello, you must be Irene Whelan's daughter."

She nodded as she shook his hand. "Jamie Whelan Woodward. I have an appointment with Mr. DeGuerre."

"I'm David Musgrave. I don't know if you knew that Mr. DeGuerre is retiring and I'm taking over the practice."

"Oh. No, I didn't."

"I'll be sitting in on the meeting, if that's okay?"

"Sure."

With that, he led her to an inner office at the back end of a short hall. As she entered, she saw it took up the full width of the building and had a view out the windows toward Mt. Hood, its snow-capped top just peeking above a line of clouds whose soft gray color and fluffiness gave them the look of a row of pussy willows.

Elgin DeGuerre was white-haired and slightly stooped, but a pair of lively gray eyes assessed Jamie from head to toe. "You look like your mother," he said as he shook hands and exchanged greetings with her.

"Most people say I look like my sister."

"I knew your mother when she was young. And your father." He gestured for her to take a seat. "We're without a receptionist right now as Amy's on vacation. Would you like a glass of water? Or coffee, tea?"

"I'm fine, thanks."

"Then, let's get to it."

DeGuerre looked to Musgrave, who outlined the details of Jamie's mother's estate, which were in surprisingly good order. Jamie had been named as personal representative and beneficiary, with the caveat that Emma be provided for, though that was not specifically laid out. There was a sealed, manila envelope in the file with Jamie's name and Los Angeles address handwritten on its face in her mother's handwriting. Musgrave handed it to her, and Jamie grasped it with nerveless fingers, her heart suddenly pounding hard. DeGuerre appeared to have checked out.

"You can read it later," David Musgrave said, understanding what she was feeling. "I wasn't sure whether we were supposed to mail it to you, but when we reached you and you said you were coming home, we decided to wait. Your mother was wise, putting her assets in a living trust, so there'll be no probate."

The estate consisted of the house, which had the mortgage paid off, a small IRA, which named Emma as the beneficiary, Mom's aging Outback, and a checking account with several thousand dollars that already had Jamie's name on it. Vaguely, she remembered her mother having her sign a signature card when she was still in high school. She hadn't thought about it in years.

There was a lump lodged in her throat. They'd been on such uncomfortable terms for the better part of Jamie's adult life, yet her mother had taken steps, almost from the moment Emma was hurt, to take care of both of them.

"I can write checks on this account," Jamie said, staring at the bank statement.

Musgrave nodded. "You're a signer."

"You'll generally be dealing with David from here on out, as I'm retiring at the end of the year."

"Is this . . . the extent of the money for Emma?" Jamie asked, a little surprised it was so small, because her mother and Emma, too, had acted like it was set up to take care of Emma after her death.

DeGuerre looked at David Musgrave with some confusion. Jamie sensed that a lot of the business was in Musgrave's hands, that maybe Elgin DeGuerre's retirement wasn't coming a day too soon.

David said, "This is your mother's full financial picture."

They talked a bit more, and then Musgrave and DeGuerre laid out all the particulars required for Jamie to assume the deed to the house, etc. By the end of the hour, she was sufficiently informed to assume control of her mother's estate, but she headed back down the stairs from the offices feeling emotional in a way she couldn't quite define. She opened the manila envelope with her name scrawled on its face and drew out a handwritten card the size and shape of a thank-you note.

When she unfolded it, the contents made the hair on the back of her neck stand on end.

> *If you're reading this, I'm gone, and that means Emma's alone and needs you.*
> *Come home, Jamie.*

The buzzing in Jamie's ears made her deaf. She stood in frozen fear for seconds that felt like eons.

"Jamie?"

The female voice snapped Jamie back and made her jump. She'd stopped halfway down the stairs and now had to grab for the handrail to steady herself.

"Oh, I'm sorry. I didn't mean to scare you."

A woman in her late thirties or early forties stood just inside the exterior door to the building. It took Jamie a long moment before her heartbeat began to slow and she could focus on the newcomer. "Gwen?" she asked, aware how unsteady her voice sounded.

Gwen Winkelman reached out both hands to her as Jamie made it down the last few steps. "Your hands are so cold. Are you all right? I heard you were back. How are you?"

"I . . . just met with the lawyers about my mom's estate." Jamie swept a hand vaguely toward the second floor.

"Bad news?"

"No . . . no . . . I'm just processing."

"Do you have a moment? Come into my office. I'm at the end of the hall. I have herbal tea." She didn't wait, just led the way, looking back to see if Jamie was following.

Jamie did, gratefully. She realized Gwen's office was the

one with the ferns showing through the window. She almost laughed. She should have known.

The rooms were half the size of Elgin DeGuerre's, which was right above it, but it had a small reception area and an office. Gwen held open the door and pulled over a plush client chair for Jamie.

"It's my therapy room," Gwen said, "but don't let that scare you. I'll be right back with some chamomile."

Jamie practically collapsed into the thick cushions. There was a small desk to one side and a couple of other chairs. She could hear Gwen in the reception area, tinkering, and a few minutes later she reappeared with two cups of steaming tea. She handed one cup to Jamie and took one for herself. She then seated herself in one of the other cushy chairs and flipped up the hidden footstool on the recliner, showing Jamie how to do the same, which she did.

Jamie let out a huge sigh. She wanted to cry, for no good reason she could discern.

"What is it?" Gwen asked.

"Nothing."

"Nothing?"

Jamie drew a breath and looked at her long-ago classmate. Gwen was more of what she'd been in high school, and less, too. She had that same otherworldly quality her parents possessed now. Maybe it was a function of her appearance: long, somewhat wild hair, shot with gray and corralled in a brightly colored scarf; white peasant blouse; hoop earrings teamed incongruously with a pair of black yoga pants. Or, maybe it was the office, with its plants and faint, musky scent. She was a throwback to another era, as her parents had been.

"How are your parents?" Jamie deflected.

"They're fine. They moved to Chile. Patagonia. Way, way south. Practically the tip of the continent. They live in a small village and work with the local people. It's really a wonderful way to live in this world, you know?"

Jamie had a vision of living in a place with none of the complexities of her life and momentarily saw the appeal . . . yet knew it wasn't for her.

"Do you want to talk about whatever it is?" Gwen pressed again. "Something about the estate bothers you."

"It's not that." There was something so open about her, so fresh and different, that Jamie's guilt was twigged again. Gwen wasn't the norm, and Jamie, as a high schooler, had been threatened by that. She glanced down at the note, which she'd practically crushed in her hand when Gwen scared her. Now she smoothed it out and tucked it into the rest of the papers she'd been given.

She thought about telling her about the note, but couldn't bring herself to. Instead, she said, "You've worked with the River Glen police."

"That's true. Did you talk to someone there about me?"

"Cooper Haynes."

"Ah. Cooper, yes. Well, I didn't really do that much for them. They were on the right track. I just gave them a profile of a killer. The kind of thing you see all the time on television these days." She smiled.

"Cooper said you helped."

"That's good to hear."

Jamie went back to something she'd said. "You profile killers?"

"Mainly, I help people work through problems by understanding their own psychology. Their motivations, their fears. Like that."

"Is this a session?" Jamie asked.

She laughed. "Well, I guess it could be, but I see it as two old friends getting together who haven't seen each other in a while."

Jamie relaxed a little. The tea helped.

Gwen said, "You know, I was just thinking about the night of the Stillwell party, when your sister was babysitting the Ryersons. A lot of people have been affected by what happened. Some in small ways, some in quite large. Emma, for certain, but there's been a ripple through this town ever since. With certain people you can feel it."

"Like who?" Gwen didn't immediately answer her, and Jamie realized she may have stepped into privileged information, so she asked instead, "Are you feeling it with me?"

"I know you've been affected."

Though she'd had no intention of revealing what was in the note, or that she'd been "called" in her dream, Jamie suddenly changed her mind and showed Gwen the note and what both she and Harley had "heard" the night Irene died.

Gwen looked at the note for a long time, then her gaze locked hard on Jamie. "Your daughter received this same message?"

Jamie nodded. "The same night."

"At the moment of your mother's death?"

"Well, there's no way to know that for certain."

She drew a breath and exhaled slowly. "That's interesting."

"Crazy, you mean? Impossible? In the realm of 'Your imagination is getting the better of you, Jamie'?"

"No. I've known of some strange things."

"Like what?" Jamie challenged.

She shook her head. and the hoops at her ears danced. "You aren't my first unicorn, Jamie. I had a client with a similar experience. Not as wonderfully pinpointed as yours, but a message from a dying family member nevertheless. Sometimes, in ways we don't understand, people are able to send out messages to their loved ones when death or great peril is imminent."

"Yeah? Well . . . it's creepy," said Jamie.

"Yes. It is. But you're so incredibly lucky. I'm very jealous."

"Oh, yeah. Right."

"I'm serious."

Jamie lifted her hands in surrender, then dropped them. "I don't know why I told you. I've kept it between Harley and me until now."

"Do you think your mother had a message for you, beyond 'come home'?" she asked.

"No . . . other than she wanted me to take care of Emma."

"And you are."

"Yes." Jamie heard the conviction in her tone and so did Gwen.

"Did you just make that decision?" Gwen asked curiously.

"I think I made it a while ago. I just didn't know it till now."

"That'll make your mother happy."

"Happy's not a word I would use to describe my mom," said Jamie. "Strong. Pro-active. Single-minded. Always sure of the right course of action. And . . . dead, so I don't know how much she's feeling right now. . . ."

"I knew your mom. She also loved you and Emma very much. And your daughter."

"Yes . . ." Jamie's voice petered out. Although it wasn't even noon yet, she felt like she'd already put in a full day.

Gwen discreetly checked her watch. "I have an appointment coming. Actually, they're late. . . ."

"Oh, thanks, Gwen. Really. It was great to see you," Jamie said hurriedly, rising from her chair. "I'm at Mom's house, if you want to stop by sometime."

"I'd like that. I'm at my parents', too."

She left Gwen a few moments later, heading into a watery, midday sun. There'd been a wash of rain and the pavement was wet, but Jamie made it to her car. She had a sense of being watched and looked around from inside the Camry. There were several pedestrians on the street, but they were just walking, one on his phone, another climbing into her vehicle.

She drove back to her house, parked the car, and walked into the backyard, looking at the garden. While she stood there, the clouds opened up and rain poured down, soaking Jamie as she ran for the back door.

Letting herself inside, dripping water on the floor, she looked around and thought, for the first time, *I'm home.*

Jamie Whelan.

I watch her get into her car and, after a few moments of looking around, drive away.

Has she been to my therapist? I don't like that idea.

I enter the office room full of ferns. I know plants suck up carbon dioxide and provide oxygen, but they feel invasive. I always feel claustrophobic.

Gwen is there, greeting me with a smile, though it looks somewhat forced today. She's been looking that way more and more.

"You were with Jamie Whelan," I say. No reason to beat around the bush, if it's indeed true.

She's taken aback by my attack. Although Gwen's good at disguising her feelings, she's not perfect at it. I can detect the little nuances.

Gwen decides to be honest by saying, "Jamie's a friend of mine from high school." Like I don't know that.

They're all treacherous, these women. I've seen them for what they are. They never give up. They start young, targeting good men and throwing them away . . . stealing them from their wives and children . . . cheating on their

own spouses. They feed off men and then throw them away.
It's happened to me before. I won't let them do it again.

Jamie Whelan looks just like her sister.

I'm almost sorry Emma's become what she is.

I'd rather she was dead.

Chapter Twelve

"I'm babysitting for Mr. Ryerson Saturday night," Marissa said to Harley in between classes. "They live about three blocks over from me. You want to join me? I'll ask him. I'm sure it'd be okay."

Harley's gaze was on Greer Douglas and Tyler Stapleton, who were in a serious confab at the other end of the hall. They hadn't been expelled, despite some hard-ass parents, but they were in some trouble; Harley wasn't sure how much. The truth was, she had a crush on Tyler. Who didn't? He was *that guy*. She'd had an almost-relationship with *that guy* at her old high school, but it had ended badly, with him spreading rumors about her that weren't true. Like, oh, sure, she'd let him go to third base on a first date. They hadn't even kissed, but that asshole Kyle Carver had blown it all up and—

Greer suddenly turned around and looked straight at her. Harley ducked her head and pretended to be digging through her backpack. She had a crush on him, too . . . she'd even said as much to her mom, which was hard to believe now. That had been a really low point. The truth was, she liked him, even more than Tyler, but he seemed like he was serious trouble.

"Did you hear me?" Marissa asked a bit impatiently.

"Yeah. I don't know. My mom's a little weird about me babysitting."

"Seriously?"

"But I need the money. I *need* a phone." Harley looked up again. Tyler and Greer were moving down the hall together away from them.

"I'll split it with you. C'mon. I hate babysitting alone."

"I'll ask," Harley said in a tone that said, *Don't get your hopes up*.

She went to Language Arts and dropped her backpack on the floor beside her desk. She wasn't sure what to think of Greer. He'd been okay at the mixer, at first. But then he and Troy had realized that Emma was her aunt and Troy had asked, "That Down syndrome woman at the Thrift Shop? God, my mom goes there all the time. It's just a bunch of leftover junk, but she thinks it's great."

"She doesn't have Down syndrome," Harley had shot back, her blood boiling at his dismissive tone.

Greer had murmured something, trying to change the subject maybe, but Troy was oblivious. "You ever been there?" he asked her.

"Theo's Thrift Shop . . . ? Yeah, I've been there with my mom to drop my aunt off," Harley said tersely.

Troy had caught her tone and really looked at her. "Your aunt . . . oh, wait . . . she's the one that got"—he circled his finger by his ear—"when she got attacked, or something."

"Hey," Greer protested, seeing something in Harley's face.

But then they were staging their stunt on the stage and she and Marissa were grabbed to be part of it. Greer's hands were on her arms, placing her forward, and he was whispering in her ear, instructing her, and so she let it go and went along with the prank, but the whole thing had left a bad taste in her mouth. She should've stuck up for Aunt Emma more. Said something. Greer should've stopped Troy sooner. It was all wrong. But she hadn't wanted to blow everything up on her first day of school, and she hadn't wanted to lose her connection to Greer by making a scene.

Now, she listened vaguely to the teacher's instruction over their reading list for the year. She was already behind two books, but one of them had been part of her last curriculum, so she should be able to catch up, no problem. Reading was easy. She wasn't bad at math either, as a rule, but again, she was behind in this particular section of algebra.

Still, her mind wandered and she struggled to look attentive when all she could think about was Greer Douglas and what Troy had said and how Tyler was really good-looking, but maybe kind of full of himself. Also, Marissa had told her mom about why she'd come over to their house and the shit had truly hit the fan. Her stepdad was cool, she said, but Harley was worried that her mom would try to end the friendship. Parents were tricky. They could just sooooo get in the way.

She made it through class and then was in the hall, aware that half the kids were on their phones. It made her mad. She was going to have to get a phone. Have to. They couldn't be that broke, could they?

She needed a job.

She caught up with Marissa after school. "I'll do the babysitting. I'll just do it. Mom'll have to let me."

Marissa gave her a look, like she knew Harley had no power, because, well, who really did? Adults had all the power.

A couple of other friends of Marissa came over, and they chattered about the upcoming game on Friday night.

"Will Tyler even get to play?" Lena, the short-haired Asian girl asked.

"They'll wipe the field with us if he doesn't," Katie said.

"They better let him play," Marissa said. "It's just not fair if they don't."

There followed a discussion about what to do on Friday night. The game was at River Glen's home field. Harley tuned out. Katie and Lena were Marissa's friends, but they'd only warmed slightly to her. It was always a bitch to move schools and try to make new friends. Some of the sophomore boys had been nice to Harley, but nobody but Marissa was stepping up to be a real friend.

She looked around for her mom, who'd said she would pick her up in the side parking lot.

"Oh! There's Tyler," said Lena.

They all looked. He was standing near Dara Volker. She had a hand on one hip and looked pretty pissed. Greer purposely grabbed Tyler and dragged him away, but Tyler shook him off and went back to Dara, to finish their conversation, it appeared.

"Wonder what that's about?" asked Marissa.

Katie half-laughed. "You, probably. And you." She slid a glance toward Harley. "The senior girls were pissed that the boys pushed you guys off the stage."

"We didn't ask for it!" Marissa declared.

"Oh, don't worry," said Katie. "They always do weird stuff when a new girl's around."

"Me?" Harley asked, surprised.

Katie shrugged. Harley worried she may have stepped over an invisible line, but Marissa ignored it all and went back to her own defense. "I just really want Tyler to be able to lead the team," she said. "These fucking rules."

"Whoa," said Lena.

"Is Greer on the team?" asked Harley.

"Yeah. But he's not the quarterback. If Tyler's out, the next guy is . . . who?" Marissa looked around at them.

"I don't really care about football," said Lena.

"Do you care they're in trouble?" Marissa shot back.

"Boys are stupid," observed Lena. "I've got two brothers. I know."

Harley was starting to feel uncomfortable. She was trapped with a clique of Marissa's friends who may or may not be on Harley's side. They could blast her as well as defend her. It was too early to tell. They were all planning to go to the Friday night game, and they hadn't asked Harley to meet them. She probably could just join in, but she still felt like an outsider.

"Uh-oh," Marissa whispered as they broke from the group.

"What?"

Harley looked over to see her mom talking to Marissa's. Harley braced herself, too; Marissa had told her how her mother had gone nuclear upon learning about the spreading of Grandma's ashes.

"Why'd you tell her? You said you weren't going to tell her," Harley had reminded her fiercely.

"It just came out, okay? She was grilling me. And your mom said not to make it a big deal!"

By the looks of things now, it was a big deal. The two women were facing off.

"It wasn't appropriate," Laura Haynes said sharply for about the tenth time. "I really hardly know how to talk to you if you can't see how inappropriate that was."

Jamie, who'd been accosted as she was getting out of her car, had weathered about five minutes of this conversation. She'd apologized and agreed with Laura, saying yes, she should have said something to her earlier, but after admitting she was wrong, she refused to engage further. Though the last thing she wanted was to make an enemy of the mother of Harley's closest friend and Cooper's ex-wife, she'd basically dropped out of the conversation and was currently just waiting for Laura to wind down, which looked like it could take a while.

"I understand this was an important family rite, but my daughter should not have been there, and I should have been told what was happening." Laura looked at Jamie through wide hazel eyes. She had blondish-brown hair like Jamie's own. She was trim and fit in yoga pants, a ponytail, and sneakers. And she felt empowered.

"Mom!" a female voice cried.

Marissa.

Jamie looked over to see their daughters approaching. Thank God. Laura fixed her attention on Marissa.

"Get in the car. We're going to be late for class," Laura told her.

"What class?" Harley asked.

"Tae kwon do," said Marissa. She and Harley exchanged a look that could have meant anything.

Marissa climbed in Laura's car and Harley followed Jamie to theirs. They both watched Laura head out of the parking lot from inside the Camry and Harley asked, "What were you two talking about?"

"One guess."

"Oh." Harley made a face.

"Yeah."

At the house, Harley grabbed up her backpack and waited for Jamie as she got out of the car. "I . . . uh . . . Marissa wants me to go to the football game on Friday."

"If Laura lets that happen, okay," Jamie said. She wished she could park in the garage instead of in the driveway, but her mom's car was inside. It seemed strange to think the Outback was really hers now.

"And she wants me to babysit the Ryerson twins with her on Saturday. Is that okay? Please? I need to make some money. I really, really need a phone. All the kids have 'em, and I *know* that's not a reason, according to you, but I really want one."

Jamie looked into her daughter's anxious face. She didn't

know how to tell Harley that she wanted that for her, too. It just hadn't worked out so far. But now, with her mother's money . . . maybe there would be enough after the dishwasher was fixed. "Maybe we can work something out," she said slowly. "I could get a new one, perhaps, and you could have mine."

Harley's mouth dropped open. "Seriously? Oh my God! Really?"

"I think we can manage it," Jamie said and Harley emitted a whoop of joy.

"I'll tell you all about the meeting with the lawyer today. And my old friend, Gwen, who's a psychologist or therapist. It was an interesting day."

But Harley was already gone, having bounded up the back steps and using her own key, which Jamie had copied from the one under the gnome, shoved into the house.

Theo was bringing Emma home tonight, so Jamie followed in Harley's wake, wishing she didn't feel so bad about Laura Haynes. A text came in on her phone as she was pulling out the salad in a bag and makings for homemade chili. They'd been having pasta practically every night and Jamie needed a change, even if it was Emma's favorite. She had ended up using the bucatini for spaghetti, not for carbonara, much to Emma's chagrin, and had promised she would buy some more . . . later . . . after they had something else to eat.

Checking her phone, she saw it was from Icky Vicky and several other phone numbers on the chain, likely her friends.

Leander's. ASAP.

Can't make it, Jamie texted back. Dinner for the family.

In an hour. We have to talk about last Friday! It's hit the fan!

Jamie stared out the kitchen window, which overlooked the driveway. She was thinking how to respond when Harley, still jubilant, slid into the kitchen on sock feet.

"What?" Harley asked.

"Oh . . . one of the moms wants me to join them at a wine bar, but I said—"

"Go. Go! I can make chili," she added, looking around the kitchen at the supplies spread across the counter.

"I don't know if I want to go."

Harley gave her a stern look. "You need friends if we're going to stay here. And I don't think it's going to be Marissa's mom."

Jamie gave a short laugh. "Yeah . . . likely not."

"Go have fun. I've got this. I'm in charge," her daughter said, with a smile that was somehow a little worrisome.

"Fun," Jamie repeated, but then went upstairs to change her clothes.

All the women were already at the wine bar when Jamie entered: Vicky, Jill, Alicia, and Bette. They all looked over at her, and there was something in their collective stare that chilled her blood.

"What?" Jamie asked.

There was a charged moment where they all glanced at one another, and then Bette said, "The Haynes girl said she went to your house to spread somebody's ashes. Tell me that's an early Halloween thing?"

"Sit," Vicky said, pointing to a chair. No scooting over on the bench today.

Reluctantly, very reluctantly, Jamie crossed the last few feet and sank down in the empty chair nearest Vicky. The other women gazed at her in a mixture of horror and awe.

"That was . . . really out there," said Vicky.

"No judgment, but why did you do it?" Alicia asked.

"Isn't that something you do as a family?" Jill asked. "Walk along a beach . . . spread ashes . . . everyone says something about a family member? Kind of one of those really personal things?"

No judgment? Yeah, sure. How could she explain? Did she even want to try? Looking at their faces, Jamie decided to take a stab at it. "Harley wanted a friend. She was a little afraid . . . put off . . . by it all, but my sister was adamant. Emma knew Mom wanted to be in the garden."

Vicky pursed her lips. "Emma."

"I would rather have had it be just our family, but . . ." She turned her hands palms up, then dropped them to her lap.

"Laura Haynes is buying a house in Staffordshire with her boyfriend. She's . . . well, she's pretty upset with you." Though Vicky's words were a rebuke, she seemed to be distracted.

Alicia put a hand out to Jamie, touching her fingers. "Don't let it get to you. Laura's nice, but she's strung tight where her daughter's concerned. She's lucky Marissa's stepdad is Cooper Haynes and he's so good with her. She could have my ex. He's a problem."

Deon Stillwell of the grab hands. Yes, he was a problem.

Jill said, "That girl's on the edge of trouble."

"Who? Marissa?" Bette glared at Jill. "She's just like every other high school girl. The drama. The angst! I've met her a number of times. I've seen her with Cooper. She's like a true daughter to him. She's *fine*."

"You planning to get to him through his daughter?" Vicky asked with a sidelong look.

"If that would work," Bette agreed without compunction. "But I'd rather just go right up to him and say, 'You need to know me' and take it from there."

The women all chuckled and the moment of recrimination passed. . . . Jamie was already regretting coming. It wasn't like these women would necessarily be her friends, not like Camryn or even Gwen. Still, she was relieved they'd apparently forgiven her her gaffe with Laura Haynes. She sensed that this "wine klatch" could turn on her very quickly. Navigating female friendships never seemed to get any easier.

The talk moved to the school, and the fury the women felt over possible suspensions.

"They were *costumes*," Vicky declared. "It was fun, and no one got hurt. It was your daughter, right? Who was part of the skit?"

She was looking at Jamie, who said, "Um, yes."

"Troy wasn't part of it," Alicia said, in a tone that suggested she'd been saying this a lot.

"Troy was, too," Vicky flashed, showing a deadlier side. "He just didn't get caught."

Alicia's lips tightened.

"Girls, girls," Jill admonished. She didn't have any children, apparently a choice she and her husband had made.

"We've got to figure this out," Vicky insisted.

"Well, what are we supposed to do?" Alicia asked. "If this got back to Deon and he thought his son couldn't play football . . . ?" She shuddered.

"It's only Monday," Jill said breezily. "It'll be worked out by the end of the week."

Would it? Jamie wondered, and from that point on she checked out of the conversation, waiting for her chance to escape.

"The old hags with the freshman girls better mind their own business. Edina and Marty What's-her-name and Caroline. They need to get their fat asses out of it."

Alicia said, "They're trying to take over the PTA."

"Let 'em," said Bette.

"Easy for you," Vicky snapped. "Alex isn't on the football team."

"He's a musician in the band," Bette declared.

Jamie wanted to edge out the door.

"What about Greer?" Jill asked, although Jamie thought she was just trying to divert from what was becoming a tense moment among the women.

They all took a moment to back off. Hearing Greer's name, Jamie's ears pricked up.

"Who knows?" Vicky shook her head, her lips still pressed together. "Dug'll have a fit if he can't play, and he's the best defensive player on the team."

Dug? "Is Greer Dug's son?" Jamie asked.

"Yep." Vicky gave her a smile that was more like a grimace. "Small world, huh?"

"And both Greer and Troy have had their problems," Bette reminded them, drawing a killing look from Alicia. "Well, it's true."

"Nothing big," Alicia said.

"Yeah. Grand theft auto. Nothing big." That was from Jill.

Alicia looked like she was about to cry. She swept up her purse, and everyone immediately begged her to stay and Vicky apologized for being bitchy. She was just so worried about Tyler and the team.

Jamie left as soon as she could, her head full of new information. Greer Douglas was the boy Harley seemed most interested in, and he'd stolen a car?

As she drove home, she reminded herself not to jump off the deep end until she knew more. Paul had had a series of scrapes with the law that she'd found dangerous and romantic as a teenager.

Chapter Thirteen

By Friday morning, the question about the boys involved in the Halloween prank at the mixer was resolved. None of the boys were suspended. The parents had lobbied hard and there were only a few who'd objected, the small group of parents who'd been called out at Leander's wine bar. Because neither Jamie nor Laura Haynes were demanding some kind of justice for their daughters, the outrage over the costumes and props had dissipated. Only one parent had complained, and that particular parent was known for always kicking up a fuss, so it was decided she was crying wolf . . . again. Jamie, after meeting with Icky Vicky and friends, had later connected with Camryn, who kept her ear to the ground and lived in the same neighborhood of said wolf-crier, Cathy Timbolt, a single mom who was running for the school board and whose daughter was likely to be valedictorian of the senior class. She also had a daughter in the sophomore class named Katie.

"Cathy's a pain in the ass, but she often has a point," Camryn admitted. "Just so you know, in case you start substituting."

On that, Jamie was still waiting to be called and hoped it would be soon. With her mother's estate getting settled, her immediate money crises had eased, making it easier for her to breathe more easily. While Harley was at school, she'd gone to the local Verizon store and purchased a new iPhone, set it with her phone number, then had a new number assigned to her old phone for Harley. She planned to bestow her old phone on her on Friday evening, before the football game.

Against her better judgment she'd also agreed to let Harley babysit with Marissa at Teddy Ryerson's. Jamie had called Teddy herself and checked to see if it was all right, which he'd assured her it was. Jamie had still been reluctant. Who knew what Laura would do? Maybe this would be another black mark. But beyond Cooper's ex, Jamie had other misgivings. Since the fateful night of Emma's attack, she'd had the heebie-jeebies where babysitting was concerned. She'd always had trouble leaving Harley with anyone other than the Mexican nanny who lived in their apartment complex and was basically Harley's other parent, and she'd struggled to let her daughter babysit for any children.

Emma didn't learn of Harley's babysitting gig until Theo dropped her back home on Friday evening. Jamie had just bestowed the phone on Harley, who was gripping the phone and shouting, "Oh my God, oh my God, oh my God, oh my God!"

"Harley needs to be able to contact me," Jamie explained to Emma, who was looking at Harley with alarm.

"Mom said I would lose a phone," Emma answered. "I wouldn't lose a phone."

"We'll work on that," Jamie said.

"Oh my God!" Harley's voice was a delighted shriek.

"You have to be careful," Emma told her. "People put bad things on phones. You can get caught. Sometimes you have to use other phones."

"That's why we have the home phone," Jamie assured her, wondering where she'd gotten that information.

Emma cocked her head, thinking about that.

Harley said, "I'm going to call Marissa right now! No, I'm going to text her." Her fingers were all over the cell phone's keyboard. "Oh my God. I can call you from the game, and from babysitting, and I don't have to use somebody else's phone!"

"You're making me feel bad that it took so long," said Jamie with a smile, sharing in her daughter's delight.

Emma asked, "Babysitting?"

"At Mr. Ryerson's." Harley didn't look up from her phone. "Oh my God! I have to tell her who I am! She doesn't recognize the number!" She laughed.

Emma's blue eyes, which had a tendency to look into the distance when you were talking to her, zeroed in on Harley. "Where?"

"Where am I babysitting?" Harley asked.

"The Ryersons," Jamie answered for her.

Emma shook her head. "You shouldn't go. They'll come after you. Blame you. Try to kill you."

"Emma." Jamie's blood froze.

"Bring them here," Emma told Harley in all seriousness. "To our house. Where you will be safe."

Harley's grin stayed on her face, but she blinked a couple of times and slid a look Jamie's way, to see how she was taking this advice. "I'll be with Marissa," she assured Emma. "I won't be alone."

With that, Harley clutched her phone close and hurried away, clambering up to her room, slamming her door behind her.

"He shouldn't have done that to me," Emma said.

"He?" questioned Jamie. Emma had rarely spoken about the attack and she'd never specifically pinpointed her attacker's sex as male apart from her cries of seeing "his eyes." "You mean the man who hurt you . . . at the Ryersons'?"

"Mom said he should've died for it," Emma stated matter-of-factly.

* * *

"What're you doing tonight, man?" Howie asked Cooper as Cooper was shrugging into his jacket. It wasn't raining, but the temperature had taken a nosedive.

"I'm taking my stepdaughter and a friend to the high school football game."

"Rah, rah, River Glen?" Howie grinned at him, his white teeth gleaming. He'd grown up in Portland, at a school with a football team that seemed to always win their division.

"If they can field the team," Cooper said with a shrug on his way out. There'd been a question all week of whether the boys who'd worn the costumes at the mixer would face suspension or be expelled or some other sanction. At least Laura hadn't flipped out about this particular transgression; she wasn't completely without understanding of teens, apparently, but she had a chip on her shoulder about his relationship with Marissa, even though she'd been the one who'd wanted out of the marriage.

But that was because of you.

Cooper made a face as he drove back to his father's house. *Your house*, he reminded himself. *Yours now.*

He didn't have a whole lot of time until he was due to pick up Marissa and Jamie's daughter, Harley. Laura had apparently confronted Jamie about Marissa being invited over to spread Mrs. Whelan's ashes. He would have loved to have been a fly on the wall for that one. He hoped Jamie could handle herself and had a feeling she could, although whether that was the truth or just the way he remembered her being, he couldn't say. And Laura had a tendency to leap first and ask questions later when it came to anything outside her narrow view of rights and wrongs, but you didn't become a cop without learning there were different strokes for different folks.

He changed his clothes and stored his Glock in the small

safe he'd had installed in his father's—his—bedroom closet. No one knew the combination but him. He didn't like carrying a gun off duty. Just wasn't going to do it.

He'd called the family from Vancouver—the DeProsperos—whose daughter had been killed in the apparent robbery while she was babysitting. He'd spoken with the deceased girl's father, who'd surprised him with information that had been kept out of the papers, more because it was the man's opinion than because it was based on any real fact.

"It was her boyfriend," DeProspero told him flatly. "He was the robber. They got in a fight and he killed her. And he's dead now, too, so it's over."

"Are you certain? Nothing ever came out about that."

"I just know it."

Cooper let that one go. "How did he die?" he asked.

"Gunshot. Killed by the next guy whose girlfriend he was trying to steal. Maybe you don't call that justice, but I do."

After asking if it was all right if he called on him again and getting an okay, Cooper had then checked with the Vancouver police, who'd turned him over to the detective who'd worked the case, now retired. The detective hadn't totally agreed with Mr. DeProspero when he'd first heard his theory, but after all this time he'd mellowed a bit and allowed that maybe there could be something there. "I thought he was a grieving parent who wanted to lay the blame on a kid he didn't like anyway. But now, with the hindsight of twenty years, I think he was right," the detective told Cooper.

"There was talk of the Babysitter Stalker that summer."

"I never really bought that," the detective admitted. "Did you?"

I was a kid, Cooper thought. He'd almost wanted it to be true. Some explanation that took the crime away from him and his friends. But he'd shaken his head and thanked the detective for the information.

Now, he grabbed up his keys from the hook by the back

door and headed for his Explorer. He was inordinately glad Laura had tasked him with taking Marissa to the game because Laura and her boyfriend were planning to have a date night before a weekend of purging stuff from their house in preparation for moving to Staffordshire Estates. He was glad, because he was going to see Jamie again.

Is it just because she's Emma Whelan's younger sister? he asked himself again. Then, *If so, why does it matter so much?*

He forced himself to explore that. Guilt, for sure. He'd been attracted to Emma in high school and now, years and events later, he was attracted to her younger sister. A lot of the reason he'd gone into law enforcement was because of what had happened to Emma, but was his attraction to Jamie for the same one?

No. Though there were definitely elements of Emma in Jamie, his attraction to her was more than that. He'd been unable to get her out of his thoughts since seeing her again, now as a woman. Yes, he could admit he was drawn to a certain "look"—*thanks, Howie, for pointing that out*—but looks only went so far.

He thought back to high school, to Emma. He'd liked her, a lot, but the truth of it was, Emma had been that girl who wouldn't really date any of the guys in high school. He and all his classmates had mostly been relegated to the friend zone. Rumor had it that Emma was seeing an older guy, out of college or maybe even closer to thirty, but that was likely an excuse they'd all wanted to believe. Race Stillwell had had a thing for Emma, too. Race's obsession had been a big reason they'd all gone to the Ryersons'. And while all that was going on, Jamie Whelan had been at the Stillwell party. Race and Dug had run into her, in fact, just as they'd been heading out to pick up Robbie and head to Emma's babysitting gig. That had come out during the interviews at the police station following the attack. The question had been floated that maybe the wrong Whelan girl had been the targeted victim, but there was no evidence to support that theory, then or now.

But why had Emma been targeted? Now that he'd learned the babysitter attack in Vancouver had likely been a deadly lover's quarrel, he found the burglary idea harder to swallow.

Was it really just a terrible, random crime?

He tightened his jaw. He didn't want it to be random. There was no protection against random. He wanted there to be a reason. A real motive. A way to keep what had happened to Emma from being such a terrible, senseless act that could occur again.

He told himself to check with the family in Gresham whose daughter had fallen to her death. He pretty much knew the details of that event; the boyfriend had confessed. Neither of the so-called Babysitter Stalker crimes of twenty years ago appeared to have anything to do with Emma's attack.

Five minutes later, he wheeled into Laura's house. The garage was open and packed with boxes. The moving had already commenced. Cooper felt a small pang of regret. The marriage was long over and the biggest reason was that they'd grown apart, that the hours of his job had gotten in the way of Laura's future plans, that Cooper had never fully committed in the way she'd expected. She'd warned him that they weren't making it. She'd thought that they would get married and she would get pregnant again, but that hadn't happened. And as Marissa had grown older, Laura had resented the bond Cooper shared with her. It all added up to a bad brew neither could stop drinking.

He texted Marissa: I'm here. During the first phase of his split with Laura, he'd made a point of walking to the front door and asking for Marissa, as if he were a boy asking a girl out on a date. Laura had been icy and abrupt if she spoke to him at all. Now, he just texted.

Marissa didn't bother texting back. She flew out the door and into the passenger seat of his SUV. "I thought you'd never come," she declared. "She thinks I shouldn't go to the game. That I should protest those boys! The ones that 'ruined the mixer.' That's what she said. Swear to God!"

"She just wants you to stay safe," Cooper said.

Marissa choked out a laugh. "Yeah right."

"It's what all parents want."

"*She* wants punishment. She wants them off the team. I had to *beg* her to stay out of it. She's just overall pissed and taking it out on all of us. Swear to God, David looks like he wants to run!"

"I hope not."

Marissa looked at him. "Oh, you're right. If we lose David, Mom'll be crazy."

"That's not what I said."

"Don't worry. I won't throw you under the bus. You don't want her bugging you either."

"She's your mom. Give her a break."

"Fine. But I know we're on the same side," she said with confidence.

They drove to the Whelan house, and Cooper climbed out of his seat, surprising Marissa, who'd already jumped from the car and was heading to the front door. She stopped short and looked back at him.

"You're coming in?" she asked, brows knitted.

"Yes."

"Why? We're kinda late."

"Don't worry. I'll get you to the game."

Jamie scrubbed at the pan with its baked-on egg and cream sauce. Emma had gotten tired of waiting and attempted her own carbonara from the new bucatini Jamie had picked up at the grocery store. Jamie had been hovering around her sister, trying to guide and help. Unfortunately, the carbonara took a little more skill than Emma could muster, and the eggs had scrambled rather than melting into the sauce. Emma had eaten it anyway, and Jamie had followed suit. Harley had politely declined, saying she would get something at the game.

Now Emma was on the couch, watching one of her DVR episodes. Beside her sat Theo's dog, Bartholomew, "Dummy"; Theo had dropped off the dog with Emma at Emma's request. When Bartholomew had bounded into the Whelan house and Emma had announced that Dummy was spending the night, Jamie had looked at Theo with questions in her eyes, to which Theo had signaled for Jamie to walk her back to her van.

"I didn't realize Emma liked your dog so much. It was hard to tell," Jamie admitted.

"Oh, Emma's a huge fan. Bartholomew, and his predecessor, Seymour, have 'babysat' Emma for years. Your mom worked nights and the dogs were sometime companions for Emma. Mostly she was fine. But whenever she asked if she could keep 'Dummy'—which was also her name for Seymour, by the way—I sent her home with the dog. It allayed her anxiety, although your mom was not a dog person."

"You got that right. Thanks, Theo. You're a good friend," Jamie said, her throat tight.

Theo patted Jamie's arm. "So, you're staying?"

"Yes."

Theo couldn't hide her relief, though she quickly masked it. "Emma can almost be by herself."

"Almost" being the operative word.

"Did something happen today, for her to ask for the dog?"

Theo made a face. "Nothing really new. . . . There's a homeless man who stops by to see Emma now and again. He has an interest in her. I don't think he's . . . a problem, but I keep an eye out whenever he's around. He tries to engage

Emma, but she ignores him, mostly. He came by today and she was a little rattled. I told her to go in the back and straighten the inventory—which she loves to do—and I waited till he left. But she's been kind of anxious ever since. It wasn't long after that that she asked if Bartholomew could spend the night with her. This is the first time since you've been here that she's wanted him."

Jamie had thought that over as Theo climbed into her van and waved a goodbye. She wondered if she should talk to Emma about it, but she'd let the matter slide through the bucatini experiment.

Now, Jamie looked at the back of her sister's head and wondered. Emma didn't hug or touch Bartholomew, but she liked the dog sitting right beside her, which he did. The current television show was Halloween-themed, and they were making a dish of orange pumpkin and black bat-shaped ravioli.

Jamie's gaze drifted toward the television and the cable box. Harley was begging for a streaming device to plug in to the TV because Mom's television was ancient by the standards of a fast-changing digital age. Jamie had called the cable company to change the name on the account and had run into a raft of red tape, which she'd been prepared to plod through, but the company had also wanted to upgrade her system with new boxes. But that would mean losing all the programs already taped. Jamie had put the brakes on that, knowing Emma might go into full meltdown if her programs were wiped out in the name of progress.

Headlights glowed through the window and Emma's head jerked around. Bartholomew, too, grew alert.

"It's Harley's ride to the football game," Jamie said.

Emma and the dog both kept staring. Bartholomew started growling low in his throat, picking up on Emma's tension, maybe.

Jamie walked to the bottom of the stairs. "Harley!" Jamie yelled up to her.

"Coming!" was the muffled reply, then Harley's door flew open and she was hurrying down the steps. She wore jeans and sneakers and a rather nice red blouse Jamie could see beneath her black jacket. Her hair was tied back at her nape and there was the hint of makeup on her eyes.

Hmmm, Jamie thought.

Emma said, "Boys are bad."

"Boys are not bad," Harley snapped back, taking offense. Then, remembering who was dispensing this advice, she relaxed a bit, saying, "Well, maybe sometimes."

The doorbell rang, and Harley swooped over to answer it. Marissa was on the other side . . . and so was Cooper.

Immediately, Jamie wondered what her own makeup looked like. And her hair. And her clothes.

"You ready?" Marissa asked.

"Yep," Harley said.

"You want to come in?" Jamie asked them both.

"We've got to get going," Marissa threw out before Cooper could answer.

"Hi, Cooper," Emma said. She had slowly risen to her feet. Bartholomew had jumped down and was clearly torn between wagging his tail and growling as he waited to see how things broke.

"Hi, Emma." Cooper smiled at her as Bartholomew, having apparently decided Cooper was a friend, came to the door to sniff at the newcomers.

"You got a dog?" Marissa asked, staring accusingly at Cooper.

"He's just visiting. He's Theo's. From Theo's Thrift Shop," Jamie explained.

Marissa bent down and Bartholomew began wriggling and half-jumping and licking her face.

"Dummy," said Emma.

"Maybe after dropping them off, you could stop back by?" Jamie heard herself suggest to Cooper, shocked by the words. Her heart was pounding a mile a minute.

"I'll do that," said Cooper. The smile he sent Jamie kick-started her heart.

A lot of wattage you're still very susceptible to.

After they left and Bartholomew was back on the couch beside Emma, Jamie asked her sister, "Is that all right? That I invited Cooper?"

Emma shrugged, but didn't look away from the screen.

"We'll just go to the back porch and not bother you."

"He came with the other boys, but they didn't mean to hurt me," she said after a moment.

"That's right, but I thought you blamed them?"

Emma turned to look directly at Jamie, something she rarely did. It gave Jamie a strange, uncanny feeling.

"I know the truth," she said, then turned back to her cooking show.

Chapter Fourteen

Cooper returned to Jamie's place and she invited him in for a glass of wine. Emma was still on the couch, watching TV with Theo's scruffy-looking black-and-white dog. When Jamie suggested heading to the back porch, he followed her outside. The temperature had dropped along with nightfall. A low-hanging, crescent moon looked as if someone had placed it right above the gardens.

They each held a glass of red in a tumbler. "Mom didn't drink in her later years," Jamie explained. "I picked this bottle up a couple of days ago, after I met with her lawyer."

Cooper took a swallow. He was no wine connoisseur. They all tasted about the same to him. But he'd seen the label and knew it wasn't quite of the chichi tier David preferred.

Thinking of him, Cooper asked, "It's none of my business, of course. But was your mother's lawyer Elgin DeGuerre?"

Her brows lifted. "Yes."

"You met him, then?"

"Yes," she said more cautiously, clearly wondering where this was going.

"Laura's boyfriend is an attorney with the firm, David Musgrave."

"Oh." That threw her. "He was there. He's taking over for Mr. DeGuerre."

"It's still a small town in a lot of ways," Cooper said dryly.

Jamie nodded. "He seemed . . . okay."

"I've heard he's a good lawyer. Just thought you might want to know."

"I do. Thanks."

A few moments later, he asked, "How is it, coming back?"

"Fine."

"Is it?"

"Harley likes the school. She likes Marissa. Emma . . . needs care, and I've got my name in to substitute teach."

"So, the change is basically a good one?"

"I didn't have all that much to leave," she confessed. "I wasn't really sure what I thought about coming home until it happened, and I definitely had my doubts at first, but . . ." She shrugged lightly. "It's River Glen. I know this place. And . . . there's Emma."

Cooper nodded. "I want to know what happened to her. I'm doing my own investigation," he admitted.

She turned sharply his way. "You mean now?"

"Yeah. It's been too long already. I want answers." He heard the cold determination in his voice and sought a lighter tone, "But we don't have to go over it again."

"No, I'd like to go over it. I want answers, too. I'd like to know exactly what happened. I've never heard. I just know a bunch of the guys from Emma's class pranked her, and that her attacker came afterward. I thought . . . I used to think, that she was targeted by the Babysitter Stalker, like that girl in Vancouver and the one in Gresham, but the Gresham girl's boyfriend confessed."

"Yes."

"So, no link between the deaths that summer and Emma's attack?"

"Seems unlikely from what I can tell so far."

"What made you decide to investigate now?"

You . . . your return. Cooper couldn't really say that, though it was what came to mind. He thought about Emma, sitting on the couch watching television. The blank way she'd greeted him.

"I've always wanted more answers."

"Me too. Can I help?"

He looked into her eager face. "Sure," he heard himself say, then added, "By coincidence, I did some recent follow-up on Emma's case."

"You did?"

He nodded, then told her about his conversation with Mr. DeProspero. "I'd never heard that maybe it was his daughter's boyfriend before."

Jamie took another swallow from her barely touched glass. Cooper was just holding his empty glass.

"What can I do to help?" she asked.

"I don't know yet, but I'm just getting started."

"Does that mean the attack on Emma was a random attempted burglary? Wrong place at the wrong time?" She inhaled deeply, closed her eyes, then exhaled. Her arms were wrapped around herself. It was pretty cold out.

"I'm going to check with Mike Corliss. He was the detective on the case for River Glen, now retired. I want to go over everything he did."

"You think there's something he missed?"

"I don't know. I was a kid when he was interviewing us all, and I was pissed, and then nothing came of it all. When you got back . . ." He trailed off, realizing he'd done what he'd told himself not to: let her know she was the impetus to his renewed interest in the case. "I just decided it was time to revisit the investigation."

She was silent for a long beat. Then she said, "Good," with a determination that matched his own.

* * *

"Tell me about what happened when you guys pranked her," Jamie said. The chill had reached inside her and she'd started shivering uncontrollably, so they'd headed back inside. Emma was just finishing another one of her cooking shows and was standing in front of the couch, turning off the TV with the remote. She and Bartholomew then headed toward the stairs, and as Cooper and Jamie entered the kitchen, she heard Emma's bedroom door shut.

Cooper ran a hand through his hair, hesitating. Throughout their time on the back porch, Cooper had been determined and forthright, but now, inside, with everything almost said between them already, Jamie saw him take a huge breath and hold it in for a moment, letting it out slowly, giving himself time to think.

She invited him to take the seat Emma had relinquished, and then she perched on the ottoman of the leather chair that had been her mother's favorite seat. In the few times Jamie had visited, she'd chosen a kitchen barstool rather than get in the way of her mother and Emma's set routine.

Cooper stared at the now-blank screen of the television as Jamie had turned it off. A floor lamp near him cast shadows on the planes of his face. Jamie realized how stern he looked and for the first time really thought of him as an officer of the law more than the boy she had such a serious crush on in high school.

"I'm not sure whose idea it was," he began. "All of us, at some level. Race was expecting Emma at his party, and she stopped in, but she told him she was babysitting. That threw everything off. Race was not happy. He was really into her, but she was distant. So, we changed our plans. I was with Tim Merchel and Mark Norquist. Race was with—"

"Dug Douglas," Jamie stated flatly.

Cooper nodded. "You ran into them when they were leaving Race's party."

"You knew that?" Jamie's brows lifted.

"It came out when they were interviewed by the police. Race and Dug picked up Robbie Padilla. I don't know if you know, he's now the phys ed teacher at the high school."

"River Glen High? No, I didn't know."

Cooper went on to explain that Tim Merchel lived in Sacramento and Mark Norquist was deceased, which she'd already known. That night, they'd rung the front bell of the Ryerson home and seesawed a squeaky window, but Emma was neither fooled nor scared.

"She knew it was us and what we were doing. Race was kind of pissed and Merchel razzed me about having a crush on her. Emma came out on the porch and called us out. Told us we were like fourth-graders. We decided to leave . . . well, most of us. Dug wanted to stay. Race brought him back in his car, along with Robbie. There was a rumor that Emma was seeing a college guy and that really ate at Race, who thought she was his. He was devastated when he heard what happened. Made a lot of noise about finding that college kid and making him pay."

"Emma wasn't dating anyone," Jamie said.

"Maybe secretly?" Cooper looked at her. "It's an area that never really was explored."

Jamie shook her head slowly, thinking. Did she know what her sister had been doing in those days? She thought she did, but did she? The truth was, she hadn't paid much attention to Emma's life except when it intersected with her own.

"If she was, it was very secret," Jamie said.

"No college guys?"

"No college guys," she repeated. "I remember that she was babysitting, working a lot, saving her money, and studying. She wanted to go away. It's ironic, actually, because I didn't feel the same way. I wanted to stay home, and yet I was the one who left." She looked at him, finding it sort of hard to believe that they were having this conversation after all these years, that she was sitting down with the boy of her dreams and discussing the terrible events that had changed all their lives. She asked if he'd like another glass of wine, but he declined. She, on the other hand, felt like she could use a drink and got up to pour herself one.

"What do you think happened after you guys left?" she asked him after she'd refilled her glass.

"It was written up as a home invasion, though nothing was taken, but maybe Emma got in the way of a burglary."

"He tried to kill her. The cuts were deep. The scars are still . . ." She'd been going to say "visible," but that wasn't a strong enough adjective. What she wanted to say was the scars were malevolent, because someone had wanted to kill Emma, yet she couldn't quite find the right word to capture the depth and horror of the attacker's intent.

They heard a noise from the second floor and both turned to look toward the stairs, but after a few moments, Emma still didn't appear.

Jamie said softly into the quiet that followed, "I haven't tried to talk to her much about it since I've been here. She's popped out with random comments she won't elaborate on, so it's more maddening than helpful. My mother pushed and pushed, but all it did was upset her, so she quit trying."

"Your mother pushed the police, too. I've read the report."

"She blamed them for not digging deep enough. Thought they dropped the ball. She said it enough times: 'They dropped the ball.'" Jamie made a face. "I remember telling her to stop saying that. I was a teenager. I just couldn't handle it."

"I drove the police crazy. I wanted them to find the perp and I wouldn't listen to any excuses."

Jamie half-smiled. "Mom swore she'd find out who did it if it was the last thing she ever did."

"I feel the same way."

They looked at each other for a long moment, and Jamie's

heart began a heavy beat. Cooper finally broke eye contact, saying, "I'll dig into the report, recheck with some of the names in the file. I'll know more when I connect with Corliss. Just a warning: You may hear complaints from the people I interview."

"They can complain all they want," Jamie said with some heat. If she could learn anything, *anything,* about her sister's attacker, it would be worth it and more. "Who are you thinking of specifically? Your classmates?"

"And other people at the party. The Ryersons: Teddy, Serena, and their parents . . ."

"The Ryersons split up afterward," said Jamie. "Remarried other people and moved out of state."

"If there's anything you can find out about what was going on with Emma at that time. With friends, or family, or relationships . . . ?"

Jamie thought about Icky Vicky and the others in the wine group. Emma's classmates . . . did they know anything about the attack, even something they may have forgotten? "I'll ask around. I could try to talk to Emma, too," she said slowly. "Don't know how much good that will do."

"Let's check in with each other in a few days." Cooper got up from his seat.

Jamie looked at the time. She doubted the football game would be over yet. She longed to ask if she could go with him to pick up the girls, but she couldn't leave Emma without letting her know . . . and with the homeless man coming into the thrift store today . . .

"You said you had a crush on Emma," she said, almost surprised that she'd let that out.

"Oh. Yeah. Everybody did."

I had a crush on you.

"Do you have to leave . . . just yet?" Damn. She hoped she hadn't sounded as desperate as it felt like she had.

"I thought I'd check out some of the game."

"Oh, okay."

"But I don't have to." He looked at her, and she felt the full weight of his gaze.

"You have a partner at work?" she asked, casting about for anything to talk about.

"Eversgard. Howard . . . Howie. I had a different partner till about a year ago, when he moved to Eugene."

"Are there any women in the department?"

"Dispatch. Front desk. Six officers, and Elena Verbena, who's also a detective." He lifted his chin, as if he'd just re-membered something, and then said, "You know Gwen Winkelman. She was at River Glen when we were there."

"Oh, yeah. She was in my class . . . a friend. I saw her earlier this week, as a matter of fact."

"Then you know she's a psychologist. She's helped on a couple of cases. We had a child who was an eyewitness to a crime, but was too scared to talk to us. Gwen convinced her to trust us and we got the guy. He'd broken into a number of houses and stolen money, jewelry, small items."

Jamie felt a tinge of regret all over again, for how cal-lously she'd thought of Gwen when they were younger. "She's not a child psychologist, though."

"She just sort of made a connection. Hard to explain, really. A little woo-woo, as my sister says."

Jamie gave an involuntary shiver and covered it up with, "Maybe Gwen could talk to Emma."

"Maybe."

Neither one of them put much serious hope into their words.

A moment later, Bartholomew started working his way down the stairs. Jamie looked up to see Emma standing at the top step. "Are you okay?" Jamie asked.

"Dummy needs to go out."

"Oh."

Emma followed the dog down the stairs as Jamie headed

with him toward the back door. She looked back to see Emma staring hard at Cooper and Cooper gazing back at her. He was still in the kitchen, leaning against the counter, giving Emma lots of space.

Jamie would've liked to stay with them both. She was worried, a little, that Emma might do something untoward. But Bartholomew whined in his throat and she opened the door. The little dog jumped down the steps and into the yard. He circled around and found a spot on the side of the garage and away from the garden, much to Jamie's relief, though knowing her mother, she might have been amused if the dog had chosen to use her resting place as his toilet.

She hurried back inside to find Emma waiting at the bottom of the stairs for the dog and Cooper looking for Jamie to return.

As Emma and Bartholomew headed back upstairs, she asked Cooper a bit anxiously, "Everything okay?"

"I think so. She told me she knew I didn't do it. Then she buttoned my top button."

Jamie saw that Cooper's shirt was buttoned up to his throat. "She does that," Jamie said. "She puts things in order, as she thinks they should be."

"Do I look like a dork?"

She looked up into his blue eyes. She wanted to kiss him. She wanted it more than she'd wanted anything in a long time.

Instead, she quickly unbuttoned the top button and said, "Not anymore."

When he left a few minutes later to pick up the girls, she exhaled. It felt like she'd been holding her breath for a millennium.

Harley shivered in her jacket. She and Marissa were standing on the track that encircled the football field, along with a lot of other classmates and students from the school. It was somewhat mind-boggling how many people she'd met over the past week. A lot of them were really nice to her, going out of their way to say hi, though she sensed she had drawn the attention of the senior girls, through no real fault of her own, in a way that made her pulse jump with low-grade fear.

Marissa looked over at the senior girls and said, "Dara Volker and her crowd. They think they own Tyler and all the guys."

Marissa liked Greer Douglas and Tyler Stapleton and probably others. After last Friday's mixer, she and Harley had vaulted into the senior class's collective consciousness. Marissa had learned there was a party at Troy's house after the game, a possible beer bash, as it was known that Troy's dad tended to look the other way and his mom didn't live there.

"Are you in for the party?" she asked now.

"No. I can't." Harley had already put her foot down and now she did it again. There was no way she was going to make things worse for herself. She'd just gotten her cell phone. She couldn't screw things up without risking losing it. "If my mother ever learned I was at the Stillwells' . . ." She drew an imaginary line across her own throat.

"She doesn't like the Stillwells?" Marissa asked, but her attention was on the game. River Glen was wiping the field with the other team.

"You have to know the history."

Harley wasn't interested in going into everything, but she need not have worried because Marissa was only half-listening. "Did you see that pass?" she said in awe. "Tyler's going to get a scholarship."

Harley had heard very similar things at her last high school about their own outstanding quarterback. She'd believed them once, but now, not so much.

"Look! Look!" Marissa screamed as the crowd erupted in cheers. Harley had to peer around the heads of other people to get a good view. A River Glen player in green and gold was racing down the sideline toward the end zone. The crowd was going wild. The player was knocked out of bounds only a few yards from making a touchdown.

"That's . . . that's *Troy!*" Marissa cried.

Immediately, the team huddled, reformed, took position, and the ball was passed off to a player of the same number: Troy, according to Marissa. Harley had no reason to doubt her. Another few seconds and the shrieks and hollers filled the stadium air as the player scored. Harley looked toward the sky, above the bright and blasting football field lights, to a sliver of a moon, barely visible above the light pollution—something they'd been learning about in science—below.

A chant rose up. "Tyler! Tyler! Tyler!" Harley glanced over and saw it was a group of senior girls, led by Dara Volker.

And Troy, Harley thought, but she was glad the running back wasn't part of the girls' spontaneous cheer. He'd been kind of mean and uncaring about Emma. Harley still felt bad about not sticking up for her aunt, yet she knew she would be risking what little acceptance and popularity she possessed if she made a big stink.

She thought about Greer Douglas as the River Glen Pirates kicked off to the opposing team. He was on defense, she knew; she'd made a point of knowing. She had a mini-crush. "Mini" being the operative word. He was a senior and she was a sophomore, and the senior girls could make her life miserable if he even looked at her, which he wouldn't, but she wasn't following any of her own advice since they'd been singled out for the mixer prank. Greer had taken an interest in Harley, and Marissa had moved her affections toward Tyler and maybe Troy. Though she'd warned Harley they could be stepping on toes, she'd seemed to conveniently forget her own advice since that night.

"We gotta get to that party," Marissa said as the clock wound down on the game. The outcome had pretty much been decided by the first quarter. River Glen had pulled ahead and the other team hadn't had a chance.

"I just told you. I can't."

"Don't you want to go?"

"'Course I do." Harley wasn't actually all that certain she did. She didn't want to make any more mistakes and find herself friendless. "But we have tomorrow. Babysitting."

Marissa gazed longingly at the team as the last play was run and the cheerleaders and people in the stands started screaming, a loud roar that drowned out everything else. Marissa yelled as well, and so did Harley. When the sound finally died down, Marissa said, "Okay, you're right. We can maybe figure out something tomorrow."

"What do you mean?"

"Maybe the guys'll stop by the Ryersons'."

Harley's heart lurched, but she didn't say anything. It wasn't that she didn't want to see the guys . . . but . . .

"Oh, Jesus," said Marissa as they were walking with the throng heading toward the gate. "There's my mom."

"I thought your dad was picking us up."

"He was. He is . . . Did something *happen*?"

She started pushing her way through the crowd, and Harley followed after her. When they reached Mrs. Haynes, they both stopped. "What's wrong?" Marissa demanded. "What are you doing here?"

She looked taken aback. "Nothing's wrong. I just came to pick you up."

"Dad's supposed to pick me up."

"Well, I beat him to it," she said tartly.

She had blond hair in a casual ponytail and wore gray yoga gear with a thin black jacket. She had a coffee or a latte in one hand as she glanced toward Harley. "You must be the new friend? We haven't really been introduced."

"Hi. I'm Harley Woodward," Harley said.

"Nice to meet you."

"Does Dad know you came to get me?" Marissa demanded.

"I just texted him. Don't worry. It's okay for you to leave with your mother. Are we giving you a ride?" she asked Harley.

"If it's all right."

"No problem." Her smile seemed a little practiced, but Harley told herself it was going to be okay.

They climbed into her charcoal Land Rover. Marissa got in the front and Harley got in behind her friend.

The conversation was desultory, mostly consisting of Mrs. Haynes asking questions and Marissa supplying one-syllable answers while she looked at her phone. "I texted Dad, too," Marissa revealed. "You coulda just let him pick me up."

"Don't make a federal case of it," Laura said on an exasperated sigh. "I'm your mother."

"Like I don't know that."

Silence for the rest of the trip. Harley was glad when they pulled into her drive and she could throw open the door and skedaddle.

Marissa rolled down her window and said, "See you tomorrow," with a knowing wink that her mom couldn't see.

"What's happening tomorrow?" Laura asked.

"Oh, nothing."

Harley was out of earshot by then. The front door opened, and Mom stepped out. Harley was halfway to the front steps and her mother came down to meet her.

"Oh." Mom looked surprised. "I thought Cooper was bringing you back."

"No, it's Marissa's mom."

"Okay." She waved at Mrs. Haynes, who suddenly turned off her Land Rover and stepped out of the car. Mom's smile, like Mrs. Haynes's earlier, looked a little fixed as she came farther down the front porch steps to meet up with Marissa's mom.

Harley didn't take her eyes off Laura Haynes. As if sensing trouble, Marissa erupted from the car. "Mom!" Marissa yelled. "Mom!"

"Thank you for bringing Harley back," Jamie began.

"I just heard that the girls have worked out a babysitting gig for tomorrow night." Mrs. Haynes stopped a couple of feet in front of them as Marissa practically slid into place beside her.

"Don't get weird," Marissa warned, to which her mother shot her an angry look.

"Harley told me. I checked with Ted Ryerson to see if it was okay," Mom said.

"It's not okay. I don't care what his answer was. I don't want Marissa distracted. She has a job to do when she's babysitting, and with someone else there, it doesn't get done the same way. I don't want to be *that* mother, but I really think Marissa should babysit on her own."

This was what Mom had said, too, and now she flicked Harley a look. Harley wanted to protest, but Marissa was already in the fray.

"Mr. Ryerson said it was fine!"

"Marissa," her mother warned.

"He said it was *fine*!"

"I understand," said Mom. "Harley can stay home. Let Marissa babysit on her own."

"You understand?" Mrs. Haynes questioned.

"Yes," Mom said, in that clipped way she used whenever she was really pissed but was pretending she wasn't.

Mrs. Haynes looked at her, too, assessing. "So, we agree on this?" she asked.

"Yes."

"*Mom!*" Marissa gazed at her mother angrily.

"Come on," Mrs. Haynes snapped at her, heading back to the car.

Marissa threw Harley a can-you-believe-this look, then, with the slow gait of a prisoner heading to her doom, followed after her.

When they were gone, Harley said, "This is shitty."

Mom didn't answer immediately. When they were back inside the house, Mom turned the lock on the door and said, "Yes. It's shitty."

"And don't swear," Harley added, hoping for a smile, but all Mom did was head upstairs.

Chapter Fifteen

The return phone call from Mikes Corliss came in just after Cooper was informed by Laura that she was already at the football stadium and picking up Marissa. Cooper had texted Laura back about collecting Harley as well, and that he was on his way to get both girls when Laura responded that she was taking care of it.

And then the retired River Glen detective's call came through, and Cooper chose to let Laura do what she would—when she made up her mind about something, she was nearly impossible to dissuade—and answered the phone.

"You wanted to talk about the Whelan attack," Corliss said. "I remember it as if it was yesterday. Beautiful girl. Terrible, what happened to her."

"I was one of the kids who pranked her," Cooper reminded him, still finding it hard to admit his part in the events that transpired.

"I remember you, too. What's on your mind?"

Cooper told him that he'd been going through the old files, seeing what he could find. When Corliss asked what had brought on this review, he admitted that Emma's mother had died and that her younger sister had returned to River Glen to help.

"You want to meet somewhere, son?" Corliss asked.

Son. Cooper vividly recalled Corliss calling him that when he and his friends had come in to the station to be interviewed. Corliss had calmly taken their statements, even while hysteria had been the order of the day for a number of the townspeople. Irene Whelan, though vocal, had kept her head. She'd flat-out said it was not a bogeyman who'd harmed her daughter. It was a flesh-and-blood, evil man.

Cooper had first seen her in Corliss's office while he was waiting to be interviewed, where she'd radiated anger.

"The Waystation?" Cooper asked Corliss now.

"Be there in forty-five."

Cooper checked his clock and decided to take a quick shower before meeting Corliss. He was disappointed that he wouldn't see Jamie again tonight. He kept thinking about the soft touch of her fingers undoing the top button of his shirt.

Jamie came out of the shower to find Emma sitting on the bed in Mom's bedroom, waiting for her. Bartholomew was beside her, tongue out and panting after running up the stairs, apparently.

"Who was that lady?" she asked flatly as Jamie, wrapped in a towel, searched through her suitcase for some clean clothes. "You need to unpack."

"Yes."

"Who was that lady?" she asked again.

"She's Marissa's mother. She's dropped Marissa off before."

"She doesn't like you."

"Yeah . . . well . . ."

If she doesn't like you now, how's she going to feel if she finds out you're interested in Cooper? she asked herself, then argued back: *He's her ex-husband. Ex.*

Like when does that ever change how a person feels?

"You still like Cooper," Emma said.

"Still?" Jamie questioned.

Emma smirked.

Harley came to the doorway. She'd changed into her pajamas, but there was a thundercloud over her head. "Marissa's mom is really a—"

"Uh-uh-uh," said Emma, tsking her finger.

"She has every right to feel the way she does," said Jamie.

"You don't like her either," Harley retorted.

"I don't know her. We've started off on the wrong foot. That's all."

"Uh-uh-uh," Emma repeated, this time looking at Jamie. To Harley, she added, "Jamie's in love with Cooper."

"*What?*" Jamie lost it. "You said 'like' a minute ago. I don't even know Cooper Haynes anymore. He seems like a nice enough guy, but that's as far as it goes."

"I think he's cool," said Harley.

"Jamie went to the party so she could see him, but he came to the house with his friends." Emma looked up at the ceiling and closed her eyes, but kept her head tilted. "He wasn't the one, though."

Jamie had wriggled into her jeans, but she paused in the act of hooking the eyes of her black bra. "The one?" she asked, finishing the task, then reaching for an oversize sweatshirt. She was going to go downstairs and have another glass of wine, or two.

"The one who scared me."

Harley was looking from Jamie to Emma and back again.

Now Jamie asked carefully, "The one who hurt you?"

Emma opened her eyes. Jamie hadn't turned on the lights, and in the semidarkness from the hall illumination, Emma's eyes looked huge and black. "I see . . . his eyes. . . ."

"Mom," Harley whispered, alarmed.

"Whose eyes?" Jamie asked. Jamie could feel Harley's tension and her own stretching between them, tight as a guide wire. When her sister didn't immediately answer, she asked again, "Whose eyes, Emma?"

"He came to the front door to scare me."

"Race? Race Stillwell?"

"He didn't scare me, though."

"Was it Race's eyes you saw?"

She regarded Jamie soberly. "Race Stillwell doesn't scare me." She then pointed at Harley and warned, "Don't babysit them. They are scary."

"The . . . Ryerson twins?" Harley asked.

"I'm glad Dummy's here. I want Theo to give him to me."

With that she got up, walked through the bedroom door, and headed downstairs, the dog at her heels.

Corliss had corralled one of the few booths that ran alongside the rough board wall opposite the bar. Cooper took a look around, his gaze catching on Dug Douglas, who was warming a barstool. Corliss made eye contact and Cooper headed his way.

The retired detective was silver-haired, with a bushy mustache and dark eyes beneath thick, gray eyebrows. He had a glass of dark beer in front of him, untouched as yet. He gave Cooper the once-over as he slid into the seat across from him.

"I remember you," he said. "You wouldn't give up."

"I still haven't."

"All my notes are in the file. I don't know what you think I can help you with, but go ahead. Ask what you want."

"After you ruled out any of us kids, how did the investigation into the attack on Emma Whelan go?"

"Like I said, it's all in my notes."

"I've read the notes. I'd like to hear it from you."

He shrugged and gave up arguing about it. A barmaid whose weathered face said she'd seen it all looked at Cooper. He pointed to Corliss's glass and asked for the same. Once she was out of earshot, Corliss said, "I'll be honest. Even though we decided it wasn't any of you, we didn't completely, if you know what I mean. We moved on, but there was always the suspicion that one of you, one that maybe she rejected, had come back at her with the knife."

"The knife that was never found."

He nodded. "Nothing was taken from the house other than the knife, as far as we could determine. Whelan's purse was on the counter, untouched. None of the Ryersons' belongings were missing, nothing lost to sticky fingers. That was per both Dr. Ryerson and his wife, Nadine. They were horrified about what had happened to Emma. They'd been at a charity event at the Hotel Lovejoy in Northwest Portland, which is now the Lovejoy Apartments, and the meeting room is a restaurant. Nadine was the first to find Emma on the living room floor, unconscious. Dr. Ryerson came in after her. They were both shaken to the core. You probably know their marriage didn't survive the stress. They split up and moved away. I believe they're both remarried and are living in California or Nevada. . . . I heard Ryerson retired to Palm Desert at one time. She stayed in River Glen for the kids and then left after they graduated."

Cooper knew most of the facts about the Ryersons, but he made a mental note to check up on them, see what they remembered about that night. "Anything else about the case? Something that caught your attention at the time?"

Corliss slowly shook his head. "Like I said, I always thought it was one of you boys."

Cooper finished his beer, whereas Corliss had barely touched his. There was a distant light in his eye, as if he were thinking hard about something else.

"You had in your notes about Emma having a possible 'secret life'," Cooper said.

"You all kept trying to blame the attack on an older boyfriend," Corliss said with a snort. "The Stillwell kid said she stopped in to his party late and wouldn't say why. His assumption was that she'd been to see this boyfriend and it hadn't gone well. She was in a bad mood, barely spoke to him before going to her babysitting gig. Maybe she just didn't want to see Stillwell."

This was close in line to Cooper's own thoughts. He pressed Corliss for any further information, but the man drank his beer down nearly in one long draught, then shook his head and scooted back his chair. Cooper threw down enough money to pay for them both. He thanked Corliss for his time as they both got up to leave. He hadn't learned anything he didn't already know, but it was worth the effort. If he was lucky, maybe something would shake loose that was buried in the man's mind. If it didn't, no harm, no foul.

"Hey, man."

Cooper was in the Whistestop's parking lot, heading for his Explorer. The voice came from a dark corner that immediately put Cooper on alert.

Dug Douglas materialized from the shadows into the cold light from the riot light on the top of a pole that lit up most of the lot. He was finishing a cigarette, and it was the red glow from its tip that Cooper saw before Dug showed himself.

"What are you doing lurking back there?" Cooper asked the insurance man.

"Saw you come in and decided to wait for you." He ground out the butt against the cracked tarmac. "You're becoming quite a regular here, huh?"

"Same could be said of you."

Doug smiled. He'd put on a few pounds over the intervening years and his hair, though he'd hung on to most of it,

had silvered. He wore it a little longish for the current style.
"You were with that cop who interviewed all of us all those
years ago."

"Yeah."

"He gave my son some grief a few years back. Acted like
Greer had been stealing out of garages down on Oak Street."

Oak Street . . . where the Ryersons lived. "I remember."
Cooper had been on the force, but hadn't yet made detective.
Mike Corliss had just retired, but he'd been called back in on
Greer Douglas.

"It wasn't Greer. It was Troy Stillwell and Tyler Stapleton.
No one wants to believe the two best players on the football
team are lowlife thieves. Easier to blame it on Greer."

*And there was that joy ride with the neighbor's car that
both Troy and Greer had been involved in.* The neighbor had
screamed grand theft auto, Dug had found a way to soothe
the man with a nice settlement. Tyler Stapleton may have
been part of that spree as well, but Troy and Greer had covered for their team quarterback.

"Your son was never charged," Cooper reminded him.
Dug's expensive lawyers had seen to that.

"I'm telling you this because it's the truth. Think what
you will. You always kind of were a self-important prick. But
it wasn't my boy. Keep that in mind."

Self-important prick . . .

Cooper thought about Dug's wife, a pretty, somewhat insecure, stay-at-home mom who spent a lot of time around
the high school, according to Robbie, trying to ease her son's
way through school. The little Cooper had seen of Greer he'd
thought the kid could go either way. He had the grades,
brains, and skills to make something of himself, but Dug, for
all his business successes, was still insecure and somewhat
unformed, at least in Cooper's biased opinion, and if Greer
took a page from Dug's book, he'd never reach his potential.

"You see Corliss often?" Dug asked.

"Not really."

"Something in particular brought you two together tonight?"

Cooper decided there was no reason not to tell him. "I'm looking into the attack on Emma Whelan. Wanted to see what he could remember."

"What the hell, man. That's ancient history."

"It was never solved, though."

"Why now?" he asked.

"Her mother just died and her sister's back, taking care of her. Just seemed the right time."

"I hear the sister's a looker. Like Emma."

"She is," Cooper allowed.

"You got a hard-on for her, too?" he asked, that slow smile widening across his lips.

Cooper said evenly, "I just want to know what really happened that night. I think Emma and her family deserve to know, too."

"Cooper Haynes to the rescue."

"One thing Corliss said . . ."

He stiffened a bit. "Yeah?"

"He still thinks one of us had something to do with Emma's attack."

"Hell no. We were all cleared. Totally cleared," he added with some heat.

"He doesn't have proof. That's just what his gut is telling him."

"Well, his gut's wrong." Dug glowered at him a moment, then asked, as if he couldn't help himself, "What have you got so far?"

"Nothing, really. I'm just going through the reports from that night. Doing some interviews. Maybe I'll catch up with you later," Cooper added.

"Hah." He turned away then, and Cooper watched him head to his vehicle, a black, Jeep Rubicon.

On the way home, Cooper thought about Douglas's body language. He'd definitely reacted to Corliss's belief that there was more to the story from Cooper and the guys who'd spooked her that night. *Was* there more to the story?

Dug had been with Race, and Race had had it bad for Emma, who'd yelled at them disparagingly from the porch, which hadn't sat well with any of them, but not with Race in particular. Could Race have done something in a fit of jealousy and rage? And, as Race's right-hand man, could Dug have known about it?

But Race had been devastated over Emma. Cooper would swear that wasn't faked. Race wasn't that skilled of an actor. But maybe it was devastation of another kind . . . a manifestation of guilt and regret?

Cooper shook his head. No. Race, for all his faults, would never hurt Emma. He'd had a number of girlfriends over the years since. Nothing that seemed to pan out into something lasting. Cooper knew a couple of them, and none of them had anything bad to say about Race, other than that he'd never really grown up and was basically unreliable. If anything, they acted like he was disengaged. Not in the moment. Not involved enough to care whether he was in a relationship or not.

"His feelings just aren't that deep," one of them had said with a huge sigh. "I wasted too long on a guy who never matured past junior high."

That was an improvement on fourth grade, but not by much.

But Dug . . . Dug had wanted Race's approval more than about anything else in those days. Could Dug have confronted Emma in a misguided attempt to win favor with Race?

Or are you just trying to pin something on Dug because he pissed you off?

He let himself into the house and flipped on the kitchen lights, then wandered toward the living room and the hallway that led to the bedrooms. There was a bookshelf recessed into the hallway wall. He rarely noticed it, but tonight, his eye was drawn to the tall books on the top shelf, one of which was his high school yearbook. He snagged it and took it with him to his bedroom. There was a desk in one corner. His father's, now his. He opened the book and turned to the senior pictures. The book practically flipped open on its own to the correct page, it had been so well used.

There he was. Cooper Haynes. Looking directly at the camera with a stupid, cocky grin on his face. He flipped back, and there was Patrick Douglas, his expression serious, as if he were trying for an actor's headshot rather than a senior picture. He went past his picture and found Race Stillwell, chin jutted forward, but there was something wooden in his expression, stoic and somewhat forced. He didn't know how to take a picture and look relaxed. He checked Tim Merchel's picture. And Mark Norquist's. And Robbie Padilla's. They all looked like he remembered them. Robbie hadn't changed all that much, just a different mustache, and Tim, the last time he'd seen him, had that same time-can't-change-us look as well.

Lastly, he turned to Emma's picture. She'd had it taken before the accident and the school had put it in the yearbook, even though she hadn't finished senior year. Her blue eyes were full of confidence and there was something almost mischievous about her smile, like she had a secret she didn't want to share.

He stared at the photo a long, long time, determined to make good on his promise to find out what really happened to her.

* * *

Saturday night, Jamie had everything she needed to make spaghetti. Maybe bucatini carbonara had been a bit of a disaster, but spaghetti was in her wheelhouse, and probably Emma's, too. She was just getting ready to cook up the hamburger for the meat sauce when her cell phone rang.

She glanced at the screen, but didn't recognize the number. "Hello?" she answered cautiously.

"Hi, Jamie. It's Ted Ryerson."

"Teddy," she responded, surprised. "Well, hi. What's going on?"

"My sister and I are going out to dinner tonight, meeting another friend, and we wondered if you'd like to join us. We're heading into Portland. Pearl District, maybe? Pick up Serena and then meet at a restaurant. Maybe catch a film afterward."

Jamie was nonplussed. Maybe he was just being nice, or maybe he thought she had money to invest, but either way, she didn't want to take him up on the invitation. It just felt weird. "Well, thank you, but I'm sorry, I've got other plans," she lied. "Maybe another time?"

Teddy and Serena were only seven years behind her, but it felt like a full generation to Jamie. She really didn't know them, and anyway, she'd half-hoped, though it was maybe silly, that she might connect with Cooper tonight, somehow. He'd called and told her he'd met with the retired detective on her sister's case.

"That's too bad. I thought if Harley was at my house, maybe you could use some company."

"Harley's not going to be there," Jamie corrected him. "It's only Marissa. We had a change of plans."

"Oh . . ." Now he was the one who sounded nonplussed. "All right," he said reluctantly. "Next time."

"Next time," she agreed.

"Who was that?" Emma asked when Jamie was off the phone. She was in the kitchen with her apron on and Jamie had tasked her with opening the jars of tomato sauce while she browned the hamburger.

"It was Teddy Ryerson. He asked me to join him and Serena for dinner."

The open jar slipped out of Emma's hand and thunked on the counter. In a surprisingly swift move, Jamie lunged for it and grabbed it before it fell to the floor, slopping a glop of red sauce onto her hand.

"I don't like them," Emma said, her face screwing up as if she were about to cry.

"I know. You said so before. But I'm not going out with them. And Harley's not babysitting for them tonight. But Emma, we have to be able to do things that we think are okay, and if that means being with the Ryersons, well, we're going to do that."

"Okay."

Her sudden capitulation raised Jamie's eyebrows, but she let it pass. Half an hour later, Harley wandered downstairs, phone in hand, just as Jamie served up the spaghetti, a green salad, and the garlic bread Emma had prepared. Though the garlic was a little heavy-handed, both Jamie and Harley complimented her on the bread.

"I've been talking to Marissa," Harley admitted, out of earshot of Emma. "She's really pissed at her mom."

"Hmmm."

"Do you really like Mr. Haynes?" she asked curiously.

"I hardly know him."

"He called you today."

"Are you checking up on me?" She gave her daughter a look.

"I think it'd be cool if you liked him, that's all." Harley fingered her phone's keypad. "I kinda like somebody."

"*Greer?*" Jamie didn't know if she was more surprised by the speed of this new attraction or the fact that Harley had willingly brought it up to her again.

"He barely knows me. He's a senior. It's not anything." She shut down as fast as she'd opened up.

"Okay. If you want to talk more, let me know."

But Harley clearly felt she'd said too much already. And she had, in a way, because Jamie, having been given another kernel of information, was curious about this boy who had tickled her daughter's fancy, so to speak.

The three of them ate the spaghetti and garlic bread and an Italianesque salad with an oil and vinegar dressing; then Jamie headed upstairs, leaving Emma downstairs watching her DVR'd cooking episodes with Harley, who was watching with her . . . and texting with Marissa. Jamie warned her to let her friend be. Marissa was foremost in charge of Oliver and Anika, and the last thing Jamie needed was to hear more about it.

Camryn called and asked if Jamie was free to go out. Jamie almost said yes. She could visit her friend and also make good on the excuse she'd given Teddy Ryerson. But she felt unsettled. It didn't feel right leaving Harley and Emma alone tonight. She begged off, but she and Camryn confirmed plans for the next weekend.

She then took a bath and tried to put Laura Haynes out of her mind. It bothered her that things had gone so sideways with Cooper's ex. Icky Vicky's tribe had said how nice Laura was, and they'd been half-scandalized that Jamie had allowed Marissa to come to their house while spreading Mom's ashes and not warn Laura in advance.

That had been a mistake. But she wasn't sure how to ameliorate the situation beyond the apology she'd already given.

"Maybe she's not as nice as everyone says," Jamie muttered to herself.

Later, after Emma was in bed, Harley was in her room, and Jamie had settled down with a suspense novel by a first-time author who'd received good reviews, there was a *thud* from Harley's room and a sudden pounding of feet, and the door to Jamie's little sleeping alcove was thrown wide.

"Mom! Mom!"

"What? I'm right here. What?" Jamie had half-fallen asleep while reading, but now she sat straight up, wide awake from Harley's shrieking voice.

"It's Marissa! Someone broke into the house and came at her with a knife!"

Chapter Sixteen

"What? *What?*" Jamie leaped out of bed. She was still in her clothes, having fallen asleep in them.

"She's . . . she's . . . in the bedroom, hiding with the kids. . . ." Harley's voice was shaking and tears stood in her eyes.

"Did she call 9-1-1? Is he still in the house?"

"I don't know."

"Jesus Christ!" Jamie was full of horror.

"I'll text her."

"I'll call 9-1-1," Jamie said, waking fully to the horror of the moment, her hand scrabbling on the bedside table for her phone.

"She did! She called 9-1-1," Harley declared in relief, staring at the screen of her phone. A rush of sudden tears ran down her face.

"Good. Good. Oh my God. Oh my God." Jamie hardly knew what to do.

She glanced down the hallway to Emma's closed door, then pulled Harley inside her tiny room and closed the door. "We need to . . ."

"We need to do something!"

"Cooper. Um . . . I'll . . ." She was already scrolling through her favorites for his number.

He answered almost immediately. "Jamie?"

The lilt of expectation in his voice made her nose sting. "Cooper, Marissa called 9-1-1. She says someone broke in. She called Harley."

A beat. "When?" His tone had changed to hard and cold.

"Just a few minutes ago?"

"My phone's ringing . . ." And he was gone.

Harley looked at Jamie. They stood frozen for a moment, then Harley hurled herself into Jamie's arms, sobbing wildly.

Cooper broke all records driving to the Ryersons'. He'd been called by Marissa, who'd told him the police had arrived from her 911 call and that everyone was safe. There was no one there and no sign of an intruder. Her voice was shaking. He'd asked her about the kids, who'd been asleep through most of it and now were wide-eyed, crying and staring at the police: two officers who hadn't realized Marissa was Cooper's stepdaughter.

"Did you call your mom?" he asked her.

"No. But I did call Mr. Ryerson." He could hear the unshed tears clogging her voice.

"Good. Call your mom. I'll be there in ten."

He made it in five.

As soon as he entered, he saw Marissa on the couch, a twin under each arm. She bounded up and ran to him, burying her face in his chest. The twins' crying grew louder, and Cooper gently unwound Marissa from his arms and told her she needed to make sure they were okay. She followed his advice but kept tight hold of one of his hands. The officers, Crake and O'Hara, stood to one side. Crake lifted his chin at Cooper, indicating he wanted to talk to him.

"I need to talk to the officers."

"I need to tell you what happened," said Marissa.

The twins, a girl and a boy, were sniffling and staring at him with wide, scared eyes.

"Stay with the kids. I'll just be a minute."

"You're not leaving?" she asked on a gasp.

"No. I'm just talking to them."

He gently moved away from Marissa. She was clearly traumatized. But she stayed put, rubbing the kids' backs absently, her eyes seeing some other horror.

Crake gestured for him to come through the kitchen and into the small access room by the back door. Cooper remembered the layout from the pranking. Nothing much had changed with the decor since. The creaky window by the back door was closed, but he suspected it would still creak if he opened it.

"She said a guy in a ski suit and mask came after her with a knife."

Cooper felt a distinct shock. "What?"

"Came in through the back door," Crake went on. "There was no sign of anyone when we got here. No break-in. Your daughter ran into the bedroom both kids were sleeping in, shut the door, and jammed a chair beneath the knob. She was on the phone with a friend. Got off it to call 9-1-1."

"You came in through the back door?"

"Yeah. Front was locked. We cleared the place. She and the kids were in the bedroom. Nobody."

Something in his tone caught Cooper's attention. "You think she just got scared and called and now's making it up?"

"I don't know."

He could buy that she might've gotten scared and called 911. Marissa was imaginative enough. But she wasn't an out-and-out liar to cover up a mistake. "If she says someone was here with a knife, I'm going to believe her."

Crake bent his head. "She's certainly scared enough," he agreed.

Cooper went back to Marissa, who grabbed his hand again. The kids clung to her.

"Why?" Marissa asked him, her voice teary.

"I don't know." Cooper squeezed her hand.

Why was the question he still asked himself about Emma. And now a second time? At the same house? While someone was babysitting?

A screech of tires sounded from outside, and suddenly Laura was there, hugging Marissa hard and scaring the twins. The two children, Oliver and Anika, Marissa managed to tell him, allowed Cooper to kneel in front of them and talk to them. Then Ted Ryerson was there, rushing in from the back, looking wild-eyed. Upon seeing their father, the twins burst into fresh tears and jumped forward to meet him.

"I've got my daughter," Laura told Cooper when he turned his attention to Marissa again.

"Mom . . ." Marissa protested weakly.

"Can I talk to her a moment?" Cooper asked. The two officers, upon checking with Ryerson and making sure everyone was fine, left the scene to Cooper, and Ted Ryerson took his twins into his bedroom because they refused to be away from him.

"Tomorrow." Laura put her foot down.

"It'll be quick," Cooper promised her.

Laura wouldn't let him talk to Marissa alone, so he ignored her and concentrated on the teenager.

"You okay?" he first asked.

"You're asking her that now?" Laura demanded. She was practically shivering with rage.

"I'm okay," Marissa said in a squeaky voice.

"No, you're not. God, how could this happen?" Laura was breathing hard.

"Tell me what happened," Cooper asked Marissa calmly.

"I told the officers everything already . . ." she said uncertainly.

"I know. I just want to hear it from you."

"Don't you think she's been traumatized enough?" Laura demanded.

"When did you first see him?" Cooper asked Marissa, ignoring his ex.

"I was in the living room. I was looking out . . . that window." She glanced fearfully toward the front of the house. "I was . . . the kids were in bed. They wanted to sleep in the same room. It's what they like to do whenever there's a babysitter. I put them down and I was in the living room. I felt something . . . cold air . . . I turned around and . . ." Her voice was rising to a high squeak. "He had on a ski mask and . . . and a *knife*!"

Laura's hand flew to her own mouth. Hearing it from Marissa brought the hairs lifting on Cooper's arms as well.

"What did you do?" Cooper asked quietly.

"I ran to the kids' bedroom. I was . . . I was on the phone . . . with Harley. . . . I screamed! I threw the phone down and grabbed the chair and shoved it under the doorknob. I grabbed up the phone again and called 9-1-1 and I . . . called you. . . ." She swallowed. "I could hardly hear, my heart was pounding so loudly. He rattled the door and I screamed again and it woke the kids. . . . I didn't come out till I heard the officers. . . ."

"Okay," he said as Marissa started shaking some more.

"That's enough," said Laura.

"Who was it?" Marissa asked rhetorically.

"I'm going to find out," Cooper said, just as Ted Ryerson returned from the bedroom. Immediately, his kids started calling for him.

Ted said, "I want to know what happened from beginning to end."

"We'll go over it tomorrow," said Cooper as he glanced back to the bedroom door.

"Fine." Ted was white-faced.

Cooper herded Marissa and Laura to the back door and Ted followed, locking it behind them with a distinct click.

"He could've been more concerned for Marissa," Laura said tightly.

Cooper wasn't going to argue with her as he walked with them to her Land Rover. He asked Marissa, "Was the back door unlocked?"

"I don't . . . think so," she answered uncertainly.

"Is that how you entered the house?"

She nodded slowly.

"And how Mr. Ryerson left?"

"Yes."

"You don't remember locking it behind him?"

"I don't know!" she wailed.

"Stop badgering her, Cooper," Laura said angrily.

He lifted his palms. "We'll pick it up tomorrow."

"We're going to be at the new house all day. Marissa's with us," Laura said.

"Then I'll see you there." Cooper shut Marissa's passenger door behind her and waited till they pulled away from the curb.

In his SUV, he put in a call to Jamie. She answered right away. "Everything's okay," he told her, then launched into the details of Marissa's babysitting scare.

It was close to midnight when the text came through on Harley's phone. She'd been lying in bed, trying to get to sleep for over an hour. She and Mom had stayed up talking for a while after receiving the news that Marissa and the

Ryerson kids were fine. The relief had been huge. Mom had poured herself a glass of wine and then gripped the glass's stem as if her life depended on it. She'd then told her that the circumstances of Marissa's scare were very similar to Aunt Emma's attack—*and at the same house!*

Harley had been so freaked out, she'd almost asked for a glass of wine herself, except she hated the taste. Horrible, foul stuff. She'd told herself she could sleep now that she knew Marissa was okay, but she'd stared at the ceiling, wishing she'd kept her night-light on as the dark seemed to press around her.

Harley was charging her phone on the dresser. For a moment, she didn't want to get out of the warm safety of her bed. But only one person would be texting her, most likely.

She slid out from under the covers. Tiptoed rapidly to her phone. The screen had gone dark, but she touched it awake.

She could read the start of the text: **I'm scared shitless don't say anything I don't think it was the guys, they'd left. But if it was them why—**

Harley had to plug in her code to open the phone and read the rest of the text.

—did they bring a knife. God I'm scared!!!

Harley listened for her mother. She didn't want her coming into her room unexpectedly. When she determined the house was quiet, she quickly texted back.

It can't be the guys, they wouldn't do that

Would they?

Harley thought back to Marissa's scream. It had scared her shitless, too. But some of the guys had come by the Ryersons' earlier. They'd tossed pebbles at the windows, and Marissa had gone to the back door and been able to catch sight of them running down the block. She'd been pretty sure one of them was Troy Stillwell and one was Greer Douglas. She thought Tyler was there, too, but she hadn't seen clearly. Harley had wondered—hoped, actually—that Greer had come because Marissa had let it be known that she would be babysitting, too . . . until she wasn't.

But to come with a *knife?* They'd had props at the mixer. Freddy Krueger's fingers . . . the Grim Reaper's scythe . . . but with Marissa . . . the sudden appearance of the guy in ski gear with a *knife* . . .

"It wasn't them," she whispered aloud, hopefully, not totally convincing herself.

Marissa texted back: gotta go . . . talk tomorrow . . .

Harley signed off with an "OK" emoji.

She felt cold inside. Afraid. Afraid there was someone out there who'd threatened her friend. Maybe the same guy who'd attacked *Aunt Emma?*

She shivered violently, then breathed in and out, in and out, in and out, calming herself down.

But what if it was a prank? A stupid, terrible prank, but still a prank? That was way better, but still really bad. Marissa had called 911 and Mr. Haynes, the police detective, had gotten involved. Marissa had poked a hornet's nest and the boys could be in real trouble. . . . Greer could be in real trouble.

She chewed her lower lip. She didn't want that to happen.

Maybe she would just keep the information that the boys were there to herself.

Marissa had texted don't say anything

An excellent plan.

But as she fell asleep, her mind hooked on the scars on Aunt Emma's back that she'd caught a glimpse of one day when she'd inadvertently opened the bathroom door as she was getting in the shower. Big, jagged scars along her shoulder blade, faded now, but the first thing you noticed against her smooth, white skin.

* * *

Jamie arose around four a.m., unable to sleep. She kept thinking of what Cooper had said: that a figure in a ski mask had come at Marissa with a knife. Each time she'd dozed off, her brain had slipped an image of the attacker into her dreams and she'd woken with a start, heart racing, gasping for air.

She took a shower and washed her hair, then stood under the spray. She needed to wake up, and even though she knew she was going to feel dull and out of sorts all day, she couldn't stay in bed one more minute.

Why had the intruder come after Marissa? Was it something to do with Teddy Ryerson, or the Ryerson family as a whole? Was it something to do with there being a babysitter? That made no sense at all, but these two bookended crimes over twenty years apart couldn't be completely random, could they?

No. They were too similar. A knife wielded against a babysitter at the very same house. There had to be a connection. But what? Why?

Poor Marissa . . . *lucky* Marissa, actually, that things weren't worse. She'd escaped physical harm, and though God knew what kind of mental distress she was now under, she hadn't suffered the same fate as Emma.

Emma . . . Jamie had wrestled all night over whether she should alert her sister to what had happened. Emma had already mentioned that she didn't like the Ryersons. She still seemed slightly bemused by the fact that Teddy and Serena were grown and that Teddy had twins of his own.

Her gut told her not to tell Emma anything that had happened last night. But on the other hand, if Emma found out from some other source, someone who might not know her full history . . . Jamie had a vision of Emma yelling, "*It's his eyes . . . his eyes!*" and inwardly shuddered. She didn't want to hurt her sister, and bringing up the attack would surely do just that, but the chance of someone else bringing it up first . . . that just couldn't happen.

Two hours later, while Jamie was seated at the table, Emma came downstairs, once again wearing her Scottie dog pajamas. She eyed Jamie, who'd lifted her cup of black coffee to her lips.

"Mornin'," Jamie greeted her.

"Where is Harley?"

"Still in bed. It's Sunday. I wouldn't expect her till noon."

"The Thrift Shop's closed on Sundays." Emma walked to the drop-in range top and arranged the spices that were lined behind it against the back wall, placing the salt and pepper at the end of the row.

Jamie looked away from her sister, fretting over how much to tell her.

Emma asked, "Are we getting the dog today?"

"The dog?"

"Harley wants a dog," Emma reminded her. "Mom is in the garden. We can get a dog now."

Jamie started to respond, then stopped herself. After the events of the night before, the idea of a dog had new merit. It had been Emma who'd insisted they couldn't have a dog because "Mom" wouldn't allow it. Clearly, she wasn't feeling that way any longer.

"When Harley gets up, let's talk about it."

"That will be at noon."

"Or thereabouts," Jamie corrected. "Could even be earlier."

Emma pulled out a box of Cheerios and set about getting herself breakfast. Jamie was starting to feel hungry as well.

"Want me to make bacon and eggs?" she asked.

"Pancakes," Emma said. She'd been about to pour milk on her cereal, but now she hesitated.

"I could make pancakes," Jamie agreed.

"Mom made pancakes on Sundays."

"Then let's do that."

Twenty minutes later, Jamie was just setting a plate in front of Emma, who'd brought out both maple and boysenberry syrups from the pantry, when Harley stumbled into the kitchen in a gray sweatshirt and a pair of gray-and-white-striped pajama pants. Her hair was sticking up in spots, and Jamie watched as Emma's gaze swiveled toward Harley and glued on her hair. As Harley sat down, she wasn't surprised to see Emma get up, go to Harley, and press her hands to Harley's crown, trying to tame the errant locks. Harley locked eyes with Jamie, and there was something in her gaze that made Jamie say a tad sharply, "Emma. Let's let Harley wake up."

"Her hair is not good," said Emma.

"It's all right," Harley responded.

After another minute of failed ministrations, Emma went to the sink, washed her hands and returned to her seat.

"Pancakes?" Jamie asked her daughter.

Harley started to shake her head, then stopped and said, "Yeah. Sounds great."

Emma poured boysenberry syrup in a circle on her pancake, followed by a circle of maple syrup. She cut into the pancake with the edge of her fork and took a bite, slowly spinning the plate as she worked her way around the pancake.

Harley watched her in silence. Jamie wondered what she was thinking, but she wouldn't meet her eyes again. After a long minute, she tucked into her own pancake after Jamie slipped it in front of her.

It was an oddly quiet scene. Jamie tried to make a little conversation, letting it be known that the dishwasher repairman was coming on Monday. Neither responded. She then asked them both if they would like a second pancake. Harley shook her head and Emma, eyeing Harley, shook her head as well.

Jamie made herself a pancake and joined them at the table. She ate without tasting. Nourishment more than the joy of a meal.

"Harley is awake," Emma pointed out.

Harley frowned at her aunt. "Yeah. Why? Were you waiting for me?"

"You want a dog," said Emma.

"Umm . . ." Harley flicked Jamie a look, her brows still furrowed.

"Emma would like a dog, too," Jamie explained.

"Now that Mom's in the garden," Emma clarified.

"Oh," said Harley. She stared at her half-eaten plate, then swallowed hard. "That would be great." Her eyes filled with tears.

Jamie's heart hurt for her daughter. "Should we go to the shelter in town? Camryn's involved with Love . . . pets . . . or something?"

"Luv-Ahh-Pet. You spell Luv with a 'u,'" said Emma.

Harley nodded her head vigorously.

"I'll give Camryn a call."

"Who is Camryn?" Emma asked.

"A friend of mine. From high school."

"Camryn Watts," said Emma.

"That's right." Jamie was impressed that she remembered.

Emma said, "We will name him King. No dummy names for our dog."

They both looked at her, and Jamie asked, "What if he is a she?"

"We will name her Queenie."

"What if she already has a name that she knows?" Harley

posed. She'd dashed her tears away and now finally looked more awake and in the moment.

Emma frowned at Harley. Clearly, that thought hadn't occurred to her. "We will answer each challenge as it comes," she announced, and in her tone, Jamie heard an echo of her mother's voice.

As Emma left to get ready, Jamie asked Harley, "Have you heard anything more from Marissa?"

"Why would I?"

"Because you're her friend. Because you were on the phone with her. Because she's scared."

Harley shook her head. "I don't really want to talk about it anymore."

"I just want to make sure she's all right."

"She's fine. Can we drop it now?" Harley swept up her plate and put it in the sink with a clatter.

"How about you? How are you doing?"

"Mom!"

"Give me a break, Harley. I just want to make sure we're all okay."

"We're all okay!"

With that, she turned away and ran up the stairs.

Sunday morning.

Normally a day off for Cooper, but the attack on Marissa had changed everything. Howie had been put in charge of the investigation by Chief Bennihof himself, as Cooper, being Marissa's stepfather, was considered too close to the victim to be dispassionate enough to do the job.

Bullshit.

Cooper was knocking on Laura's door at 8:30 a.m. Laura answered in her bathrobe, tucking it tighter around herself upon seeing Cooper on her doorstep. He didn't wait for her to speak. "I want to talk to Marissa."

"You talked to her last night."

"I want to talk to her this morning. Howie will be interviewing her later."

"Howie? Why? She doesn't know anything. Leave her alone."

He just looked at her. Laura knew, from her years with Cooper, the steps of an investigation. How many times had he complained to her about parents whose instincts to shield their child got in the way?

"She should never have gotten hooked up with that new girl," Laura declared, throwing the door wide and walking away.

"What's Harley got to do with this?"

"I don't know. Something. Everything's gone sideways since Marissa adopted her."

"Do you hear yourself?" Cooper asked her as he followed her to the back of the house and the kitchen. It always felt a little strange to be in the same rooms he'd shared with her during their marriage. Maybe it was a good thing she was moving.

Laura shook her head to him, but didn't turn around. She moved to the coffeepot on the counter. "Want some coffee?"

"Sure."

She poured him a cup into one of the flowered mugs she'd purchased at the start of their marriage and hung on a mug tree. She gave him hyacinths. The interior color of the cup was purplish blue. It was the mug she'd always given him when they were living together. He wondered if she'd done it on purpose, or if she even noticed. She didn't say anything about it.

She didn't bother offering him cream or sugar. She knew he took it black.

"Marissa's not up yet. Last night was . . . harrowing. Are you supposed to be talking to her before Howie?"

"No."

Their eyes met. Laura correctly read what he wasn't saying—that he, too, was a parent who wanted to protect their kid.

"What do you think happened?" Laura asked. All pretense was gone. They were talking about Marissa now.

"I think she was attacked by a stranger who meant her harm. . . ."

"But?"

"I don't know."

Laura inhaled, then nodded. She went to the bottom of the stairs and yelled upward. "Marissa! Cooper's here. He's got some things to talk about with you." She looked at Cooper and said in a quiet voice, "I'm in the room, too."

He wanted to protest. He would, if he'd had a leg to stand on. Instead, he gave her a curt nod.

Marissa came downstairs in her pajamas. She looked pale and her hair was mussed. "What?" she asked a bit resentfully.

Cooper explained that his partner would be interviewing her soon about the events of the night before.

"Why can't you?" she asked, her eyes widening.

"Because I'm your stepfather."

Marissa immediately had a fit, saying she wouldn't do it. She even appealed to her mother, but Laura had gotten the lay of the land and wasn't going to fight with Cooper on this one, like she normally might.

The three of them walked into the living room. "Where's David?" Marissa asked, which Cooper had been wondering about as well.

"He's on a run," said Laura.

David Musgrave was religious about his exercise. He ran several miles a day, every day, sometimes longer.

"I'm not talking around him," Marissa told her mother.

"Well, he's not here, is he?"

"I already told you everything," she said, turning to Cooper. Her lower jaw was set.

Cooper knew Marissa well. The belligerence in her demeanor was a cover-up for something else. Maybe nothing bad, but a cover-up nevertheless.

"Did you recognize your assailant?" he asked.

"No! Of course not!"

"It wasn't anyone from the school?"

"*No!* Oh my God. You think I'm lying?"

"No. No, I don't think you're lying," Cooper said swiftly. "I believe you were attacked."

"I was. I was! He *scared* me!" She started crying, and Laura tried to gather her in her arms, but Marissa struggled free. She gazed at Cooper bitterly. "I thought you . . . I thought you were different."

He wanted to tell her he was. He wanted to keep their special relationship special. But more than that, he wanted to keep her safe. "Was anyone from the school at the house at any time?"

There was the briefest hesitation. Barely noticeable. Then she was outraged. "This *man* came in, in big, bulky ski gear and a mask and he had a *knife*! I ran to the bedroom and grabbed the chair and I was screaming on the phone. He *rattled* the door handle!"

"Did he try to push in?"

"Yes!" She blinked. "But . . . I think he heard me on the phone. . . . That's why he stopped."

"What kind of knife was it?" Cooper asked.

"I don't know. It was a knife!"

"A steak knife? A butcher knife?"

"Umm . . ." She clasped her hands together and thought hard. "More like the one Mom uses to cut up apples?"

"A utility knife," said Laura, rising from the edge of the chair where she'd been seated. She went to the kitchen and pulled out a five-inch knife with about a one-inch blade.

Marissa shrank away from the sight of it and Laura put it back in the drawer. "Maybe not quite as big."

Cooper asked her a few more questions, but after the knife she didn't have much more to say.

"You're going to get him, right?" she asked when the questions ran down.

"Yes," he stated positively.

She relaxed a little, and this time when Laura put her arms around her, she let it happen.

"If you think of anything else. Anything. Tell me, or tell Howie," he added.

"I'm not telling him anything," Marissa declared.

"No, you need to. And if there's anything you're holding back, or you remember something later? Don't keep it to yourself. We need to find this guy. Even things you don't deem important very well could be. Don't leave out anything."

Again, that faint hesitation. "Okay," she said.

As Cooper was heading out the front door, David jogged to a stop beside the garage door, checking his Fitbit. He was breathing hard. When he saw Cooper, he said, "Six miles."

Cooper nodded.

"What are you doing here so early? This have to do with what happened to Marissa?"

"I wanted to see how she was doing. My partner's going to be interviewing her later."

"I'll make sure she's okay," the lawyer said.

There was something a bit pompous about the man Laura had chosen after Cooper, but Cooper was grateful that Laura had moved on. She'd been the one to end their relationship, but it had only been after several years of Cooper working longer and longer hours. He'd told himself there was just a lot to do, but it hadn't been the complete truth. Laura had complained bitterly about his hours in the beginning and, when things didn't improve, had basically told him to get out, which was rather presumptuous considering they'd bought the house together. But he'd gone, relieved it was over. He'd used work, and his father's illness and subsequent death, as an excuse to explain his distance, but the crux of the matter was, the marriage had run its course.

Chapter Seventeen

It was late morning before Jamie, Emma, and Harley were ready to meet Camryn at the Luv-Ahh-Pet Animal Rescue Shelter. Jamie hadn't brought up Marissa and the intruder who'd threatened her again. She'd tried, with limited success, to put it out of her mind. Cooper and Laura were taking care of Marissa, and Harley had shut down on her. The best thing to do was move forward.

As they were about to head out to the car, Jamie received a call from the high school staff. One of their senior Language Arts teachers had suffered a fall on his outdoor steps and broken his ankle. Could Jamie fill in the next day and likely for several more?

"Yes," Jamie said with enthusiasm.

When Harley realized her mother was substituting she looked pained.

"It's not for your grade. It's the senior class," Jamie said, a bit exasperated.

"You'll be teaching the seniors?" Harley moaned, as if it were her last day on earth.

"I won't embarrass you. I promise."

"You can't promise that," she said from deep in the doldrums.

"Do you want to look for a dog or not?" Jamie demanded.

"Yes!" said Emma. She had her coat on and was standing by the short hall to the back door.

"Yeah. Yeah, I do," said Harley. Shoulders hunched, she shuffled toward Emma. She'd managed to change into a pair of jeans and another sweatshirt, but that was about as far as her personal appearance went, whereas Emma had taken a shower and washed her shortened hair and was also in jeans and a favorite blue, long-sleeved tee and her dark-gray nylon jacket. She looked ready to go to work, as she did every day. In many ways, she was self-sufficient. A product of years of training by their mother, Jamie guessed.

Camryn was inside the shelter when they arrived, chatting with a young man on the other side of the counter whose name tag read "Burton." Her short blond hair was damp and she admitted she'd dashed through the shower after an earlier workout. "Glad you're getting a dog. I'm on the board here and I've vouched for you. We usually do a home check, but I know your mom's house and the fenced backyard. It's perfect for a dog."

"Mom's back there, too," said Emma.

The young man at the counter's brows lifted in a silent question, but no one filled him in as he lifted a section of counter and showed them through an inner door to the cages beyond.

They looked over all the dogs at the shelter. There were far fewer than Jamie had expected. "It waxes and wanes," another young, male worker told them.

"That one's cute," Emma said, pointing to a medium-sized, reddish, long-haired dog with a fanlike tail. As if realizing she'd singled him out, he bared his teeth and growled low in his throat.

Camryn said, "I was here when he came in. He's adjusting, but he was very neglected."

Burton added, "Probably needs some more time."

"What about that one?" Harley asked. The dog in question was black and white, with half its face black, the other white. It silently watched them, making no sound.

Camryn looked at Burton. "I don't know her. She's new."

"That's Duchess," Burton said. "Don't let her quietness fool you. She's pretty vocal sometimes. She was just dropped off by a couple who were divorcing and moving into separate apartments. She was their watchdog."

"Is she friendly?" Harley asked.

"Pretty much. She's a little more trusting. She's just getting used to things."

Harley squatted down in front of the dog, who eyed her from behind the cage. She held the back of her hand near so the dog could smell her. Duchess stepped forward cautiously, took a few sniffs, and seemed to relax a bit.

"Duchess," said Emma.

"Meant to be," said Harley.

"Do you want to fill out the paperwork and take her on a test basis, just to make sure she's the right fit?" Camryn asked.

"Yes!" declared Emma.

Burton took Duchess from her cage and the dog went to Emma as if they were long-lost friends. There was a grin on Emma's face as she rubbed Duchess's head.

It was kind of amazing to Jamie how quickly that bonding took shape. "Well, we need to go get some things. Like dog food and a dog carrier," she said, watching Emma and Duchess bond.

"I'll come with you," said Camryn.

"Oh, wait." Jamie stopped short on her way out of the shelter. "I'm working tomorrow. Duchess will be by herself. Maybe we should wait before we—"

"*Noooooo!*" Emma cried.

Camryn said quickly, "We have volunteers who will help with the transition."

Burton said, "I could do it. I don't work tomorrow."

"Okay . . ." Jamie was starting to worry she'd bitten off more than she could chew. "I realize we're going to need a dog door, too."

Hearing a "no" in her words, Emma began to breathe fast, like she did when she was about to have a fit.

"We'll figure it all out, Mom," Harley jumped in. "Please!"

Jamie held up her hands in surrender. "I want the dog, too," she told both Emma and Harley. "Let's go to the pet store and get her stuff."

An hour and a half later, they were on their way back home, with Camryn following after them in her car. Emma had calmed down and Harley's mood had elevated. Jamie could tell already that not only was Emma in love with their new pet, but Harley was as well. Though Duchess was in the carrier for the ride home, both Emma and Harley talked to the dog encouragingly the whole way. Duchess seemed to take it all in stride. At least, she wasn't whining or barking. Though they were ostensibly "testing things out," Jamie knew they'd crossed the Rubicon as far as the dog was concerned. There was no turning back for either Harley or Emma.

Jamie invited Camryn to hang out with them for the rest of the day. She said she would stick around for a while as Duchess got the feel of the house, but she had to leave by four. While she was at the house, she and Jamie discussed what had happened to Marissa the night before as best they could, given both Harley and Emma were around, though the two of them were distracted by the dog. Before she left, Camryn held her hand to her ear, thumb, and pinkie outstretched in classic phone receiver style and mouthed, *I'll call you.*

Jamie nodded and was waving at her as she pulled out of the drive when her cell phone buzzed. When she saw it was Icky Vicky, she almost didn't answer. In the end, she took the call in her sleeping room, closing the door tightly behind her so she couldn't be heard.

"Hello?" she answered.

"Jamie! I heard what happened to Marissa Haynes . . . um, Dalworth! Oh my God. At the same house *as Emma*? Is she all right? Do you know? I know she and your daughter are friends. . . . Do you know anything?"

So, it was a gossip call.

"I know Marissa and the Ryerson twins are fine." *Did she?* "Physically unhurt," she amended.

"Was it a burglar?"

"I don't really know."

"A prank?"

"A prank?" Jamie repeated.

"Bette called up Ted Ryerson. She invested some money with him and they dated briefly about a year after his wife's death. He said it could be a prank."

Teddy and Bette? Bette was older than Jamie and Teddy was at least seven years younger than she was. Not that that mattered, but they seemed like an unlikely couple.

"He told Bette about it. I guess he met with Cooper today. Do you know anything about that?"

She was fishing. "No," Jamie said truthfully.

"Oh, I'd heard you were seeing him."

"Me?" she asked. "Who told you that?"

"I think your sister told Jill. Did you know Jill's part of the charity that works with Theo's Thrift Shop? She stopped in and talked to Emma, who said you were dating. That won't make Bette happy."

Jamie groaned inwardly. "It's more like we see each other when we're picking up or dropping off our daughters."

"Okay. Well . . . not the word on the street. Laura Haynes

certainly thinks something's going on with you two, too.
You've really crushed Bette's aspirations as well, I can
tell you."

"Nothing really to tell."

"Your daughter wasn't there last night? I thought the two
of them were babysitting together."

"Where do you get your information?" Jamie asked on a
forced laugh. "No. She . . . couldn't go." Jamie wasn't about
to tell her that Laura had called off the girls' babysitting together. After the events of last night, she almost owed
Cooper's ex a thank-you. She'd thought about calling her
today and checking on Marissa, but Laura would undoubtedly disbelieve Jamie's motives were pure.

You just chickened out.

Vicky was rattling on about getting together with wine.
Jamie demurred, suspecting they would all be pumping her
for information, but Vicky was insistent. "If not Leander's,
somewhere else."

"I have family dinner tonight," Jamie said.

"Oh, pooh. Come on. Happy hour somewhere. I know.
The Waystation. Say around four? Let's slum it in the name
of letting our hair down. Bring a friend."

That last line was what turned Jamie to thinking maybe
she would. "All right. I'll see what I can do."

As soon as she hung up, she called Camryn back. She
told her about the women's date and asked her to join her. "I
know you said you were busy. Just thought I'd try," Jamie
told her.

"Oh, man. I just can't. But next time, okay? I'll break
whatever plans I have, I promise," Camryn pleaded.

"Okay."

That took the wind out of Jamie's sails, even though it
was what she'd expected. She thought hard for a moment.
Before she could debate with herself on the wisdom of her

next move, she called Gwen Winkelman and invited her to join her.

"Thank you. I'm intrigued. Yes, I'll come with you. What an unexpected treat," the psychologist agreed.

Cooper had planned on calling Ted Ryerson as soon as he was back at the station, but when he'd walked in, he'd learned that Ryerson had already beaten him to the punch: There was a message waiting for him to call the man. Cooper punched in the number and Ryerson picked up right away.

"Cooper Haynes, returning your call."

"I thought you wanted to interview me." Ryerson sounded a bit peeved.

Cooper had checked the time and seen it was about eleven. Ryerson was raring to go. "My partner, Howard Eversgard, is lead on the case, but I'd like to talk to you, too."

"I know Howie," Ryerson said. "If you want to talk now, I could get away for an hour or two. My sister's here and said she'd take care of the kids. Does it have to be the station? How about that coffee shop off Aspen Court?"

Cooper knew the place by reputation only. It was on the fringes of the city, closer to Jamie's neighborhood than the city's downtown area. "I'll meet you there," he said.

The Coffee Club was a throwback to the seventies, with rough wood siding in the interior and ferns hung in several skylights. They sold a limited variety of sandwiches, along with coffee and a surprisingly long list of teas, considering their name. Cooper, who'd skipped breakfast, ordered a turkey sandwich and a cup of coffee.

Ted Ryerson came in just as Cooper was taking a seat at a table for two toward the rear of the open room. It was about all the privacy he could hope for, given the surroundings.

Ryerson was in a white shirt, open at the throat, and slacks. He was as tall as Cooper and probably had ten to twenty pounds on him. His blondish hair was darkened from being slightly wet, and Cooper suspected he'd been working out and just gotten out of the shower. He had that kind of muscular build.

Cooper stood up and shook the man's hand. Ryerson was about ten years younger, and he had a hard grip. Cooper wondered if he was telegraphing his strength.

He hadn't taken a measure of him the night before; there'd been too much going on. But he did now. If you met him on a dark night, you might be glad to have some kind of defense.

"I've been thinking about last night full-on nonstop. Latch on the back door's been a problem for a while, but I had it fixed. That's a good, strong lock now. No one would have gotten in unless she let them."

"She didn't let anyone in," Cooper said.

"Maybe not on purpose, but by leaving the door open? Maybe by mistake? I fixed that latch," he said again.

Cooper wondered if he was worried Laura might sue should the door latch's defect come to light. Ryerson was clearly making sure Cooper knew it had been taken care of . . . maybe to cover his ass. He seemed to want Cooper to know that he wasn't responsible.

"Let's get back to the fact that someone came in, dressed in ski gear, and threatened Marissa with a knife," Cooper said.

"Yeessss . . ." He looked Cooper right in the eye. "I know that's what she says and she's very convincing, but isn't it awfully coincidental, given what happened at my house with Emma Whelan?"

"Emma Whelan was attacked and it changed her life," Cooper reminded him evenly.

"And it's a horrible, terrible crime. My sister and I have been affected by it, too. All our lives. I'm just saying that I'm not sure I believe we had a second attacker at my house. Doesn't make sense. I don't know who Emma's attacker was. Maybe you know more than I do."

"What's that mean?"

"You were there, man." He spread his hands. "You and your friends. Hell, it's part of River Glen lore now."

"But none of us attacked her." Cooper could feel himself growing hot under the collar.

"That was the department's conclusion. I know. I've spent a lot of time on this, Detective Haynes. Was it the truth? Is it the truth? Maybe. But what if it isn't? What if one of you guys came back and stabbed Emma Whelan? What if—"

"Everyone liked Emma. We all did. No one would hurt her," Cooper interrupted.

"—Marissa invited some boys to come over and one of them thought it would be a great joke to come after her with a knife?"

"No."

Ryerson just looked at him. Cooper knew he was being irrational. Ryerson wasn't saying anything that hadn't swirled through Cooper's own subconscious. He just didn't want to believe it.

And that was death for an impartial investigation.

"You're saying you don't believe it happened like Marissa said." Cooper was terse.

"Isn't that more reasonable than to think the same thing that happened at my house twenty years ago happened again?"

"Marissa was terrified last night. So were your kids. That doesn't sound like a prank to me."

"Well, as Detective Eversgard is the lead, I'll talk to him," Ryerson said.

Cooper finished his cup of coffee, watching Ryerson walk out the door. The man met someone on the sidewalk, an older woman in earrings and a scarf artfully swept over her shoulders, and leaned in to her, smiling and talking. She seemed to come alive at the attention.

Ted Ryerson was in investments. Watching this interchange, Cooper sure hoped he was on the up and up and wasn't some kind of scam artist. There was something a little slick about him.

Or is that just you being annoyed because he pointed out an important piece you refused to investigate? Your friends.

"Not refused," he said aloud. He just hadn't gotten to it yet. Either for Marissa or Emma, who'd already waited twenty years.

Mike Corliss believed Emma's attack had been perpetrated by one of her classmates. Ted Ryerson believed the same held true for Marissa.

He sighed, dropped some money on the table, and headed out. He had to let Howie interview Marissa. Maybe he would learn something Cooper wasn't going to like. For now, he would believe his stepdaughter. If there was any truth to what Ted Ryerson believed, it didn't seem like Marissa was aware that the attack had been staged by her schoolmates. She'd been truly frightened last night.

In the meantime, he was going to delve into the report on Emma's attack, the interviews he and his friends had given twenty years earlier. If the department hadn't gotten it on computer yet, it was still in paper form.

He planned to spend the rest of Sunday, and however much longer it took, to scour those old reports.

Jamie beat Gwen to the Waystation, but not by much. Her old friend blew in the door in a rush of cold air from a wind that had suddenly cropped up, shaking the leaves from the trees and blowing them into neighborhood yards and pressing them against buildings.

Vicky and Jill were already seated, and it turned out Alicia was in the bathroom when Jamie arrived. She'd just greeted the other women when Gwen appeared, having to pull the door shut behind her.

"How wonderfully lowbrow," Gwen said with appreciation, looking around as she came to the table.

"Isn't it, though? You have to order at the bar here," said Vicky. She smiled at Gwen, albeit with forced warmth. Jamie wondered if, in spite of what Vicky had said about inviting a friend, she'd overstepped her bounds with these women.

Jamie went with Gwen to the bar. The three other women had ordered wine, so Jamie did the same, but Gwen asked for herbal tea. The look she got from the man with the beard made them both chuckle. "I've got coffee," he said. "Maybe instant decaf."

"How about a sparkling water?" Gwen asked.

He poured Jamie's wine and handed Gwen a can of soda water and an empty glass.

Alicia had returned from the bathroom as they regrouped around the table. She looked a little taken aback by Gwen, whose hair was once again pulled back by a scarf and who wore a sacklike dress in blue cotton and flip-flops, even though the temperature was in the low fifties outside. She had, Jamie realized, taken up the same style as her mother, who'd worn colorful Hawaiian muumuus almost exclusively when Gwen had been growing up. Jamie made introductions, even though the women mostly knew one another.

Vicky immediately quizzed Gwen on her work with the police. Jamie gave Gwen a worried look. She hadn't meant to subject her friend to a full-on third degree. Gwen, however, could handle herself.

After a few minutes of this, when it became clear Gwen

wasn't going to cough up anything, Jill turned her attention to Jamie. "So, tell us about last night's attack."

Gwen looked at Jamie with questions in her eyes, and Jamie realized she hadn't heard about it yet. Jamie gave the women a perfunctory rundown of how Marissa had been accosted and frightened, to the gasps and cries of everyone. When she was finished, Gwen asked urgently, "How's Marissa doing? Fear can really injure a person's psyche."

"Okay, I think. I mostly know what Harley's told me. She's been in contact with Marissa, but she doesn't want to talk about it with me."

"God no," said Alicia. "Parents just can't be trusted."

"No kidding," said Vicky.

Jamie said, "I imagine Cooper, being Marissa's step-father, is making sure she's okay."

A discussion about who had terrorized Marissa ensued. Jamie was uncomfortable throughout, as the women kept turning to her, as if she were holding back on them.

"You don't think . . . she could have made it all up?" Vicky asked. "For attention, maybe? Kids do crazy stuff."

"What makes you say that?" Gwen asked, unintentionally putting Vicky on the defensive.

"Well, Tyler said that she let it be known where they were babysitting together, Marissa and Jamie's daughter. I know Harley wasn't there," Vicky said quickly to Jamie, "but that's what they'd said to the boys. Tyler thought the girls were kind of hoping the guys would show up."

"Well, did they?" asked Jill, looking from Vicky to Alicia.

"Not Tyler," Vicky said quickly. "He was home. I don't know about the others, but Tyler wasn't there."

Alicia shook her head. "Troy isn't interested in the younger girls. He thinks they're all drama queens. Maybe some of the other guys . . ."

"Not Tyler," Vicky said again.

Their rapid-fire defenses didn't ring true. Jamie was starting to realize that maybe the boys had been at the Ryersons'.

"Why wasn't Harley with Marissa?" Jill asked.

"Laura, Marissa's mother, didn't think it was a good idea," Jamie told her. She had the sinking feeling that Harley had held things back from her.

Gwen asked, "Does anyone know if the boys were actually there?"

"From what Cooper said, Marissa was honestly scared," said Jamie.

"You and Cooper check in with each other?" asked Vicky.

"I talk to Cooper and to Laura. Our daughters are friends," Jamie reminded her. "I don't know much more about what happened, though."

"Yet," said Jill.

"You'll tell us if you learn anything?" Alicia sounded somewhat strained. She was addressing Jamie.

"Well, sure, but won't it be on the news?"

"I would think so," said Gwen, which made all three women look at her as if she'd just uttered a dire warning.

"Hopefully, your little darlings aren't all lying to you. . . ." Jill looked down her nose at Vicky, Alicia, and Jamie in turn, but this time it seemed more like a warning.

"Let's not talk about it anymore." Alicia picked up her glass of wine, tasted it, made a face, set her glass back down, and asked, "Where's Bette?"

Jamie had tasted her own wine and knew how she felt.

"Out . . . with a guy, probably," Vicky answered. "She said she can't stand sitting around and looking at Kearns's dull face."

"They'd better get divorced and fast, before they try to kill each other," said Jill.

"Oh, it's not that bad," Alicia scoffed.

"Nearly," Jill snorted.

"What do you think, Gwen?" Vicky asked curiously. "Our friend Bette's still married, and living with her husband—Phil Kearns, from high school; maybe you remember him?—but she's been going out like three nights a week and sometimes comes home in the wee morning hours. I've told her to be careful. Kearns might finally get off his ass and do something crazy. He doesn't seem the type, but Bette's pretty darn *open* about the whole thing. That seems like a bad idea, doesn't it?"

Gwen thought for a moment. When it was clear she wasn't getting off the spot, she said, "You never really can know what someone else is going through. Some people live out loud, like maybe your friend, Bette? I don't know her, so I can't say. Other people keep everything bottled up inside, which, in my experience, is far more dangerous."

"You try to draw them out, right?" Jill asked. "In therapy?"

"Examining a problem—talking it over—is almost universally better for a person's psyche."

Gwen had grown more serious as the discussion went on, and a bit drawn in, Jamie felt.

"But when you touch on people's deepest fears, you need to be careful," Gwen added.

"Like . . . you think they'll flip out?" asked Vicky.

Alicia saved Gwen from having to answer. "Yeah, they'll flip out. If I do anything that makes Deon feel like I've dissed him somehow, he gets mean."

"That's not fear, that's being an asshole," said Vicky.

The rest of the evening, the talk centered around Tyler and Troy and Alex, Vicky, Alicia, and Bette's senior boys. After a while, Jamie glanced at the clock and made excuses, and she and Gwen walked out together, leaving the other three women at the table.

"Sorry they grilled you," Jamie said. "It's kind of what they do."

"How did you hook up with them?"

"I ran into Vicky at the school and she invited me to their wine klatch and it went on from there. I'm Emma's sister. I think that had something to do with it."

Gwen inclined her head in tacit agreement.

"Did you . . . you asked if the boys were there. Do you think . . . they could have something to do with it?"

"I haven't talked to Marissa myself, so I don't have any way of gauging what happened," Gwen responded.

She realized her friend wasn't about to conjecture about last night's attack, and she didn't want to either. But Gwen had raised the question, which had caused immediate pushback from Vicky and Alicia.

"I'm just glad Marissa's all right," Jamie said, and Gwen seconded that.

As they parted to head to their respective vehicles, Gwen hesitated and added soberly, "Stay safe, Jamie."

"Thanks. You too," Jamie said, wondering if there was more than just a well-wish in her words.

Fifteen minutes later, as Jamie opened the back door, growling and barking greeted her. She stopped short. She'd already forgotten about the new addition to the family. Duchess came racing around the corner, but from the kitchen, Emma yelled in her flat voice, "Duchess. Stop."

The dog cocked an ear and slowed down. Upon seeing the newcomer was Jamie, she came up and sniffed her hand and seemed to relax. She then allowed Jamie to rub her head and scratch her ears before bounding back toward Emma. Jamie followed and found Emma and Harley standing side by side at the counter, putting together sandwiches from some of the deli meat Jamie had purchased at the store. Harley was quiet and Emma was looking at her, apparently trying to figure out what was wrong. Duchess wedged herself between them, her nose up as she gazed at one and then the other, as if trying to figure out which one would be most likely to give her some of the wonderful-smelling meat.

"You got a sandwich for me?" Jamie asked.

"You didn't eat?" Emma asked her, frowning.

"I just had a glass of wine."

"Just one?" Harley asked somewhat accusingly, looking up.

"Yes, just one." Jamie looked at her daughter hard. "What's that about?"

"Nothing," she muttered, casting her eyes downward again.

Something going on there. Maybe she was taking her fear for Marissa out on her mother.

Jamie let it go for the moment. Emma was in the process of putting together a sandwich for her. She lined the bread up carefully. If she'd had a ruler, she would have placed the tops of the slices against it. She tucked the knife into a jar and worked to get just the right amount of mayonnaise on the blade.

By the time Jamie got her carefully constructed sandwich, a good five minutes had passed in what should have taken one. Theo had warned her of Emma's need for control. "She doesn't always become so exacting, just sometimes. She needs to be able to handle things her own way," Theo had told her.

Emma said, "I'm going to feed Duchess and take her outside." She hardly even had to look at the dog for it to follow after her.

Jamie suddenly realized she wouldn't be home tomorrow for the dishwasher repairman, and she called and left a message that she needed to change the date unless he could come after four p.m. She didn't expect to hear back today, but at least she'd alerted him.

Harley put her plate in the sink with less noise and drama than earlier. She turned to leave the room as Jamie was ending her phone message. "Hey, I wanted to talk to you about something," Jamie called to her.

Harley stopped and looked back at Jamie with a careful expression. "What?"

"You know I went to see Mom's lawyer about her estate . . ."

"Yeah, you told me. That's how I got my phone."

"I got a note from Mom along with the papers from the lawyer." Jamie was starting to hesitate. All week she'd been deciding how and when to talk to Harley about a number of things, like her crush on Greer Douglas, but hadn't figured out how or when. But before much more time went by, she wanted to inform her about the note.

"I also ran into my friend Gwen. She has an office in the same building."

"What did the note say?"

"I'll show it to you, but it basically said I needed to come home and take care of Emma."

"Come home?" Harley whispered.

"And I told Gwen about it . . . about everything . . . and that's what I wanted to say. Gwen said it happens sometimes. A person can get a message through to their loved ones telepathically."

"I don't believe that!" Her eyes were wide, her body tense. "Do you believe that?"

"I'm just telling you what she said. In fact, what she really said was that I wasn't her 'first unicorn.' I guess what I'm trying to say is, it's not that far out of normal."

Harley's gaze dropped to the floor. "I think it's effin' creepy. And so do you."

With that, she left Jamie standing in the kitchen, staring

out the window to the backyard and the brittle, leggy stems
of the Mr. Lincoln roses.

*The teenager had to be put in her place. That's how it
starts . . . when they're young. Did I want to kill her . . . ? I
thought so. I took the knife to the house with that intent. But
it all got away from me. She ran to the children.*

*Next time . . . if there's a next time . . . I hope there isn't a
next time . . .*

But if there is, I won't fail again.

Chapter Eighteen

Monday morning, Jamie arrived early at the school, where she was handed the day's assignments for the students of her Language Arts class, and then one of the senior students who helped out in the office showed her around the school and to her classroom.

Jamie felt a few butterflies. Always the case on the first day at a new school. She stood beside the teacher's desk and smiled at the students as they filtered in. One of the boys slid a look at the others, but then stopped and said to her, "You're Harley's mom?"

"Yes, I am. And you are?"

"Greer," he said.

Jamie tried not to react. She surreptitiously checked him out as he headed toward a group of boys at the back of the room. He was nice-looking and had a confident way about him that she suspected had been the draw for Harley.

Once they were all in their seats, Jamie told them about their teacher's unfortunate accident and that she'd said that today's class would be used for writing their semester essays, the theme of which concerned future career choices. A collective groan rose from the back of the room where the boys had congregated. Jamie didn't have a seating chart. Maybe there wasn't one. But all the boys gathered together seemed like a no-go. Still, until it became a problem, she wasn't going to make waves.

Class went pretty well for the first twenty minutes, then the whispering started.

It wasn't, as Jamie had suspected, the boys. Mostly it was a group of girls who were trying to get the boys' attention. Jamie slid a look at the main girl, who gave her a sheepish shrug of her shoulders and a big smile when she caught Jamie watching her, before turning her attention back to her paper.

Jamie pretended she hadn't heard, but she knew what the girl had said. It was a comment to the tallest boy in the class, who she'd heard Greer call Tyler. Was this, then, Tyler Stapleton, Icky Vicky's son? She glanced down her class roster and found his name.

"You were there, too," the girl had accused, to which he'd shaken his head.

"Try Troy and Greer," Tyler whispered loudly back at her.

Jamie thought she heard another female voice say, "Fuck those sophomore girls," but wasn't sure.

As if they recognized she was about to step in, they all put their eyes on their papers and started writing. She cruised around the room a few minutes later and learned that most of them were actually working. The girl with the smile was writing about her plans to go to the University of Washington. Jamie noted that was also the college of choice for Tyler. She'd seen Dara Volker's name on the list and thought maybe she was the one who'd spoken. Greer had plans to take a gap year off and snowboard around the country. Whether that was feasible or not was not for her to judge. His father was Dug Douglas, who'd been Race Stillwell's sidekick in high school and now was a successful businessman with a collection of independent insurance agencies. Was this, then, the boy Harley was interested in? She wasn't sure how she felt about her daughter hanging out with a senior.

The rest of the day was fairly uneventful until her last period, where she ran into Troy Stillwell, Deon Stillwell and Vicky's friend, Alicia's, son. Troy was good-looking and he knew it. There was something off-putting about his attitude toward the girls who were embarrassingly interested in catching his eye. She'd seen it before. The cool guy who knew he was cool, who enjoyed the adoration of the girls, but regarded them as pawns in his life.

But she didn't know him. It was too early to make such a damning assessment.

Just because you don't like his father doesn't mean the son shares the same bad behavior.

Yet Troy looked enough like Deon to bring back that dreadful night when he'd grabbed her crotch and Emma had been attacked. And his behavior around his classmates did not bode well for indicating what kind of person he was.

You were there, too, the girl in her first-period class had said to Tyler Stapleton, and he'd responded, *Try Troy and Greer.* . . .

Where had the boys been and when?

Her mind went to whomever had scared Marissa. Could that be what the girl had been referring to? Were the boys involved? Had they taken a joke too far and now wanted to act like it hadn't happened? Already Vicky was putting space between that event and her son. Maybe it wasn't what it was all about . . . but maybe it was.

After school, Jamie gathered up her belongings. She hadn't heard yet whether she would be on for another day, but she thought she might be. It was good to be working, bringing in some income.

She was outside, walking by the gym, intending to meet up with Harley at her car, when one of the gym's double doors were flung open and a boy stomped out with Robbie Padilla on his heels. "Where are you going?" Robbie demanded.

"Home," the boy snarled. Troy Stillwell.

"I told you, your father's coming here," Robbie reminded him.

"I don't give a shit." Troy locked eyes with Jamie. "What are you looking at?"

Jamie had dealt with teen aggression before, but she felt ill-equipped this time, being that Troy was Deon Stillwell and Alicia's son.

She looked past him to Robbie, whose anger had reddened his face. Troy swept past Jamie and crossed the parking lot, breaking into a half-run.

"What happened?" Jamie asked, knowing full well Robbie had no reason to talk to her about anything if he didn't want to.

Robbie angrily shook his head, then said, "Jamie," as if belatedly realizing who'd spoken up. "That was . . ." He stopped himself, flapped a hand, and muttered, "I just get tired of all the knuckleheaded behavior," before retreating back inside and closing the door behind him.

When Harley showed up with Marissa, both of them were inordinately quiet. Jamie dove right in. "Okay, which boys came to the Ryersons' on Saturday night?"

Immediately, both girls looked taken aback, then outraged. "What are you talking about?" Harley demanded.

"You don't think I was attacked?" Marissa cried at the same moment.

"I'm guessing Troy and Greer."

Harley's mouth dropped open and her eyes widened. Marissa sputtered a couple of times, then she snapped her jaw shut. The corners of her mouth dipped downward and tears filled her eyes.

Jamie sighed. "Oh, Marissa. We only want to help. No one's going to blame you."

"Oh yes they are!" Marissa was sure about that as she started to sob. "He came after me! It wasn't the boys. It was *him*. He wanted to hurt me!" she wailed.

Out of the corner of her eye, Jamie saw Laura Haynes marching her way. Oh, no. This was all she needed. Another chance to dig a deeper grave with Cooper's ex.

"I believe you," Jamie assured her. "I'm glad you're okay. The boys were there, though. They're not keeping it a secret. The senior class is wise to it. And Mr. Padilla knows, too." Jamie was extrapolating, but she figured she was close enough to the truth.

It was at that moment that a silver Dodge Charger sped into the lot, stopping with a screech of brakes. Deon Stillwell stepped from the car. Heavier, but she could tell it was him by the shape of his head. She hadn't realized she'd committed that aspect of him to memory after he'd sexually assaulted her. Her stomach clenched.

"Mom . . ." Harley murmured, pained.

"Don't say anything to my mom," Marissa begged Jamie, eyes huge.

"You need to tell her," Jamie said, dropping her voice as Laura neared.

"I'll tell my dad about the guys. I'm not talking to her."

Deon Stillwell glanced Jamie's way. Did a classic double take. Though he was across the lot near the gym door, she could see him stop short and hear him ask in surprise, "Emma?"

At that moment, Laura reached them, capturing Jamie's attention as she sent a scathing look across Harley and Marissa that landed fully on Jamie. "What are you keeping from me?" she demanded.

Jamie resented always being on her heels around this woman. She shot a look Deon's way, but his back was to her now as he charged up the steps to the gym door, yanked it open, and stepped inside. "Talk to your daughter," she said shortly to Laura, then touched Harley's arm and added, "Time to go."

"You and Cooper and everyone else seem to think I don't deserve to know what's going on with my own child," Laura leveled at her.

"Everyone deserves to know about their own children." Jamie wanted to grab Harley, who seemed rooted to the spot, and bodily shove her into the Camry, but she didn't touch her.

"What did you tell her?" she demanded of Marissa.

"I don't know! Leave me alone!" She turned as if to run off, but Laura snagged her arm. "Marissa," she said in a warning tone.

"I'm talking to Dad. Not you. Not anyone else!" She jerked her arm free and trudged away, head down.

"Mom . . ." Harley said again. She was now by the passenger door and looking across the top of the car at her mother.

"Get in," Jamie said, tense. She yanked open her own door, slid inside, and jerked the door closed. Harley fumbled with her door, then put her backpack in the footwell, and tried to get her legs over it as she climbed awkwardly inside.

"Jesus Christ," Jamie muttered, beyond exasperated as Harley finally closed the door after her.

"Why are you so mad?" Harley said on a sniff.

"Why didn't you tell me about the boys? Oh my God, Harley. This is . . . with what happened to Emma . . . *at the Ryersons'*!"

"That's why we couldn't say anything! Marissa was attacked. That's no joke! The boys were just . . . they just came by earlier."

"You knew this and you didn't tell me. Even after someone . . . came in . . . and your friend was terrorized."

"Okay. I'm awful! What do you want me to say?" Harley demanded in a high voice.

"The truth! All of the truth! And if Marissa doesn't tell Cooper, I will."

"Great. Good for you." Harley subsided into wounded silence.

Jamie clamped down on her own fury. She wanted to argue and scream and badger and keep on pointing out all the flaws in Harley's teenage logic, but it wouldn't prove anything useful.

They drove in silence the rest of the way home. At the house, Harley leaped from the car and tried to yank her backpack free, and it was all she could do to get the book-filled bag free from the footwell.

"Don't say anything," Harley snapped as Jamie got out of the car. She ran up the back steps and fumbled with her key. She glanced back at Jamie, as if expecting her to say something. In fact, Jamie had a lot to say that she was forcibly keeping to herself.

"And *you* don't swear," Harley added, before pushing open the door and disappearing into the house.

Cooper sat at his desk, the twenty-year-old binder with the notes on Emma's attack open in front of him. He'd gone through the pages on his classmates and found a few discrepancies from his own memory. These he planned to follow up on with each particular classmate to see how they recalled the events of that night today. One in particular was Dug saying he and Race had gone home together, and Race saying he'd gone home alone. Later, Dug had said the investigator had gotten it wrong, that he and Race had arrived at the Ryerson house together, but he'd been dropped off on the way home, to which Race concurred. Race had also dropped off Mark Norquist, which was how Cooper, who'd been in his own car with Tim and Robbie, remembered it.

The book also held the notes on the interviews Detective Corliss had had with Dr. William and Nadine Ryerson, Ted and Serena's parents, and with Dr. Alain Metcalf, who'd dropped Nadine home that night because she and her husband had had a big blow up at the River Glen General Hospital "Glen Gen" Donors Night party. After the fight, Nadine had left with Dr. Metcalf. Several hours had passed before she had him bring her home, which Mrs. Ryerson had not wanted to talk about, apart from saying she'd fallen asleep on the good Dr. Metcalf's couch. Nadine had asked Metcalf to drop her off; she hadn't wanted him to come in, in case her husband had beaten her home. As it turned out, Dr. Ryerson was not there. Nadine was the one who'd discovered Emma on the floor, bleeding, and had called 911. Dr. Ryerson had appeared on the scene about the same time as the ambulance, still somewhat inebriated, apparently one of the sources of the earlier fight between his wife and him.

There were additional notes added later. One being that although the Ryersons had initially projected a united front, within the year of the attack on Emma Whelan, they were divorced. Dr. Ryerson left the area soon afterward for Palm Desert, California, with a woman named Kayla, another source of the fight at the charity event. Ryerson had subsequently made Kayla his second wife.

The final note was that, after staying in River Glen until her children, Ted and Serena Ryerson, were through high school, Nadine Ryerson moved to Lake Tahoe with her fiancé, Dr. Jay Campbell, an anesthesiologist. After that, there were no further additions to the case binder.

Cooper looked up Nadine's information and learned she and Campbell were now married and had moved from

Lake Tahoe to Bellevue, Washington. Ryerson and Kayla were now residing in Bend, Oregon. Both of them were within driving distance, so it would be easy to have face-to-face interviews at some point.

Cooper eventually came up for air. He didn't really have a workload as Verbena was writing up a domestic violence, he said/she said case and Howie was deep into Marissa's attacker. He was being cagey and uninformative with Cooper about what Marissa had told him in yesterday's interview because she was his stepdaughter. Howie had called her on the phone. Not really the ideal way to depose her, but about the only way Laura would allow him to do it. He'd griped a bit about Cooper's ex to him this morning, but not much. He wanted to keep the investigation into Cooper's stepdaughter carefully neutral, although he had admitted he'd mostly gotten the same description of the attacker from Marissa that Crake, O'Hara, and Cooper had: big man in bulky, black or gray ski gear, a knitted ski cap over the face with eye holes. Blue eyes, she thought . . . or maybe brown. Cooper had tried to ask further questions of Howie, but his partner had lifted his hands and said that was all he knew.

But what it really meant was that was all he would talk about.

As if divining that one of his investigators wasn't busy, Chief Bennihof stuck his head out of his office. "Patrol's on its way to Theo's Thrift Shop. A homeless man came in, waving a weapon, and scaring the women working there. He's gone now. You want to take it? I think you said you know them."

Cooper was already snatching up his coat, his pulse speeding up. "Yeah. I'm on my way."

"Okay, I'll call them off."

Cooper wondered if Emma was at work, and then learned as soon as he got there that yes, she was, and it was she who'd become the most upset by the homeless man. Theo was attempting to calm Emma down as Cooper entered the store. Emma was seated behind the counter, staring off trancelike.

"She's been this way since he left," Theo said. She gave Cooper the eye and inclined her head toward the door. Cooper understood that she wanted to talk to him alone.

"Where did he go?" Cooper asked.

"He should go to hell, where he came from," Emma suddenly blurted out, causing Theo to jump. "That's what Mom says."

"Are you okay?" Theo asked her.

She nodded slowly. "I'm okay."

Theo turned back to Cooper. "He turned right. He might be heading for the bus stop." She had a hand resting lightly on Emma's shoulder. "He's been here before . . . um . . . he's okay."

"He's not okay!" Emma argued back.

"What kind of weapon was he carrying?" Cooper asked.

"A knife." Emma suddenly covered her eyes with her hands.

"A table knife," Theo added. She looked at Cooper beseechingly. Clearly, there was more going on here that Theo wanted him to know, but not in front of Emma.

"I should go and see if I can find him," he said slowly, his eyes on Theo.

She nodded. "He's probably okay now," she said.

"He smells bad," Emma stated flatly.

"How often does he show up here?" asked Cooper.

"Too often!" declared Emma.

"It was kind of whenever Deke was in the area, but more so recently," Theo said. Her gaze was on Emma.

"Since Mom died," Emma stated flatly.

Theo's brows lifted. "I guess that's true."

"His name's Deke?" Cooper asked.

"I don't know his last name. He thinks of himself as Emma's . . . friend."

"He's *not* a friend!" Emma dropped her hands and glared at the room at large.

"I just said that's what he thinks, hon," said Theo.

"I'll take care of it," said Cooper. He pulled out a business card and handed it to her.

He left them a few moments later, and he was barely thirty feet away when Theo came rushing out of the Thrift Shop's front door and called to him. Cooper reversed his steps until he was near enough that she could speak softly.

"Deke isn't really threatening, usually. He's just very interested in Emma, but it's more like protection, if you know what I mean? He wants to be near her, but he stands too close. Emma can't see it for what it is. She gets nervous and sometimes calls 9-1-1 before I can intervene."

"Got it."

"But this time was a little different. She yelled at him, which she never does. She usually ignores him. But this time she said, 'My sister's here and I have a dog.' I think she was calling him off, maybe? Telling him to leave her alone."

"Okay."

"He went that way." She pointed. "Thank you," she added, and then, "And well, yes, he does have body odor."

Cooper drove his Explorer past the bus stop and saw a man in rumpled, stained clothing seated on the bench. No one else would get near him. The others stood in a group about ten feet away. Cooper parked in the Park and Ride lot and sauntered over just as the bus appeared. Cooper saw it was on a route that went into River Glen proper and beyond. Everyone boarded but the guy on the bench. As Cooper grew closer, he could smell the ripe scent coming off the man. He stopped a few feet away. The man looked over at him. He had piercing blue eyes in a dirty face. Even from where he stood, Cooper could also smell the alcohol fumes. The man was dead drunk.

"What choo want?" he asked Cooper.

"Is your name Deke?"

"Sure is." He smirked. "Deke's my name. Drinkin's my game."

"Deke, you were just at Theo's Thrift Shop and you scared a woman there."

"Who? Emma? No. No, no, no. Emma knows me."

"You had a knife with you?"

He reached in his pocket and Cooper tensed, but sure enough, he pulled out a table knife. "It's mine," he said, sounding like he was warning Cooper should he attempt to take it away.

"Deke, it scared Emma."

"Nope." He wouldn't accept that. "I just have to protect her. That's my job. That's my duty."

"Well, maybe you should leave the knife at home next time."

"Gotta protect myself, too."

"Where do you live, Deke?"

"Here and there."

"River Glen?"

He squinted up at Cooper.

"I saw the bus was heading that way," Cooper explained.

"Used to live there. Used to work there. Now I don't do neither."

"How do you know Emma? From the Thrift Shop?"

He shook his head.

Cooper gauged Deke's age to be somewhere in his fifties. "How'd you meet her?"

He waggled a finger at Cooper. "If I told ya, I'd have to

kill ya." He cackled again, then broke into a coughing fit that doubled him over.

"You okay?" Cooper asked.

Deke nodded, and once he'd got himself under control, pointed his finger at Cooper. "Real sorry about what happened to her. I look out fer her now. Someone has to. She knows that."

"I'm not sure she does. Like I said, you scared her." When Deke just shook his head, he asked, "So, you know about what happened to her? Twenty years ago?"

"She got hurt."

"Yes, someone hurt her. Back a long time ago."

"He never got over her," he said.

"Who never got over her?" Cooper asked quickly.

Deke looked up at him blearily. "You got any spare change?"

Cooper shook his head. It was a likely scenario that Deke would be drinking any money that came his way. "Who never got over her?" he repeated.

"I dunno, mister." Deke looked around a bit nervously.

"Who did you mean?" Cooper pressed. "Someone from her past? You know, we've always wanted to find out what really happened to her."

Deke just stared down at his worn shoes.

"When was it that he never got over her?" Cooper asked. Deke was shutting down, and though he didn't expect miracles, any new information about Emma was worth getting. "Now . . . ?" When Deke didn't answer he asked, "Or are you talking about when Emma was babysitting and was attacked?" It was a long shot, but like Theo had said, he was very protective of Emma. Sure, it could be because he knew her from the Thrift Shop, but if it was something else, Cooper wanted to know about it.

"My bus left." Deke looked longingly down the street, where the bus had disappeared around a corner.

"Do you need a ride somewhere?"

Deke squinted and asked again, "What choo want, mister?"

"I'm looking out for Emma, too."

"You don't know her," he said scathingly.

"I do. We went to school together. We were classmates."

Deke licked his dry lips. "I'm goin' to the Logger Room. Jes down the street. You could gimme a ride there."

"Where do you live? I'll drop you there."

Deke snorted. "You jes leave me be, mister."

At that point, Deke got up and started shuffling away. Cooper tried to get him to get in his car, but he'd decided he'd had enough and flapped his hand at him and went on. The Logger Room was probably a mile away, across the line into Portland. Cooper didn't see how the management was likely to let him in, given his smell and dishevelment.

"What's your full name?" Cooper called after him.

Deke didn't answer. Just kept walking.

"If you know something about Emma, something that would help her, I'd like to know it, too," Cooper called after him.

Deke didn't respond, and Cooper was torn between following him on foot and climbing into the SUV and picking him up.

His cell buzzed at that moment and he saw it was Jamie. He answered, "Hey, can I call you back? I'm in the middle of something."

"Yes. But I think some of the senior boys might have been scaring Marissa on Saturday night."

Cooper's attention snapped to the phone. "What?" he demanded. Jamie repeated what she'd said as his mind whirred to catch up. "You think one of them scared her into the bedroom?"

"I just think they were there. I substituted today and overheard some things, and then I talked to the girls."

"Is Marissa with you?"

"She's with her mom now. Harley's with me."

"Does Laura know this?"

"Yes. Marissa said she wanted to talk to you, not anyone else. We were all at the school at the same time."

He could just imagine that confab. "I'll come by to see you later," he clipped out. "I'm going to follow up."

"Okay."

Cooper clicked off and climbed back into his Explorer. Deke was working his way down the street toward the bar. He wanted to follow up with the guy. Maybe he knew something. Maybe he didn't. Either way, now was not the time. He was angry, and not sure at whom. The senior boys, for certain, but even more so at himself. He'd been with friends trying to spook Emma and tragedy had struck. Now history had repeated itself. He was lucky . . . they were all lucky . . . that Marissa was okay.

Cooper threw a last glance at Deke in time to see him suddenly topple over and collapse in a heap halfway into the road. "Shit," he muttered, then punched the accelerator in order to get to him before he was hit by a passing car.

Chapter Nineteen

It took Cooper an extra hour before he could get home after calling for an ambulance to take Deke, who was unconscious, to Glen Gen Emergency and extricate himself from the event. One look at Deke and the ER staff hurried him to a partitioned room and started an IV. "He's been here multiple times," a male doctor in his forties with a hangdog face told Cooper.

"You know his full name?"

"Deke Girard. He sobers up and then falls off the wagon, but it's less sobering up lately."

Cooper said, "He passed out while walking."

The doctor, Dr. Wertz according to his name tag, admitted, "He doesn't look good."

"Meaning?"

"Meaning he doesn't look good," he repeated. "He's on a downward trajectory."

"Does he have any family?"

"He has a girlfriend. I don't know her name. It's in his file and she'll be called if she hasn't been already."

"I'd like to talk to him some more."

"As soon as he's stabilized and awake."

Cooper nodded. The doctor's abrupt manner may have been his normal way, but the ER was busy this afternoon.

An early Halloween party had apparently resulted in a collapse of a Halloween display that had landed on several children, causing contusions and minor burns from the look of it, and one adult with broken fingers. The cacophony in the waiting room was from angry parents who all apparently wanted to blame the guy with the broken fingers. He looked a little dazed and smelled of beer. The angry parents seemed alcohol-fueled as well.

"Can I get someone to call me when that happens?" Cooper asked, pulling out a card.

"Do you mind giving it to Darla?" He jerked his head to indicate a woman at the intake desk.

Cooper went over to her. He waited in line rather than interrupt the tearful mom who was telling her about the burn on her daughter's arm from the candle wax inside the huge, "enormous" pumpkin, whose weight, apparently, was the source of the crashed display. The daughter, who looked to be about eight, sat by, her eyes large. Her right arm was covered by a cold pack that she was holding in place. As Cooper waited, the daughter lifted the pack and examined the red spot. Painful, he believed, but it looked superficial, luckily. He was no doctor, but he'd seen a really bad burn or two.

When it was his turn, he showed his badge and gave Darla the same request he'd given Dr. Wertz. Darla assured him that she would let him know, then gave him the extra information of the girlfriend's name: Hillary Campion.

Cooper then headed back to Laura's for a talk with Marissa. When he got there, Laura made it clear that he was unwelcome. When Cooper pushed that he wanted to talk to Marissa about the boys, Laura's lips drew into a tight, white line.

"I'm tired of you hijacking *my* daughter. I'm tired of this game. You're not her father. You're not my husband any longer. Just get out of our lives. Get out of *my* life!"

"I want to find out who attacked her. I would think you would, too."

"Talk to your partner! It's not even your case!"

And then she slammed the door in his face.

So much for their earlier detente. Cooper had to work hard to keep his anger in check. Sure, Marissa wasn't his, at least in the biological sense, but in every other way she was. They recognized themselves as father and daughter, and that relationship couldn't be denied just because Laura wanted it that way.

Hell.

He started back toward his house, then turned around and drove straight to Jamie's. The binder of notes on Emma's attack was in the car with him. It wasn't his to take home, but he'd done it anyway rather than take the time to copy everything.

He just wanted to talk to someone about it all. In person. Not on the phone.

He'd told Jamie he would stop by, which was great. She was just the person he wanted to talk to.

Jamie had left Harley alone to stew in her bedroom with Duchess as she headed to the store to buy some groceries. She had a note from Burton, whom she'd reluctantly told where to find the outdoor key, that said Duchess had been taken outside once during the day and that she seemed to be adjusting well. She texted him back, thanked him, and asked if there was anyone else this week who could help out as she would be substituting for the next few days at least. He'd texted back and offered to come on his lunch breaks for the rest of the week.

Dog door, she reminded herself.

She'd also gotten a call from the dishwasher repairman

who'd said he might be able to stop by around five today, so Jamie was hurrying to be home by that time.

She ended up buying a rotisserie chicken, a variety of greens for a salad, and some premade mashed potatoes. Her phone rang its tone for a text, and she saw that the repairman was outside her house. **Be there soon**, she texted back, and then drove as fast as she dared to bump up the driveway. A white truck was on the street with Gold Appliances stamped in black letters on the driver's door, so she threw a wave to the man sitting behind the wheel. He waved back.

She hurried up the steps and through the back, then hurried through the house to meet him at the front door. "Thanks for waiting," she told him.

His name tag read Allen, and he looked about forty, with brown hair and an easy smile. "No problem."

She showed him the recalcitrant appliance and then ran upstairs to tap on Harley's door to let her know she'd picked up dinner.

"I'm not hungry" was the muffled response.

The dog whined a bit. "You'd better let Duchess out and feed her soon," Jamie said. "The repairman's down in the kitchen."

"Tell me when he's gone."

Fifteen minutes later, Allen said, "You need a new dishwasher, ma'am. This one's . . . old. Sorry."

"Not a surprise."

"You can check them out at the store, if you like," he said, handing out a card for Gold Appliances.

"Thanks." She paid him with her credit card, the balance of which was finally at zero again, and he headed out.

She let Harley know that he'd left. Harley came down the stairs with Duchess, took her to the backyard, and filled her bowl. She waited while Duchess chowed down her food, then the two of them went back upstairs and Harley barricaded both of them in her room again. Well, fine, Jamie thought. That would only work until Emma came home. She'd planned on picking up Emma as soon as she was done with the repairman, but Theo had called and said it was another bad day with the homeless man who seemed to frighten her so, and that she would be dropping her off.

Jamie was beginning to wonder who this guy was, and if Emma should even be going to work until he was somehow stopped from coming into the shop to see her.

Cooper arrived about an hour and a half after his phone call. Seeing him coming up her walk sent Jamie's pulse racing. It drove her crazy, her reaction to seeing him. How could it be after all these years? She'd told herself she wasn't the romantic type. Even eloping with Paul she hadn't felt this way, but then, she had used him as a means of escape. Had he not died, she didn't doubt they would have divorced.

But still . . .

She pulled herself together and answered the door with a smile. "Hi."

"How's everything going?" he asked.

"I don't know how to answer that. Harley's in her room and Emma's still at work. There was an incident there with a homeless man who harasses Emma, I guess, but Theo took care of it and is bringing her home tonight."

Cooper hesitated. "When is that?"

She looked at the clock. It was already after six. "Soon."

He exhaled a deep breath. "Mind if I sit down?"

"Sure. Anywhere."

He chose a seat at the table. She could tell something was on his mind and imagined it was about Marissa. "Can I get you anything? Are you off duty?"

"Yes."

"I've got cheap wine, or . . . water?"

He smiled. "Cheap wine's fine. I have some things I want to talk about before Emma gets here."

"I've also got dinner that no one seems to be eating but me."

"I don't know that I can. Thank you."

She could tell he was distracted. "Okay. Shoot," she said as she grabbed one of the bottles of red she'd purchased, a medium-priced blend, and worked to get the foil off.

"I was at the Thrift Shop today . . ." Cooper began, and then, as she set down a glass in front of him and one for herself, taking a seat across from him, he told her about his adventures with Deke Girard, the homeless man with a fixation on Emma who was now at Glen Gen, and then he went on to the details of what he'd learned by refreshing himself with information from the binder the police had on Emma.

When he finally slowed down, Jamie recovered from the narrative to realize she hadn't touched her glass of wine and neither had Cooper. "What does it mean, about this Deke guy?" she asked at the same moment she heard Theo's van pull up on the street in front of the house.

"I don't know yet. It's a lot of information to go through. I haven't had time to really digest it all. Just wanted to talk it through."

"Good. Me too." She nodded. "But Emma's here."

"It might have to wait till later. Meantime, I'm going to talk to those high school kids about Marissa, and I'm going to check with my 'friends' from high school. I just wanted to get it all out there. For another person's ears . . . your ears . . ."

"We're in this together. Are you working on finding the man who came after Marissa?"

"Not officially. My partner, Howie Eversgard, was assigned the case."

"You and I are working on Emma's case."

"Again, not officially. But yes, we are." He smiled faintly, and she noticed that his top button was undone. Remembering unbuttoning it for him brought a warmth spreading through her.

The front door opened and Emma came inside, followed

by Theo. Emma zeroed in on Cooper. "Did you get that Deke?" she asked in her flat way.

Cooper said, "He's in the hospital, Emma. He collapsed, so an ambulance took him there."

"Glen Gen?" She stopped, frozen, staring at him, her head half-cocked in a way Jamie had learned meant Emma was thinking deeply.

Jamie almost intervened. She knew how uncomfortable Emma could make people, but she stopped herself. Cooper was a police officer, and he'd known Emma in some capacity for years.

He nodded. "I left him in Emergency. His name is Deke Girard."

Cooper had informed Jamie about the particulars, but Jamie didn't know how Emma would take it, so she kept her eyes on her sister. Theo, too, was watching Emma.

"Is he dead?" Emma asked.

"He was being attended to when I left," said Cooper.

"He smells bad."

"That's a fact," Cooper said with a nod.

Jamie hadn't realized she was holding her breath until she had to inhale hard. She half-expected Emma to go into one of her panicked states. Theo clearly was worried, too. But Emma seemed extraordinarily stable, and Jamie wondered if it had something to do with Cooper. He silently emanated strength and capability.

"You were there that night," Emma said, as she had before.

"I was. I'm sorry for what happened to you."

"Race was there," she said. "Race Stillwell."

Jamie looked at Theo, who shook her head, her brows lifting. Emma rarely if ever talked specifics about that night. She might remember that Cooper was there, but she'd never named names to Jamie's knowledge.

She wanted to let Cooper know how unusual this was, but he was focused on Emma. Maybe he knew.

"Race was there," Cooper agreed. "And Tim Merchel. Robbie Padilla. Mark Norquist."

"He's dead," she stated.

"Yes, Mark died on tour in Afghanistan. And Dug Douglas."

"Patrick Douglas."

Now it was Cooper's turn to lift his brows. "Yes, Patrick Douglas."

"No one calls him that," she said.

"No," Cooper agreed.

Emma finally dropped her gaze and turned to Jamie. "You made a chicken," she said, walking through the living room to the kitchen. "I can smell it."

"I had to put it in the refrigerator to save it, but I can heat you up some."

"I'll head out, then," Theo said.

"You're certainly invited to stay," Jamie said.

"No, no. I've got a dog. And so do you, apparently."

Duchess, who'd been softly whining from inside Harley's room, suddenly went into full-scale barking. Harley opened the door, and the dog streaked downstairs, sliding to a stop just outside the kitchen and staring at Cooper with laser eyes.

"Who's this?" Cooper asked.

"Duchess," said Jamie as she stepped to the refrigerator, where she'd put the rotisserie chicken.

Theo said, "She's a beauty."

A beauty was not what Jamie would have called the black-and-white dog. Comical, maybe. A little goofy-looking. But Theo was a dog lover from way back, and Duchess, apparently recognizing that trait in her, went to Theo, but made a wide berth of Cooper. She growled faintly at him, almost a worried sound, but then sniffed and licked Theo's hand.

"My sister thinks I need a dog," said Cooper. "I worry that I'm going to come home one day and one's going to be dropped on my doorstep, courtesy of Jeannie."

Theo said, at the door, "Then maybe you should beat her to the punch." She waved a goodbye to everyone and closed the door behind her.

Emma had called Duchess over and the dog was standing beside her, still regarding Cooper like an interloper. "I don't want to give you our dog."

Immediately, Jamie and Cooper started talking at once.

Cooper: "I would never take your dog."

Jamie: "That's not what we're saying."

"I love Duchess," Emma said and the dog, seeming to understand, finally released Cooper from her hot gaze and laid her chin on Emma's lap.

Cooper, after first demurring, agreed to stay for dinner. The three of them dug into the food and Emma warned Cooper about not giving the dog treats, telling him it wasn't good for the animal. They were just finishing up when Harley appeared in the sweats and T-shirt she slept in and a heavy-duty pair of socks.

"Can I get you a plate?" Jamie asked, rising from her seat.

Harley slid onto a barstool, pointedly choosing not to sit with them. "Sure," she said. "Thanks."

Jamie knew her daughter wanted to somehow blame her for the way everything had come down. Her appearance in the kitchen stopped all conversation. Jamie really wanted to talk to her alone, but Harley had made certain that wouldn't happen. Jamie wanted to ask her if she'd spoken to Marissa, but with Cooper in the room, she knew Harley wouldn't be forthcoming.

Emma said, "I want to watch my programs."

Jamie explained to Cooper that Emma had a number of cooking shows on DVR as she set it up, even though Emma could generally do it herself. Just as the first episode was coming on, Emma turned to Cooper and said, "Mom knew. And you will, too."

"What will I know?" he asked her.

"How to get him."

The show started and Emma tuned in. Cooper got up from his seat and joined Jamie in the kitchen. Harley, who had nearly finished her meal, picked up her plate and took it to the sink with Duchess trotting after her, still giving Cooper a wide berth.

"I've got homework," Harley muttered and headed upstairs. Duchess chose to stay with Emma.

In his earlier conversation, Cooper had told Jamie how Laura had prevented him from talking to Marissa now that they knew for certain that some of the senior boys had "pranked" her. Neither of them spoke of it now, because Emma was within earshot.

Jamie said, "We could go on the back porch again?"

Cooper's gaze lay heavily on Emma's blond head for a moment before he nodded and followed Jamie down the short hallway and outside. It was nippy, and Jamie immediately rubbed her upper arms. She was always forgetting how cold it was here after years of living in Southern California.

Cooper said determinedly, "I'm going to find whoever scared Marissa."

Jamie shivered a bit.

"You want my jacket?" he asked.

"No . . . no . . ." Half of the reason she was shivering was because of his nearness.

The breeze ruffled his hair and he ran a hand through it and looked back toward the rear door to the house. He then turned back to Jamie. A moment passed between them, one that made gooseflesh rise on her skin.

"You said the senior boys involved were Troy Stillwell and Greer Douglas?"

"I . . . that's . . . those were the two names I heard. One of the senior girls named Tyler Stapleton, but Vicky insists he wasn't there." She hesitated, then added, "Robbie Padilla was having some kind of issue that involved Troy Stillwell today. Deon showed up at the school and went straight to the gym, I assume to see Robbie about him."

"Deon and Race live together at the Stillwell house."

"That's what I heard," Jamie said.

"I'm going to talk to both of them, too. Race doesn't have any kids. Neither one of 'em ever got married. They just moved into the house after their parents died and stayed there. But Troy's there quite a bit of the time."

"I've met Alicia, Troy's mom."

Cooper nodded, waiting for her to go on.

"There's a group of women, organized by Vicky Stapleton, who meet for wine and catching up. They've invited me to join them. Jill and Alicia and Bette Kearns, Phil Kearns's wife."

Cooper gave a deep nod of understanding. Seemed about to say something more, but thought better of it. "Emma's friends," he finally said.

"Classmates," Jamie corrected. "I don't know about friends."

"How'd you get connected with them?"

"I ran into Vicky. She's invited me out a few times and the friends were there. I heard about their kids from them, then, today, I met a few."

"They were the kids who singled out Harley and Marissa for the Halloween prank."

It was Jamie's turn to nod. She almost told him that Harley had a crush on one of them, but knew that would be a bridge too far if her daughter ever found out.

"What?" Cooper asked, sensing she was holding back.

"Any chance it was one of the boys, who maybe didn't mean to go that far and it just got out of hand?"

He didn't answer for a long moment, then he said, "I need to talk to them."

She understood just how he felt. She wanted him to talk to them, too. She said, "Vicky was pretty clear that her son wasn't involved; Tyler."

"And you believe her?" His smile was faint.

"Jury's still out on that one."

They stared at each other for a moment, and he raised his hand as if he were going to touch her face, but stopped himself with a jerk, as if coming to. "I'd better go. I'll just head down the driveway to my car rather than back through the house."

With that, he practically jumped down the two steps to the yard and strode around the corner of the house and down the driveway to the street. She heard a beep when he opened his vehicle's door, then the sound of the engine turning over, then the crunch of tires over the cracked blacktop as he backed out, a hesitation when he put the vehicle in Drive, then the hum of the engine slowly disappearing into the night.

She wrapped her arms around herself and stared over the darkened backyard, then up to the sky, where the wind had blown away the clouds and the diamond-hard stars winked down at her.

Something caught her peripheral vision. A trail of glimmering light that flitted from the rear of the yard to the corner of the garage and disappeared.

Jamie looked around, eyebrows up. What was that? She stepped down the stairs cautiously and walked into the yard, looking back for the source of the light. Apart from the illumination inside the house, there was nothing. The nearest streetlamp was a hundred yards away and gave off a dull cone of light only in a specified area. As she stood there, a car drove by, the glow from its headlamps never reaching into the backyard.

She quivered. A whole body spasm sparked from fear.

She ran back up the stairs and into the house, slamming and locking the door behind her.

Cooper went home and took a cold shower. With everything going on, he could scarcely believe that Jamie Whelan had such an effect on him. Was it some kind of concoction of guilt and desire and regret that played on his senses, making him more susceptible? A memory of what could have been, playing out in front of his eyes? Or was it that he wanted her . . . Jamie . . . and his twenty-year-old crush on Emma was just an excuse?

He'd been off work for several hours, having crossed the line into overtime when he was dealing with Deke Girard and then spending the early evening at Jamie's. He'd wanted to stay. He'd wanted to stop everything for a while and make love to her. He hadn't felt that way in years. When Jamie had mentioned Vicky Stapleton and her friends, he could have told her that he'd been propositioned by nearly all of them, married or otherwise, along with Meghan Volker, who'd wanted to jump from her unhappy marriage to a relationship with him. He'd tried to let her down easy, but it hadn't worked, and to this day she gave him the cold shoulder whenever they chanced to see each other, mostly at school functions. He steered clear of married women as a general rule, but even if they'd all been single, none of them had done it for him.

But Jamie . . .

He remembered that small moment in high school when he'd invited her to the party. She'd just reminded him so much of Emma. A coltish Emma. The brilliant smile of disbelief she'd given him at the invitation had been burned on his retinas. He'd walked away from that encounter with a smile on his face, thinking about her, but then he'd seen Emma by her locker, talking with Race, and he'd felt instantly competitive. He'd been glad Emma had turned away from him, slamming her locker, throwing some comment over her shoulder that had Race staring after her with frustration.

She's dating an older guy.

Cooper dried off his hair with a towel, then slung it around his neck, walking naked to his closet. He dressed in clean jeans and a light blue shirt. He needed to do something. Something constructive.

He grabbed the binder of notes on Emma's case and flipped through them blindly. He already had most of them memorized. There wasn't that much there that he didn't already know.

Thinking of Race, he called him up to talk. Race answered his cell with, "Cooper Haynes," in a tone that was half amused, half . . . stoned, maybe?

"Mind if I stop by and talk with you and Deon?" Cooper asked. It was closing in on nine p.m.

"Sure, man. What's up?"

"I'll tell you when I see you."

"This about Troy? Deon's not really in the mood."

"Partly. See you in twenty."

Cooper grabbed his jacket, checked for his keys, and headed out. As he climbed into his SUV, he thought about Deke Girard. He called the hospital to check on him and was transferred several times before he was cut off. Rather than waste any more time, he decided he would stop at Glen Gen on the way and had turned in the direction of the hospital when his cell rang. He looked at the screen and saw it was the number he'd just called. Race. Pulling over to the side of the road, he answered, "Hey, Stillwell."

"Look, um, I talked to Deon. He's not going to talk to you. Your partner's already been all over him about Troy. Leave it be, Haynes. Just kids being kids. You, of all people, know how it is."

So, Howie was on to the boys, too. "I have some other things to talk over," Cooper told him.

"I don't know, man. Deon's had some tough times since Mom and Dad died. I don't know if you know about the business, but it went tits up."

Stillwell Seed and Feed had been a huge operation at one time, selling products like grass seed across the nation and internationally as well. But with the death of the Stillwell parents, the sons, Race and Deon, had never seemed to be able to manage the company in the same manner. Sales had dropped precipitously, and they'd finally sold out and been swallowed up by a larger company. Word had it that they were burning through the money they'd made on the sale. Like a lot of people, Cooper had wondered how long they could live off the proceeds until there were no proceeds left.

"I heard you're in a lawsuit," he told Race.

"No shit. And it's sucking up cash like you wouldn't believe. Those fuckers stole our company from us. You want to investigate Troy? Go on ahead, but Deon's out and so am I."

"I'd like to talk about Emma Whelan."

"Emma? Thought this was about your daughter."

"Both."

"Well, man. Good luck to ya," he said in a voice that said Cooper was on a fool's errand. And he clicked off.

Cooper exhaled. "Well . . . shit," he muttered. That shot that.

He thought about Jamie. A part of him wanted to go back to her house so badly it felt like a tractor beam had caught him in its grip. He wrestled with himself for a while, then decided to go on to the hospital. He would catch up with Race and Deon during the day, maybe tomorrow, when he had some extra time. He couldn't tell Howie about it. He didn't want his digging to find its way to the chief's ears. Bennihof ran the department by the book. He liked things neat and tidy, which wasn't the way police work was. Everyone who worked beneath him understood this, however, and everyone tried to give him complete, neatly typed, and organized reports. Neither Cooper nor Howie was particularly proficient in the neatly typed and organized realm, but they cleared cases on a regular basis, so their basic hunt-and-peck skills and terse remarks were accepted.

He strode into Emergency after parking at the far end of the lot, away from the path that an ambulance would take if it should come wailing beneath the portico outside the ER main doors.

He saw that Darla was no longer on the job. He knew that shifts changed at seven. Employees at the hospital worked twelve-hour shifts, seven to seven, which made their forty-hour weeks about three and a half days. They worked long hours when they were on the job, but it made for a good amount of time off.

He went up to the woman who was seated at one of the ER intake desks and introduced himself. He explained he was checking on a patient who'd been brought into Emergency earlier, but who had likely been admitted to a room.

"Or he could have been released," Cooper finished. "His name's Deke Girard."

She was young, probably in her twenties, with a diamond-esque stud winking in the curve of her nose and short, dyed, black hair. Her name tag read Kris Dietrich. She blinked several times. "Let me call Dr. Russman. He's on duty tonight," she said, reaching for the phone.

"I talked to Darla when I was here. I came in with Deke Girard, and I just want to know if he's awake yet."

"I know."

"Is there a problem?"

She looked away from him and spoke into the phone, explaining the situation, apparently to Dr. Russman. "He'll be right with you," she said, hanging up, and then made a point of ignoring him.

Cooper walked away to stand on the other side of the room. One side of the ER was the double doors that opened to the portico. Two sides were offices and hallways, and the outside wall that connected at a ninety-degree angle was a row of floor-to-ceiling windows facing the front parking lot. Beyond, he could see one of the maple-lined roads that ran through River Glen. Once upon a time there had been elm trees, but Dutch elm disease had taken its toll. Maples had been planted in the last twenty to thirty years. He remembered how small they'd been when he was in high school.

"Detective?"

He turned around to face a man with thick silver hair and bushy black eyebrows and brown eyes behind wire-rimmed glasses. "I'm Dr. Russman. Nurse Dietrich said you were asking about Mr. Girard."

"That's right."

"Mr. Girard passed away about an hour ago. We notified his emergency contact, Ms. Hillary Campion. She may be downstairs at the morgue, if you would like to talk to her."

Cooper was getting over the shock of Deke's death. In the space of a few hours, he'd learned of the man who felt protective about Emma, had placed him on a list of interviewees, needing to know what connection he had with Emma and what his motivation was. Now the man was dead.

"I want to talk to her," he told the doctor, and was directed to the nearest elevator bank, which was down the hallway that led to the main hospital, through an inner set of glass doors.

He'd just slammed his palm on the elevator button, lost in thought, when one of the cars opened, having come up from the lower floors. A woman in a stained coat and once white, now splotchy gray suede boots stepped out. Her legs were bare. Her face was clean but heavily lined, as if she'd gone through some hard living over the years. Her hair was scraped back into a ponytail at her nape. There were wavy lines across her forehead, etched deeply, as if she had many worries. It was an educated guess that she might be Deke's girlfriend.

She made eye contact with him. Cooper asked, "Hillary Campion?"

"Who's asking?"

"I'm Detective Cooper Haynes. I saw Deke collapse and called the ambulance that brought him to the ER."

"He was fine this morning," she said, glaring at him as if it were his fault.

"He was walking to a bar when he collapsed."

He hadn't meant it to sound like a disparagement of his lifestyle, but that's how she took it. "You don't know us." Her jaw quivered. "You didn't know him."

"I know. I wanted to talk to him. I—"

"What the fuck do you care? Harassing him. You . . . *pigs.*"

She swept by him and he caught a little of the body odor Emma objected to in Deke. He couldn't remember the last time he'd been called a pig.

He called after her, "He knew Emma Whelan. Said he needed to protect her. I was a classmate of Emma's."

"Bully for you." She was heading for the doors to the main parking lot.

"I just wanted to find out what he knew about Emma."

She stopped short and looked at him with loathing. "Well,

he's dead now, so you can't. Go back to your life and leave me alone."

With that, she pushed the bar on the door and let herself out into the dark night. He watched her walk almost all the way to the skeletons of the maple trees.

Chapter Twenty

Jamie spent the next three days substituting for the same absent teacher, but the injured woman was able to return on Friday, her foot in a boot, releasing Jamie from duty. She took Emma to work. Cooper had returned to their house briefly on Monday night to let Emma know the man who'd caused her so much anxiety had passed away. Jamie had thanked him for coming by, and he'd accepted that, but then he'd left again. He'd alluded to the fact that he was planning on interviewing the Stillwells and said he would keep in touch, and he'd managed a couple of phone calls to check in. They'd briefly discussed parts of Emma's case, but the circumstances weren't great on her end; she often had listening ears around her when he called. He also couldn't relay much about an active investigation, which meant the attack on Marissa, although Jamie also understood it was not his case. He did ask her to rethink about whether the first Ryerson home invasion could have anything to do with her, rather than Emma. They'd dismissed the idea more than once. But try as she might Jamie couldn't see any scenario where someone was after her sophomore self.

Emma, for her part, had taken the news of Girard's death in stride. She hadn't commented, apart from saying, "Mom would be glad," then acted as if nothing unusual had happened. Jamie had contacted Gwen and asked her to talk to Emma, and Gwen had agreed to stop by the house on Wednesday night. Harley, who'd been on the phone with her friends but wouldn't give Jamie the slightest inkling of what was being discussed, had wanted to witness the meeting between Gwen and Emma, but Jamie had put the kibosh on that. Even she wasn't invited into Emma's room, where the meeting had taken place. Instead, she took Harley out for ice cream—ignoring her protests of having homework, being tired, needing to be alone, whatever else she could dream up—so that they could have some privacy.

Jamie had tried to get Harley to open up, to no avail. She'd mentioned that the seniors had, after that first day, clammed up tight about what had happened to Marissa around her. She'd used that information to hopefully prod her daughter into communicating, but Harley's answer had been, "What did you expect after you ratted them out?"

What Jamie didn't tell her was that the staff room at the school hadn't been so tight-lipped. The boys involved in the pranking had been interviewed by the police, and though Deon Stillwell had threatened lawyers and lawsuits and all kinds of legal action, Troy's mother, Alicia, had managed to override him. It helped that Troy himself wanted to talk to the police. The two boys involved, Troy and Greer Douglas, admitted they'd gone to the house to scare Marissa, but that Marissa had seen them and knew who they were. They'd thought that a friend of hers was going to be there, too, but when they learned Marissa was alone, they left. It was sometime after that that Marissa said the intruder had entered the house. She thought she'd locked the back door, but under questioning had broken into tears and admitted that maybe she'd forgotten.

There had also been talk that Tyler Stapleton was part of the group, but the other boys had insisted he wasn't, so that question had been dropped, although Jamie could tell some of the staff weren't so sure Tyler was as innocent as they all claimed.

In any case, everyone believed Marissa had been frightened by a home invader, not either of the boys.

Unless one of them had gone back in ski gear and with a knife.

While Jamie was sitting across from Harley in the ice cream store, she'd asked her, "So, are you friends with any of the boys in your own grade?"

"I know 'em" was the sullen response.

"Maybe you should work on making friends with them?"

"Why?" Harley had been carefully eating along the edges of the cup of salted caramel and fudge ripple ice cream.

"I just know that you know the senior boys, and I wondered about your own class."

"You don't like the senior boys now that you know they scared Marissa. Why don't you worry about the creep who scared the shit out of her?" She waved around her plastic spoon. "'Language, Harley,'" she intoned, as if she were Jamie, then added, "I mean it, Mom. You're focused on the wrong stuff."

"I don't want to get in an argument with you. We're all concerned. If someone's out there—"

"If? *If?* See! That's the problem!" she cut her off.

"What about Greer?"

"What about him?" Harley had glared at her, daring her to continue.

"I heard he's been in trouble with the law."

"What? Who told you that?" she demanded.

"Apparently, he stole a car."

"That's not true!" She had her spoon gripped in her hand so tightly, Jamie imagined it would leave marks.

"That's what I heard. If it's not true, I'm sorry for spreading gossip, but if it is true, you might want to rethink how you feel about him."

That had done it. Harley had shoved her spoon in her remaining ice cream, gotten up, and stomped out of the store, waiting by the car until Jamie had paid and joined her. The trip home was made in silence. Jamie had wanted to talk to Harley about the state of Marissa and her friendship, too, but that wasn't going to happen. She'd overheard enough of Harley's telephone conversations to realize Harley and Marissa had cooled it a bit. Harley, being new, was suffering without the battalion of other friends Marissa possessed. It didn't appear to be a serious rift between the two girls. It seemed more that circumstances had made it difficult for everyone and, truth to tell, Marissa was dealing with some PTSD-like symptoms.

After they'd returned from the ice cream trip and Harley had once again shut herself in her room with Duchess, who'd been lying outside Emma's door, her chin on her front paws, both Emma and Gwen had come downstairs to the kitchen. Jamie had looked at Gwen, but it was Emma who said, "She can talk to you about me. I told her she could."

"Are you certain, Emma?" Gwen had asked, clearly rechecking.

"I don't have a mom anymore," Emma explained. "You need to talk to Jamie."

Jamie noticed Gwen was carrying a piece of paper from a notepad with some writing on it. "Is that for me?" she asked as Emma ensconced herself in front of the television.

Jamie glanced down at the words she had written in cursive: *She's not hiding. Likely lost memories.* "It's more a note to myself," Gwen explained as she and Jamie walked away from the living room together. Rather than stand in the hall below the stairs, where their voices might carry, they once again stepped onto the back porch.

"This appears to be my meeting room," Jamie said. She darted a look toward the back fence and around the yard, the same examination she'd done all week, but the area was unremarkable. No strange light flitting through the darkness. She was beginning to think she'd imagined the whole thing. Maybe she needed to have her eyes examined.

"I don't think it'll be a surprise to you that Emma doesn't seem to have deep, dark secrets," Gwen revealed. "What you see is what you get. She doesn't seem to be adversely affected by this man's—Deke Girard's—death. I can't even completely say she's relieved. It's just in the past for her."

Jamie nodded. "I think that's good."

"She did say he smelled bad."

They both chuckled softly, then immediately sobered. After a moment, Gwen said, "A lot of people were traumatized by what happened to her. It has tentacles that still reach into a lot of River Glen families."

"Are you thinking of any in particular?"

She gave Jamie a you-know-better look. "I can't really say." She seemed to contemplate something, then added, "Emma said you and Cooper Haynes are looking into the past."

Jamie was surprised Emma even knew that. "Cooper was here on Monday. He's also trying to learn who broke into the Ryerson house and scared his stepdaughter."

"Tell him to be careful," Gwen said seriously.

"I will."

"And be careful yourself," she added, clearly choosing her words. "I applaud you and Cooper for reexamining what happened to Emma, and for searching out who came after Marissa. The truth needs to emerge."

"But . . . ?" Jamie asked, recognizing Gwen was trying to say something without really saying it.

"It's always dangerous when revelations come to light that someone's trying hard to hide or suppress."

"You know something about *Emma's* attacker?" Jamie asked, feeling her way.

She shook her head. "No. I'm just saying that people have different hot buttons, maybe even different realities, and you have to be careful how far you push them. Tread on their reality, try to dissuade them from it, and you might be in for a battle royal you didn't even know was lurking there."

"What do you know?"

"Nothing. Just remind Cooper to be careful, too."

"Is there someone in particular I should look out for?" she couldn't help asking as Gwen turned back toward the house.

She hesitated a moment, fiddling with the scarf tossed artfully around her neck.

"I don't think so."

"You're scaring me a little."

"I don't mean to. All I'm saying is that you never completely know what's in another human's mind. Perceptions are hard to change. Like, for instance, you and I know Emma doesn't have any deep secrets, but we're the only ones who really know that."

"Someone might think Emma knows something about them?"

"I'm using her as an example." She shook her head and half laughed. "Stay safe, Jamie," she said as she headed out, her usual sign off. Jamie had walked her to the front porch and watched as she opened her driver's door. Another vehicle, a black SUV, cruised by the house slowly, and Gwen glanced back at it sharply. Jamie glanced at the SUV again as it turned the corner at the end of the block, then back at Gwen, who'd shut her door and started her engine. She drove away in the opposite direction from the black SUV.

Jamie had involuntarily shivered. Gwen's "I don't think so" when Jamie'd asked if she should be afraid of someone in particular wasn't quite a denial, and she seemed on edge . . . as if she wasn't quite certain everyone in River Glen was on the up and up.

Or are you just being paranoid? Jamie asked herself now. She was back at the house after a trip to Gold Appliances, having picked out a medium-grade dishwasher, which would be installed the following week. She hoped no further extraordinary expenses cropped up.

She decided to head to the grocery store again and try to find some of the items Emma had said she needed to make what she wanted to do next, another pasta dish: lasagna rollups. Jamie had been planning to get the fixings for a taco bar, but figured maybe she should get both. As she drove to the closest market, she thought over Gwen's warning again. Had she possibly been referring to Emma when she referenced an "own reality"? That didn't make sense, because Emma didn't seem to harbor deep-seated fears and memories. Emma had been sanguine upon learning of Deke Girard's death, so maybe with the homeless man's death one of her worst fears or worries had ended. With Emma, it was hard to say.

She was just finishing up at the cash register when she saw Teddy Ryerson enter the store. He seemed to be looking around, and then his gaze fell on her. She lifted a hand in greeting and smiled, though she didn't want to engage. She just wanted to head home, and not do another meet and greet.

Or maybe it was that she felt bad about Teddy and Serena. It was an uncomfortable memory, her last babysitting duty and how it had turned out for them and, of course, for her sister.

"Hi, Jamie," he said with a smile. "Just the person I wanted to see."

"Oh, hi," she said as she handed the checker her empty grocery bags to fill.

His expression sobered. "I've tried to reach out to Marissa, but her mother has blocked me."

"Well, the police are looking into everything that happened. How are Oliver and Anika? Are they okay? I've been thinking about them." She looked at him as she finished paying and the checker placed her bags in her cart.

"Echoes of the past, huh?"

"Yes indeed." She started pushing the cart toward the door and Teddy followed after her.

"The twins are pretty good, I think. They didn't see anything that happened. They were scared because Marissa was. They knew someone had come in, but they didn't actually see the intruder. As long as Marissa's okay, they're okay. We've called Marissa a couple of times. She's been great, allaying their fears, but I haven't been able to really talk to her. I just want to make sure she's all right myself. She's babysat for me dozens of times. I feel terrible about what happened."

As Jamie reached for one of the bags from the cart, he picked up the other one and walked with her to her Camry. Jamie opened the back door and put down her first bag. Teddy handed her the second one, and she placed it on the floor.

"It's just wrong," he said as she shut the door. "And after all these years and what happened with Emma? What do you make of it?"

She shrugged. She wasn't sure she wanted to talk about both attacks, Emma's and Marissa's, with him. But when she finally glanced at him and saw how tortured he looked, she let her guard down a bit. "I don't know."

"I think it could be the boys. Those senior boys," he said.

"But Marissa says it was someone else. The boys are friends. It just doesn't sound like them."

Teddy nodded. "But doesn't it seem unlikely that there would be a repeat, you know? A babysitter at my house? Doesn't it read that it would be someone who knows what happened to Emma, and maybe thought it would be fun to do the same thing to scare Marissa?"

"Fun?"

"I'm just saying, whoever scared her was in disguise. She might not have recognized them. Maybe they didn't mean to scare her that bad."

"With a knife?"

Teddy looked pained. "She's not sure about the knife. . . ."

"What do you mean?"

"I heard she can't really recall it . . . what kind it was."

"Well, why would she? When you're frightened and you think someone is going to kill you! Harm you. And besides, I think the police have determined it wasn't the boys."

"Maybe you're right." He sighed heavily.

"I don't know what to think," Jamie admitted.

He seemed to appreciate that as he looked at her hopefully. "Come and have a coffee with me," he urged, pointing to a small café in the same strip mall as the grocery store. "Have you got a minute? I'd sure like to talk to you."

Her first instinct was to turn him down. She only wanted to talk over the frightening events with close friends. But she'd told Cooper she was in on delving into Emma's cold case and Teddy Ryerson was part of that cold case. It was his house they had broken into both times. And since she and Teddy had already greeted each other and discussed Marissa's attack, maybe this was the time to learn something more.

"Half an hour," he said, pressing.

Jamie smiled and shrugged. "Okay, sure."

The café was foremost a bakery that sold a few assorted sandwiches. Teddy ordered them each a medium-sized coffee and brought them to a table by the window. He'd been texting while he was waiting and now said, "Serena's in River Glen. I told her where we were. That okay with you?"

"Of course."

"So, how's it been, coming back?" he asked. He sat across from her, his brown hair having been tousled by the breeze. He looked very young and seemed somewhat tense.

"Different, but okay. Good and bad, I guess. Kind of what I expected. What about you? I know you were married and your wife died of . . . leukemia?"

"Yeah, that was hard," he admitted. "I still miss her. So do the kids, of course. Serena's been a real help."

"That's good."

"I've tried dating some, since. Don't know if you've heard. It's a small town."

"I think Vicky Stapleton mentioned that you were seeing a friend of hers."

Teddy looked surprised. "Who was that?" he asked.

"Bette Kearns."

She watched the flush crawl up his neck to his face. "Ummm . . . I know Bette. She's in a tough marriage. Don't get the wrong idea about me, Jamie. I . . . uh . . . try to leave married women alone. Bette made some investments with me, and I . . . okay, I listened to her problems to make a sale. And I like her. We're friends."

"No judgment."

"It isn't really like that."

"What about your parents?" she asked. "I heard they moved to Palm Desert or somewhere."

"No, they're back in the Northwest. My dad's in Bend with his wife, Kayla, and my mom's in Bellevue with Jay."

"Much closer. Makes it easier to see them."

"There she is." He'd been looking out the window and now he waved to Serena, who saw him and lifted a hand to let him know she'd seen him. She entered the café a few moments later. In a black trench coat and high-heeled boots, Serena had the height of a runway model.

She came directly to their table and sat down beside her brother. They had a similar look: blondish hair, blue eyes, darker eyebrows. "Hi, Jamie," she said.

"Hi." Jamie smiled.

Teddy said, "We were just talking about Mom and Dad."

"What about 'em?" Serena frowned.

"That they moved closer to us," he said.

She made a face. "Not sure what I think of Kayla."

"We don't like her much," Teddy admitted to Jamie with a rueful smile.

Jamie said, "We don't like my dad's wife either."

Serena looked at her sharply. "Your stepmother?"

Jamie nodded. She'd just brought Debra up as a means of being part of the conversation.

"Emma doesn't like her?" she asked.

"No."

"I haven't seen Emma in a while," said Teddy. "How is she?"

"Oh . . . okay . . . I don't know how well you know her now, but she's fine. Happy, I think. She loves her job, and we just got a dog. . . ." Jamie went on to explain about Duchess, and a little about Emma and the Thrift Shop.

"How's Harley?" Serena asked, once she'd finished.

"Good. Scared, some, after what happened to Marissa."

"Man, I wish they'd figure out who broke into my house," said Teddy.

Serena said, "I thought the back door was open."

"I don't think Marissa latched it," Teddy agreed. "I just meant that I hope they find whoever got in and threatened her with a knife. They didn't take anything that I can tell. I don't get it."

"Maybe they were after her," Serena suggested.

"Why would they be after her?" Jamie asked. "Who knew that she would be there?"

"Well, the senior boys," Teddy said, going back to his earlier theme about the crime.

"But, if it wasn't them, who was it?" Jamie asked. "Was she targeted, or was it the house? A burglary that went awry when Marissa called 9-1-1, maybe?"

"Why was Emma targeted?" Teddy asked rhetorically. "I've never understood that one, either."

Jamie thought of Cooper and his high school friends. Even as she denied that the senior boys had terrorized Marissa, she remembered the boys that had all had a crush on Emma and the way she'd blown them off. "Maybe it was supposed to be a burglary, too?" she suggested, not really buying it.

"Maybe someone was after her . . . or . . . you?" Teddy posed.

Jamie just shook her head.

"Emma was pretty," said Serena somewhat wistfully. She closed her eyes. "But all that blood . . ."

Teddy shot his sister a worried look. "You're not going to go there, Serena."

"No." But she didn't open her eyes.

Jamie asked, "You saw Emma that night?"

"No." Teddy was emphatic.

Serena slowly opened her eyes. "The blood was still on the floor later. It scared me, but Dad was there."

"Serena has a strong imagination," said Teddy.

"It's memory," she corrected him. "The blood got into the wood. They couldn't get it up. It's still on the floor, under the new rug. That's why Dad left," Serena said.

"And because he and Mom weren't getting along," Teddy corrected. He gestured with his hand to push the whole idea aside. "This attack on Saturday brought it back for all of us.

It was hard, but I needed to be there, especially for Anika, like Dad was for Serena."

Jamie made a sound of agreement. "I haven't told Emma. None of us have."

"That's probably a good idea," said Teddy.

The conversation waned and Jamie decided it was a good time to wrap things up. "I've really gotta go. Thank you for the coffee, Teddy."

"I would've bought lunch, too."

"I'm good. Thanks again."

"If you have any financial needs . . ." He lifted his palms and smiled. "With your mom's estate, possibly? Call me. I'll offer free advice, if nothing else."

"Thanks," she said with a smile, then hurried back to her car. Most of her mom's assets were tied up in the house. She didn't really need investment advice. And there was something off-putting about Teddy Ryerson's approach that she couldn't get past.

Harley shivered, practically bent over from the weight of her backpack as she waited for her mom to pick her up. She'd had a few moments with Marissa alone today. Finally. Such a huge relief. *Huge*. The whole week had been shit from beginning to end. Marissa was freaked out and thought Harley had told the parents about the boys being there, which wasn't true, but it took a while for it to come out that it wasn't Harley, and it was great that it had, but by that time everything was terrible. Greer and Troy were dragged down to the police station. Mr. Padilla, the gym teacher, had figured out Troy had been there and had called in his dad, and then that pulled Greer and Tyler into it, too. But Tyler's parents had sworn he was with them, so he couldn't have been there, so it all fell on Greer and Troy.

And Greer had been there to see *her*, not Marissa. Her heart lifted a bit, just thinking about that, except that everything was really shitty and it wasn't going to get better until they caught the creep who'd scared Marissa. It wasn't the senior boys. It just wasn't! Mom had been hinting that that was the case and said Greer was a *criminal* and it just wasn't true . . . she didn't think. She was going to ask him about it, but now no one was talking to anyone. *Total hell.*

And who was that guy who tried to get Marissa?

Harley's shivering intensified. She took off her backpack and dumped it on the ground. Jesus, they were going to give them all scoliosis from the weight of their bags! Or was that a genetic disease? It might be a genetic disease . . . but they could get it anyway!

She suddenly wanted to cry, but fought it back. Bold. Daring. In the vanguard. Yeah right.

What was taking Mom so long? She'd texted that she would be right here, right away.

As if hearing her thoughts, her cell phone gave out its text trill. Harley grabbed the phone from her back pocket. It was from Mom: Got hung up. Be there soon.

"Well, crap." She hiked up her backpack and slipped her arms through the straps. Now she had to pee.

With a cloud over her head, she trudged back into the school. There was hardly anyone around. Friday, and they were all heading to whatever fun thing was next on the agenda. Not her. Not Harley Woodward. Nope. Marissa was staying in this weekend, and the football game was away, and Greer and Troy weren't playing, the last she'd heard, so it was all crap.

Harley trudged into the empty restroom and into a stall, dropping her backpack on the floor. She peed with alacrity. This was her superpower. Fast peeing. At her old school, she'd raced a good friend one time and they'd both laughed themselves silly.

She felt a pang of loneliness. Yes, she'd wanted to move, but hell . . . she'd run into different problems here. Weird ones.

Out of the stall, she washed her hands, looking at herself in the mirror. She was pale, the freckles on her nose standing out against her white skin.

The door to the bathroom opened and Dara Volker walked in. She stopped short upon seeing Harley, and Harley froze as their eyes locked. Immediately, she remembered hearing how at last Friday's party—the one after the game that neither she nor Marissa had been able to go to—Dara and Tyler had been having sex in one of the bedrooms and then they got into a huge fight where Dara had slapped him in front of a whole bunch of people. That story had gotten lost after the attack on Marissa, but it slipped across Harley's mind in the nanosecond when both of them looked at each other.

"You're that new girl . . . Harley," said Dara.

"Uh-huh."

"Greer likes you."

She didn't know what to say to that, so she said nothing.

"He liked Michaela last year." She moved farther into the room and slipped a small black purse off her shoulder. She wore jeans and a black turtleneck and her blond hair was tied back in a loose ponytail. Somewhat terrified, Harley made note of the older girl's appearance for future consideration.

"Do you like him?" she asked as she rummaged through the purse for a tube of cover-up. She dabbed at a zit on her chin that Harley hadn't even noticed.

"I don't know him very well. Apart from being pushed off the stage, that is."

Dara turned and gave her a long look. Harley wished she hadn't said anything.

"It doesn't matter anyway. We're all graduating. We'll hardly ever see one another again. Tyler can go fuck whoever he wants."

With that, she turned back out of the room, stopping long enough to add, "And he wasn't at that house where your friend was babysitting. He was with me."

She pushed through the door and Harley stood there for a moment in silence. Tyler had been with his parents, according to them. Well, he couldn't have been with both of them, so who was lying?

She felt cold all over. Could *Tyler* have been the one in the ski gear who'd come after Marissa with a knife?

Chapter Twenty-One

Cooper had started out the week in serious frustration about being kept out of the Ryerson home invasion, but by Wednesday, Howie finally laid out everything he'd discovered about the teens who had pranked Marissa at the Ryerson house in a meeting that also included Chief Bennihof and Detective Verbena. "I don't think it was Troy Stillwell or Greer Douglas," Howie concluded. "I thought it was. Tried to be fair, but I really thought it was. They were there, but they left. They gave me a blow-by-blow account of what they did and when, but they left together in Stillwell's car, which needs a muffler. Neighbors heard 'em leave and saw the car with the two boys in it, about an hour before the Ryerson home invasion."

"Couldn't they have gone back?" Verbena asked. She posed the question that had been on the tip of Cooper's tongue.

"They could've," Howie had agreed. "But they went to Deno's and ordered pizza. Hung out there for quite a while, then headed to the Stillwells'. Deon Stillwell swears they were there the rest of the night, and his ex, Alicia, who was also at the house, concurs. She and Deon got into a huge fight about Troy. I got the feeling there was drinking, maybe dope smoking going on with the teenagers and she was ready to blow the thing wide open. Now that the law's involved over the attack on Marissa, she's changed her mind. She did tell me to check and see where the boys' phones were after ten o'clock."

"Did you?" Bennihof asked.

"Not yet. But I will."

"Was there anybody else with them?" Cooper asked.

"Only the two guys in the car. Marissa, once she realized that we knew that Troy and Greer had been there, admitted she wasn't sure if they were the only ones. They were in dark pants and hooded sweatshirts. She only caught glimpses of them. Admitted she wasn't really scared. She knew who they probably were, and it turns out she was right."

"So, our attacker is someone else," said Verbena.

"I think so," Howie agreed.

They'd discussed the case some more. Cooper had wanted to jump into it, but Bennihof had thought it would be better if he let the other detectives handle it, and Howie had agreed, reminding him, "It keeps you one step out from your ex-wife."

Cooper had been left with a vandalism case at the Staffordshire development. Someone had written swear words into new concrete with a stick in front of an almost finished home at the far end of the development. The lots around it were for sale. The builder of the vandalized property was fit to be tied. He was going to have to replace the ruined concrete at great expense. An empty bottle of Tito's vodka had been left on the site. The glass of the bottle would be great for fingerprints. Cooper had looked around a bit and found a place at the back of the lot, where it was mostly brush and briars, and a copse of trees where the ground was disturbed, the vegetation flattened. He concluded something had been laid atop it, possibly a blanket, and the used condom tossed into the briars looked like it answered that question.

He'd gone over the Emma file again and had lingered over his information on the Ryerson parents, William and Nadine. They'd arrived separately at the house that night. Initially, they'd said that William had wanted to stay and Nadine had caught a ride with Dr. Alain Metcalf. The timing had been a little off, however, and eventually, it came out that the Ryersons had had a huge fight, with Nadine accusing William of cheating before leaving with Metcalf. William had proceeded to keep on drinking and, yes, had been flirting, rather unsuccessfully except for Kayla, his current wife, throughout the night, both before and after Nadine left.

There had always been a question about William's practices. He was a little too liberal with his prescriptions, according to a few sources who'd requested anonymity. Now in his sixties, he'd moved to Bend a few years earlier and was still practicing.

Nadine was married to another physician, Dr. Jay Campbell, and had moved to Bellevue from Tahoe fairly recently. Campbell's kids, only a few years younger than Ted and Serena, lived in the Seattle area, and Cooper guessed that may have had something to do with their choice of location. Like Ryerson, Campbell hadn't retired yet.

Dr. Alain Metcalf, Nadine's ride home the night of the charity event and the big fight between the Ryersons, had died a few years later outside Glen Gen, where he worked as an orthopedic surgeon. He'd been attacked in the hospital parking lot, bludgeoned, his wallet and prescription pad stolen. He'd died on the spot. The police had waited for either his credit cards or the prescription pads to be used, but neither had. The killer, seen all in black on the security cameras, had hidden late at night behind another car when Metcalf came out of the hospital to get into his. He'd come around to attack Metcalf, then run off across the lot to a wooded area which stood on a short hill. According to the notes in the file the tape was grainy and the night was somewhat foggy. The killer had never been found. Like Dr. Ryerson, Metcalf was suspected of being free with his prescriptions, and there was thought that one of his "patients" may have killed the golden goose in some kind of dealer/addict dispute.

Cooper made a note to recheck that. He thought about calling Jamie, but decided to wait. He'd taxed her with thinking whether she could have been the intended target and wanted to let that percolate awhile. If it wasn't one of his classmates who'd attacked Emma, why had the Ryerson house been targeted twenty years earlier? If it wasn't one of the senior boys who'd come at Marissa, why had the Ryerson house been targeted last Saturday? Random home invasion . . . ? Someone capitalizing on the Babysitter Stalker story that long ago summer? Someone reenacting that now?

Or was Mike Corliss right, and Emma's attacker was indeed one of his classmates?

He just couldn't believe that.

Thursday morning, Cooper determined he would interview Race Stillwell after work whether Race wanted him to or not. He put in a call to Tim Merchel in Sacramento not long after he got to the station, but Tim was busy. However, the lawyer called back within the hour.

"What's up, Coop? Long time no talk to," Merchel said, sounding distracted.

Cooper could hear conversation in the background. "I'm looking into Emma's case again."

"Yeah? Hope you figure it out. I'm at the courthouse. Got a trial going. We're on break."

"I won't keep you. I'm just checking in. Seeing if there's anything you might remember about that night that we haven't gone over."

"Haven't thought about it in a while. Do you know I'm

getting married? Finally got smart enough to ask her, and she said maybe." He snorted a laugh. "Made me pay for taking so damn long, but it's on now. I'll send you an invitation."

"Congratulations."

"And if I think of anything, I'll let you know. You should talk to Race . . . and Dug."

"I plan on it."

"They never were on the up and up. I'm still sorry about Emma, you know."

"Yeah."

"And I'm sorry for being such a shit. We all liked her. You just got farther than the rest of us."

Cooper heard Tim's name being called by someone, and Tim told him he had to go.

Cooper was still thinking about that call, about how Merchel had zeroed in on Race and Dug and their story about Dug walking home on his own. He'd said the same to the police twenty years earlier and he'd even wanted them to give him a lie detector test, which hadn't happened, to Cooper's knowledge. There was nothing in the file about it. Mike Corliss had always believed it was one of Cooper's classmates and had developed tunnel vision about any other possibility. Maybe he was right.

Around noon, a call came in about a domestic dispute at the Kearns home. Patrol responded to the 911 call from a frightened young girl named Joy, who turned out to be the Kearns' seventh-grade daughter. Joy tearfully claimed her parents were killing each other. When the officers got to the home, Phil and Bette Kearns were at two different ends of the house and Joy, who'd been home from school with a sore throat and watching TV in her room—something the parents had apparently forgotten about when their fight escalated to blistering war—was standing by the front door, waiting. She hurried the officers in, and eventually, Phil and Bette were coaxed into meeting in the middle, coming into the living room. According to the officers' report, Phil's face sported a dark red handprint where his wife had slapped him. She also showed bruises on her wrists where she claimed he'd held her against her will in a hard grip. She swore he was overpowering her. He swore he was just holding her away from him. That was when Bette started wailing that she wanted Cooper Haynes. When Phil seconded that, the patrol unit happily sent out the request, and Cooper, though loathe to get involved, nevertheless took over for the officers, even though it wasn't strictly part of his job description. The lines were blurred some at River Glen Police Department, but he said/she said disputes generally didn't require a detective.

It was part of the irony of the job that what kept him out of the investigation of the attack on Marissa was what made him lead man on his classmate's domestic violence case: Cooper knew Phil from high school and Bette from being introduced to her when she was with Phil. She was overly friendly, one of those people whose behavior bordered on inappropriate. He could almost see an "I'm available" sign flashing over her head.

When Cooper arrived at the house, he relieved the patrolmen, then entered through the foyer to find both Bette and Phil seated in chairs in the living room. As soon as Bette saw him, she leaped up and ran to him like they were old friends, crying and claiming Phil was a monster. The daughter was standing at one end of the room, pressed against the wall. Cooper ignored Bette in favor of Joy. "Are you okay?" he asked the girl, which brought big, fat tears rolling down her cheeks. He kindly suggested that maybe she could head back to her bedroom, which she gratefully did, practically running from the room.

He then turned to Phil and asked crisply, "What happened?"

"If my wife could unwrap herself from you, maybe we could have a serious discussion."

"You're the one having the fucking affair!" Bette hissed.

"What happened to our 'open' marriage? It was okay for you, but not for me?" Phil snapped back.

"Meghan Volker?" she practically screamed.

Cooper, who'd carefully extricated himself from Bette's embrace, knew he was in over his head. River Glen was sometimes too small a town.

Phil lifted a hand and began ticking off each finger. "Tom Gideon, Lanny Dufernal, Ted Ryerson, Lawrence Stapleton—"

"I did not sleep with *Lawrence Stapleton*!" Bette shrieked.

"Only because he turned you down."

"Wait," Cooper held up a hand.

"You fucker! You absolute fucker! You . . . you slept with *Meghan Volker*. Her husband will kill you. He'll kill both of us!"

"Ex-husband. And I've already talked to him about marrying Meghan Volker once this whole divorce thing is over."

Bette screamed so loudly it made Cooper's ears ring.

Phil stood up from his chair and advanced on her.

"Hold up." Cooper put his body between the two of them, half-convinced he was going to be beaten up by one, the other, or both. Emotions were hot, spewing like lava. "Calm down, both of you, before something happens that'll send you both to jail or worse."

"I hate you. I hope you die!" Bette screamed.

"You first, bitch."

"Sit back down." Cooper pointed Phil to his chair. "You too." He turned to Bette.

She looked wounded that he'd turned on her. "You would really send me to jail?" *In a heartbeat,* he thought, but what he said was, "You need to stop escalating this fight before somebody gets really hurt. I suggest one of you leave the house."

The Kearnses stared at Cooper for a moment, then slowly looked at each other.

Phil made a sharp motion with his arm. "Fine. I'll go. I don't want to stay here anyway."

Her lip quivered, and Cooper could practically see the air go out of her. "No, I'll go. The kids like you better anyway," she added, starting to sob.

Phil got up from the chair again. "I'll pack a bag." As he passed by Cooper, he asked in a lowered voice, as if he suddenly was worried what his daughter could overhear, "Did you sleep with her, too?"

"No."

"Y'sure?" He lifted his brows.

"Shut up, you asshole," Bette said, also in a quieter voice, but her eyes burned with fury.

Phil brushed past him and Bette, alone with Cooper, seemed to finally feel some embarrassment at her behavior. Her face flushed pink and she looked down at her toes. Cooper waited while Phil packed a bag, then after making sure he was on his way, he got ready to leave himself.

Bette jumped up and begged. "Please stay. Please!"

Very carefully, not wanting to send her into a screaming virago once again, he explained that he had work to do.

"Come back later," she then invited.

Hell no.

Away from the scene, he'd gone back to the station and written up the report on the incident. He hoped that would be the last of it. After work he drove first to his place, calling Jamie on the way. He'd wanted to go over to her house. Had hoped she would invite him, even though he told her right from the get-go that he was working on a number of things, but it hadn't happened. Instead, they ended up having a fairly meaty conversation about Emma's attack and his efforts to basically reopen the cold case. He told her that he wanted to set up some interviews, both with his old classmates and with Ted and Serena's parents. Also, he related the murder of Dr. Alain Metcalf, a crime she knew about from her mother who'd worked with the man. She, in turn, told him about Gwen Winkelman's meeting with Emma and then Gwen's warnings to be careful and stay safe and to tell Cooper the same.

"Always," Cooper said, a stock answer.

"No, she was serious. Like she knew something, something dangerous, but she wouldn't say what that was."

Cooper considered. Gwen had really helped out the department, but she was a tad out there for him.

The department had let it be known through the press that they were still looking for Marissa's attacker, thereby backhandedly clearing the senior boys, so Cooper had felt comfortable telling Jamie that they were searching for a different man entirely, no one from the school, at least none of the kids.

He almost asked her if she wanted to take a trip to Bend with him, to drop in on Dr. William Ryerson, but he held himself back.

This morning, Friday, he'd learned about a burglary that had apparently taken place about three blocks from the Ryersons' on Saturday night. The couple hadn't initially noticed items had been stolen when they got back from a night out at a party. It was over the course of the week that they'd recognized that money had been taken from the drawer in the kitchen, where they kept spare change, some relatively inexpensive jewelry couldn't be found, and their newest television, in their living room, had been oddly askew. Originally, they'd each thought someone else in the household had moved it and put it back, but now, as more missing items came to light, they wondered if the thief had tried to take the TV and, upon realizing it might be too difficult to get away with, had had to abandon it. Cooper had directed fingerprints to be taken, and they'd found where the thief had gained egress; a pane of the window in the kitchen door was easily removed and put back, which was how the couple let themselves in when they were locked out.

Someone likely had that information, so maybe it was an acquaintance, possibly someone in the neighborhood?

Oh, and a bottle of Tito's vodka seemed to be missing.

Cooper told them he would meet them at their house when they got home from work, and Ryan Pendelan said he'd be back by four, so Cooper decided he would make it his last appointment of the day. The crime team had already dusted for prints when he got there and not found any. He listened to Pendelan, who was somewhere in his late twenties or early thirties, and his myriad complaints about the terrible state of "today's youth." It seemed more like the kind of charge someone much older would level.

As Pendelan showed him around the house, pointing out where items were missing, Cooper was already half-convinced there might be a connection between this burglary and the vandalism case, both of which could have happened the same night. The way the Pendalan's television was moved, but not taken, seemed like the work of an amateur, and the vandalism and vodka tryst in the weeds read like teens.

And it was also the same night the Ryerson's home had been invaded by an intruder who had accosted Marissa. Was it a teen? He didn't want to think so. He knew the boys who'd spooked her, and they weren't bad guys, but they were walking that thin line between right and wrong. He didn't want them choosing the latter.

On the other hand, he didn't want to believe it was a criminal intent on harming her. It was what Marissa believed, and he was going with that, but that thought turned his insides to ice because it might very well mean whoever it was would try again.

"Anything else you've noticed missing?" Cooper asked as Pendelan wrapped up his tour.

"My wife says a blanket, an extra one we use in the den."

Cooper added that to his notes, but didn't tell him about the evidence they'd found outside Staffordshire Estates.

Checking the time, Cooper decided to stop into the station before he left for the day. His mind was still churning over what he'd learned. The Pendelan burglary and Staffordshire defacement both bore the earmarks of someone young: stolen liquor, pointless vandalism, a blanket on the ground during a cold night rather than indoors. Though Staffordshire was far enough away that you might want to drive, the Pendelan burglary was only a few doors down from the Ryerson home invasion. All three crimes were either the same night, or only a few days apart.

He wondered if any of the houses at the new development had a security camera system. Based on the prices he'd seen, he guessed a lot of them might once they were finished. Unfortunately, only a couple of them were nearing completion, the one his ex and David Musgrave were in escrow over being one of them.

He called Laura to ask her. She answered on the second ring and said urgently, "Did you find him?"

He knew she meant Marissa's attacker. "No. Howie's on that case, as I told you."

"So, you didn't find him." Her disappointment was great.

"Not yet. Check with Howie. He's the one with all the updates." This wasn't entirely true; Cooper had been let in to the investigation once the boys were removed as prime suspects. "I wanted to ask you if you have security cameras at your new house in Staffordshire."

"Yes, of course. I'm not letting anything like this happen at my house."

"Are they operational?"

"I don't—" She stopped herself. "Why?"

"I was hoping to see some footage from Saturday night. There was vandalism at one of the houses."

"Oh. Yes. I know about that one." She paused. "I don't think so, but I'll ask our builder."

"Thanks, Laura."

She didn't respond for a moment, then mumbled a good-bye. Since their divorce, Laura was always uncomfortable with Cooper when she determined he was being gracious.

At the station, Howie said, "Phil Kearns came in."

"What for?" Cooper asked.

"To lodge a complaint against you. He thinks you've been having extracurricular activities with his wife."

Elena Verbena, leaned back in her chair, several desks over. "Haynes," she said in a tsk-tsk voice.

"He's mad because he's the one who had to leave and blames me." Cooper sat down at his own desk.

Elena shook her black curls. "I really hate dealing with he said/she saids."

Chief Bennihof came out of his office. "Got a lot of pressure from the Douglas and Stillwell kids' fathers. They both, by the way, said they didn't want you bothering their sons." He looked at Cooper.

"Me?" Cooper was surprised.

"I told them that Eversgard and Verbena were handling the case. That's right, isn't it?"

"Yes." Cooper wondered where this was coming from.

"I know you said you wanted on the case." Bennihof regarded him intently from beneath bushy, gray brows.

"The fathers are classmates of mine, but I'm not asking them about their sons."

"Okay. Keep it that way."

Bennihof went back into his office and closed the door. Elena, Howie, and Cooper waited till he was gone then looked at each other. They all felt Bennihof's was a political appointment. He wasn't a bad guy, but he wasn't much of a cop.

Howie cast an eye back to the chief's office. He said quietly to Cooper, "You need to know anything, ask me."

Cooper appreciated it. However, he knew he needed to play by the rules for the time being. "Thanks. I'm okay for now."

On the way out of the station, Cooper took a detour to cruise by Deke's girlfriend's address, which he'd looked up after they'd brushed by each other at the hospital. He'd done the same thing almost every day this week. He wanted to talk to her but knew she already resented his intrusion, so he was biding his time, waiting for a better opportunity.

Now he turned onto her block. Hillary Campion lived in one half of a rather run-down duplex. Cooper had learned she rented the place from the owner, who lived in the other half. She worked nights in the kitchen of a Portland restaurant. Her Dodge Neon in the driveway. Fifteen years old or more and dented in several places along the side and rear. He could push it with her, he knew, but he was hoping to get her on his side enough to open the door about Deke's connection to Emma. Even though they'd been a couple, Deke had apparently preferred homelessness to cohabitating with Campion. Or maybe she hadn't been able to handle his drinking, which clearly hadn't been under control.

Thinking about Bennihof's warnings, Cooper nevertheless decided to keep with his plan to interview Race. True, it could be sticky if Deon was around and decided to get twitchy about Cooper being at their house. But Cooper had no intention of talking to him about Troy. Sure, he'd like to, but he had other reasons for being there. It could get him in hot water with the chief, but he would take his chances. And he planned on checking with Dug Douglas, too, although it would be about Emma, not Greer.

Chapter Twenty-Two

Cooper drove up the long drive to the Stillwell house, planning what he was going to ask. Even knowing that things had started deteriorating around the place after the Stillwell parents' deaths, he was a bit surprised to see how far things had gone down. He eyed the moss-covered roof, the missing bricks on the house, the holes in the driveway. It didn't look like there'd been any upkeep since the sale of Stillwell Seed and Feed, and that had been years back.

He rang the bell and waited, then rang it again. Deon finally appeared, looking as if he'd just rolled out of bed, though it was close to six p.m.

"What, man?" he said, somewhat belligerently. "I'm not talking to you. I told your chief that. You're in big trouble. I'm just saying."

"I'm here to see Race."

"Race ain't here."

Cooper had seen Race's car. He knew which one it was. The same Mustang from twenty years earlier. For all the decrepit disrepair, Race kept that machine well-tuned. "I'll wait."

Deon looked like he was going to deny him, but Cooper just kept his eye on the man. Finally, Deon shrugged and wandered back down the hall. It wasn't much of an invitation, but Cooper took it as such, letting himself in and closing the door behind him.

They met up in the kitchen. Cooper saw that Deon's lackadaisical invitation was really a means to let his anger build up. He eyed Cooper with barely contained fury and went off on him, the police, the travesty of justice for his son, the people of River Glen who'd gleefully helped contribute to the Stillwell family's dwindling fortunes, and so on and so forth. Cooper let the man rant as he looked around the kitchen. Half of the cabinets were without doors and those with doors were cockeyed on their hinges or gapped open. The counters were scratched and stained and a built-in butcher block cutting board had chips of wood missing. Deon slowed down when he saw Cooper's silent assessment and said, "Those shitheads took us for everything. But we'll get 'em back. Our lawyer says it's guaranteed."

Cooper made no comment on that. He started to ask where Race was when Deon cut him off.

"My boy had nothing to do with that break-in. He was just goofing with Dug's kid, and they were fuckin' around like you and Race and the rest of 'em when Emma got stabbed. Same thing."

"Both crimes were home invasions," Cooper said.

"What I'm telling you is, back off. All of you *cops*. Leave my boy alone or I'll sue. I told your boss that. I think I could get you fired." He smirked.

"I saw Race's car. He upstairs?"

At that very moment, a thud of feet hitting the floor was heard overhead. Cooper looked up at the ceiling.

Deon was clearly thinking about how to play this. Cooper waited. He'd never really liked Deon Stillwell. He was a younger, meaner, louder, cruder version of Race.

Finally, he made his decision. "Race? *Race*? The po-po's here!" he yelled.

He then walked away down a short hallway, and moments later, Cooper heard a door slam shut.

Footsteps sounded on the stairs, descending to the first floor. Cooper stepped into the hallway just as Race turned the corner, heading toward the kitchen. Race stopped short upon seeing him. "Haynes. What are you doing here?"

"Decided to stop by because I still want to talk to you."

Race grunted, then said, "Troy's at school. He's going to his mother's tonight, I think. Ask Deon."

"I'm not here about Troy."

"Well, River Glen PD's been all over him. Why don't you go after Dug's son? He's the one who instigated it all. Troy just went along."

"I want to talk about Emma," Cooper reminded him.

Race rolled his eyes and moved past Cooper to the kitchen. Cooper slowly followed and watched as Race pulled a longnecked Budweiser out of the refrigerator.

"Want one?" Race asked.

"No, thanks."

"You still on duty?" He didn't wait for a response as he headed to the small adjoining family room with two leather recliners, stained and split, a couple of side chairs, their fabric also stained. Cooper spun around one of the wooden chairs around the kitchen table and sat down carefully. The chair wobbled on uneven legs but held his weight. Race dropped into one of the recliners and reached for the remote, then, as if remembering Cooper's purpose, set it back down. "So, what do you want to know?"

Cooper decided to try to approach Race as a friend, rather than one of River Glen's lawmen. He wanted Race to remember their shared past. "I ran into Dug outside the Waystation the other night. Kinda got me thinking about Emma."

"Emma." He sighed. "What a fucking shame." He took a pull on his beer.

Cooper tried to read him and felt he was being sincere. "When we all left that night, Dug walked home on his own. He stayed behind because he wanted to keep pranking Emma to impress you."

Race half-laughed. "Dug just wanted a clear head before he showed up back at his parents'. He was messed up."

Dug had been no more messed up than the rest of them. Cooper had always known in his gut that Dug had gone back to keep after Emma as a means to make Race happy. "The truth is you came back and picked him up."

"You're way off base," he denied, but his tone was careful.

Cooper was pretending to know more than he did. He'd never believed Dug had anything to do with hurting Emma, but he'd thought there was more to the story than either Dug or Race was telling.

"You left the Ryersons', dropped off Robbie, circled around, and came back for Dug."

"That's not what happened." Race shook his head. His hair was still dark, but there were flecks of gray just beginning to show.

"Dug got in your car and then you took him home."

"That's just not true, Haynes," he said with more heat, but he wouldn't meet Cooper's eyes.

"What part did I get wrong?" Cooper asked coldly.

"What do you mean?" Race paused in the act of taking another swallow.

"It always bothered me, Dug not leaving with the rest of us. What did he do?"

"Nothing."

"Come on, Race. What sort of pranking did he do?"

"I told you. Nothing!"

"Emma had shut you down and Dug knew you were mad. Maybe he went too far?"

"Nothing happened with Dug," Race shot back. His face

had suffused with a dark red color. "He liked Emma. All of us liked Emma. She shut you down, too," he reminded him, glaring at Cooper as if it had just happened.

"Emma was just friends with all of us."

"Because of that college guy!" Race expelled.

"There was no college guy."

"Yes, there was," he insisted.

"I talked to Jamie. She said there wasn't anyone in her sister's life."

"And you believed her?" Race looked at Cooper with a smirking grin. "You got it bad for her, too? Wanna get in her pants? Deon said she looks just like Emma."

Cooper put a check on his own anger and just waited.

"There was somebody Emma was seeing. Maybe her baby sister didn't know about him, but her friends did. I told the police he was the one who tried to kill her."

"Could have been an accident."

Race made a growling noise that summed up his frustration with the subject. "If I ever find the fucker, I'll kill him myself!"

That felt real. And Cooper could relate. He'd felt that way when Emma had been attacked and he felt that way now about the intruder who'd threatened Marissa.

"Find who she was seeing and you'll find the guy who attacked her," Race stated flatly.

Cooper took a mental step back. He wanted to press on the Dug issue, but it was clear Race believed Emma had been attacked by her supposed older lover. Irene Whelan had pushed that theory for a while as well, but it had never been proven and seemed to be a dead end. A few of Emma's girlfriends had been interviewed and asked the question, but none had offered up anything about Emma and any particular lover and no one had ever said she had a "secret life."

Race had grown quiet, and Cooper realized he was deep

in thought. It was the look of someone who was carefully thinking something over.

"You should talk to Dug," he finally said.

Cooper stayed very still. Something unexpected here. "What'll he tell me?"

He seemed to wrestle with himself for a while, then he sighed. "I did go back for him, but I didn't find him. He walked home, like he said."

"You didn't tell the police you went back for him."

"No. Of course not. They woulda made more of it than it was."

"Did you go back to see Emma?"

"*No*. I circled the block, looking for Dug. He was already gone. Then I drove back to the party and got everybody out of there. Told 'em the police were on the way. I was . . . pissed."

"What'll Dug tell me?" Cooper asked again.

"Nothing!"

"You just told me to talk to him."

"Yeah, to confirm that it wasn't him who hurt Emma. I know it wasn't Dug. You know it wasn't Dug. I didn't see him. I saw . . . I don't know, it was dark, but it wasn't Dug."

"Jesus, Race." Cooper was on his feet. "You *saw*? What did you see?"

"*It wasn't Dug!*" he yelled as Cooper strode down the hall. "I'm going to find Dug."

"Don't go off half-cocked, man. It wasn't Dug, because I saw somebody else!"

Cooper slowed his steps and stopped by the front door. He turned around and regarded Race, who'd followed after him. Race had bleated out the truth, but now looked like he was going to start covering up again. "Who?" Cooper demanded.

"I don't know, man. That college guy, probably. In a ski mask. But it wasn't Dug."

"What?" Cooper bit out.

"Maybe I'm wrong. I didn't see him that well. But it wasn't Dug."

"You saw a guy in a *ski mask* the night Emma was attacked?"

"I don't know. It was hard to tell. I thought so. I was looking for Dug, and I saw him, Dug, I thought at the time. But this guy wasn't on the street . . . he was kind of staying close to the side bushes . . . and he didn't walk like Dug. I told Dug about him later, and he said it wasn't him."

Cooper stared at Race, his thoughts tumbling over one another.

"They were trying to hang us all, remember?" Race declared. "Wanted to blame the whole thing on us. They woulda strung Dug up without a trial. I know how these things go. The police are a friend until they're not. So don't go making this bigger than it is."

"If this is true, you covered up for whoever attacked Emma."

"I *told* the police it was that college guy!"

Cooper's blood was pounding in his ears. He was as angry as he'd ever been. With an effort, he tried to cool his fury, but he wanted to slam Race up against the wall. Race could be lying, he reminded himself. He could have manufactured this ski-masked intruder because he'd heard that was who'd chased Marissa and it gave him a desperate alibi for his friend or himself. . . .

"I'm going to find Dug," Cooper said again.

Race sighed and closed his eyes. "I loved her, man. I would have done anything for her. And I'd do anything to find the fucking psycho who did this to her. I'm on your side on this, Haynes. I'm just telling you, Dug didn't go inside that house and hurt Emma. It wasn't him."

But Cooper was already outside the front door, yanking

it closed behind him. Whatever the truth was, he was going to find out.

Jamie was late to pick up Harley from school and was relieved to see her waiting by the back doors that led to the parking lot, her back to Jamie. Jamie waved her over, but Harley didn't see her. Her head was down, and Jamie belatedly realized she was texting. Muttering under her breath, Jamie slammed out of the car and hurried toward her. "C'mon," she yelled as she reached her, circling her arm in a classic, let's-get-going move. "I bought a new dishwasher and it's getting installed today! I have to be back for when the guy shows!"

She glanced down at Harley's phone, but Harley clicked off in midword. She'd been typing, "... just saying what she said. Tyl—"

"Who were you talking to?" Jamie asked.

A hesitation. "Marissa."

"Good. I'm glad you two connected. It's been a tough week. How is she?"

"Fine."

"Glad to hear it. Okay, well, come on. We gotta go."

Harley followed her to the car and Jamie rushed to get home. She was relieved the dishwasher repairman wasn't there yet. He'd given her a two-hour window, which was fine. She was just glad it was getting done today.

Harley made kissy-face noises at Duchess, who returned the exchange with little barking sounds of delight as she quivered all over. Jamie hadn't substituted today, so she'd been able to take care of the dog's needs. According to Burton, Duchess could apparently make it from the morning till late in the afternoon, but Jamie told Harley to make sure Duchess was taken out and fed.

When her cell buzzed at about five-thirty, she thought it

was a call from the installer, but it turned out to be Cooper. She answered with a smile in her voice that she couldn't contain. "Hi, there."

"Hi. I just wanted to . . . see you," he admitted.

"Fine by me." She heard the lilt in her voice and silently scolded herself for being so obvious.

"I've got a few things to do, but maybe later?"

"Sure."

"It probably won't be till after seven."

"I could make dinner? Or we could go to Deno's with Harley and Emma . . . ?"

"Any chance I could take you out?"

"Well . . . yeah . . ." She quickly ran through what she would need to do.

"I'll text when I'm on my way."

"Perfect."

Jamie checked the time, then, with cell phone in hand, ran upstairs to put herself together.

Dug Douglas was out of town, according to his wife, Teri, who was also his girl Friday, apparently; she answered the phone calls for Douglas Insurance. Cooper explained who he was and that he wanted to get in touch with Dug right away. Teri wasn't going to give him Dug's number just because he was a friend and a police officer. Whether she knew something that kept her from divulging the information because Dug had asked her not to, or if she was just naturally reticent, Cooper didn't feel like wasting time. He gave her his cell number and told her to have Dug call him ASAP.

He knew he needed to cool down. He was mad at both Race and Dug, and himself, too, for sensing there was more and not following up on it when he was younger, or any time in between. He didn't believe Dug had hurt Emma, certainly not on purpose, but he and Race had lied and covered up and knew far more than they'd ever mentioned.

Because they were afraid of getting in trouble.

But that was no excuse.

He could easily get Dug's phone number on his own, but maybe it was better to let Dug contact him rather than blasting into the guy, demanding answers in any way he could get them, which was what Cooper really wanted to do.

And . . . there was a chance Race was lying. About the ski mask and maybe more. There was also a chance that Dug didn't know anything at all. That he had, as he'd said, just walked home.

But Cooper didn't believe that. Dug had been Race's right-hand man. He would've wanted to contact Emma for Race. To either appeal Race's case to be her guy, or to give her a mean-spirited warning for being a disinterested bitch. Cooper could practically hear Dug calling her names.

Still, that was a long way from stabbing her in the back with a knife. Was that what last Saturday's intruder had planned for Marissa? Coming into the house with a knife? The thought sent a cold chill down his spine.

It's better you can't talk to Dug yet. You need to think this through.

Cooper knew he was giving himself good advice, but he didn't know if he would take it. He wanted to go after Dug Douglas hammer and tongs and pound the information out of him, if that was what it took.

Pushing his anger aside, he drove back to the station, where he had the file on Emma's attack locked in a bottom drawer of his desk. He pulled it out and took it home with him. He looked at the clock and gave himself about an hour and a half before he would meet up with Jamie.

* * *

Jamie looked at herself in the mirror. Too much makeup? She would have liked to take a shower but didn't have time. She worked a smudge of eyeliner off the corner of her eye, checked the white sweater and black slacks. She'd pulled her hair into a loose bun at her nape. Too schoolmarmish?

Not with those red lips . . .

Making a noise of frustration, she swiped off the lipstick and applied a lighter shade of pink. Better.

"Oh, for God's sake." She lifted her palms from her makeup tray and left the bathroom.

Harley popped her head out of her cracked bedroom door at that moment and Duchess did the same, trying to squeeze out toward Jamie.

"Where are you going?" Harley demanded.

"I'm just getting ready."

Jamie headed toward the stairs.

"For what? Are you meeting those women?"

"No."

"Who, then?"

Jamie drew a breath and exhaled. She wanted to lie, but that would be counterproductive, and it would all come out anyway. "Mr. Haynes."

"What? Really?"

Jamie hurried downstairs. Where the hell was the delivery-man? It was after six. She paced the kitchen. Theo was bringing Emma home tonight and that should be any minute, but what had happened to the dishwasher delivery?

Ten minutes later, she heard a large truck outside and hurried to the front windows to see it was Gold Appliances. Finally. At the same time, she saw the Theo's Thrift Shop van slide to a stop on the street in front of the house. Theo got out and looked at the delivery truck, and Emma pushed out from the passenger side and also gazed curiously at the large, rumbling vehicle in the driveway.

Jamie threw open the front door. The sunlight was fading

and the clouds were rolling in. "It's the dishwasher," she yelled to Emma and Theo.

Emma took a look toward the sky and hurried inside. She immediately called for Duchess, who, having escaped Harley's room, had followed Jamie around as she paced, then, tired of that, returned to Harley's room. Hearing Emma's voice, the dog whined loud enough to be heard outside Harley's door. A few moments later, Harley let her out and she bounded down the stairs and damn near knocked Emma over. Emma giggled, which brought Jamie's head around with a snap. Emma never giggled. Or laughed. Or chuckled.

Theo was watching the man who was bringing in the appliance, which was strapped on a dolly, backward down a ramp out of the back of the truck. Jamie realized it was Allen just as Theo sketched a wave goodbye to Jamie.

"It was a pretty good day today," Theo yelled at her. Jamie nodded her appreciation and waved back. No more Deke.

Allen immediately apologized for being late as he came up the front walk. Apparently, the man who was supposed to come to her house had suffered a family emergency. His wife had been in a fender bender and was in the hospital.

"Is she all right?" Jamie asked as she held the door for Allen, who gently bumped the dishwasher up the porch steps and into the house.

"Last I heard it was a broken arm, so yeah . . . I think she's okay."

He set to work pulling out the old dishwasher and replacing it with the new one. He had to turn off the circuit breaker to get the job done, and the kitchen and part of the living room went dark.

Emma had gone upstairs with the dog and into the bathroom—Jamie expected her makeup items to be lined up when she returned—but now she came back down with Duchess in tow. Duchess hung back from Allen.

"Oh, come on, you remember him," Jamie chided the dog. "He was here on Monday."

Emma was frozen in place, staring at Allen. Jamie, realizing this, touched Emma's arm, hoping to break into her fixation, but Emma wouldn't move as Allen muscled the first machine out of the way and set the new one in place. Luckily, there was enough room in the cabinet space for it to fit.

"What's wrong?" Jamie whispered to Emma.

Her sister didn't say anything, but Jamie could feel her tension.

"Let's go in the living room," Jamie suggested, gesturing to the far side of the room, away from the kitchen.

"It's dark . . ."

"We could go upstairs."

There was a long pause. Emma couldn't seem to drag her gaze from Allen, who'd flicked her a look, aware of her odd behavior.

"Emma, come on." Jamie would have pulled her arm, except that never worked with her. It only made things worse.

"I see his eyes . . ." she intoned flatly.

Jamie caught her breath. "Emma!" she said sharply.

"*I see his eyes!*" she yelled, ignoring Jamie's attempts to distract her.

"Emma, stop!" Jamie snapped.

It didn't do any good. "*I see his eyes! I see his eyes!*" she cried. Then she lifted her arm and pointed a shaking finger at Allen, who stood in stunned surprise, his mouth dropping open.

Jamie gave Allen a hard glance. She tried to see what Emma saw, but Allen was just a young man in Gold Appliance coveralls and boots, his name stitched on a front tag, looking at them through blue eyes wide with shock. To

Jamie's knowledge, Emma had never actually pointed at anyone before.

"That's Allen. Our dishwasher repairman. We have a new dishwasher. He's helping us," Jamie told her.

Emma's lips started trembling and Duchess, picking up on her distress, started growling. The dog stared Allen down, as if he were a criminal.

"No. No, Duchess. Emma, we're going upstairs." Jamie spoke sternly. "Emma, do you hear me? We're going upstairs *now*."

Emma came out of her trance. She blinked several times, then turned blindly toward the stairs, accidentally knocking one of Mom's pictures cockeyed on the wall. She stopped, straightened it, then marched upstairs. Duchess didn't want to give up on Allen and barked at Jamie.

"Go on up," Jamie shooed her.

Reluctantly, the dog finally dropped her protective stance and obeyed, trotting up the stairs after her mistress.

Once they were alone, Allen looked at Jamie and asked, "What was that?" He was clearly shaken.

"I'm sorry. My sister has cognitive issues. It sometimes happens this way."

"I didn't mean to scare her."

"No, it's really not you. It's just . . . I'll go up and see that she's okay."

"Okay." He turned back to his work.

Jamie climbed up the stairs, throwing a look back down at Allen. What had Emma seen? Something about him. It couldn't be about Allen himself. He was way too young to have had anything to do with Emma and what had happened to her. Was it his eyes that had cued her? Their color or shape? Something about his looks, or being? Her reaction was definitely different than anything Jamie'd seen before.

She knocked on Emma's closed bedroom door. "Emma? Can I come in?"

No response.

"Emma?"

Footsteps, and then Emma cracked open the door. "Is he still there?"

"He'll be gone soon."

"He's not the guy."

"The guy? I know he's not. . . . He's the repairman, Emma. Just the repairman."

"He's not the guy," she repeated.

"Good. I'm glad. He's just the repairman. Can I come in, Emma?"

Emma stepped back from the door and pulled it open, then she latched it behind Jamie quickly. "I don't want him here, but he's not the guy."

"I agree. But . . . what guy do you mean? The one . . . with the . . . eyes that scare you?"

She shivered.

"Is it the man who hurt you whose eyes you see?"

Her teeth started chattering and she shoved her knuckles in her mouth. It took a few moments, but then she was able to pull her fist back and say, "It wasn't Cooper Haynes. It was the other one."

This was more than Jamie had ever heard before. Mouth dry, she asked, "Was it one of Cooper's friends?" When she didn't answer, Jamie asked, "One of your classmates from high school?"

"No."

"No?"

Emma went to her bed and Duchess followed. She patted the comforter and the dog jumped onto the bed beside her. Emma then practically buried her face in Duchess's fur. Duchess licked her hand and settled down.

"Emma . . . ?"

"I don't want to talk, talk, talk," was the muffled answer.

"Could I ask one more question? Just one more? Are the

eyes you see, the eyes of the man who came after you when you were babysitting?"

Emma didn't respond. Jamie hesitated, wondering how far she should push. Her cell phone dinged that she had a text. She ignored it for the moment, deciding to try once more.

"Emma, when you 'see his eyes' are you talking about the man who stabbed you?"

"You should leave me alone now. Mom knew."

"What did Mom know?"

"She knew." Emma heaved a deep sigh, then slowly lifted her head. "She has money for me. For when I go to Ridge Pointe."

Emma had said something like this before. Jamie hated to break it to her, but their mother did not have enough money to send Emma to the nearest assisted living facility to their home in River Glen.

"I don't know if that's going to happen," Jamie began.

"Goodbye." Emma cut her off.

Jamie knew she wasn't getting anything further out of her sister. She stepped back into the hallway, closing Emma's door behind her. Back downstairs, she was glad to see Allen was making real progress. She wanted to apologize again for her sister, but decided enough had been said.

Remembering the text, she plucked her phone from her back pocket and saw it was from Cooper.

See you in thirty?

Yes, she texted back. Thirty minutes would give her enough time to let Harley know that she was heading out and to make certain Emma was aware of what was going on as well.

* * *

Bette Kearns poured herself a glass of Pinot Gris and let her tears fall into the light gold depths. She drank the wine with the tears. Why not? What good would it do to pour herself another only to have the same thing happen?

She wandered back into the living room. Joy had run away to a friend's house overnight and Alex was with his buddies, doing their "garage band" stuff, which Bette thought was cute but Phil believed was a waste of time when you could be involved in sports. Bette knew her friends felt the same way, though they'd never said so. If your son wasn't in football, what good was he?

She snorted and swiped at her rainfall of tears. She'd started to dry up, but then she thought of Phil with that *whore* and she wanted to throw herself on the floor and beat her fists or pull out her hair or take a fistful of Valium or . . . drink another bottle of wine. She was almost through the first.

She wandered to the sliding doors that led out to the back patio. They had a nice view of one of the rivers that fed into the Willamette, East Glen River, from which River Glen derived its name. Their house wasn't in a new development, but it had character.

And if you divorce, you lose all this . . .

And that *whore* gets it all.

There was some faulty logic in there, Bette recognized, though she was starting to feel distinctly fuzzy. Good. She wanted to quit thinking about Phil on top of that *whore* with the big boobs and lush, golden-brown hair and catlike eyes. That woman just oozed sex. And Dara, the little slut, was going to be just like her.

Bette allowed herself a moment of supreme jealousy.

You fuck around, too. . . .

"That's what happens when your husband stops looking at you that way," she said on a quiet sob.

She gazed at herself in the bathroom mirror. There were hardly any wrinkles. Victoria had far more than she did, although Botox did for her what nature could no longer provide. But Bette believed she looked ten years younger than any of her friends and, well, she could still turn the heads of younger men. Case in point: Ted Ryerson.

"Call me Teddy," he'd whispered to her when he'd been pounding into her against the wall of his bedroom. She'd been worried the kids would come home, but his sister had taken them out to a movie and he'd assured her they would be alone for a while. She'd learned he had quite a sexual appetite, which had been fine with her. She'd mentioned as much to Victoria once, who'd croaked out a laugh. "Didn't we all once?" and then, "Sounds like he takes after his old man."

Bette had questioned that, and Victoria had said Dr. William Ryerson was known for screwing his patients and being a bit free with his prescriptions, so maybe there was a little quid pro quo going on, pills for sex? That was one of the rumors going around before he left town, although it had never been substantiated.

She wondered if she should call Teddy now. She felt broken. How could Phil take up with that *whore* when he wouldn't even have sex with his own wife? Was she that pathetic?

Her vision blurred with tears. She knew her eyes and nose were red from crying. No. She would not call Teddy now.

But she would refill her empty glass.

She walked back inside. She tried to close the slider, but it stuck a little. Fuck it. She was heading outside again as soon as she opened another bottle anyway.

She caught a glimpse of herself in the stylized mirror above the wine refrigerator. A sun made out of shards of glass that radiated from a center point. She sniffed. She looked terrible.

She bent down and searched in the undercounter refrigerator for a bottle of Pinot Gris. Lots of red, Phil The Bastard's favorite. No Pinot Gris. But there was a rosé left over from the summer . . . from that little patio party she'd had for the girls. That was before Jamie Whatever-her-name-was had been invited to their group. She'd had a pink tablecloth and her best china and they'd drunk themselves silly over canapés and desserts.

But when Jamie Whatever had shown up something had changed. Not just because she was turning Cooper Haynes's head, as Jill and Victoria had told her, but because everybody who'd gone to River Glen High seemed weirded out about Jamie's sister, and the tragedy that had befallen her. Bette had heard the story from Phil, which had been corroborated by her friends, though none of 'em wanted to talk about it that much.

Emma Whelan's ghost hung over them all . . . even though Emma was still alive.

But . . . but . . . *Phil* and that *whore* . . . Her heart ached. No, she didn't want a divorce. What could she do, then?

"You can't have one," she muttered aloud, twisting off the screw-top. Amazing how good some of these twist-top wines were these days.

She refilled her glass and screwed the top back on the bottle, then bent down again to put it back in its slot so that it stayed cold. She stumbled a bit, accidentally, hit her cell phone on the counter, spinning it around to where it nearly fell to the floor. The door shot back on its hinges, slamming into the cupboard. Luckily, she'd left her glass on the counter and it was intact.

"Shit."

She stood up.

In the mirror shards, she saw a tall, masked figure standing behind her. A ski mask. Bette automatically whipped around and saw the knife.

She screamed, and he slashed at her. She backed up, kept on screaming, her hand hitting her wineglass, grabbing it as it fell. He charged her, and she threw the glass at him, hitting him in the head. He stumbled. She tried to turn, slipped, and her knee buckled as he slashed forward. Missed her face. Jabbed her throat. He drew back, and Bette reached up in shock, covered the wound with her hand. Her other hand was gripping the edge of the counter. She was sinking, sinking. Her fingers moved, slipped a bit, touched her phone.

Her attacker had fallen back. He lifted the knife again, caught sight of himself in the sunburst mirror, and hesitated. Bette used the moment to grab her phone. She hit Favorites and pressed randomly. Got Victoria's number.

Her attacker came at her again.

"Call 9-1-1," Bette whispered as she fell to the floor. "He's in my house . . . I'm dying. . . ."

Chapter Twenty-Three

"What's so urgent?" Dug Douglas growled into the phone as Cooper drove over to Jamie's.

Cooper had answered the phone even though he hadn't recognized the number. Teri, Dug's wife, must've gotten him Cooper's message. He jumped right in with, "Race told me he circled back to the Ryersons' the night Emma was attacked but couldn't find you."

"Oh, for . . ." He cut himself off. "So, what of it? Now you're going to say I'm the guy who attacked her?"

"You and Race lied. To us, and to the police."

"Race lied," he corrected.

A fine distinction. "He told you he came back for you. You both held back vital information."

"So what? You fucking cops. All you wanna do is bust people. You don't care about the truth."

"Race said he saw somebody in a ski mask."

Dug grunted. "Yeah, he told me the same."

"He's not just making that up? You're not making that up together?"

"Hell no. What the fuck, man?"

"Marissa was attacked by a guy in a ski mask."

"So?"

"It just seems kind of convenient."

"I don't know what you're getting at, but Race told me—"

Cooper's cell started buzzing. He had another call coming in. From the station.

"—at the time that he saw this guy in a ski mask, in the neighborhood. I didn't see him. I walked home, and it took a long fucking time, let me tell you. You want to know more, talk to Race."

"I've got a call coming in that I need to take."

Dug snorted his disgust. "I'm done talking anyway."

"We're not finished," said Cooper.

"Yeah, we are." He clicked off.

Cooper answered his call and learned a 911 call had come in from Victoria Stapleton about a possible attack at the Kearns'.

He'd just turned onto Jamie's street, but now he kept going right by her house. At the first opportunity, he circled back around and headed for the Kearns' home, the second time in as many days. He called Jamie and had to cancel their date. She sounded let down and he swore it was work.

"The life of a policeman," she said lightly.

"I've got an emergency. It's . . . it happens. I'm sorry. I'm not sure how long it'll take."

"Okay."

He was left with the feeling she didn't believe him. He wanted to call her right back and plead his case, but it wouldn't do any good. He focused instead on the task at hand.

He arrived at the house just as the ambulance was pulling away. "What have we got?" he asked Crake, the officer in charge.

"Attacked with a knife. Stabbed in the throat, but she's still alive. Missed the carotids, maybe nicked one?"

"Bette Kearns?"

"That's what it looks like."

Cooper's phone buzzed again and he glanced at it as he

headed into the house. Another number he didn't recognize. He answered abruptly, "Haynes."

"Cooper?" A woman's voice, quavering, half-hysterical.

"Who is this?" he snapped.

"Victoria . . . Stapleton. Bette called me and I called 9-1-1. She said she was dying!" Her voice rose in panic.

"Take it easy. Take a breath," he advised quickly.

"He's at her house! You've got to go there!"

"I'm here. I'm on the scene. Tell me what happened. . . ."

"Oh . . . okay . . . you're there? Good. She called me. Is she okay? Is she okay?"

"She's in an ambulance, on her way to the hospital."

"But she's alive?"

"Yes."

Victoria broke down and sobbed with relief as Cooper, recognizing she would be little help, quickly got off the phone.

Jamie stood frozen in place from where she'd been loading the new dishwasher for the first time. Vicky had just called and begged her for Cooper's number, saying there was an attack on Bette, that she wanted to talk to Cooper and knew Jamie would probably have his number. Jamie had given her the cell information, then asked her what she was talking about, but Vicky was already off the phone.

Jamie had a pretty good idea that this emergency was what had taken Cooper away. She was selfishly glad that his reason had been legit. She was used to Paul's inveterate lies about almost everything, especially if he'd felt she would get in the way of whatever he wanted to do. But she was stunned about Vicky's news. Bette? *Attacked?* How? Was she okay?

"Mom?"

Jamie looked over at Harley without really seeing her. Her head was too full of terrible, imagined pictures.

"Can I talk to you a minute?"

Jamie came back to the moment with a bang. She examined her daughter. Harley's face was taut with tension. "What happened?"

"Nothing." A return of the old spark. "Nothing to me anyway," she said. Her shoulders slumped and she moved the toe of her sneaker on the floor.

"Tell me." With an effort, Jamie pushed her immediate fears for Bette aside and motioned Harley to come sit down at the kitchen table. Harley moved like an automaton, seating herself stiffly on one of the chairs. "What's this about?"

"I told you I liked a guy . . ."

"Yes. Greer Douglas."

"You don't have to say it like that," she objected. "He's not *bad*. He went there to see me. He told me so. And I couldn't be there because of Marissa's mom."

"He and Troy Stillwell pranked her."

"But they didn't go after her! That wasn't them!"

"Okay."

"You don't believe me." Harley subsided into injured silence.

Jamie exhaled. Tried to stay in the moment. "All I know is that someone came after Marissa. I'm not blaming the boys. I don't know what happened. I'm just . . . I don't want you to get in some kind of trouble because of all this."

"How would I get in trouble?"

"I don't know. Bad choices could be made?" Harley glared at her, and Jamie lifted her hands in surrender. "I'll reserve judgment."

"Will you?" She'd been looking down at the table, and now she gazed at her from the tops of her eyes.

"I'll try. That's it. That's all I can offer."

Harley thought that over. She chewed on her lower lip, clearly working something out. Jamie waited. It seemed to take forever, and Jamie was on pins and needles anyway, before Harley exhaled heavily and said, "I think Tyler was there, too."

"At the . . . Ryersons? Pranking Marissa?"

"He was with them, but then he wasn't. Greer didn't say it exactly, but there's maybe another girl he's seeing besides Dara? Tyler was looking for her that night?"

"You're not saying he went into the house and—"

"No. I don't know. I don't think so. I think he was . . ." She made a face and said in a higher voice, "Maybe using them as cover?"

"For . . . ?"

"Drinking and having sex with this other girl?"

Jamie held her daughter's gaze. "And they don't want to rat out their friend and have him maybe off the team, or at least mad at them for telling? Neither of them thinks that Tyler went after Marissa, but somebody did, and they're worried they'll get blamed for it."

Harley nodded. "Yeah . . ."

"And Greer Douglas let you know this because . . . he likes you?"

She lowered her lashes. "I don't know."

"Or because he knows you're connected to Marissa and her dad and maybe thinks you can help get both of them off the hook?"

Harley jerked involuntarily, and Jamie realized she'd scored a direct hit, at least to her daughter's psyche. "But they didn't do it," Harley insisted.

"Do they know who did? Have some idea, at least?"

"No . . . I don't know."

"Does Marissa know this?"

"I don't know."

"I think you need to tell Cooper."

She looked at Jamie in horror. "No! I can't. They'll know it was me!"

"Maybe they want you to tell him."

"*No!* You can't tell. You promised!"

"I didn't promise anything."

She leaped to her feet. "If you tell him, I'll never tell you anything again. I never will! I promise!"

"Harley, this is a police matter."

"No, it's not! They didn't do it! And neither did Tyler! He just cheated on Dara. That's all!"

"His mother says he was home that night with them."

"And Dara says he was with her, but it's not because of Marissa. It was cheating. That's all."

"Who's the girl?"

"*I don't know!*"

"But you have an idea. And if you give me a name, I can go from that angle."

"What'll you do?" Harley stared at her.

"I'll check with the mom. Find out what's going on. See what I can learn. I'm not a cop, I'm just a person, a concerned parent."

"Mom . . ."

"What?" Jamie was starting to feel impatient.

"Greer said . . . this girl is kind of a thief."

"Thief, meaning . . . ?"

"She knows how to get into houses where she was a babysitter and steals stuff. She babysat these people with a dog . . . she babysat the dog . . . and after that, she could go in and steal money and booze and stuff. . . ."

"What's her name?"

Tears filled her eyes. "She's one of Marissa's friends. Katie Timbolt. Marissa doesn't know about her."

"Harley. The police need to know."

"You said you wouldn't tell. You promised!"

"You keep saying that, but it's not true. Cooper needs to know."

"You said you'd come at it from another angle!"

"Don't you see it's bigger than that?"

Harley turned away from her and ran for the stairs.

"Harley . . ."

"*Leave me alone.*"

Jamie's temper began to rise. She forced herself not to chase after her daughter.

Cooper's phone rang again as he was waiting for the tech team to arrive to go over the scene for evidence. He was making sure the room wasn't trampled any further. He saw that the call was from Jamie and was going to press the button to answer when one of River Glen PD's SUVs pulled up with a squeal of tires and Howie slammed out.

Cooper sent the call to voice mail.

"I was on my way home and got the message. What happened?" Howie asked.

Cooper explained about Bette being attacked, Vicky getting the message and calling 911, and Cooper arriving to see Bette already in the ambulance.

"Was she conscious?" Howie asked.

"Not really. I didn't get near her. They were working on her."

"What happened?"

They walked into the house together and looked at the large patch of blood soaked into the living room carpet. Both of them stayed ten feet away. "Any security cameras?" Howie asked.

"No. There's an alarm system, but it wasn't activated."

Howie grunted.

"Victoria Stapleton said Bette said she was being stabbed,"

Cooper revealed. "I think we should send someone to the Stapleton house. She was on the edge of hysteria."

"Want me to go? You got this handled?"

"Yeah, I'm just waiting for the techs." Their department was too small to have its own crime scene investigators, so they relied on the county to provide the forensic team.

"Okay. I'll check with you later."

As soon as he was gone, Cooper listened to the message from Jamie. "I'm sorry to bother you," she apologized. "Vicky called for your number and I think you might be helping Bette. . . . I just have some other information. When you're free, call me. Thanks."

He wondered what that information was. His mind automatically went back to what Dug had said. Was it true, or was it mixed with lies?

The tech team arrived and began setting up. Cooper knew Ray McClane and brought him up-to-date on what he'd learned, which wasn't a hell of a lot at this point. He then left McClane and his team and headed to Glen Gen where Bette Kearns was in emergency surgery. Her husband had been called and gave them the okay; she'd needed immediate attention. He was on his way to the hospital.

About the time Cooper learned that information, Phil showed up, looking wild-eyed. Spying Cooper, he strode over to stop directly in front of him in the waiting area outside of the OR. "What happened?" he demanded. "What happened?"

Cooper assessed the man carefully, looking for tells. The last time he'd seen Phil was as he was leaving the house, virtually kicked out, his wife screaming at him about his purported affair with another woman, an accusation he hadn't denied. Spouses had killed over less.

"Bette's in surgery?" Phil gazed around the room.

"They sent her from ER straight to the OR," said Cooper.

"What the hell happened?" he asked, his shoulders slumping. He looked like he'd been running on pure adrenaline and had just run out.

"Until we talk to Bette, we won't know for sure. Victoria Stapleton got a call from her, asking that she call 9-1-1. Bette said she'd been stabbed . . . and that she was dying."

Phil sank down heavily in the nearest chair. "Oh, God."

"Phil . . ."

"Yeah?"

"Can you prove where you were at about six-thirty tonight?"

Phil raised dread-filled eyes to Cooper. "You can't think I had anything to do with this."

If the man was acting, he was giving an Oscar-worthy performance. "If Bette can identify her attacker, it won't be necessary. Otherwise, it would just be easiest to cross you off the list."

"But you don't think she can identify him."

"I don't know yet. It's usually the first thing out of a victim's mouth, unless they're covering for them."

"I was at my hotel alone," he said.

"Did you use your cell phone?" Cooper asked, knowing it could help prove where he was by where it was located and to whom he was communicating.

He slowly shook his head. "I was thinking about the kids. How to tell them. Well, Joy obviously already knows, but I was just sitting in my room, not even watching TV." He looked toward the OR doors. "Who would do this? I don't understand." A moment later, Cooper saw him blink as a thought hit him.

"What?" asked Cooper.

"Volker. Meghan's ex-husband. He still thinks he owns her."

Bette had remarked that Volker was a jealous ex. "What's Volker's first name?"

"Eric."

Cooper stepped away from Kearns and called Howie. "You at the Stapletons'?"

"Yeah, but they've got everything under control. The wife, Victoria, looks sedated. Nice house here. West end, outside of Staffordshire, but old school nice, y'know?"

"Lawrence Stapleton makes money in real estate development. The wife's a real estate agent," Cooper said. "Can you sit on the hospital? Bette Kearns is in surgery. Her husband's here, but I want to interview another guy."

"Phil Kearns, your classmate, is at the hospital?" asked Howie.

"Yeah. I want one of us to be there when Bette first wakes up. I could call Verbena."

"Let's give her a night off," said Howie, which was Cooper's way of thinking, too. "Okay, I'll be there in about twenty."

Cooper walked back to where Phil was seated, staring at the floor. Before Cooper could alert him that Howie was on his way to the hospital, Phil said, "I should tell my kids. They should be here in case . . . in case . . ." He buried his head in his hands.

While he was waiting for Howie, Cooper called Jamie back. "Just wanted to let you know I got your message, and yes, I'm on the Kearns case."

"Is Bette all right?" Jamie asked anxiously.

"She's in surgery. That's all I know."

"She was attacked . . . ?" She asked the question as if she really didn't want to know the answer.

"That's what I understand."

"I know you can't talk about it. I'm just worried. Bette's an acquaintance, but one of the few people I know. I'm just . . . stunned . . . and worried."

"In your message you said you had some information for me?"

Jamie exhaled a long breath. "Oh. Well. It's on something else. My daughter wanted me to swear not to tell, but I'm going to. Probably a bad idea for our relationship, but I think you need to know. . . ." She then related that a friend of Marissa's appeared to be burglarizing the houses of people whom she'd babysat for and possibly sleeping with Tyler Stapleton behind his girlfriend's back and also making Tyler an accomplice to her crimes. When Jamie mentioned stealing liquor, Cooper went right to the Tito's vodka bottle. If there were fingerprints on the smooth glass surface, maybe there would be a match.

He said, "I know of a theft of liquor, but the people who live in the house don't have any children."

"Harley said this girl, Katie, also babysat a dog."

Cooper had an immediate vision of Marissa's friend, Katie Timbolt, whose mother, Cathy, was running for school board and whose senior daughter was on the short list for valedictorian. The political blowback on this would be big, if it were true. "How'd Harley get this information?" he asked.

"A friend . . ."

"Not Marissa."

"No. Harley says Marissa doesn't know." She paused for a moment, then added, "She also said Dara Volker told her she was with Tyler last Saturday, which, according to Harley, wasn't the truth."

"Dara's protecting him? Maybe doesn't know about Katie?"

"Maybe . . . But also, um, Vicky made a point of saying her son was home with the family that night."

Cooper had also heard Vicky spell that out multiple times, leaving Greer Douglas and Troy Stillwell to face the music. "Does . . . Harley's source . . . have any feeling that Tyler was the intruder who came after Marissa?"

"I don't think so. What I'm hearing . . . what she's saying by not saying it . . . is that the boys have been covering for Tyler for this other thing. Not the attack on Marissa. That's separate, and they're adamant they were never involved with that."

That was how Howie had described Greer and Troy in the interviews he'd had with them: adamant that they weren't involved in the Ryerson home invasion targeting Marissa. He would bet Harley's mystery caller was one of the boys involved, either Greer or Troy, which also meant other kids were likely to know about Tyler's extracurricular activities. Maybe Dara Volker herself. He doubted Vicky and her tribe would cover for Tyler if they knew what he may have been up to.

May, might, maybe . . .

He needed to learn the truth about Tyler Stapleton. And he also needed to know if it had any bearing on the attack on Marissa.

"I'm on my way to the Volkers' now," said Cooper, which caused Jamie to sweep in a sharp breath.

"You're going to ask Dara straight up?"

"Nothing like that. I'm going there for a separate reason. The Bette Kearns case."

"Oh," she said. "Of course. I don't understand what happened there. It's all terrible, but she's going to be okay."

She didn't seem to be looking for a response and he couldn't give her one anyway. "I still want to take you to dinner . . . in fact . . ." He trailed off, realizing he was getting way ahead of himself.

"What?"

"Never mind, I'll—"

"No, what?" she insisted. "You were going to say something."

"I was going to say I'm planning on going to Bend to interview William Ryerson. I was going to call him, but a face-to-face is better, and after all this time, I want everything he'll give me. That's easier in person; he won't be able to just get off the phone. I'm thinking about heading out tomorrow for the day."

"And . . . ?"

"And . . ." He trailed off again.

"And you want me to go with you?" Jamie finished for him.

She was way too perceptive. He thought of a lot of things he could say. Some kind of long-winded explanation. In the end, he said simply, "Yes."

"I'd love to. What time?"

"I've got to make sure I can do it," he said, thinking of Bette Kearns, and also that he'd not contacted Ryerson to find out whether he was available. A lot of ifs.

"When will you know?"

"Tonight. Later. I'll call you as soon as I do."

"Okay," she said

"Okay," he said back.

Bette Kearns was quicker than I'd thought she'd be. Smarter. I am ashamed of myself because I couldn't finish what I started. I had to hurry out of there. But I thought she'd die by now anyway. These women . . . these women who lie and cheat and feel no compunction!

Bette is the worst of them . . . No. Not the worst. Just the most blatant, the most active. Emma was the worst.

Will they make me do more? I don't want to . . . I really don't want to . . . but if they make me . . .

My head hurts with the thought. I press my hands to the sides of my head and hold myself together.

Gwen wants another appointment with me. I haven't been "serious" about my problems. She knows. Deep down, she knows. Has she heard about Bette yet? If not, what will she do when she finds out?

I don't want to contemplate killing her.

But it doesn't matter. The victims, the men, need to be avenged.

Chapter Twenty-Four

Cooper learned Eric Volker's number and address from the police database. The man had moved into an apartment about a mile and a half from where Meghan and Dara Volker now lived. Neither living arrangement was in River Glen's chichi West End, nowhere near Staffordshire Estates. The house was a two-bedroom ranch in a quiet neighborhood and the apartment was on the east edge of River Glen near Portland's westside city limits.

On his way to Eric Volker's, Cooper put in a call to both Dr. William Ryerson in Bend and Nadine Ryerson Campbell in Bellevue. He got them both, and when he explained that he was looking into the twenty-year-old attack on Emma Whelan, they both sounded underwhelmed about meeting with him. Understandable, but he wasn't going to let that deter him. He made an appointment with Ryerson for Saturday and Nadine for Sunday. At first, she turned him down, but as the interview looked like it was getting pushed into the workweek, she'd changed her mind.

Cooper called Volker on his cell, but he didn't pick up. When he got to his apartment, he found Eric was not at home. Volker called him back just as he was getting into his SUV and said he was at the River Glen Pirate's game in

Gresham, on the other side of the Willamette River and a good forty-five minutes away even without traffic. From the background noise, it appeared he was telling the truth. Easily found out. And if Volker had been there at kickoff, he couldn't have attacked Bette.

Dara was also at the game, but Meghan Volker was home and answered Cooper's call by inviting him over. He demurred. She was an outside cog and he wanted to make plans for the next day with Jamie. But then he realized he was putting off the woman when she might offer up something about her ex-husband, or Phil Kearns, or maybe even Bette, that would give him insight. Maybe, maybe not. But not meeting with her could very well just be putting her off.

He almost called Jamie again. He hadn't told her what Race had said about the man in the ski mask. His more immediate issues were the attack on Bette, which could or could not relate to the attack on Marissa, the possibility that both Dara Volker and Vicky Stapleton had lied about Tyler Stapleton's whereabouts the night of the attack on Marissa, and the rumor that Tyler had been with Katie Timbolt for a night of sex, burglary, and vandalism. A lot of mischievous, dangerous, and downright evil doings for River Glen, where the occasional bust of teen drinking and recreational drugs, DUIs and accidental deaths, made up the bulk of his detective work.

He kept himself from calling Jamie, though the urge was strong. He realized he'd already moved her to a level of trust he rarely allowed with other women. If he wasn't careful, she would be as close to him as a lover and they hadn't even shared one kiss. He was already thinking of her as a partner in some ways.

Meghan Volker met him at the door. Her hair was long and lush. Her dress was low-cut and short, revealing shapely legs. Her shoes were black platforms with tiny ankle straps.

Her lips and face were Botox or something similar. She looked well put together, but there was that element of fakery in the background that somehow could never be fully erased.

"Detective Haynes," she greeted him with a small smile.

She'd made a play for him once, shortly after he and Laura split. She'd been still hooked in with her now-ex at the time, and Cooper had steered clear even though she possessed a kind of tractor-beam pull that reached into his male core. He'd needed his bruised ego soothed some, but luckily, he'd kept his head. Not so a number of other men. And Eric Volker had gotten in physical fights with most of them.

She invited him in and led him to a living room done all in white with black accoutrements: a pole lamp straight out of the sixties, a lacquered tray upon which a silver carafe and two wineglasses sat, a white, fuzzy, wool throw draped across the end of an ottoman.

"What can I help you with?" she asked. "Would you like a drink? It would only take me a jiff to shake up some martinis."

"Thanks, I'm fine."

"Yes . . . but do you need a drink?" Again the small smile. It was clearly a practiced line.

"Bette Kearns was attacked by someone this evening in her home. She's in the hospital, in surgery."

The smile disappeared. She blinked in shock. "That's why you want to . . . talk about Eric?"

"You knew about his relationship with Bette?"

"I don't keep tabs on him, but he's Dara's father and he sees her occasionally. . . . Hospital? What happened to her? To Bette?"

"She was stabbed in the throat."

"Oh my God!" She'd perched on the edge of the ottoman and now she jumped to her feet. "Well, it wasn't Eric! He's a brawler, not a killer. I mean, yes, he's punched people, but it's . . . not like *that*!"

"What's it like?"

"It's a game. That's all. He's a caveman. Wants to hold on to his woman. He picks fights with my dates. I don't like it," she added quickly, though Cooper was thinking that she liked it very much, "but I can't control him. He's stepped over the line a time or two, but he would never hurt a woman."

"Would he enter a rival's house, expecting to confront him, and run into the wife instead?"

"Of course not! Okay, maybe he'd go in, as I said, but he would never hurt a woman. Never."

"He's never hurt you?"

"No . . ." She turned away, taking a few steps toward the kitchen. The tenor of her voice had changed, however. "I don't know why you're blaming this on Eric," she tossed over her shoulder, now sounding angry. "What about her husband? Phil?"

"We're talking to him. He told his wife he was seeing you."

"Well . . . it's only been a few dates. He's still married."

"He made it sound like more."

"You talked to him about it?" she accused.

"He told his wife he was going to marry you and that he'd already talked it over with Eric."

She whipped her head around to look at him, clearly surprised. "*Phil* talked to Eric?"

"That's what he said."

"Well, it's not true. Eric would never stand for that."

There was a gold-filigreed clock atop the white fireplace mantel, the only other color in the black-and-white room. He saw it was closing in on nine p.m. He sensed he'd gotten all he could out of Meghan Volker, and though he still needed to interview her ex-husband, he thought he had a pretty good idea of what was going on between Eric and his ex-wife. Did it rise to the level of an attack on Bette Kearns? He doubted it. It wasn't part of their game. But could she have gotten in the way between Eric and Phil? Possibly. Although this seemed like something else.

Cooper thanked Meghan for seeing him, then headed for the door.

"That's it?" she asked, peeved.

"For now."

On the way out, he put in a call to Howie, who said Bette was through surgery and doing okay, as far as he could tell. Phil had called his children. Alex had rushed over and was at the hospital already and Joy was being brought over by the friend's family with whom she had been spending the night.

"I'll come spell you," Cooper said. He wanted to be there when Bette woke up. He wanted to be the first to hear what she had to say.

"All righty." Howie didn't argue.

Cooper got another call. He saw it was from Vicky Stapleton. He answered and she said thickly, "How's Bette? Is she okay? Oh, please tell me she's okay."

Cooper explained that she was out of surgery and he was on his way to the hospital now.

Vicky said, "Oh, good. *Good.* I'll go see her in the morning; is that all right?"

"Depends on what her doctor says."

"I'll call the hospital first. Thank you, Cooper." As she was hanging up, he heard her say to someone else, "No . . . he couldn't play . . . my head is so dull . . ."

Clearly Vicky hadn't attended the game because Tyler wasn't tonight's quarterback. Maybe Coach Padilla had learned something of Tyler's suspected illegal activities the previous weekend. Marissa hadn't gone to the away football game either. Laura had insisted she stay close to home, but Cooper had talked to Marissa and she'd shown no signs of interest anyway. He understood she was scared about what had happened to her. He wanted her to take as much time as she needed. He just didn't want her to pull away so far that it would be hard to come back again.

I'm gonna find that asshole.

He set his jaw. Whoever had hurt Marissa would pay.

Ten minutes later Cooper pushed through the hospital doors to the waiting area outside the OR where the Kearns kids were seated in the chairs, looking glassy-eyed. Howie was talking to one of the nurses. Upon seeing Cooper, Howie waved him over.

"This is Nurse Cargill—Angie—and she says Bette just woke up. She's having trouble talking, but she's coherent."

Angie said, "We told her not to talk."

"But she did manage to say something first, right?" Howie looked at the nurse. "Tell him," he said.

Nurse Angie pursed her lips, seemed to want to deny him, then turned to Cooper. "She said 'ski mask.'"

Cooper's blood ran cold. "Anything else?"

"No. Just that."

Cooper absorbed that in silence. Amazing how all roads led back to the ski mask.

He phoned Jamie and spoke to her briefly. "I'm going to have to postpone meeting with Ryerson. I need to be in River Glen right now." He told her Bette was through surgery and what she'd said. As Jamie absorbed that, he added, "I'll call you tomorrow. Maybe I can cut out a block of time and we could meet."

"I'd like that," she said warmly. Then, "Stay safe, Cooper."

* * *

Saturday morning dawned gray and gloomy with a mist in the air. It was a week before Halloween, but if there was ever a day that seemed fit for that holiday, it was today.

Jamie had spent a sleepless night after talking to Cooper. She was disappointed about the cancellation of the trip to Bend, but not surprised. There was too much going on in River Glen for Cooper to chase after a cold case. Also, it would have been tricky for her to leave for an entire day as well, abandoning Emma and Harley to their own devices. That was a recipe for disaster.

Didn't mean she didn't want to go. She'd managed to hide her disappointment. It was way out of proportion to an un-planned trip that had just popped up. Still, it was gratifying to know Cooper wanted to take her somewhere. It just couldn't happen in the midst of two home invasions in River Glen within six days of each other. Cooper was bound to be involved with a police department as small as theirs; it was all hands on deck.

She glanced at the oven clock. 6:11. Before she'd learned for certain the trip to Bend was scratched, she'd texted Camryn: Any chance you could babysit Emma and Harley tomorrow?

"Babysit" was the wrong word. She'd been thinking of correcting herself when the text from Camryn came back: Oh, I wish I could but I've got company.

Jamie had thought about checking with Theo; maybe after Emma and her shift, Theo might come over and take care of Emma for a few hours more, but then Cooper had called everything off.

She was pouring herself a cup of coffee when Emma and Duchess came downstairs and headed outside together. "You're up early," Jamie observed.

"Duchess needs out," she said.

A few minutes later, Emma and the dog stepped back

inside. Emma was shivering when she entered the kitchen. "Cold out there," she said, and then, looking Jamie up and down, added, "Where are you going?"

Jamie hadn't said anything about her plans and her clothes were her usual jeans and a sweater, so she said, "I'm not going anywhere."

"Why are you so happy?" Emma asked, carefully preparing Duchess's bowl of dry dog food. Each bit of kibble had to be carefully added to create an even amount. Duchess dove past her as soon as the bowl was on the ground and kernels went flying.

"I don't know that I'm happy . . ." She'd purposely kept the range of bad things that had happened in the past week from Emma, though she wasn't certain how long that could continue.

"Is it because of Cooper?"

Jamie was saved from answering when her phone beeped for an incoming text. She glanced at the screen and saw it was from Vicky: We're all going to see Bette at the hospital this morning at about ten.

Jamie could well imagine how Bette's doctors might feel about a posse of women descending on her. Getting in to see her was likely a pipe dream, and she really felt she should stay away until she learned more about Bette's condition.

However, Vicky had given her a golden opportunity to have a talk with her.

She texted back: Good. Any chance we could meet for coffee first?

Vicky wrote back a few moments later: How about nineish at the Coffee Club, off Aspen Court? I'll let everyone know.

"Perfect," Jamie said aloud, texting back.

Emma slid her a look. "Be careful," she warned.

"I'm just meeting Vicky for coffee."

She wagged her head slowly back and forth while she dipped into her cereal with her spoon. She was still wagging it as Jamie left the room and headed upstairs. A frisson slid down her back, a cold finger of fear. Sometimes Emma's ESP-like sentience was downright spooky.

Harley rolled out of bed early and took a shower and washed her hair. She felt grody and miserable. A hell of a week. Hearing from Greer just before the team took off for the away game had surprised her. He'd never called her cell before. But his message had been serious stuff, and a part of her wondered if she was being played: Give the new girl enough information to hang herself and see if she tells her mom.

Well, she had told Mom. If this was a setup of some kind, so be it.

He called you!

Even all her second-guessing of his motives couldn't totally blunt the fact that Greer had called her.

You. You. *Harley Woodward. Greer Douglas called* you!

What he'd said about Tyler was sobering, though. Okay, he hadn't *said* it, he'd just hinted. Strongly. Tyler was screwing around with Katie . . . *Katie* . . . whom Marissa had known since grade school. Katie's mom was running for a position on the school board, which decided all kinds of shit about the schools, and Marissa considered her a good friend, and both of those things were going to cause big trouble.

But Greer called you!

She drove the hairbrush through her hair in deep sweeps through the tangled strands. He'd wanted to know if she was coming to the football game. Without Marissa, Harley hadn't really had a way to go. She didn't know anybody well enough to ask for a ride. She had, for a really crazy moment, thought about calling Lena or Katie, but had chickened out, thank God. If Katie was really stealing, with or without Tyler—*could he really be with her?*—then Harley was lucky she'd stayed away.

Harley thought about her bathroom meeting with Dara. Did Dara know? She must suspect. Otherwise why would she say she was with Tyler last Saturday? Greer had said . . . *practically* said . . . that Tyler was with Katie and they'd broken into that house and stolen liquor and jewelry. Good God.

She quivered inside from head to toe, knowing she'd ratted them out to her mother. She regretted that. Had regretted it all night long. If Mom told . . . if the other kids found out, she'd be thrown out of the group. A pariah.

She already knew how that felt: terrible.

Cooper was in the station early, as were Howie and Elena Verbena. Elena's bouncy, dark curls were tied back and she looked fresh and ready to work. Howie, on the other hand, was wrinkled and yawning. Cooper, too, had spent a long night even after he'd gotten home, rethinking what had happened and writing up notes.

"I hope I look better than you," Cooper told him.

"I slept on the couch," Howie said. "Gonna take a shower here."

"You do look better, Coop," Verbena said. Then, to Howie, "What happened to you?"

"Wife's sister and husband are aboard the divorce train, so the sister and her kids moved in last night. I lost out on a bed." He glanced over at Cooper. "We're the interim hotel."

"A lot of that going around," Cooper said.

Howie picked up the small overnight bag he'd brought

with him and headed down the hall to the break room and the men's bathroom/locker room.

"Bring me up-to-date," Verbena said. She'd been almost pissed that they'd left her out of last night's events.

Cooper gave her the full run-down and a copy of his notes. She'd heard some of it, and Bennihof had called her this morning to ask her to be the liaison with the media. Marissa's intruder had gotten some play on the local station, but with Bette Kearns's attack, it had become more sensational. Cooper thought of the ski mask, which had yet to be made public. When it did, the shit would really hit the fan.

"I gotta make a phone call," he said, taking his cell and heading outside.

"Personal?" Verbena asked. It wasn't like Cooper to seek privacy for a call when it was police business.

"Yeah."

He phoned Jamie from outside the station's back door. She answered immediately, as if she'd had her phone in hand.

"Think we can get together, depending on how my day goes? Maybe we could make that dinner tonight."

"Sure," she said, brightly.

He could feel himself relax a bit. He yearned to be in her company. "I'll call or text this afternoon."

"Okay."

If Cooper came through on his dinner invitation—which she'd learned could change with the weather—that was more than okay. She'd fallen on Gwen as a possible babysitter, but hadn't called her yet. Now that it was only dinner, she could probably leave Emma and Harley for a while. Probably . . . or maybe Theo could stay late.

She looked up Gwen's number on her phone and called

her before she could change her mind. She hadn't talked to her since she'd had her session with Emma and wanted to touch base anyway.

Gwen's number went to voice mail. Both disappointed and somewhat relieved, Jamie left a message asking her to call her back. "No big message," she told her. "Just checking in."

Harley cruised into the kitchen. She was dressed and her hair was drying following a shower. After her heartfelt confession to Jamie the night before, she was being extremely quiet and circumspect.

"Everything okay?" Jamie asked, watching as Harley pulled down a bowl for cereal.

"Did you tell anybody what Greer said?" She poured Frosted Flakes into the bowl and turned to the refrigerator for milk.

When Jamie didn't answer immediately, Harley poured the milk on the cereal, set the half-empty plastic carton on the counter, slammed open the silverware drawer for a spoon, then sat down heavily in the chair and looked at Jamie accusingly.

"I told Cooper."

"Jesus Christ!" She waved around her spoon. "Go ahead. Tell me not to swear. And I'll tell you not to tell a secret!"

"What about this *person* who went after your friend with a knife? Don't you want to get him? Don't you want Greer and Troy and whoever out of the way, exonerated, removed from the picture, so that real detective work on this guy can be made?"

Harley jerked back as Jamie's torrent of pent-up frustration came at her like a fire hose. "You said you wouldn't—"

"I said I would try another angle *before* you told me about the breaking in and stealing," she cut in.

Harley lapsed into silence, spooning up her cereal in a kind of glum funk.

Emma, who'd been getting ready for Saturday at the Thrift Shop, came downstairs with Duchess at her heels. "Somebody's yelling," she said.

"I wonder who," muttered Harley.

"Jamie." Emma stated.

"Are you all ready?" Jamie asked her as she picked up her purse and headed toward the back door. She paused, looking back. Emma was in her line of sight, still standing in the kitchen. She seemed to be staring at Harley. Feeling Jamie's eyes on her, she finally turned and headed down the hallway after her sister.

Chapter Twenty-Five

Jamie was the first one at the Coffee Club. She'd never been to the coffee shop before and liked the greenery and throwback feel to the place. She chose a table with a fern hanging in a skylight above her head. A waitress came by with menus and Jamie asked for a latte. The woman left the menus and was just returning with Jamie's drink when Vicky came through the door. The real estate agent looked like hell. Her hair was out of its usual chignon and tangled by the fitful wind that had flung spatterings of rain at Jamie when she'd raced from her car to the interior of the café.

"Where's Jill?" Vicky frowned as she pulled out a chair across from Jamie and shrugged out of her coat. Her blue blouse and slacks looked pressed, but her makeup seemed only half-on.

"I'm the first one here," Jamie said.

"We won the game last night. Did you hear?"

"Um, no. Good. Go team," Jamie added.

"Tyler wasn't there." She sighed and snapped up one of the menus. Jamie watched her eyes and realized she wasn't even reading it.

"I think Harley wanted to go to the game, she just wasn't able to." This was a bit of a lie. Harley had made it clear that she had no interest in going unless Marissa did, and Marissa was staying home.

"Can you believe what happened to Bette?" Vicky set down the menu. "I'm just in shock. It was terrible. Yesterday was surreal. I think I'm still processing. I guess we all are."

"It was good you could pick up when she called."

"Right? I mean, I could have had my phone off, or who knows what." She shuddered. She then eyed Jamie in a more calculated way. "I was glad you had Cooper's number. You two have been hanging out together."

"Talking on the phone," Jamie clarified.

Vicky seemed to take that in, but then she looked past Jamie and said heavily, "I think I have a commission going sideways. Laura Haynes and David Musgrave."

"The house they're building?" Jamie asked in surprise. She'd thought that was a done deal.

"The builder still owns it. We've just been working to get their loan in place. But . . . oh, I can't really talk about it. I don't even really know; it's just sometimes you get that feeling. Has Cooper talked to Laura recently, or have you?"

Jamie realized things must be bad if Vicky couldn't even get through to them. "It's been a rough week for Laura."

"Absolutely. Nobody's concentrating on the house. I get that. It's just . . . oh, it'll work itself out." The waitress came by, and Vicky ordered black coffee. "How's Emma?"

"Fine. I dropped her off at work this morning." Jamie was trying to figure out how to broach the subject of Tyler. She wished some of Vicky's other friends would get there and break into their usual gossip and take the pressure off her. "I guess Troy Stillwell and Greer Douglas admitted to being at the Ryersons' last Saturday."

"Seems like a century ago, doesn't it?" Vicky sighed again. "Are you all right?"

"I'm worried about Bette. I just . . . want to talk to her. I don't think it could possibly be the same guy who went after Marissa. I don't understand it."

"Both of those boys deny going into the house to scare her."

"I never thought it was them. And now the Bette intruder? What does Cooper think?"

"I heard there was another boy out there the night Marissa was pranked." Jamie held her breath after her provocative comment.

Vicky avoided Jamie's eyes as she pushed a loose strand of hair behind her ear. "Where did you hear that?"

"I worked at the school last week."

Now she met Jamie's gaze. Some of her fire returned as she said, "There are a lot of terrible, unsubstantiated rumors flying around. I wouldn't give them too much credit."

Jamie heard the warning. She also heard how worried Vicky was that those "unsubstantiated" rumors might be true. Was that why Tyler wasn't at the game?

At that moment, Jill cruised in, looking around the Coffee Club in her usual disdainful way. Seeing Vicky and Jamie, she sauntered over. "Do you really think we'll see Bette?" she asked as she sat down.

"No." Vicky was blunt. "We're probably wasting our time. I just want to make sure she's all right."

"Well, of course." Jill's brows raised at Vicky's manner. A far cry from her normally breezy demeanor. "Is Alicia coming?"

"No." Vicky was abrupt. As if realizing she'd silenced both Jill and Jamie with her unusually harsh tone, she explained, "She apparently was with Deon at the game last night. I never talk to her when she's with him, but she did manage to say that she was busy today. I didn't text her."

"She was with Deon?" Jill repeated. "I didn't think they talked."

"They have Troy. And he's a handful. Just a problem all the time. Lying, cheating . . ."

Stealing? Jamie thought.

As if reading her mind, Vicky didn't finish her thought.

Jill turned to Jamie. "Your friend Gwen is certainly an interesting person. Her house was pointed out to me. Definitely different."

"You should have seen it when her parents were here. Fake Spanish moss," Jamie said, trying to lighten the mood a bit.

They both turned to Vicky, who was clearly lost in thought.

"Maybe we should go to the hospital," Jill said uncomfortably.

"Yes," Vicky agreed, rising to her feet as if she'd just been waiting to be released.

A woman came into the coffee shop just as Jamie, Jill, and Vicky were leaving. She looked at them, her gaze zeroing in on Vicky. Her lips parted and she looked stunned.

"Vicky . . ." the woman breathed. She had short, dark hair and wore a power suit in dark green with a white satin blouse. Behind slim, tortoiseshell glasses, her eyes were huge, but her mouth was thin and tight.

Who? Jamie thought, and glanced at Vicky.

"Cathy," Vicky snapped out.

"We need to talk. I was going to call you this morning. I know it's—"

"I'm heading to the hospital right now," Vicky cut her off.

"Oh." That stopped her for a moment. "I'll call you this afternoon, then."

"Fine."

The woman nodded, then looked about to say something more, but Vicky intervened. "I wouldn't believe everything you hear. And for God's sake, Cathy, it's Victoria."

* * *

Cooper was allowed into Bette's room as Phil and their two kids were just leaving. The nurse hovered nearby. "She has trouble talking. Don't force her," she warned him before she left the room.

Bette's throat was bandaged, as was the right side of her face. The knife had slashed into her temple and down the side of her head into her neck, nicking the carotid artery, as Crake had guessed. She was lucky she'd called Vicky and help had come so quickly.

"I can talk," Bette said softly as soon as the nurse was gone.

"Okay. I don't want to strain you. Let me know if it gets to be too much."

Tears filled her eyes. "Cooper, you gotta get him."

"I'm going to do my best, Bette."

"He came in through the slider," she began. "I think I left the door open . . ."

Jamie drove to the hospital behind Vicky's black Explorer. It reminded her of the vehicle that Gwen had looked at so sharply as it had cruised by Jamie's house on Wednesday. Cooper had a black SUV as well, and so did the whole of the River Glen Police Department for that matter. Thinking of vehicles reminded her of her mother's car, sitting in the garage. She hadn't even been in there but once. She wondered if she would ever really feel settled in.

Inside the reception area, they learned they would not be allowed to see Bette. Vicky looked like she wanted to argue, but they were told the no visitors request had come from the family.

"I think that was Phil just leaving," Jill said. "I think he passed me as I drove into the parking lot."

Vicky said, "Is Bette awake? I don't know if I trust Phil in charge."

Jamie was feeling like an interloper. She'd agreed to

come to the hospital as a means to talk to Vicky and that had kind of fizzled. "Maybe we should try tomorrow. I'd better get home."

"Okay." Vicky was distracted. Had been since her encounter with Cathy.

"What's going on with Cathy Timbolt?" Jill asked.

Vicky shook her head, then looked at Jamie. "Why don't you ask Jamie?" she suggested. "Her sophomore daughter's a friend of Katie's and she was pumping me for information earlier because she thinks Katie and Tyler hooked up."

Jamie's breath caught. She'd never said anything like that to Vicky. Jill looked at her, then back at Vicky. "Tyler?"

Vicky looked like she wanted to cry. "That little *bitch*. She's a fucking thief, Jill. A *thief*!"

"Who?" Jill asked, aghast.

"Katie Timbolt! And she's got Tyler mixed up in her mess. That's why Coach benched him!"

With that, she covered her face with her hands and broke down and bawled.

Cooper finished talking with Bette at around ten-thirty, wished her well, causing a tear to slide down her unbandaged cheek. He headed back to the station. A news van was parked outside, and when they saw Cooper, a young man and woman rushed over to try to interview him. He didn't want to be on the evening news, so he ducked away from them and hurried up the back steps. Once inside the detective bureau, he headed to his desk. Howie was standing and conversing with Verbena.

"It's hit the fan," Howie said.

"The attack on Bette?" Cooper asked.

"Phil Kearns is being chased by reporters, as is Eric Volker."

"I haven't had a chance to talk to Volker yet."

"I know. He called here, pissed. Said you talked to his ex, and he plans to sue."

"Sue?" Cooper repeated. "For what?"

"Damage to his reputation, putting words in her mouth, anything he can come up with. The usual . . . but there's more."

"What else?" Cooper asked.

Elena rolled her eyes his way. "That theft and vandalism case broke wide open. Cathy Timbolt's daughter and—"

"Tyler Stapleton. Quarterback for the River Glen Pirates," Cooper cut her off.

"Allegedly," Howie put in.

"How'd you know?" Verbena asked at the same time.

"I know someone at the school."

"Jamie Whelan," Howie said with a nod of acknowledgment.

"What's happening with that?"

"The Stapletons are lawyering up. I haven't heard about Timbolt yet. Katie's father lives in Phoenix."

"The people they allegedly burglarized, the Pendelans, are pissed," said Verbena.

Howie added, "The Stapletons want no part of it. They're coming in today, with Tyler, who they say was *not* with Katie. That she did this all on her own."

"It's your case," Elena said to Cooper. "What do you want to do?"

"It's my case only because I was the one who went out to Staffordshire and saw where they pressed their hands into concrete."

"Think that'll hold up as evidence?" Howie mused.

"More likely there'll be fingerprints on the vodka bottle."

"We're having that checked. By the way, no one's arguing that they put their hands into the wet concrete. The Stapletons said they'll take care of that," said Elena.

"Is Lawrence Stapleton involved in that development?"

Howie asked. "This kid's gotta be stupid if he's doing that to his old man's business."

"Or maybe that's the point," Elena said knowingly.

"What about the theft?" Cooper asked. "Have the Pende-lans pressed charges?"

"Not yet, but they said they're going to. Cathy Timbolt's ex is a lawyer, so . . ." Howie spread his hands.

"Katie Timbolt babysat their dog," Cooper said slowly.

"And then stole from them," Elena reminded him.

"She's only sixteen," Howie added.

Elena glared at both of them. "She broke in. Stole jewelry and liquor. She and Tyler Stapleton went to Staffordshire Estates, pressed their palms into the concrete, drank the stolen vodka, put down a blanket, and had sex on the grounds."

"Allegedly," Howie said more strongly. "Her sister's one of the top students of the senior class."

"Well, great," Elena snapped.

"I'm just saying, we don't know everything. We need to take our time," said Howie.

Cooper sighed. Man, oh, man, this one was going to be a bitch. "My daughter's a friend of Katie."

"I'll take the case. I'll okay it with Bennihof," Howie said. "I've already got the other boys."

"Who didn't tell you about Tyler Stapleton," Elena reminded him.

"I know," Howie snapped back at her.

"And don't go with that boys-will-be-boys attitude. That's all I'm saying. Sixteen or no, Katie Timbolt stole from people who trusted her. Allegedly," she forestalled Howie, who'd opened his mouth to protest. She turned to Cooper. "Either way, you're off this one."

"What about Bette Kearns?" Howie asked, and Cooper laid out what she'd told him at the hospital, which wasn't much more than what they'd already learned, or at least speculated, that she had an impression of bulky dark clothes, a ski mask, and gloves.

"Ski mask," Howie said.

"Maybe tech'll pick something up," said Verbena.

"I want to talk to Eric Volker," Cooper told them.

"He left his number when he called earlier," Verbena said.

Howie scooped up a paper from his desk and handed it to Cooper, who punched in the numbers from his desk phone. Howie added, "He's a hothead."

Cooper spent the next twenty minutes on the phone with Meghan Volker's ex, who had a lot to say about the police, his ex-wife, and the cheating bastard who was fucking her, Phil Kearns, and even Bette Kearns, who would spread her legs for anybody who could rub a few nickels together. Volker said Meghan was a whore and only Dara was worth anything. He'd fought for custody for years, but now at least Dara was eighteen and could make her own decisions. He felt he was the victim in the divorce and had fought hard not to pay his wife any alimony. In his mind, she shouldn't get half of the equity they would receive from selling their house. He'd allowed her to stay in it while Dara finished her senior year, but come June, he was going to throw her out on her sagging, forty-year-old ass. When Cooper asked where he'd been on Thursday night between five and eight, he'd triumphantly told him that he was at a Portland restaurant with a date and then went back to her place, a high-rise condo, and enjoyed monumental sex into the wee hours of the morning. He provided her name and phone number and finished with, "I've got no beef with Bette Kearns. She wants to screw half the town, have at it. Phil, I don't like, but he can have Meghan. She's an expensive habit. One I'm happy to be rid of."

Cooper was pretty sure that was all bluster, but he thanked the man for the information and set about checking his alibi. It turned out the restaurant in question had videotape, and

Volker and his date, a young brunette who hung on his every word, had moved from the restaurant proper to the bar and hadn't left the place till nearly nine, past the time of the attack on Bette.

Cooper stayed at work until after five, writing up notes on the attack on Bette Kearns and also what he'd learned from Race Stillwell. Though by necessity a reevaluation of Emma's case was on the back burner, Cooper hadn't given up on it entirely. He needed to talk further with Dug. Neither Race nor Dug was giving him the full story there. He also wanted to go over what had happened at the Ryersons' the weekend before with Marissa. He believed she'd known the senior boys were the ones pranking her, though she'd refused to actually name them, at least so far. Maybe, with the advent of Tyler Stapleton in the mix, she would finally reveal all. Without the burden of trying to protect her friends, she might be able to remember something more about the intruder who'd scared her into the bedroom.

Cooper had checked with the crime scene techs earlier and they had nothing for him yet on what they'd discovered, if anything, at the Kearns home. There was a backlog of work at the lab, but Cooper had put a rush on the case because Bette was in the hospital and possibly still at risk from an unknown, at-large assailant. He called the lab again and was passed around for a while before being told that there were no fingerprints and the blood on the floor was all Bette's. In other words: nada. At least so far.

He'd called Jamie once during the day, suggesting he pick her up at six-thirty for a seven o'clock dinner in Portland. Rather breathlessly, she'd accepted, and he'd asked her what she was doing.

"Being a mom and a sister" had been her answer.

Now, he was reaching for his coat when his cell rang. He pulled it from his pocket and squinted at the screen. Laura.

He chided himself for his immediate inner groan. He

wanted to see Marissa again, and he was going to have to get past Laura to do that. "Hi," he said into the receiver.

"I'm not moving. *We're* not moving. Lawrence Stapleton has canceled the contract with us. He's selling the house— *our* house—as a spec!"

"Your Staffordshire house? Don't you have some legal recourse?" Cooper asked.

His words brought a bubble of hysteria to her voice. "You'd think so," she said, half-laughing, half-sobbing. "But when you haven't paid, you don't get to buy!"

He was only partially understanding her. She was either too upset to notice, or she was happy to keep him in suspense. Either way, he wanted to ease out of the conversation. "Is Marissa there?"

"I'm calling you for help!"

"What can I do?" he asked, biting back his first response, which would have been to point out she had the floor.

When he put it to her that way, she couldn't seem to go on. Finally, she said, "David doesn't have his part of the money. We can't buy in."

"Aren't you selling your house?" he asked.

"You know I had to refinance when you and I divorced."

They had split the equity in the house, but to do that, they had needed to pay off the current mortgage with a new, larger one in Laura's name. Even so, a number of years had gone by since their split and in this time of rising home prices, the house was undoubtedly worth more than it had been.

"I can't do it on my own. David's been helping me, and now . . ." She choked out a sob.

"I'm sorry, Laura. I'm just not sure how I can help you."

"I need a hundred thousand dollars," she blurted out. "Until David gets things straightened out."

He squinted at the phone. "I don't have that kind of money, Laura. You know that."

"You inherited from your father."

"A house. Not cash." He paused a moment, then asked, "What does David need to straighten out?"

"It's not for me to say. Those are David's problems," she said bitterly.

Distant alarm bells went off in his head. "David has financial problems?"

"I didn't say that," she said. But she had, in a way.

"Well, I can't help you, in any case. Isn't Vicky Stapleton your real estate agent? Her husband's your builder. If you just need some time to work things out with the loan, I would think she'd be your best advocate."

"She can just sell it to somebody else."

"If you talk to her—"

"David lost his job," she cut him off.

Cooper frowned. At Elgin DeGuerre's law firm? "I thought David was taking over the business from DeGuerre."

"We all did." She sounded both angry and resigned.

"I'm sorry, Laura. I wish I could, but I can't." A beat, then he added, "But if Marissa's there, I'd like to talk to her."

He heard the click and was left with dead air after she hung up on him.

Chapter Twenty-Six

Jamie changed into black slacks and a blue sweater. She freshened her makeup and fought with her hair, finally leaving it down and giving it a few tweaks with the curling iron to add some life.

Downstairs, she was glad to have the house to herself, although Harley and Duchess were upstairs, but sequestered in Harley's room. Theo was once again bringing Emma home, so she had a few minutes to wait.

She'd overheard Harley on the phone with someone. At first she'd wondered if it was Greer, but then had determined it must be Marissa. She couldn't tell how things were going there, and when Harley suddenly jumped off the bed and headed for the door to catch her eavesdropping, Jamie had her own phone in hand and had hurriedly tiptoed to the top of the stairs, acting like she was just reaching the landing as the door flung inward and Harley stood in the doorway.

"What?" Jamie had asked her.

Harley shook her head and shut the door after Duchess, who came out to sniff Jamie as if she were a stranger again. The dog seemed to know what game she was up to. Sheesh. The lengths it took to parent a teenager. Maybe she was doing it wrong. Maybe she wanted to protect Harley too much from the many pitfalls of growing up.

That had been two hours ago. She'd purchased some barbecued ribs from the store and put together a salad for Harley and Emma. She hadn't mentioned that she was going out.

Her cell rang and she realized it was Gwen. She'd forgotten she'd called her and had determined over the day that it was probably all right to leave Harley and Emma on their own for the few hours she would be out. They would have Duchess and each other. It was probably okay . . . but if Gwen were available . . .

"Hi, Gwen," she answered the phone.

"You called." Her voice sounded strained.

"I was checking with you. Seeing if you were around this weekend."

"I am. I'm catching up on some work at home. What are you doing?"

"I'm . . . well, I'm going out to dinner with Cooper."

"That's promising." She seemed to perk up a little.

"Yeah, I was . . . well, if you're busy, don't worry. But, um, I was wondering if you were free, if you could check on Harley and Emma. They're going to be home alone tonight for a few hours."

"Oh. Sure. I'd be happy to."

"Great. Emma will be here soon and Cooper's coming by at about six-thirty. Harley doesn't have any plans. With what's been going on, she and Marissa have been sticking pretty close to home." Jamie chewed on her lip for a moment, aware that Gwen hadn't mentioned the attack on Bette, even though the story had hit the news. "You know about Bette, right?"

"No . . . what happened?" The tension was back in her voice.

Jamie quickly explained about the attack on her in her home. Gwen was so silent that Jamie asked, "Are you still there?"

"Yeah, I haven't been watching television today. Umm . . .

I'll come check on them a little later . . . after I get some things together."

"Are you all right?"

"Yes, of course. Just stunned. I don't know Bette Kearns personally, and yet I feel I do in some ways. We're all connected, aren't we?"

She said it in her usual woo-woo way, but Jamie responded, "Yes, we are."

"I'm sorry I didn't meet her at Leander's with the others."

"Are you sure you're all right?" Jamie asked. There was something strange in her tone. Something . . . fearful? . . . which wasn't Gwen's style at all.

"Yes. Perfectly. Go to dinner. I'll make sure Emma and Harley are safe."

Cooper showed up right on time, just as Harley and Emma were serving up their dinner. This time Duchess allowed him in with a little less vigilance on her part.

"Given enough time, she might actually think I'm okay," he said as they headed out.

Jamie smiled. Harley had looked at her accusingly, but hadn't said anything. Jamie had the feeling she was being blamed for telling about Tyler and Katie, although Vicky had popped out with her fears that morning all on her own. Jamie had barely hinted at the teenagers' exploits.

Cooper took her to a steak house that was also known for its fish selections. Jamie ordered sea bass and Cooper had a rib eye. The conversation centered around Bette for the first half of the meal. They both had a lot of processing to get through, and then it switched to Marissa and Katie and Tyler. Cooper assured her that the police knew all about it without him telling them. Apparently, Tyler had told some of the truth. Enough to get Katie in trouble, and then Katie had popped out with the rest.

Finally, Jamie was having a decaf coffee and Cooper was working his way through an apple caramel dessert when he

looked her in the eye and said, "Race Stillwell told me he
saw a man in a ski mask near the Ryerson house the night
Emma was stabbed."

Jamie nearly dropped her cup of coffee, her fingers felt
so slick. "What?" she asked in a whisper.

Cooper explained about his meeting with Race and his
phone conversation with Dug. "There's more there. I don't
know how much more, but something."

"Do you think Dug . . . or Race . . . or this guy in a
mask . . . ?"

"I don't know. Maybe Race made up seeing the guy in a
ski mask. Maybe he was telling the truth. It was Halloween,
or close to it. We had some masks with us. It seemed signif-
icant when he first said it; now I don't know. What I do know
is they didn't tell the whole truth."

"And Marissa was attacked by a guy in a ski mask . . ."

Cooper rubbed his forehead. He was clearly thinking
about something.

"What?" Jamie asked.

"We're holding something back from the press about
Bette's attack. Her attacker was wearing a ski mask, too."

Jamie put her hand to her mouth. Her fears of leaving
Harley and Emma alone suddenly intensified.

"We're going on the assumption that the attacks on
Marissa and Bette were by the same person. They happened
within a week of each other. The same MO, with a ski mask
and a knife. What Race said about seeing a guy in a ski
mask outside the Ryersons' twenty years ago is probably
either a coincidence or something he concocted on his own.
I don't see how that has any bearing on these recent attacks,
but it's in the Zeitgeist. It's of the moment."

Jamie said, "Twenty years ago, the killing of the babysitter in Vancouver was by a man in a ski mask."

"It was her boyfriend, according to the victim's family.
But maybe that's what keyed Race's imagination at the

time." He sat back as the waiter brought the check. "We don't know. Yet."

They drove home, and Jamie found she didn't want the night to end. They'd basically talked shop all night and that was fine, but she wanted something more. "You want to come in for a bit?" She glanced around for Gwen's car but didn't see it.

He looked at her. "Can you . . . stay out longer?"

"Maybe . . ."

"We could go to my place?"

Jamie yearned for it so badly she almost leaned toward him. "Let me check on Harley and Emma, okay? I'll just be a minute."

She hurried up the front walk to the door. It was locked. She rapped on the panels, then searched in her purse for her key, letting herself inside when no one answered. The hairs on the back of her neck lifted. It was nine-thirty. They could both be in their rooms, but something felt wrong.

She nearly fell over from fright when she walked toward the stairs and saw Harley frozen in midstep, halfway down.

"Jesus!" Jamie's hand flew to her chest. Then, "Are you all right?"

"I heard the front door open."

"That was me. Sorry. I just wanted to check on you."

"You always come in the back."

"I know. I'm . . ." She drew a breath. "I'm going out for a nightcap with Cooper. Is Emma in bed, I assume?" At Harley's nod, she exhaled with relief. "Is that okay? Did Gwen come by?"

"I guess."

"You guess it's okay, or you guess Gwen came by?"

"Nobody came by."

"Really? Huh. I thought . . ." She broke off. "Gwen said she was going to stop in and make sure you guys were okay."

"Why wouldn't we be?"

"I don't know. A lot of terrible things have happened. I just wanted to make sure you were safe, that's all." *So, sue me.* Jamie could feel herself getting upset and tried to crank her emotions back down. For a moment, when she'd walked in, she'd felt real fear.

Harley looked past Jamie, then back at her. "I was kind of scared," she admitted.

"Do you want me to stay?"

"Nah." They could both hear Duchess whining and scratching at Emma's door. "We've got the dog." She turned, lightly ran back up the stairs and Jamie exhaled a breath and traced her steps to the front door and outside.

Back in the car, Cooper looked at her and asked, "What?"

"I don't know. Gwen told me she'd stop by and check on them, but she never did, apparently. She sounded kind of odd when I talked to her earlier."

"She's the one who told you to tell me to be careful."

"Yep."

They drove in silence for a few minutes. Then Cooper said, "You want to stop by her house?"

"Do you mind?" Jamie looked at him with relief.

"No. It's not much out of the way."

"I'll call her. See if she answers." She placed the call, but it rang and rang and went to voice mail. "You think she turns off her phone at night? Some people do."

"Hard to say."

They got to the house. The fake Spanish moss might be gone, but the carved symbols in the trees and the odd little collection of items in various places on the lawn, wooden art pieces and religious symbols, were still there from Gwen's parents' days.

They walked up to the front porch. There was one dim light on in the area Jamie remembered as the kitchen. Maybe the oven light, she thought. She rang the bell and long, deep, solemn notes tolled within. The hairs on Jamie's arms stood on end.

"I know this sounds crazy, as if I'm trying to be like Gwen or something, but I know something's wrong. She's off beat, but reliable. I hadn't seen her in years, but she hasn't changed. She's loyal, and I was a rotten friend. But Gwen's the same."

"What do you want to do?"

She was relieved he didn't act like she was being hysterical. "I don't know. Find her."

"Let's see if her car's in the garage."

Like Jamie's mother's house, Gwen's had a detached garage to the side and rear of the house. Cooper was tall enough to look in the windows along the top of the garage door. "Not in there."

"Oh. She's out. Huh. That's weird. She didn't check on Harley and Emma."

"When was she going to stop by?"

"Well, I would've thought by now." They'd walked back to Cooper's SUV and climbed inside. "She said she had something to do first."

"Workwise?"

"I don't know."

"Maybe she's at her office?" he suggested.

"Maybe."

"You want to check?"

"I'm sorry to be so worried. It's just not like her. She knew how important it was to me to have her kind of monitor them."

"Let's just go see."

Fifteen minutes later, they were outside the building that housed Gwen's office. There was a light on at the end of the hall, where her offices were. Cooper tried the outer door and found it unlocked. "Is this the way it is at night?"

"Doesn't seem like it would be." Jamie's heart had started beating deep and hard. "Her office is down the hall."

They walked back together. There were no lights on in Gwen's office.

But the door was ajar.

"Wait here." Cooper's voice was a taut whisper as he unbuttoned his cuff.

Maybe it's nothing, Jamie told herself, even while her whole body shivered. *Maybe I've infected Cooper with my paranoia.*

He pulled his sleeve over his hand, pushed the door open farther and flicked on the light switch. Hesitating, he called, "Gwen? It's Cooper Haynes."

No answer.

"I'm coming in," Jamie said.

"No, stay where you are."

She came up behind him. "I don't want to stay in the hall."

He almost argued with her, but then let it go. He moved toward Gwen's office door, which, like everything else so far, was not closed completely. Jamie followed closely behind him. Every nerve in her body felt like it was on alert.

Cooper pushed open that door as well. She knew he was being careful not to add his prints to whoever's might be on the door handles and light switches.

The door swung inward. Jamie saw a shattered cup on the wooden floor in the same pattern as the one she'd drunk from when she'd been in Gwen's office. Spilled tea made a puddle where it had landed.

Cooper swept in a breath at the same moment Jamie saw the feet sticking out from behind the desk. He hurried around to the body.

"Is it Gwen? Is she okay? What's wrong?" Jamie asked in quick succession.

"Call 9-1-1," he ordered as he bent over the body. "Give them this address."

"What is it?" Her fingers felt numb as she pulled out her cell. "Wait. I see it." There was a notepad with the address printed on it.

"Yes, it's Gwen. She's unconscious. She may have fallen. I don't know yet. I'm getting a thready pulse."

"9-1-1," the dispatch operator answered. "What is the nature of your emergency?"

"This is Jamie Woodward. I'm at Gwendolyn Winkelman's office and she's unconscious on the floor with a weak pulse." She gave the woman the address. "I'm here with Detective Cooper Haynes of the River Glen Police Department. We need an ambulance."

"All right. One's on its way. Don't hang up."

"I won't."

She walked around the desk, phone to her ear. Cooper was leaning over Gwen whose mouth was slack. There was dribble running down her chin. Had she had some kind of attack? Her words of warning swept through Jamie's mind and she felt cold.

And then she saw a note page on the floor from the same slim pad on the desk. It read simply *Sorry.* Jamie recognized Gwen's distinctive capital "S," slightly separated from the other letters, from the note Gwen had written to herself after she'd met with Emma.

Sorry?

Cooper read the note and silently looked at Jamie.

What did Gwen have to be sorry for, and what did that mean? Jamie's eyes moved to the overturned cup and spilled tea.

"You don't think she . . ." Jamie couldn't complete her thought.

"I wish that ambulance would get here."

They waited in tense silence, and after what felt like an

eternity, finally heard the *woo-woo-woo-woo* of the siren as the rescue vehicle neared.

They followed the ambulance to the hospital. Jamie texted Harley to tell her what was going on. Harley called her back, which was a surprise. After asking anxiously about Gwen, to which Jamie had said it did not look like foul play, Harley, relieved, told her that Teddy Ryerson had stopped by, looking for Jamie, apparently. "He left a card," Harley said. Jamie cynically decided he was trying, as ever, to get her to invest with him. He didn't come right out and suggest it; he was more subtle than that. But he was persistent.

"Oh, and he asked me to babysit next weekend while he and his sister go to a Halloween par—"

"*What?* No! Not on your life. Uh-uh," Jamie cut her off. "Are you kidding? I can't believe he would dare to ask that!"

"You tell him that, then. I didn't want to, but he needs a sitter. Nobody's going to want to go there with that killer out there."

"I'll talk to him," Jamie said. "But you're not going."

"Jesus, Mom. I said I wasn't!"

Stay safe. Those were Gwen's words.

Cooper had ordered the crime scene team in to check out Gwen's office. Maybe she'd had some kind of seizure or accident, but that note . . . He wasn't taking any chances, and for that Jamie was glad.

It looked like everything was going as well as it could. Gwen's condition was unchanged. Jamie was just getting to her feet from her seat in the ER when Cooper was called into the area where they'd taken Gwen, behind security doors.

Jamie was still standing when Cooper appeared twenty minutes later. His sober expression was an answer.

"Oh, no," she said. "Oh, no."

He said in a shattered voice, "She passed away about half an hour ago."

"Oh, God. Oh my God."

"They don't know why yet," Cooper added.

"She didn't kill herself. She didn't! She wouldn't!" Jamie was adamant.

"No one's saying that."

Jamie heard the unspoken "yet."

Cooper pulled her into his arms and pressed her face against his chest. She was shaking so badly, she thought she'd collapse if she didn't hold on tight.

Jamie felt like she was having an out-of-body experience, much like she'd had awakening to her mother's voice saying *Come home*. Only this time it was less shock and more pure misery. Gwen . . . gone . . .

Why?

"What's she sorry about?" she asked.

"I don't know," Cooper admitted. "Come on. I'll take you home."

She wanted to say she needed to stay. She wanted to fight and rail and scream. But what was there to say, really?

They were halfway back when she said, "Can we go to your house?"

He looked at her through the gloom of the car. "You want to?"

"Yes."

That was all that was said. From the moment Cooper shut the back door of the kitchen behind them, they were in each other's arms. Jamie wanted to make love to him. Fiercely. And he seemed to feel the same way.

Their clothes were tossed on the floor in ripped-off pieces as they stumbled their way to the bedroom. And then she was on the bed, pulling him to her, wanting, needing the heat of him. They were kissing, wildly, all over each other. Her hands were in the bedcovers, gripping and twisting. Not a word was uttered. The only sounds were their breathing, the squeak of the bed frame, the hard beating of two hearts. Jamie hadn't made love in years and she was drowning in desire. She practically clawed him to her and he answered by spreading her legs and thrusting inside her with a passion that drove them both. The rhythmic motion of lovemaking fed her soul. She was reaching, straining, focused on a point of need so great that when the climax came, it almost caught her by surprise. She cried out, digging her hands into his back, hugging him to her as hard as she could. Dimly she heard him groan as well, feeling the spasms of his own fulfillment, lost in her own world.

And then the tears came and she was sobbing and shaking. He pulled back slightly to look at her.

"Gwen," she forced out.

He gently brushed her tears aside, but they were coming faster than he could remove them. He pulled away from her onto his side, bringing her with him. She cried on his shoulder for what felt like hours, but was only minutes.

Eventually, spent, Jamie joined him beneath the covers and between the sheets. She knew she needed to go home, but she didn't want to leave. Couldn't leave. They held each other in silence, almost as if neither could bear to break it.

Finally, Jamie sighed and pulled back a bit. "They'll be waiting for me and wondering about Gwen. I don't know if I can tell them."

"Maybe it can wait till tomorrow?"

"I hope so."

But when Cooper pulled up in front of Jamie's house, the lights in nearly every room were still on.

"I'll come in with you," he said.

"No. I think it's better if I'm alone. . . ." She started to reach for the passenger door handle.

"Hey."

She looked back and he touched her arm, tugging her closer. She came back willingly for a long, lingering kiss.

"I'll see you tomorrow," he said.

She smiled faintly. She wanted to tell him how much it

mattered that he was in her life, how much she suddenly needed him, but all she said was, "Tomorrow," as she let herself out of the SUV.

Harley heard the key in the lock of the front door. *Mom.* She flew out of her bedroom and toward the stairs. Duchess started whining, so Harley stopped and released her from the confines of Emma's room. She stifled a scream when Emma appeared like a spirit rising out of the gloom. Only the sight of her Scottie dog pajamas kept Harley from shrieking and running blindly away as if she were possessed.

Her mother was turning off lights as she walked through the living room and into the kitchen. Duchess barked once and ran down the stairs. Harley and Emma followed.

"Hey," Mom said, looking at the three of them. "Everybody's awake."

Mom looked . . . different. Like she'd been asleep, sort of. Put together, but not, too.

Emma said, "You had sex with Cooper Haynes."

Mom jumped as if she'd been goosed. "Good God."

"Harley was scared," Emma added.

Mom turned to Harley. "Scared?" she asked.

Now Harley felt a little like an idiot. "I thought I heard something outside. Maybe not. Duchess was acting weird. Growling. I don't know. I didn't want to turn off any lights. It was . . . I don't know, maybe I'm just crazy."

"No. It's scary times," Mom said. "Is that why you're still in your clothes?"

Harley was in sweats, and yes, she'd felt like she needed to be ready at a moment's notice. "What took you so long?"

"I shouldn't have left you alone," she said, frowning. Then she pressed her hand to her lips in a gesture that made Harley's heart stutter.

"What?" Harley cried. "Something happened."

Tears filled Mom's eyes and she couldn't speak for a moment. Emma went to her and put her hand on her shoulder, which really started the waterworks. Harley could scarcely breathe.

"It's Gwen. She's gone. She left a note, so . . . I don't know . . ."

"What do you mean? *Suicide?*" Harley gasped. "No! *Why?*"

"It makes no sense." Mom was shaking her head and Emma was awkwardly patting her on the shoulder.

Harley ran forward and threw herself into Mom's arms. "Do you think we started this?" she quavered. "By coming here?"

"Oh, no." Mom was firm. "It was already here. Whatever's going on, the seeds were already planted."

"In the garden," Emma said. "The seeds were planted, but our mother rooted them out."

"That's not . . . I was speaking metaphorically," Mom explained. "Our mother loved weeding, but Gwen's death . . . is something else. I'm sorry to tell you about it tonight. I wanted to wait till tomorrow. Right now, I think it's time for bed. I'm just so tired."

"Me, too," said Emma as she let Duchess out one more time. Harley would have liked to talk more, but they all traipsed upstairs.

Harley kept her sweats on. She lay in bed, thinking hard, testing her feelings. It had really seemed like someone was watching them and in her fear, Harley had texted Marissa, telling her she was scared to be home alone. Marissa had texted right back, thank God, totally commiserating with her. They hadn't communicated as much as Harley needed since the creep had come after her. Marissa thought maybe she was agoraphobic now. She didn't want to go anywhere and she refused to be by herself. She'd actually been sleeping in her mom's room because her mom's boyfriend wasn't around.

Texting with her had calmed Harley down and made her feel relieved. Marissa wasn't mad at her. Greer had texted her, too: Tylers in big trouble. You didnt say anything, did ya?

Harley had gone cold all over. She'd just been freaked at every level. She'd texted back: Oh no! Then added a series of emojis depicting worry and concern and left it at that.

Maybe she'd blown it by telling Mom. She hoped not. She really, really hoped not.

Hearing an engine outside, she tiptoed to her window and peered out. She had an angled view of the road and could see a dark car stopped at the end of the driveway and across the street. Was it her imagination, or was the driver wearing a *ski mask*?

She ran back to her bed and dived in, bringing the covers over her head. She must be imagining things. Had to be. She shivered from head to toe.

It took her a long, long, *long* time to fall asleep.

Chapter Twenty-Seven

Cooper called Jamie on Sunday morning, and the sound of her voice sent a flood of good feelings through him, even though their main topics of conversation were Gwen's death and the recent home intrusions and attacks. They made a plan to meet later in the day. Meanwhile, Cooper intended to talk to Marissa again. She'd gone to school all week, but otherwise had practically been sequestered. He'd tried to reach her directly, but Marissa's texts had made it clear she did not want to talk about the attack.

It was his day off but he couldn't just sit on his hands. He put a call in to Phil Kearns, asking about Bette, and learned that she was doing fine. Then Phil gave him an earful about not arresting Eric Volker, and the fact that Volker's alibi held no weight with him. By the time Cooper disconnected he'd heard about fifteen minutes more of character assassination and griping, which Volker and Kearns both appeared to be masters of.

Howie called and discussed Cooper's finding of Gwen Winkelman and her death, whether it was an accident, suicide, or something else. The crime techs and lab work would hopefully be able to offer some clarification. Howie moved from that to the Stapletons and the Timbolts who were both staunchly defending their children. The Pendelans were still

holding firm on charging Katie and possibly Tyler for
burglarizing their home and stealing from them, but Howie
thought that might all go away.

"Those charges are going to be dropped. They'll work
out a deal. Don't know whether that's good or bad, but I'm
betting on it."

Cooper felt he was probably right.

Midmorning, Gwen's death came through on the local
newsfeed on his phone. It was described as an accident,
pending further investigation.

At noon Cooper put a call into William Ryerson's home
phone, figuring if he wasn't already retired then Sunday was
most likely the man's day off. Cooper wasn't meeting the
doctor face-to-face, but neither was he giving up on digging
into Emma's cold case either.

Ryerson's current wife answered the phone. Kayla,
Cooper remembered from Emma's file. She was reluctant to
put him through when she understood the nature of the call,
but eventually, she set down the receiver and went in search
of the doctor.

A few minutes later Ryerson answered, "Hello," in a
gravelly voice. Then, "What's this about again? You're that
policeman who called."

Cooper re-introduced himself, adding, "I was one of the
kids who pranked Emma the night she was attacked."

"You're a police detective now? What do you want
again?" He sounded somewhat alarmed.

"Background. I'm going through the chronology of what
happened that night. I planned to come to Bend and try to
meet with you personally, but things have kept me here. I
wondered if you would mind answering a few questions."

"I've said it all before."

"I know. I'm working the case again. Just wanted to hear
what you remember."

"Just a minute. Kayla! Get me that cup of coffee? Put

some more cream in it. Don't skimp. I'm going to be on the phone for a while." He cleared his throat. "Go ahead."

Cooper looked down at his notes. He was having trouble moving past both Gwen's death and his lovemaking with Jamie. Memories of her filled his head. It was all he could do to come up with some questions as he remembered the curve of her back, the line of her collarbone, the soft scent of her skin, the fullness of her breasts within his palms. . . .

With an almost physical effort, he set that aside. "You were at the River Glen General's charity event with your wife, but she left early."

"Nadine left with Metcalf." The brusqueness of his tone suggested that her defection might still have some power. "She said I drank too much. Maybe I did. We all did in those days. She said I flirted too much with Kayla. Well, why not? Nadine was a cat in heat around Metcalf. She left and I kept drinking. Had to sober up before I drove home, so I just stayed until the place rolled up the carpets. Then I got home and . . . well, you know what happened. It was hard, seeing Emma on the floor."

"What time was that?"

"One o'clock? Two? Whatever I said at the time."

"And Nadine arrived at the house before you did."

"Metcalf took her home. She went to his place from the auction, spent a few hours in his bed, then finally went home to our kids. Got there right before I did, I guess."

"Do you have any kind of thoughts about what happened?"

"Thoughts? It's a crying shame, that's what it is."

"Do you think the attack was random? Or, that Emma may have been the target?"

"I don't think Emma was the target," he stated flatly. "I think she was just in the way."

"In the way of what?"

"I don't know . . . a robbery? They didn't expect her to be there."

Cooper listened to his tone. Ryerson was sure of his opinion today, but per the notes, the man wouldn't even make a conjecture twenty years earlier. "Nothing was taken, if it was a burglary, but you sound pretty certain."

"Well, hell no. Of course I'm not certain." He backed away quickly, as if Cooper'd tried to pin something on him.

Cooper let that go. "You and your wife came together after the attack on Emma."

"We tried to make another go of it. Bad idea from the start. Nadine's got money, I'm sure you know that. She's a trust fund baby. Had her money and she wanted Metcalf, but I guess that didn't work out. She ended up with Campbell. He's a decent enough guy," he added grudgingly. "Metcalf wasn't. But then, I may be prejudiced, and I suppose I shouldn't speak ill of the dead. Somebody killed him in the hospital parking lot about five years after that night. Bashed his head with a rock, or something, broke into his car, and stole some pills, I think. Anyway, Nadine and I called it quits for good a year or so later."

Cooper asked a few more questions, but Ryerson was losing interest along with his affable mood. He didn't offer up anything further and mostly just reiterated what Cooper already knew.

"Thank you," Cooper finally said.

"Anytime," the older man responded, though Cooper was pretty sure he didn't mean it.

He next put in another call to Nadine Ryerson Campbell but only reached her voice mail. He left his name and phone number, reminding her about his purpose, then clicked off. Maybe she would get back to him.

He made himself a sandwich of turkey deli meat, lettuce, and two slices of wheat bread that was just shy of turning to mold. He remembered his dinner the night before, and that

brought him back to Jamie, which in turn brought him back
to their lovemaking. He had to practically shake himself out
of that memory.

"You got it bad," he muttered.

Cooper forced his mind back to the case. The Vancouver
babysitter killing from twenty years earlier and the two
recent home invasions and attacks had been perpetrated by
someone in a ski mask. Race had said he'd seen someone
in a mask near the Ryersons' the night Emma was stabbed.
Was that true? And if so, were the two crimes connected?
Maybe today's attacker was a a copycat, just using props
from the past.

"Knives . . . and ski masks . . ." Cooper mused.

Jamie called Teddy Ryerson on his cell on Sunday afternoon. She was heavy of heart over Gwen, puzzled and tense
about the attacks on Bette and Marissa, and over the moon
about last night with Cooper. With all of that, she didn't need
to worry about a babysitting gig for Teddy's twins.

"Jamie," he greeted her with relief. "I've been thinking
about you all week. All these terrible things. How's Emma?
And Harley? I spoke to Harley last night and she seemed
worried. I guess, kind of like we all are."

"Hi, Teddy. Harley told me you'd called about babysitting
next weekend—"

"You're going to say no," he interrupted. "I can hear it in
your voice. It's like my house is cursed."

"Well, your house isn't the only one . . ."

"Might as well be," he said bitterly. "Serena and I have
been invited to this party every year. Friends of friends in
Portland. I wanted to ask you, too. We can bring anyone we
like."

"Oh, um, thank you. I just can't. I've got . . . stuff." Jamie
fumbled around.

"I figured you'd say that." He hesitated. "Can we meet, though? I'd like to talk to you about something."

"What?"

"Well, your finances. Specifically, your mother's estate."

She actually burst out laughing. Hysteria, maybe, after everything else. "Teddy, I'm sorry. I'm not really interested in investing with . . . well, I'm leaving things as they stand."

"Okay. I understand. I really do. It's just that . . . I spoke to Irene a couple of times."

Oh, did you?

"She, like you, wanted to leave her finances in the hands of Elgin DeGuerre. DeGuerre did great things for a lot of people for a lot of years. Guided them toward good investment companies. But that law firm is changing management. DeGuerre's retiring."

"I know, Teddy."

"I'm just asking you to pay attention. That's all. I don't want you to lose your money, or somehow be . . . cheated out of what's yours."

Jamie wanted to laugh some more, but she held herself back. She didn't know for sure that Ted Ryerson was preying on people—women—and for all she knew, he could be doing a great job for anyone who invested with him. She just didn't trust him.

As if reading her mind, he said, "You don't trust me, do you?"

She felt a little bad, but she wasn't going to change her mind. "Thank you, Teddy. I'll bear in mind what you said."

"Please do, Jamie. Your mom and I actually got along, more than you might believe. She said she'd set up an account for Emma. Her goal was to save up enough to take care of her after she was gone."

Jamie felt an icicle of fear stab her heart. There'd been no separate Emma account.

"Let me know if I can help you in any other way."

"Thanks." She wasn't sure what his deal was, but if there was any chance he was actually trying to help her . . . ?

"Wait," Jamie said quickly, before he could hang up. "If you can't find a sitter for your party why don't I bring Oliver and Anika to my house?"

"You mean it?" He perked up.

"I don't like leaving Emma alone, or Harley, for that matter these days. I'll be home next weekend. We can all take care of the twins."

"Oh, man. Thank you, Jamie!" he said in a rush of gratitude. "They'd really like that."

Once she was off the phone, Jamie ran the conversation through her head again. Was there a pitfall in there somewhere? She had no problem with her decision to bring the twins to her house, and she wasn't interested in a party, but the conversation over money had left her with a bad feeling.

She'd made the call in her sleeping room, but now she stepped into the hallway. Duchess bounded toward her and circled around her, the most the dog had accepted Jamie into the fold to date. She was definitely third in line behind Emma and Harley. "Hey, girl," Jamie said.

Emma was just coming up the stairs. Jamie looked at her and asked, "Did Mom have a special account for you? You said something about it."

"Money for me after she died, and she died. You have my money now."

"Well, there's the house."

"No, it's special money."

"Special money," Jamie repeated.

"So I can go to Ridge Pointe."

Harley's door opened and she appeared in the same sweats she'd been wearing the night before. Jamie had almost knocked on her door, Harley had slept in so late, but she'd heard her playing music and decided she was probably okay and had left her alone. Afternoon was normally not an acceptable time to rise, but the old rules hadn't applied this past week.

"I'm starving," Harley said, heading downstairs.

"I'm not sure what we have," Jamie said, following her.

"I don't care." Harley grabbed a bowl and shook her favorite cereal into it. She poured milk over it, then flung herself onto one of the kitchen stools. Emma sat down beside her and looked at her. After a moment, Harley looked back and asked, "What?"

"Do you need a psychologist?" asked Emma.

Harley looked from her to Jamie with questions in her eyes.

Jamie asked, "What do you mean, Emma?"

"Harley slept very late. She could be suicidal."

"No!" Jamie gasped.

"No way!" Harley said at the same time.

"You said suicide," Emma pointed out to Harley. "I don't want you to die." She shot Harley a worried glance before her eyes slid away. Her chest was starting to heave.

"I was talking about Gwen. Ms. Winkelman, or whatever. Mom's friend. Not about me. I just feel bad about her." Harley looked at Jamie through the tangle of her hair, which she swept back with one hand. Her eyes were red. "And I feel bad about everything."

Emma darted a look at Jamie and raised her brows. "Suicidal."

"No, Emma. I feel bad, too, and neither Harley nor I is suicidal. We're just dealing with our emotions. Sometimes we feel really bad, really sad."

Emma nodded gravely, then asked, "Can I have my money now? I think I'm ready to go to Ridge Pointe."

"We need to work some things out first," Jamie said, sorry she'd twigged Emma to the supposed nest egg. "I, um, made a decision and I want to talk to both of you about it." She told them of her conversation with Teddy Ryerson about babysitting the twins from their house. She finished with, "Emma, I know you said you don't like Teddy and Serena, but Oliver and Anika are seven-year-olds who need a baby-sitter."

Harley's eyes moved from Jamie to Emma, but she said nothing, merely spooned up more cereal.

"I like kids," said Emma.

"Good." Jamie was relieved.

"Are you going to have sex with Cooper Haynes again?" Emma asked.

Harley's eyes swung back to Jamie, who dodged with, "Emma, that's pretty personal."

Emma thought hard for a moment, then said, "I don't think it was him who came back."

Jamie studied her sister. Her head was cocked, as if she were really working things out. "Do you mean when you told me 'they came back'? As in the night you were babysitting?"

She nodded slowly. "It wasn't Cooper Haynes. But it was one of 'em."

Jamie's mouth was dry. Cooper had told her that Dug Douglas had gone back to the Ryerson house that night, but he'd denied seeing Emma again. He'd also told her that Race had seen someone in the area in a ski mask. Carefully, Jamie asked, "Was he wearing a . . . ski mask?"

"No."

"No mask at all?" Jamie queried.

"No." She drew a breath and turned away. "I don't want to talk about it."

Jamie racked her brain for a way to further the conversation but then glanced at the clock and became more practical. "Harley's having cereal, but what about . . . lunch?"

Emma stopped. "Pasta?"

"I'll make some spaghetti. I think I have everything for that."

"That's for dinner. Come on, Duchess!" And she headed toward the back door.

Harley asked, "Are you sleeping with Mr. Haynes?" once they were alone.

"You heard what I told Emma. That's personal."

"I'll take that as a yes."

When Cooper's phone rang, he didn't recognize the number. He wondered if it might be Nadine Campbell, but it didn't seem like the number he'd called earlier. When he answered, the caller identified herself as Hillary Campion.

"You gave me your card," she reminded him.

He was surprised and seized on the opportunity. "At the hospital. You're Deke's girlfriend."

"Yes . . . that's right." She sounded so careful that he hadn't immediately equated her voice with the hostile one from the hospital, where he'd handed her the card.

"I heard that the psychologist died," she went on. "Winkelman. Deke went to her a time or two. I heard your name. You found her."

"That's true." Cooper looked at the time on his phone. He walked quickly to his office in search of pen and paper. The fact that Deke's girlfriend had called him after blowing him off, half-blaming him for Deke's death, was big.

"What happened to her?" she asked.

"We don't know yet. We're looking into it," he said, grabbing up a small notepad and pen.

"Man, what happened to her?" she demanded, bristling. "Tell me the truth. Was she killed?"

He thought about fobbing her off, throwing out evasions, but he knew that wouldn't fly if he wanted something more from her. "It could be an accident. Possible suicide."

She laughed without humor. "Suicide? Bullshit. She was too sane. Weird, Deke said, but *sane*. No suicide. Tell me the truth. Who killed her?"

"Ms. Campion, if I had anything more to tell you, I would. I don't even know what killed her yet."

She thought that over for a moment. "You tell me when you find out."

"I will," he promised, then asked, "Would you talk to me about Deke?"

"I don't know, mister. He asked me to keep his secrets, and I've been keeping them."

"I just want to understand his relationship to Emma Whelan. I didn't know Deke but for a few hours. What I do know is that a lot of people want the truth to come out after they're gone. Was Deke that kind of man?"

"Deke didn't like the police much." She inhaled and exhaled. "But he did like that messed-up girl . . . woman. Made me jealous of her sometimes, except she wanted nothing to do with him anymore."

"Anymore?"

Another lengthy pause, and then she said, "You know the Logger Room? It was Deke's place."

"I know it."

"Meet me there in an hour. I'll tell you about Deke and her, what he told me anyway."

"I'll be there," Cooper told her. "Do you want . . ." But she'd already hung up.

It wouldn't take him much more than twenty minutes to get to the Logger Room, but he grabbed his coat and headed out anyway.

Harley said, looking at her phone, "There's this whole thing about the 'River Glen Knifer' and Jesus, Mom . . . they've brought up the 'Babysitter Stalker' and the attack on Emma!"

They were in the kitchen and Emma was watching her programs in the living room. Jamie looked over at her sister, who was still tuned in to the episode of a show Jamie had seen four or five times already. "Let me see that," Jamie said, reaching for Harley's phone as she came around the island to her daughter's side.

"I was just trying to find something on your friend's death and all this sh . . . popped up." Harley handed over the phone.

Jamie scrolled through the article. A local reporter had clearly pulled archives on the two babysitter deaths that had occurred around the same time as Emma's attack. Emma's name was published, along with a sketchy but lurid account of someone sneaking into the house, catching her unawares, and then silencing her screams with a knife. No one knew exactly what had happened at the Ryerson house that night but this reporter wrote as if he'd been there. There was mention of Emma's head hitting the mantel and her compromised cognitive state "that affects every moment of her life."

Jamie's blood boiled. "It's this kind of half-truth bullshit that drives me insane," she hissed. "He doesn't know Emma. He doesn't know what she's like, what she's been through. She's just a *story* to him! And those two other deaths? One was definitely an accident and the other one was by her boyfriend, according to the victim's dad."

"What are you going to do?"

"Besides rip this guy a new one?"

"You're not going to do that." Harley gave her a come-on, look.

"I know. I want to, but I know I won't. I just want the truth to come out." Jamie thought about it for a minute, knowing she was too upset to think straight, but not caring. "Maybe I should ask Emma."

"About that night?" Harley asked in surprise. "She doesn't remember. You told me she doesn't remember."

"She remembers some things. We just don't want to upset her."

"But you're going to now?"

Jamie was torn. The last thing she wanted to do was cause
Emma anxiety or fear, but she also wanted to help in some
way. She couldn't help Gwen. She didn't know how to help
Bette other than to offer support. What she wanted was for
whoever was doing this to get caught.

"Emma . . ." Jamie walked into the living room, standing at the end of the couch, looking down and across at
her sister. Harley slid off her stool and moved into place
beside her.

Emma glanced at her briefly, then looked back to the TV.
"This is an Italian salad served with Italian dressing. It goes
with manicotti. They stuff the manicotti with cheese. I think
it's mozzarella, no, no, ricotta and Parmesan . . ." She trailed
off, absorbed.

"Emma, the night you were attacked. You remember?"

She cocked her head, but didn't take her eyes off the
television.

"You remember the man who attacked you?"

She looked away from the screen to a spot in the middle
distance between Jamie and the television but didn't speak.

"Was he wearing a ski mask?" Jamie asked her.

Her hands came up to cover her ears. "I see his *eyes*,"
she said.

"In a ski mask?" Jamie moved forward.

"He has a *knife*!"

"Stop, Emma. *Stop!*" Emma began rocking back and
forth, moaning. Her hands moving from her ears to over her
eyes. She made a low, keening noise that had Harley hyperventilating behind her.

"You stop it, too," Jamie ordered, whipping around to
look at her daughter. She then turned back to Emma.
"Emma, it's okay. It's okay."

"*I see his eyes!*"

"I know you do. But you're safe now. Safe with me and
Harley. In Mom's house. You're safe."

Her moaning tapered off and slowly ended in a sigh. She lifted her hands from her eyes and blinked. In a more normal voice, she said, "Mom keeps me safe."

"Yes, Mom kept you safe and we're here for you, too." Jamie reached a hand back for Harley, motioning her forward.

After a half beat, Harley moved to Emma, squatting down next to her. "I'm here," she said.

Emma bent her head forward and nodded slowly. She patted Harley on the shoulder, heaved a sigh, then picked up the remote and ran the episode back to the beginning. "I'd like to make manicotti next, Jamie," she said.

Jamie exhaled on a half laugh. "Okay. I'll go to the store."

"You need to make a list. Ricotta and Parmesan."

"I will," Jamie assured her.

Emma looked at her straight on and added, "I don't like ski masks."

The Logger Room was rough wood floors and long tables made of great slabs of wood from old-growth trees, their age putting them some fifty years before or more, when large boards were plentiful. The walls were also rough wood and covered with pickaxes, saws, and beer signs. There were no booths, just tables, about one third of them in use on a Sunday afternoon.

Cooper decided to wait for Campion to find out what she'd like before ordering. He stood at the end of the bar. Her Neon had looked like it had been driven hard. He was half-worried she wouldn't make it to the bar and was kicking himself at not offering to pick her up.

But then the door opened and she walked in. She was more cleaned up than the last time he'd seen her, in a black sweater and blue jeans. He imagined if she worked in the back of a restaurant, she'd have to present herself better for work, but then, he didn't know what kind of establishment had hired her.

She lifted her chin when she saw him and came his way. "You buying?" she asked Cooper and he nodded.

"Straight vodka. Grey Goose." She grinned at him, thinking she'd gotten one over on him. But the grin faded immediately. "You know Deke was pretty okay except when things got bad. Then he'd fall off the wagon and . . ." She shook her head. Her hair was brown, streaked with gray, straight as a sheath. It was newly washed, he thought.

He ordered her drink and a Budweiser for himself.

"You seem better now," Cooper observed.

"Cleaner, y'mean? Jobs are good. Keep the mind sharp. Out of depression."

The bartender brought her her drink and his beer. She clinked her glass against his. "Thank you kindly."

He half-expected her to knock it back. He was pretty sure he wasn't doing a thing for her health by buying her alcohol. But she sipped at the drink and even pointed to a table at the far side of the room, away from the other patrons.

Cooper sat down across from her.

"If I talk slow, will I get a second drink?" She eyed him craftily.

"Why don't we just see?" he parried. "How did Deke know Emma?"

"You know what Deke did before it got sold? He worked at Stillwell Seed and Feed. Damn near managed that company by hisself. And what did he get for his trouble? Jack shit. They sold that company and just went hog wild. Blew through the money. Deke never did find the same kind of work. I tried to help him, but I had my own problems. He bummed around for years until his dying day." She had a hand around the base of her drink, but she didn't lift it to her lips, which had pulled down in the corners as she spoke. "He was a nice guy. I know you don't think so, but he was. If those two Stillwell brothers could ever tell the truth, they'd say the same."

"Deke knew Emma from working at Stillwell Seed and Feed?"

"Ah, no. I don't think so. I'm just giving you some background. Deke . . ." Now she did swallow a hefty portion of her drink. "Deke took side jobs, too. Those skinflints never paid him enough. He did all kinds of stuff. He even fell off a roof once, treating it for moss. Really screwed up his back . . . That's how he connected with that doctor . . . Dr. William Ryerson. Gave him way too many pills. But that's how he got Deke to do stuff for him."

Cooper had brought his pad and was itching to take notes, but this wasn't the kind of interview where that would be acceptable. He would just have to wait until it was over. "What kind of stuff?"

"Well, before he was disbarred, or whatever you call it, from being a doctor . . ."

"Dr. Ryerson still practices."

She waved him off. "Whatever. Before he left town, then. He wanted Deke to be his little detective. He thought his wife was cheating on him. She had all the money, according to Deke, and this guy wanted a part of it. He told Deke he needed to catch her with her lover, and he wanted Deke to be the one to get the evidence. So, Deke followed her around as much as he could, because he was still working at the Seed and Feed at that point. And then, the big night came up."

"The hospital event at Hotel Lovejoy."

She used both of her hands to make like guns, pointing them at him. "You got it. Except it's the wife who accused him of cheating on her, instead of the other way around. Big fight. Deke wasn't there, of course, but the doctor was calling him, screaming at him to follow her. She left with some other doctor and the husband was really, really pissed."

"She said that she left after the fight because he was drunk and she was embarrassed by the scene," Cooper said.

"Well, sure, that's what she said, but she really just wanted to go home with the other doctor. Those doctors worked together and they hated each other. And the wife was a bitch. That's what Deke said Ryerson told him. A bitch with all the money. And she was looking to ditch him for this other one."

"Dr. Metcalf," Cooper said.

"Maybe. I don't know his name."

"He's the doctor who took her home that night."

"Okay, Metcalf. But Dr. Ryerson didn't know who her lover was, then. So, he had a whole different plan. He wasn't really drunk. He was fake drunk. He was planning to have a big fight to see who she chose to go home with. *Bam.* She fell for it. She accused him of being a drunk and a cheater, and then she walked out with this other doctor. So, Ryerson put his plan in motion."

"What plan?"

"He called Deke and told him to go and teach the fucking bitch a lesson, which Deke went to do. At his house. But when Deke got there, the wife wasn't back yet. She was off with the other doctor, probably at his place."

Cooper could see it all, almost as if he were watching a movie. "The babysitter was there instead."

"Yep."

"What did Deke do?" Cooper's voice was stone cold.

She looked up at his tone. "No, no, no! Deke wouldn't hurt a fly. He would never have hurt her. Never! It wasn't *him.* It was probably that kid. That's what Deke always thought."

"What kid?" Cooper asked. He tried to keep from sounding so accusing. He didn't want to stop the flow of information by scaring her silent.

"A high school kid. He was at the back door, talking to Emma. They were fighting. Arguing. So Deke left. He waited around a while, but then something happened and he decided to leave."

Dug had gone back and talked to Emma. He'd lied through his teeth about that. Cooper could feel his anger boiling up. "What happened?" he asked Campion.

She shrugged. "Don't know. Maybe nothing. Maybe Deke just left. Decided he didn't want to get involved in that. Later, apparently, the wife came home and found the baby-sitter unconscious. Luckily, the kids slept through it all. That's what Deke always thought anyway. He gave praise to God for sparing the kids, but he always felt bad about 'my Emma.' That's what he called her."

Cooper could hear the faint jealousy in her tone even now.

He knew it was Dug, but he asked anyway. "Who was the high school kid?"

"Weren't you one of 'em? You should probably know better than Deke." She tilted her head. "Do I get my drink now?" She lifted her empty glass and wiggled it.

Cooper tried to ask a couple more questions, but Hillary Campion was tapped out. He bought her another drink, dropped a tip for the bartender, and left her sipping away as he headed out to his SUV and started writing down his notes. He put in a call to William Ryerson but had to leave his name on the man's voice message. He had a lot of new questions for him.

Chapter Twenty-Eight

Cooper called Jamie on his way back from the Logger Room. "Where are you?" he asked her, hearing unidentifiable noise in the background.

"The grocery store. I'm making cheese manicotti for dinner. You're invited. Six-thirty."

She sounded subdued. Assuming it was about Gwen, he assured her, "I'm going to make sure the lab gets me the results on the spilled tea."

"Will there be an autopsy?"

"Yes. There needs to be. Her parents are on their way to River Glen."

"Do you think it was suicide?" she asked hesitantly.

"I don't know. She didn't seem the type."

"She isn't . . . wasn't. . . ." She sighed and then told him that she'd tried to ask Emma about the ski mask, ending with, "I think all I did was upset her."

"I just finished interviewing Hillary Campion, Deke Girard's girlfriend. Deke's the man who would come into the Thrift Shop to see Emma and recently died."

"Who scared her," Jamie clarified.

"Yes, but I think he really was trying to protect her, in his way." He went on to explain everything he'd learned from Campion. He finished with, "I'm sure it was Dug he saw fighting with her."

"Dug." Jamie swept in a breath.

"I'm going over to his place now. I'm going to see him, or wait till he shows. Whatever it takes."

"Be careful," she said immediately. "Gwen warned us."

"I've got another call in to William Ryerson," he said, "but Mike Corliss might have been right about it being one of us boys."

"Maybe someone should go with you to Dug's."

"I've got this. Don't worry. I'll see you at dinner, if I can. I'll call you either way."

"Cooper . . ."

He could tell she was choking up. "It's okay. We're finally going to learn something about what happened to Emma."

"I was going to say, stay safe."

"I will."

Dug Douglas . . . Patrick "Dug" Douglas . . . Greer Douglas's father.

Jamie clicked off her cell and finished buying her groceries, barely able to concentrate on the list. Had Dug stabbed Emma? Why? *Why?*

And how in God's name was she going to tell Harley?

Her phone rang and she saw it was Camryn. She immediately felt a welling up in her chest because she knew she was calling about Gwen. It reminded Jamie of how unfair to Gwen she'd been growing up and when Camryn said, "I just heard about Gwen. Oh, God, Jamie. I'm just sick." It was all she could do to keep from bawling.

Cooper drove to Dug's home with barely leashed fury. The Douglas's two-story house was white with black shutters, a modern version of a Colonial, and it sat on the edge of Staffordshire Estates. The yard was trimmed and there was a basketball hoop over the garage, a reminder that Dug and Teri had a son, Greer, a senior at River Glen High.

Cooper pressed his finger to the bell, reminding himself to stay cool. After all these years *. . . after all these years . . .*

Dug himself answered the door. He had a sour look on his face. He didn't say "You again," but he might as well have.

Cooper didn't waste time. "You had a face-to-face with Emma after the rest of us left the night she was attacked. You had a fight with her. And you never told the police. Did you tell Race? Have you both kept that back all these years?"

Dug looked like he was going to deny it. He clearly wanted to. But he took a second glance at Cooper and shook his head.

"What did you do, Dug?" Cooper asked coldly.

"Goddammit." He looked past Cooper, checking both ways, then waved him in. "Teri and Greer aren't here. Greer's hot for your daughter's friend. He's over at Emma's now."

For a moment, Cooper was distracted, but he pushed that news aside as he stepped across the threshold. Dug closed the door behind him and led him into his den, a place where every square inch of counter space and shelving held stacks of paper.

"Sit down," he invited with a vague wave. Cooper looked around. There was no place to sit that wasn't covered with paper. "I can stand."

"Oh, sit down." Dug made a disgusted sound and grabbed a sheaf of papers from a client seat that looked uncomfortable and, as Cooper learned when he sat, was.

Dug seated himself behind his desk, which faced out toward the room at large.

"What happened that night?" Cooper asked.

"Okay, look. I know you're pissed. Fine. You have a right to be."

"What did you fight about with Emma?" He practically bit off every word.

"Her *boyfriend*. Not Race. The college boy, or whatever he was. Older. I gave her hell for leading Race on."

"She didn't lead him—"

"I'm telling you what I saw, okay? And she led him the fuck on for most of high school. I told Race once I thought she was a lesbian, but he thought it was an older guy, and he was right. She *admitted* it that night."

He glanced at Cooper who held back a list of angry epithets with an effort. Eventually Dug sighed. "I went back there and the back door was unlocked and yeah, I walked right in. I scared her and she blasted me, actually shoved me out of the main house into that anteroom. I told her to get rid of whoever she was seeing and get with Race. You know what she did? She laughed. Really laughed. Hardy, har, har. I was so pissed I could hardly see straight. I told her I was going to tell everybody that she was seeing some older dude who just used her for sex."

Cooper growled beneath his breath.

"Don't worry. She didn't give a shit. You know what she said? She said, 'Go ahead. We're getting married. Do your worst, asshole!' That just burned. I wanted to kill her myself. I really did. But I didn't touch her. I was so pissed at her and I still am. I know she's compromised now. Really messed up. I'm just telling you how I felt . . . how I still feel. I'm being fucking honest, okay? Everything on the line. Make of it what you will. Give me a lie detector test. When I left her that night, she was fine. Still laughing at me."

Cooper said angrily, "If you'd told the truth at the time, the investigation would've turned toward this boyfriend. There would have been a more concentrated effort in that direction."

"They coulda looked for him anyway."

"Her mother and her sister and her friends . . . nobody thought she was seeing anyone. Only you heard it from her lips."

"I wouldn't be so sure about her friends. . . ."

Cooper stared at him, wondering if he was trying to shift blame. He wouldn't put it past him. "Who was the guy she was seeing?"

"Shit, I don't know. I think I saw her with him, maybe at Jake's Grill once, in Portland. I knew it was her. I told her that night, that I saw her, and that scared her a little. She denied it up and down. Then she turned around and called me an asshole. 'Do your worst, asshole.' That's what she said."

"Would you recognize him?"

"Twenty years later, man? Come on. And anyway, I just saw the back of him."

"What do you remember?" Cooper asked, not giving up.

Dug shook his head, then looked down at the desktop. "A guy in a gray suit. Exec type, I thought. Dark hair. Maybe some gray in it . . . I remember thinking, 'Who's the old dude with Emma?' She was really tuned into him. Just . . . ripe, you know? It was obvious."

Cooper didn't like the way Dug talked about Emma, but he pushed his own feelings aside. "She planned to marry him?"

"That's what she said. She didn't know that I didn't really see him. I was just jabbing her, but then . . . then she said that and slammed the door on me. I left there really mad, but I didn't *touch* her."

"You told Race?"

"Uh-uh. I told no one. You think I don't know what would've happened to me? The cops would've blamed it on me. That detective . . . Corliss? He wanted it to be one of us. There was no coming forward about it without consequences. I'm sorry about Emma. I really am. That should've never happened to her, and yeah, find out who the bastard is. But she was a bitch in those days. That's a fact."

He was still nursing a hurt from twenty years earlier. Cooper didn't even try to hide his disgust. Did he believe Dug? Up to a point. He still wasn't sure about Emma's secret lover, but he saw that Dug was.

"The doer might've been caught by now if you hadn't been so worried about your own skin."

"Well, find him now, then. 'Do your worst.'" His smile was hard. "I've told you all I know." Dug moved from behind his desk, indicating his patience for the interview was over.

Cooper got to his feet. "Did you see a guy in a ski mask?"

"Like Race? No."

The sound of a car pulling into the garage was unmistakable. "That's my lovely wife. I'd rather we didn't talk about this in front of her."

"The truth emerges, Dug."

"Fine. Let it emerge. Just not right now. Okay?"

Cooper left without another word. He didn't want to run into Teri right now either, or Dug's son, Greer. He looked to see how long it had been since his second call to Ryerson. An hour. He held himself back from trying again, and instead put in another call to Nadine Ryerson. Once again the call went straight to voice mail, where he left a second message.

After a heartfelt, teary conversation with Camryn, Jamie actually felt more human. She was mixing up mozzarella, ricotta, and Parmesan with an egg when Harley cruised into the kitchen. She had her earbuds in and was listening to something on her phone, but she casually pulled them out as she sat down on one of the barstools.

"What is it this time?" she asked, viewing Jamie's workspace.

"The manicotti Emma asked for."

Harley grunted, then slid a glance over to the pasta cylinders that were waiting to be stuffed. "I'm kind of sick of pasta."

Jamie said, "I've made a salad that's just waiting to be dressed. You can have some of that."

"I'd, uh, rather go to Deno's for pizza."

Jamie said, "Same flavor profile."

"Well, yeah, but it's not pasta. Maybe I can just cruise over there."

Jamie lifted her head from what she was doing and gave Harley a hard look. "By yourself?"

"It's only a couple of blocks away. We all walked there the other night."

"Harley . . ." Jamie was almost speechless. "Your friend was chased by an intruder with a knife, and Bette Kearns is in the hospital, and Gwen . . . You think I want you walking by yourself, even a couple of blocks? It'll be dark soon."

"Well, I don't have a license yet," she snapped. "Or a permit. All I've got is walking unless you want to drop me off."

"What's going on?"

"Nothing! Don't make a big deal of it!" She slid off the stool and stomped off.

"I'm not."

"You act like I'm five!" she yelled over her shoulder as she bolted up the stairs.

Emma, obviously hearing their escalating argument, came down the stairs, glancing back a time or two to where Harley had burst past her door. "Harley's mad?" she asked Jamie.

"I guess so."

"You're mad?"

"More like . . . confused. She wants to go to Deno's for dinner."

Emma looked around the kitchen. "We are having manicotti." She cocked her head and looked at the two jars of marinara sauce waiting to be opened. "You are supposed to make the sauce from tomatoes."

"That's not going to happen."

"Why not?"

"Is there anything you want to eat beside pasta?" Jamie asked. She'd learned diverting Emma's attention was the best way to get through to her.

"I like doughnuts."

"Did Mom make you pasta?"

She nodded. "Not as much as you do."

"So, you like other things, too. What kinds of things?"

"Nachos."

"Nachos. That's something different. Maybe we can make nachos later this week."

"They're just an appetizer. . . ." She looked toward the kitchen window to the backyard. "Mom only made spaghetti, but he said I should branch out. He got me rigatoni and he had manicotti."

Jamie followed her gaze toward the back window. "Who are we talking about?"

"Mom told me to learn to make my own. I think I can make my own now."

Jamie said, "Do you want to help stuff the manicotti?"

"Yes."

"Who was it that told you to branch out?" she asked as she finished mixing the manicotti stuffing and put the pasta cylinders in front of Emma with a small spoon.

Emma dipped the spoon in the cheese mixture and began stuffing the pasta shells. She broke almost every one, but Jamie tucked them back together as best she could.

"I'm not good at this," said Emma.

"Did you hear what I asked you? Who was it told you to branch out?"

"I don't know. I don't think I like him anymore."

"Mom."

Jamie looked over. Harley had dressed in her nicest jeans, combed her hair, and . . . maybe added a bit of mascara and lipstick? Jamie straightened. "Who's going to be at Deno's?" she asked.

Harley wanted to deny it. Jamie could see her expression darken. But the jig was up and she seemed to realize she couldn't lie to her mother and still hope to get what she wanted, namely going to Deno's. "Just some kids from school."

"Marissa?"

"I don't know . . . I don't think so."

"Greer?"

"Just some kids from school. Do we have to make this an inquisition?"

Emma squinted at her. "You have a boyfriend," she said sagely.

"I don't have a boyfriend." Harley was adamant, but color was creeping up her neck.

"I need to know who you're meeting," Jamie said. "I'll drive you if you want to go, but you're not walking alone."

"I can go?" She brightened.

"Tell me who you're meeting."

"Okay, Greer. And some other friends. I called Marissa, but she's like on lockdown. And she's agoraphobic now, too."

"Well, I don't know about that."

"She doesn't want to go to tae kwon do anymore. She doesn't want to go anywhere."

"She's been through a trauma."

"Maybe you could talk to her mom. . . ."

Jamie half-laughed. Harley knew better than that.

"Talk to Mr. Haynes. Tell him to tell Marissa's mom to let her come to Deno's," Harley urged.

"Yeah, like that's going to happen." Jamie slid the last broken manicotti shell smeared with the ricotta mix away from Emma, who wiggled her messy fingers.

"Why not?" Harley demanded.

"Because we've all got a lot on our plates, Harley. And Greer and Troy Stillwell and Tyler Stapleton, and your friend Katie Timbolt . . . they're all in trouble in different ways. Who exactly is going to be there?"

"I said I don't know," she snapped.

"You really want me to get between them and Marissa's mom? How do you think that's going to go over?"

"Okay, fine. Can I just go?"

"I'll walk with you," Emma said.

"No, Emma," Jamie intervened. "Then you'd be walking back alone, and that's not going to happen."

"We could all go," Emma said.

Jamie wanted to argue that she was in the middle of getting dinner ready, but apart from preheating the oven, there was nothing actually baking yet.

"Fine. We'll all walk down together and you can text me when you want to come back. And I need to know how many kids are descending on Deno's."

Harley said quickly, "Okay. I'll meet you outside," and she practically ran out the front door.

"Do you think they'll have sex?" Emma asked as she pulled her jacket from the front closet.

"Please, don't put that image in my head, Emma." Jamie grabbed her own hooded anorak.

"I know. It's pretty personal."

The three of them walked to Deno's together. As they neared the restaurant, it was Harley whose footsteps faltered. She looked through the windows, and so did Jamie. Greer

Douglas was seated in a booth, but he was alone. No other kids so far.

"Is this a date?" Jamie asked.

"Hell no." Harley was adamant.

"It looks like a date," said Jamie.

"It's not. Others are coming." Harley was positive.

"I will chaperone," said Emma.

"I don't need a chaperone. It's not a date. I'm fine. I won't leave the pizzeria until you come to get me. Okay?"

"Okay," said Emma, and turned to head back.

"Wait. Whoa." To Harley, she directed, "Go inside and wave to me and then we'll go back. You're only here for an hour," said Jamie.

Harley rolled her eyes and nodded. She headed toward the door, yanking it open. Jamie and Emma stood outside, watching through the side windows as Harley walked down the row of booths to where Greer was seated. He grinned at her as she slid into the seat opposite him.

"That's a date," Jamie said.

"Sure is," Emma agreed.

"I don't know how to feel about it."

"Mom knew."

Jamie wasn't sure what that meant, but it was part of Emma's mantra. "We'll come back in an hour," she told Emma, and they walked back together.

Cooper called Laura as soon as he was finished with Dug. "I want to talk to Marissa," he told his ex when she answered the phone.

"Good. Maybe you can make her understand. She wants to meet that Harley girl at a pizza parlor with other kids, and I think some of the ones with really bad behavior will be there."

"I've called her cell, but she's not answering."

"She only answers the calls she wants." Laura sounded frazzled.

"Tell her to call me, then." At least Laura was willing to have Marissa speak to him. That was an improvement over the last week, although it hurt a bit that Marissa was ignoring his calls.

He waited, drumming his fingers on the steering wheel. He'd driven into River Glen and parked near the town's city center. He wanted to head straight to Jamie's, but rather than having to worry about being late, it turned out he was too early. Instead, he was killing time.

His cell rang and he snatched it up, sure it was Marissa, but it was Dr. William Ryerson.

"Detective," Ryerson greeted him in his gravelly voice. "Your persistence could be viewed as harassment, but I'm choosing to keep cooperating for now. Remember that. Now, what can I help you with?"

"Deke Girard."

Cooper's blunt response was met with an intake of breath and then silence. "What about him?" Ryerson said after too long a moment, but Cooper was tired of all the careful posturing. He baldly laid out what he'd learned from Hillary Campion, finishing with, "You hired Girard to go to your house that night and find your wife. But she wasn't there. Emma Whelan was."

He hesitated, then said, "I heard Deke Girard's dead."

"He is."

"Dead men tell no tales," he pointed out.

"Sometimes those tales live on. Here's one about you. You thought your wife was having an affair, but you didn't know with whom. You were more fake drunk than drunk. Deke was supposed to even the score somehow."

"I don't have to talk to you."

"Whatever Deke was supposed to do, it never got done.

And then Emma was hurt and you needed to cover up your plan. You tried to work things out with your ex. Managed to stick with her for about a year, but you kept seeing Kayla on the side and Nadine finally left."

"I was the injured party, Detective. You've got this backward."

Cooper went on, "But she finally left you and took her money with her. That wasn't what you wanted. You needed her because your career was in trouble. You were rumored to be a 'pill doctor.'"

"That had nothing to do with it!" he suddenly burst out. "My wife was having an affair with Alain Metcalf. She went home with him that night!"

"She said at the time that she turned to him because you were drunk. She didn't know you were faking it, and probably still doesn't. She swore she wasn't involved with Metcalf."

"Well, that's a lie."

Cooper needed to tread carefully here. He'd tapped into Ryerson's anger and that could work to his advantage, as long as he didn't push too hard, too fast. "You sent Deke to your house. What was he supposed to do? Attack her? Kill her?"

"*No!*"

"You sent him there."

"To scare the shit out of her. Teach her a lesson. But he stabbed Emma instead."

"He told you that?" His cell started buzzing with another call coming in. Marissa. He hesitated, then ignored her call. He would call her back.

"No. He said there was somebody else there and he ran away. He was lying, of course. Girard was a drunk, and drunks are liars. He was supposed to scare Nadine, that's all, but he ended up attacking the babysitter. I didn't want him to hurt Nadine. Not like that. He was just supposed to make her think he would, but he wasn't supposed to go through with it. I stayed on at the hotel till the party was over. Last to leave. Everyone saw me, so no one would suspect I had anything to do with scaring her, but then . . ." He heaved an angry sigh. "Deke should've followed Nadine to Metcalf's place. That's where she was those hours in between. In his bed. He was her lover, no matter what she says. Have you talked to her? Interviewed her?"

"She's next on my list."

"Make her tell you that Metcalf was her lover. I'm not sorry he's dead, but it's too bad you can't get the story directly from him. You want a 'pill doctor'? Metcalf was handing 'em out like candy. Maybe we all were a little too loose in our prescriptions back then," he allowed, "but somebody killed him over it, so what does that tell you?"

Cooper thought about that. Metcalf's death. Though a good five years after the attack on Emma, maybe it had tentacles that reached back somehow. Could it be that both Ryerson and Metcalf, rumored to be free with their prescriptions, had run afoul of a killer, and that Emma had been an innocent victim?

Ryerson let Cooper know he was done by saying, "Deke Girard attacked Emma Whelan, but that had nothing to do with me. You want anything further, you talk to my lawyer."

Chapter Twenty-Nine

Jamie decided to wait to put the manicotti in the oven until she heard from Cooper. She checked the time. Harley had been gone her allotted hour and it would take a few more to walk down there, so she hollered up to Emma that she was going to pick up Harley as the doorbell rang.

Cooper?

She went to the door and was shocked to see Harley on the stoop. "I forgot my key and just thought I'd ring the bell because you were probably in the kitchen."

"I told you to stay there and not walk—" She cut herself off as Harley waved to whoever was in the black Mustang throbbing at the curb. The driver put up a hand, then pulled away.

"Who's that?" Jamie demanded.

"Greer gave me a ride home. You said an hour and I'm here early."

"We were supposed to text. I was supposed to . . ." She drew a breath. "You were not supposed to get into a car with a driver under age *thirty*!"

"I'm safe. I'm here. All's well."

Jamie's cell told her a text was coming in. She snatched up her phone and checked the screen. Cooper. Saying he'd be over in thirty minutes. "We need to talk about this,

Harley," she said as she marched to the oven and put the manicotti inside.

"Why?"

"You know why!" Jamie glared at her daughter. "Don't put on this act. Don't." She felt herself near tears. All day, she'd managed to hold herself together, to keep Gwen's face out of her mind, but she couldn't anymore.

"I just wanted to be with my friends. I don't know why that's so hard for you."

Jamie shook her head, not trusting her voice. She was glad Emma and Duchess were upstairs.

Harley's shoulders slumped. "Next time I'll tell you first."

Jamie's cell phone rang. It was still in her hand and she looked down at it, realizing Vicky was calling. She inhaled a calming breath and turned away from her daughter. Vicky didn't call, she texted. "Hello," she answered.

"Oh, God, Jamie! I heard about Gwen! Oh my God. Oh, dear God! What's the world coming to?"

"I don't know."

"Things have just fallen to hell." Vicky started crying, and that made Jamie grit her teeth, fighting back emotion. "I know you heard about Tyler. He's an *idiot*. I can't talk about it without crying. But Gwen . . . Is there anything I can do for you?"

"Thank you, Vic . . . toria No, I'm okay. It was a shock."

"Do you need anything?"

"No."

"Have you heard what happened?"

"They'll know more tomorrow, I think."

"I want to go see Bette. I think she might be coming home tomorrow. They throw them out of the hospital as soon as they can these days. I'll call you and let you know about her?"

"Yes. Thanks. Please do."

"Okay . . ." She was sniffling now. "Don't know if you

heard, but Alicia's taking Troy away from Deon's control. Race and Deon are about to get foreclosed on if they don't sell their house. I'm trying to get them going so they'll have something from a sale—the property is valuable—but they're not listening to me, or anyone else."

Jamie made appropriate sounds of condolence.

"Okay. If you hear anything more about Gwen, or about Bette's attack or Laura's daughter's, call me, please."

"I'll try."

Once she was off the phone, Jamie turned back around. Harley had left the kitchen. Good. She needed a moment to process.

When Cooper walked through the door a few minutes later, she stood still for a moment. *Don't cry,* she warned herself. *Don't cry. Don't do anything stupid.*

"What happened?" he asked, coming toward her.

She shook her head, her eyes burning.

After a moment, he folded her into his arms and she collapsed against him.

Harley heard the door open, and a deep, male voice. Mr. Haynes. She opened her bedroom door carefully—it had a tendency to squeak—then tiptoed down the hall. She saw her mom wrapped in Mr. Haynes's embrace, and that caught her up short. She didn't know how to feel about that. Sort of jealous, maybe.

But then she remembered how Greer had taken her hand across the table when she'd asked where everybody else was. "It's just you and me," he said. Everyone else had flaked out, he'd added, but all she could think about was his hand holding hers.

Then he'd asked, "Did you tell about Tyler and Katie?"

She'd instantly gone cold. Was torn between lying a little

and lying a lot. She couldn't tell the truth. She'd be a rat. The lowest of the low.

"Is that why you invited me to Deno's?" she'd asked in a small voice. She had to know.

"You're the only one I told."

"What about Tyler . . . and Katie? Who'd they tell?"

"I don't know."

She'd pulled back her hand reluctantly. She liked Greer. A lot. She liked his sense of humor, the way his hair fell over his forehead, the color of his eyes, the shape of his lips, *everything*. But she was afraid he might be toying with her. He was good friends with Troy, and Troy had said those things about Emma.

"Well, maybe we should just order pizza," she said, looking away from him.

She saw his eyes narrow, as if he were calculating something. A long, silent few minutes went by. Finally, he said, "We made kind of a pact. We'd see how far we could get with you guys."

"What do you mean?"

"The sophomore girls." He flicked her a look, then glanced away. "Tyler obviously got the farthest with Katie. Troy wanted you, and we were fighting about it the night we went to the house where Marissa was babysitting. We thought you were there, but then you weren't."

Harley could feel her face heat with the betrayal of it. "You didn't go inside and—"

"No," he said swiftly. "No way. That was . . . I don't know what that was. That wasn't us. But that night was the end of the pact. It was stupid. Tyler's idea. I don't know why. Maybe he had a thing for Katie but couldn't tell Dara."

"So, you just wanted to tell me that? That's why we're here?"

"I wouldn't have told you about Tyler and Katie if that was all it was." He met her gaze.

Harley's emotions were yo-yoing. One moment she was on cloud nine, the next in the depths of despair, the next somewhere in between. "So, what is this, then?" She motioned to include the two of them in the booth.

"A date?"

They'd never gotten in line to order pizza. They'd just sat in the booth and talked. Harley looked around and realized she would never make it home in time if they ordered now. "I have to walk home in like twenty minutes."

"I'll drive you. That gives us a few more."

"Okay."

He ordered them each a Coke and they sat across from each other and pretty much just stared at each other and smiled the rest of the time. When he pulled up in front of her house, he leaned over and kissed her lightly on the lips. Then they'd bumped fists and he'd said, "See you tomorrow," and Harley had tripped up the steps to the house and rung the bell.

And then . . . she'd been shitty to her mom. She'd known Mom wasn't going to like it.

Now, she looked at her mother in Mr. Haynes's embrace and tiptoed backward into her room before either of them saw her.

Was it real with Greer? She was beginning to think so. Maybe.

She pulled out her cell, deciding to text Marissa. Her fingers hovered over the alphabet keys. She started several times. She wanted to share, but she also wanted to keep it to herself. Finally, she wrote: **Met Greer at denos. Nobody showed but him and me**

Immediately, Marissa wrote back: **I shoulda gone. Sick of being home**

Harley texted: **good I'll see you at school**

To which Marissa gave her a thumb's-up emoji.

Harley's stomach rumbled. She opened her bedroom door

with a flourish to alert the adults, just as Emma and Duchess came into the hall. The dog nearly knocked Harley over with her enthusiasm before going on high alert and suddenly howling wildly.

"Jesus, don't freak me out, Duchess," Harley said.

"Yeah, me too," said Emma. "Don't freak me out. And don't swear."

Jamie pulled herself out of Cooper's arms at almost the same moment she heard Harley and Emma and Duchess enter the hall. The dog started howling, which made her jump about a foot. "What's going on?" she asked, alarmed.

Duchess ran toward Cooper and slid to a halt. She checked him out all over and finally started wagging her tail.

"You were too close to Jamie," Emma stated matter-of-factly.

Jamie looked from the dog to her sister. Sometimes Emma was almost prescient, in a weird way.

Cooper patted Duchess's head. "Good guard dog."

They all sat down at the table for dinner and Duchess, apart from some minor whining, waited until they were finished to be fed her evening meal. Harley had come downstairs and scooped herself a heaping helping of manicotti and Jamie looked at her hard.

"I didn't eat any pizza," Harley admitted. "We just talked."

Cooper looked at Harley and then at Jamie.

Emma said, "Jamie doesn't like her boyfriend."

"That's not it," Jamie denied.

"They fight," Emma added for Cooper's benefit.

Harley said around a mouthful of manicotti, "I do like pasta. I just wanted to go to Deno's."

Jamie looked at Cooper and said dryly, "Welcome to the Whelan/Woodward household."

"Are you and Jamie having sex?" Emma asked, to which Harley nearly spit out her food.

"Emma," Jamie said on an intake of breath.

"It's personal," Emma said. Cooper looked a bit taken aback, but then he just chuckled. Emma gave him a sideways look, and though she didn't quite smile in return, she said, "You and I are good friends."

Cooper slowly grew more sober, and he looked at her with warmth and a tinge of sadness. "We have been for a long time, Emma."

Harley looked over at Jamie. She was clearly moved by his words, as was Jamie. *I'm sorry,* Harley mouthed.

Jamie winked at her in forgiveness.

An hour later, Jamie walked Cooper out to his car, parked at the end of their driveway. "Emma," he said, shaking his head and smiling.

"I know. I think she enjoys being a little outrageous. She always was a little that way," said Jamie.

He nodded. "What happened with Harley?"

"One moment she's wonderful, the next she's testy and prickly and kind of gunning for a fight."

"Sounds like fifteen."

"Yeah." She then told him about Harley meeting Greer at Deno's, and him bringing Harley back by car.

Cooper said, "Marissa was supposed to go to that. I just talked to her before I got here. She feels like she's under a microscope at home, yet she's a little afraid to go out. I encouraged her, but she decided not to."

"Well, I'm glad to hear there were actually other people invited who didn't show. I thought it might be a setup."

Jamie told him about Vicky's phone call and her acceptance that Tyler had some responsibility for what had happened with Katie Timbolt. "She was commiserating with me about Gwen. She felt terrible."

Cooper said, "Hopefully, we'll know some more tomorrow. Gwen's parents should be here in a day or two."

"How terrible for them. I can't imagine it."

He nodded, and they were both silent for a minute. Then he said, "I talked to Dr. Ryerson again." He brought her up-to-date on that phone call, and they discussed his engaging Deke to go to the Ryerson house to put the scare into his wife. "Ryerson seems to believe Deke attacked Emma. He didn't mention Dug, so I don't think he knew he was there."

"It sounds like Deke saw Dug. Do you think he came back later and attacked Emma? And has spent all these years trying to make it up to her in his way?" Jamie asked.

"It's possible. Doesn't sound like the Deke Girard Hillary Campion knows, but then, she considered him her boyfriend, so she's hardly impartial."

They talked a bit more, running over more territory. He pulled her to him and kissed her hard, then set her an arm's length away. "I've gotta go. If I don't, I won't, and you have responsibilities."

"Yes," she said, throwing a glance at the house.

"Tomorrow," he told her.

"Tomorrow," she agreed, and she walked back inside as Cooper got into his SUV.

When the morning came, Jamie received a phone call from the school. Could she substitute for a sophomore Social Studies teacher? She agreed and didn't tell Harley until they were at the school that she would be substituting in her class.

"Oh, okay," Harley said. She was already outside the car and strapping on her backpack, her gaze on the school.

"Really? Okay?"

"Gotta go." She began hurrying away, and Jamie saw that she was heading toward where Marissa was just climbing out of her mother's car. Laura got out as well, and Jamie thought about her partner, David Musgrave, and his ingratiating manner at Elgin DeGuerre's law firm.

And then Teddy Ryerson's words came back to her.

I'm just asking you to pay attention. That's all. I don't want you to lose your money, or somehow be . . . cheated out of what's yours.

She'd never trusted that Teddy might know what he was talking about financially. She'd assumed he was merely trying to get her as a client to line his own pockets. Now, she realized she'd put him in that category because anything to do with the Ryersons had been anathema to her since the attack on Emma. They'd all been tarred by the same brush, but maybe that was unfair.

And could she trust David Musgrave and Elgin DeGuerre? Her mother had. But Elgin was retiring and, frankly, not doing so well.

As she went into the school, she made a mental note to talk to Cooper about it.

Cooper called his contact at the lab, Gina Rodriguez, as soon as he got to work, but was told they didn't have any results on Gwen Winkelman's death yet. "Everybody wants a rush," Gina told him when he asked for the same. "I'll get back to you this afternoon to let you know where we are."

Because Howie was handling the attack on Marissa, and that included Troy Stillwell and Greer Douglas, Cooper had handed him the Stapleton/Timbolt part of the investigation, since Tyler Stapleton had been with the other two boys that same night. Now, Howie brought him up-to-date on the situation with Tyler, Katie Timbolt, and the Pendelans. "No one's pressing charges. I don't know what those parents said or did to get their children off the hook, but it's all done."

"Offered them money," Verbena guessed.

"The school's taking a harder look than we are. Robbie Padilla, the coach, is taking heat because the Stillwell and Douglas kids are out of the game this Friday. Stapleton, again, too," Howie said.

From speaking with Robbie, Cooper knew his old friend was trying to wrangle all three boys into making better choices. Troy Stillwell's father, Deon, was no help. In many ways, he was Troy's biggest problem.

"That faction of freshman parents you met with?" Howie added. "The ones who wanted the boys expelled over the Halloween mixer prank? They've gotten wind of some of what's going on and are doubling down."

Cooper thought about Edina, Caroline, and Marty and Hal, the foursome with freshmen children who were vocal about how the school should be run. It looked like Cathy Timbolt, known for being a wolf crier against perceived wrongs at the school, had ceded her crown of outrage to those four. Katie Timbolt had probably ended her mother's run for a school board position to boot.

He turned his mind from the goings-on at River Glen High, which were small and irrelevant compared to the attacks on Marissa and Bette Kearns. If none of the teens were responsible for either of those home invasions, were the attacks related in some other way? He couldn't believe they were completely independent of each other. But if there was a connection, he didn't see it yet. Nothing had been stolen, so the doer hadn't gained personally. One was of a teenage girl, the other a woman in a rocky marriage. One took place at a home in the older part of town, the other at the newer, west end of town, on the edge of Staffordshire Estates.

And was there . . . how could there be? . . . some kind of eerie echo to the attack on Emma Whelan twenty years before?

"You really stirred up Eric Volker," Verbena said with a faint smile.

"Volker? Why? His alibi would be hard to break," said Cooper.

"He seemed to think your 'interrogation'—his word, not mine—of his ex-wife was unnecessary and 'unseemly'— again, his word—and that he's planning to sue the police and you personally."

"He can get in line," Cooper growled, recalling William Ryerson's threat to do the same.

Thinking of Ryerson, Cooper pulled up Nadine Ryerson Campbell's number again. She'd never gotten back to him. He figured he'd try her again and leave another message, if need be. He wanted her to know he wasn't giving up.

The call rang and rang, and he prepared himself to reiterate what he'd said in the other messages; namely, that, as a detective with the River Glen Police Department, he was looking into some cold cases, like the one in which Emma Whelan was attacked in her old house. He wanted to ask Nadine about her recollections of that night.

He was so prepared that he was slightly taken aback when she suddenly answered. "Hello, Detective Haynes. What do you want to know?"

She clearly had recognized his number. "Hello, Nadine. I wanted to go over the night Emma Whelan was attacked." As he had said several times before. "You arrived at the house ahead of your husband and discovered Emma Whelan on the floor."

"Detective, I don't know what I can tell you that I haven't already said. It was a terrible night from beginning to end. William was embarrassingly drunk and fell off a chair. He was flirting with Kayla and mean to me. He kept saying he knew I had a lover. Loudly. I could feel my face burning. I actually kicked him once, under the table, but he just howled and said what a bitch I was. He was the one tomcatting around, but he was blaming it all on me. So, I left with Alain. I needed a shoulder to cry on, and he was there." She hesitated, then added, "I was a little attracted to him, and I'd had more to drink than I realized, so I went to his place. *Not* for sex. I was so sick of William. Of his cheating and drinking and just everything. I was so exhausted I fell asleep on Alain's couch. Nothing happened between us. Alain shook me awake to take me home, and I didn't want to go. I wanted to stay, but . . ." She inhaled and exhaled. "You know the rest. Alain took me home and dropped me off. I didn't want him to come in, in case William was there. I didn't need another scene. I walked into the house and into the living room and there was Emma, on the floor. It was shocking and terrible. Sometimes it jumps across my mind and I can still feel the horror of seeing her, lying there. . . ."

"You called 9-1-1," Cooper said.

"Yes. I wanted to scream, but I didn't want to wake up the children. I actually clapped my hands over my mouth. I had lipstick on my right hand later, I remember. And then William was there. For a minute, I almost thought he'd done it. Like he saw me arrive, took off, and now was back and acting all solicitous."

"You changed your mind about that?"

"Yes. He was shell-shocked upon seeing Emma. That was real."

Cooper asked, "Did you ever have anybody else in mind? Someone you felt could have done it?"

"You think I haven't thought about it all these years? No. Unless it was one of those kids. That's what the detective thought." Cooper debated on telling her he was "one of those kids," but she went on before he could. "If you're seriously reinvestigating this case, you should start with them. The kids. Emma Whelan's friends. Her younger sister was supposed to be babysitting that night." She sighed. "I wish I'd never gone to the Glen Gen charity event. If I could rewind history, I would not go, and maybe none of this would have happened."

If wishes were horses . . .

"How long were you asleep at Dr. Metcalf's?" he asked.

"An hour or so. But there was nothing going on between us," she stressed. "Don't let William distract you. He always points fingers at what he does himself."

Cooper and Nadine ended their call a few moments later when she had nothing more to offer. He looked at the clock, realized it was after noon, and headed out to get himself a sandwich.

Jamie smiled at Harley when she entered the classroom, but didn't push her luck. Harley was with a friend. Lena, she thought. Harley gave her a quick smile in return when she took her seat.

Jamie passed out assignments, which was all that was required of her. Harley looked at hers and made a face. There wasn't a lot for Jamie to do apart from monitoring the room, so her mind wandered. She wanted to know about Gwen. She wanted to know who had come after Marissa and Bette, and if it was the same person.

She knew Cooper and the rest of the River Glen PD were working on those crimes, but she felt anxious. Wanted things to move faster. It did feel like everything had started happening after she and Harley had landed in River Glen.

She got a text from Vicky just as class was ending: **Leander's? Tonight? I want to cry and drink wine.**

As soon as the room emptied, Jamie texted back: **Can be there around six.**

She got a checkmark emoji in return.

She felt energized. Cooper had told her that one of the things Dug had hinted at was that Emma's classmates had known more about her "older lover" than they'd let on. Maybe they did, maybe they didn't. If she could, Jamie was going to find out.

Chapter Thirty

"I want to go to tae kwon do with Marissa to observe. See if I want to do it," Harley said as they were driving home from school. "Marissa didn't go last week, but she's feeling better and she says it makes her stronger."

"Sure," Jamie said. "Where is it?"

"I don't know for sure. You could drop me by Marissa's and her mom'll take us."

"I'll have to talk to her first."

"You could ask Mr. Haynes," she said, lifting her brows.

"And he'd have to ask Marissa's mom anyway. Don't be cheeky."

"Cheeky? Whatever do you mean, Mother?"

Jamie couldn't help but laugh a little. It felt good. "When's this class? I have a wine date at six, so maybe I could take you, if we find out where and when it is."

"I'll text Marissa."

Jamie was relieved to see that Marissa seemed to be on the road to recovery. She hoped Bette was doing the same.

"She gave me the address. She says it's closer to Portland." Harley held up her phone, but Jamie said, "I'll look at it at home."

The class was from four-thirty to five-thirty. Jamie figured she had just enough time to get Harley there and back and meet Vicky at Leander's, but that didn't take Emma into account. "You do need to take the permit test," Jamie said as she drove Harley.

"Right?" Harley agreed. "I've been telling you."

Back at the house, Jamie let Duchess out and, while waiting for her to do her perimeter check of the backyard, texted Theo to ask if she could bring Emma back after her shift. Theo sent back a thumb's-up emoji.

Jamie changed into her jeans and a black sweater and put together several turkey sandwiches for Harley and Emma. Just as she was getting ready to pick up Harley, Cooper called.

"Hey, there," she greeted him warmly.

"Are you going to be home?"

"Um . . . I'm actually meeting Vicky at Leander's at six, but I can be back by say, eight?"

"Good."

He sounded distracted. She asked. "Did you learn anything more about Gwen from the lab?"

"Not yet. I did speak to Nadine Ryerson." He filled her in on that conversation. "I didn't get anything more than I already knew from the file, but I'm going to follow up on Metcalf. About five years after Emma's attack, he was killed outside his car in the hospital parking lot. The theory was drugs, but they never found the killer. Also, I'm not sure what I think about that gap of time while Nadine was sleeping. She's adamant nothing happened between her and Metcalf, but it sounded kind of rehearsed. We talked on the phone, so I don't know if anyone else was in the room that she was playing to."

"Should I ask Emma's classmates about her maybe older boyfriend?"

"If you do, be careful," he warned.

That sounded so much like Gwen's "Stay safe" that she felt a sharp pang of memory about her friend. "You too."

Cooper hung up and she was a little bereft. She reran the

conversation in her mind and realized maybe he had some news about Gwen that she didn't want to hear.

When she arrived back at the tae kwon do school, Harley and Marissa were standing outside. Harley opened the passenger door. "Can we give Marissa a ride?"

"Sure . . ." Jamie was wary of stepping on Laura Haynes's toes by driving her child without permission.

Marissa said, as if reading her mind, as she climbed in the back seat, "I texted Mom that you would bring me back. She and David are fighting. It has to do with the new house. I don't think we're ever going to move there. She said he doesn't have the money. Something happened and he lost his job."

This was news to Jamie. "At the law firm?"

"Yep."

"I thought Mr. DeGuerre was retiring."

"I don't know." She shrugged. "But it's fine with me," she added, as Harley settled into the passenger seat and Jamie pulled onto the street. "I don't want to move. I like my room. I know it's stupid, but I feel safe there. No guy in a ski mask is going to get me."

Harley half-turned in her seat to look at her friend. "You're safe with us."

"He was crazy," she said with a shiver. "I could see his eyes."

I see his eyes.

Jamie felt a distinct shock. She slid a glance toward Harley, who didn't seem to make the same connection. But then, Harley hadn't lived with Emma during those first few years after the attack.

The girls began talking about what a shame it was that so many guys were off the team, at least for this next game. The consensus was, the opposing team was one of their toughest opponents and they were going to get creamed.

Jamie realized that Harley, who'd never cared a whit

about football before, had become a fan, probably because of Greer.

Jamie dropped off Marissa, making sure she got inside before pulling away. The extra trip was going to make her late for her wine date, but she would be there soon enough. Emma was at the house when they arrived. She'd found the turkey sandwiches and had helped herself to one. Duchess followed her everywhere.

"I'm going out for a little while," Jamie told her as Harley, too, raided the refrigerator. "You two going to be okay?"

"We three," Emma said, indicating the dog.

"You three going to be okay?"

They chorused a "yes," and Jamie climbed back into her Camry and headed to the wine bar. Halfway there, she felt pinned by bright headlights, and when she pulled into the lot, she glanced back to see a black SUV speed past and turn onto a side street. *A lot of black SUVs out there*, she thought, shivering a little as she pushed her way inside Leander's.

Vicky, Alicia, and Jill were already seated. When Jamie walked in, Vicky scooted over on the banquette to make room for her, and Alicia was in the middle of talking about Deon, saying, "—can try to come after us, but we're moving. That's it. I'm going home to Tacoma and Troy's coming with me. Troy's eighteen. I don't need Deon telling me anything!"

"You can't leave us," Vicky said, reaching a hand across the table.

"I have to."

"But you're not leaving till after football season," Vicky insisted.

Jill rolled her eyes. "Give it up, Victoria. The season is lost."

"I could kill Tyler and that little . . . bitch!" Vicky groaned. "But then I think of Bette and it's all so trivial, but is it? This is my son's future. God, I was so hard on Dara, but look what happened with Cathy's sticky-fingered little slut."

"Cathy's devastated, too," Alicia reminded her carefully.

Vicky looked like she wanted to argue some more, but held herself back. Barely. "At least she ponied up to pay the Pendelans back, too," she admitted grudgingly. "I just want it all behind us." She turned to Jamie. "You need a glass of wine."

"I can only stay a little while," she said while Vicky signaled to the waiter.

"Tell us about Bette," Alicia said to Jamie. "We know you're with Cooper. What's happening with finding her killer?"

"She wasn't killed," Jill reminded her.

"They *tried* to kill her," Alicia insisted.

How did they know she was with Cooper? River Glen was a smaller town than she'd ever credited. "I don't know anything more."

"Bette's getting sprung tomorrow," said Vicky.

The conversation circled right back to football while Jamie ordered her glass of red blend. She sipped it as Vicky and Alicia lamented, and Jill looked on, bored.

Finally, Jamie said, exaggerating the truth, "Emma's remembering little things."

They all stared at her. "About that night?" Alicia shivered. "I didn't even live here then and I know how awful it all was."

"She mentioned a boyfriend. I never knew she had one," Jamie said. "She didn't share with me."

"All the guys wanted her," said Vicky. She looked like she was about to break down and cry.

"She means the other one," said Jill crisply.

"What other one?" both Jamie and Alicia asked.

Vicky shook her head. "We don't know. Maybe he was a myth."

"Oh, he was real." Jill was certain about that. "Don't you remember? Emma told us she was going to marry him."

"Oh." Vicky thought that over. She'd apparently had just enough wine to make this a difficult process.

"Really? You never told the police about him?" Jamie asked.

"Are you kidding? We were scared that he would come after us next," said Jill. No more looking down her nose. "We didn't know his name, but he probably knew who we were because we hung around with Emma all the time. We were sitting ducks, so we kept quiet."

"He didn't hurt us." This was again from Vicky.

"But he could've," she insisted. "You didn't want to tell. You were the one who convinced me."

"You thought this boyfriend was the one who came after her," Jamie said, trying to nail down the story quickly as it seemed like they might collectively stop talking at any moment.

"We didn't know who it was," Jill said. "It was just scary."

"You never knew his name?" Jamie asked.

"I just said that." Jill looked around the room, as if checking to see who was listening.

Jamie hesitated, not knowing how hard to push. This was more than she'd expected. "Dug Douglas thought he saw him with Emma at Jake's Grill a couple of months before she was attacked."

"Jake's Grill?" Vicky seemed to surface a little from her own misery. "Not . . . Italian?"

"What do you mean?" Jamie asked.

"Oh, God, that's right. Nona Emilia's!" Jill breathed. "We thought it was a joke. Emma said something about always eating pasta. That was the Italian restaurant they supposedly went to."

"I remember . . . she said she was sneaking out to meet him . . . your mom worked nights. I thought she was making it up." Vicky stared at her wine glass. "Oh, I can't drink anymore. I'll just be a crying mess. I've got to go home and deal with things. And I've got a house to resell."

Dread settled in Jamie's chest. She had a mental picture of her sister creeping downstairs while Mom was at work and Jamie slept on, blissfully unaware.

The women were calculating how much each had spent. Jamie laid down enough money to cover her one barely touched glass with a healthy tip and walked away. Once again, she felt like she was having an out-of-body experience.

The wash of lights and the passing of a dark SUV as she walked across the parking lot woke her up. Suddenly, she was on high alert. Was she being paranoid, or was she really being followed?

She texted Cooper and told him she was on her way home, then spent the drive like a meerkat, head swiveling, eyes focused on all angles. She pulled into the drive and was relieved to see Cooper swing out of his SUV, which was parked at the curb. She ran to him, uncaring who saw, and threw herself into his arms.

"You're trembling," he said, worried. "What happened?"

"Nothing really. Just . . ." She looked over his shoulder, but the night was calm, only the faintest whisper of a breeze rustling the leaves of the trees.

"Let's go inside."

As soon as they were in the door, Duchess came to give Cooper another wary check, but he passed muster sooner this time. "I've got to get a dog door," Jamie said, slightly embarrassed that her teeth were trying to chatter.

She took Duchess outside and Cooper followed her. Harley texted her that she was in her room and Emma was in hers, and that Duchess had been too nervous to be penned up.

"The dog knows something," Cooper said.

"You were going to tell me something about Gwen," Jamie whispered as they stood on the back porch, not wanting her voice to travel upstairs.

"I got a call late from the lab. Gwen's tea was loaded with tetrahydrozoline."

"What?"

"It's found in eye drops. Enough of it slows the heart. In this case, it stopped Gwen's."

"Oh . . . no." Jamie's shoulders sagged, and once more, Cooper pulled her into his arms. She closed her eyes and drew a breath. "It really was suicide, then?"

"That's what we need to find out. The department's looking into Gwen's finances and her client record, which could fall under doctor/client privilege unless someone deliberately spiked her drink. I want to talk to her parents. Find out what they think."

Duchess came over and nuzzled Jamie's hand, even pressing her nose into Cooper's palm. "I see we're becoming friends," he said as he and Jamie headed back inside, Duchess's nails tapping alongside them.

They walked through the house and shared a kiss before Cooper headed out onto the porch. "While I'm waiting for Gwen's parents, I'm going to check into the Metcalf homicide. See if there's anything more there."

"I'm substituting again, could be for a few more days."

"All right. I'll keep in touch." He headed out the door.

Jamie stood at the window, watching him walk across the street. She heard the *chirp* of his remote lock. A car drove by and she gave it a sharp look, but it was a white sedan.

She could feel a cold spot in the small of her back. *Oh, come on. Get over yourself.*

She turned back. Emma stood, silent in her white pajamas.

Jamie gave an aborted shriek of terror, then said, "Emma! God, you scared me!"

Her eyes were wide and dark.

"What is it?" Jamie asked, as Duchess, who'd been lying on the mat at the front door looked at her mistress and froze. "Emma?" Jamie said, spooked.

"You have to be careful. They'll try to blame you. Kill you."

"Who do you mean?"

"The man in the ski mask," she said, clear as a bell.

"The man who attacked you?" Jamie clarified.

"I heard Harley. She said someone came after her friend."

Jamie nodded. It wasn't a surprise that Emma had learned of the attack on Marissa. "Do you remember the night you were attacked?" she asked cautiously.

Emma clapped her hands to her ears and closed her eyes.

"Was he wearing a ski mask?"

She slowly dropped her hands. "It wasn't Cooper who came back."

"No, no, it wasn't. We believe it was Dug."

Her eyes flew open. "Patrick Dug Douglas."

"That's right," said Jamie.

"He came back."

"We think so. Was he the one . . . or did maybe someone else come after he left?"

Duchess started whining, and Emma stepped to the window, peering out cautiously. "He's following me again."

"Again?" The hair rose on Jamie's arms.

"I see him in my dreams. You should move into Mom's room, Jamie." She dropped the curtain and started heading for the stairs.

"Did you have a boyfriend, then?" Jamie asked quickly. "Someone who liked pasta as much as you do?"

"No."

Realizing she'd been pushing because she was so certain she was on the right track, Jamie pulled herself back.

"He liked it more than me," she said.

"Who was he, Emma?" Jamie breathed.

For a stretched moment she didn't answer. She turned for the stairs and started heading that way. And then her voice floated back to Jamie.

"He was bad news."

Chapter Thirty-One

Jamie worked the next two days at the school, which Harley seemed to handle without comment, but maybe it was because she was angling to take her driver's permit test. Vicky and her husband, Deon Stillwell, and the Douglases were still lobbying for their sons to play in Friday's game, but that didn't look like it was going to happen. Alicia was intent on moving away with Troy and didn't care one iota about River Glen's chances. Cathy Timbolt had already taken Katie out of school and enrolled her in a private school in Portland. The scuttlebutt was that Cathy was moving out of River Glen entirely.

Cooper had called a few times, but he was working on all fronts related to the recent home invasions and also Gwen's death. Gwen's parents were preparing to come to River Glen, but from their village at the tip of South America to the Portland airport was a journey of over twenty-four hours, not counting prep time. They were expected anytime.

Jamie hadn't really had a chance to tell Cooper what Emma had said about the night she was attacked and her boyfriend at the time. She'd hoped to get more information out of her, and Cooper was inundated with current crimes and problems. Every time she got on the phone with him, she realized he was dealing with more pressing issues than a twenty-year-old cold case.

On Thursday, Jamie was called in to the school again, for a different teacher who was out with the flu. This one was for the seniors again. Chemistry. Once again, she was just a warm body handing out assignments. She really would like to have her own class one day, maybe at River Glen. The future felt so uncertain, it was hard to say.

Teddy Ryerson called on Thursday afternoon as Jamie was packing up her belongings and getting ready to leave the school. She had things to discuss with him, so she answered with, "Hi, Teddy."

"Hi, Jamie. Hey, um, I'm going to have to find someone else for Saturday, if I can, because you don't want to sit the kids at my house. All the babysitters are already taken, so Serena and I may not be going to the party. Anika wants to stay at the house. She's scared to leave. She feels safe in her bedroom, where Marissa holed up with them. I thought she'd like going to your house, but she feels safest at home. Oliver says he doesn't care, but I think he wants to stay home, too."

"Oh."

"So, I just wanted to let you know, you're off the hook. Thank you."

"I'm sorry . . ."

"Don't be. It's been a harrowing few weeks, hasn't it?"

"It sure has."

"How are you doing?" he asked.

"I'm okay. . . . Hey, Teddy, you mentioned that I should be careful with my mother's finances, and I got the feeling you were specifically meaning Mr. DeGuerre's law firm."

"Well, yes." He thought for a moment, then chose his words carefully, "DeGuerre has a law firm, not an investment firm, but there's been some crossover, some blending of clients' money with the firm's. That's what I've been told by some of my clients. It's why they moved their funds to my company. If it's true, it's either illegal, or just skirting the law. This is not about me being a jealous competitor. DeGuerre's old and I think he truly believes he's taken care of his clients, but he's handed over the reins to others, and I don't know what financial instruments they've got their clients invested in."

Jamie thought of David Musgrave. Marissa's words floated across her mind. *She said he doesn't have the money. Something happened and he lost his job.*

Teddy said, "I don't want to see you lose money. That's all."

"I think I'll call Mr. DeGuerre."

"Do that," Teddy urged.

"Thank you."

"No problem. Take care, Jamie."

"Teddy?"

"Hmm?"

"I'll babysit your kids at your house," Jamie said before she could change her mind. She wasn't scared for herself, just for Harley.

"Are you sure?"

"Yes."

"Well, great. If you really don't mind? See you Saturday. Thanks," he said, getting off the phone quickly as if he expected her to change her mind.

Jamie immediately called the DeGuerre Law Firm, but the line just rang on and on and on. No voice mail or receptionist. Not a good sign. Concerned, Jamie clicked off, wondering if she should run over to the law firm office. But she had her mother's assets in her possession already . . . unless there were more that had been hidden from her.

"Harley, I'll be right back," she called up the stairs, grabbing her coat and heading for the back door.

"Get some pumpkins! It's almost Halloween and we don't have any."

"I'm not . . ." She cut herself off. So she wasn't going to the store. So what? "Okay!" she called back.

At the building that housed DeGuerre's offices, she held up a moment at the bottom of the steps, glancing toward Gwen's office. Today, everything was dark. Cooper had said that her computer and files had been locked up. He'd also said she'd made out a will, surprisingly not with the law firm upstairs, although maybe Jamie now knew why, and that they were just waiting for her parents to arrive to read it.

When Jamie headed up the steps to the DeGuerre Law Firm's door she was somewhat dismayed to see a notice taped on the panels with a number to call for further information. In just the couple of weeks' time since she'd been there, it appeared they'd closed up shop, at least temporarily.

Jamie stopped at the store and bought two pumpkins, a large one and a smaller one. When she got home, she set them on the counter and called Camryn, who knew all and more about the River Glen School District. Maybe she knew about the law firm, too.

"I haven't heard about the law firm," she said, dashing Jamie's hopes. "I wonder why they're closed."

Almost the moment Jamie was off the phone, it rang, and she saw it was Teddy Ryerson again. "Elgin DeGuerre's in the hospital," he told her. "And it looks like Musgrave is no longer with the firm."

"Okay."

"Do you want me to advocate for you?"

She thought about it. There was no harm in it, as far as she could tell. She wouldn't be any worse off than she was now. Emma was certain that their mother had saved money for her to move to Ridge Pointe, but Emma wasn't exactly a sure bet on information.

"Thank you, Teddy. That would be great."

"Glad to do it," he said happily.

* * *

It took until Thursday evening before Cooper had a chance to connect with Mr. and Mrs. Winkelman. Gwen's parents had the weathered, windbeaten faces of people who lived and worked outdoors. They both wore jeans and sweatshirts and jackets meant for cold weather. The Patagonia brand of clothing was meant for harsh weather, and the Winkelmans looked like poster children for extreme conditions.

They were devastated by their daughter's death. Rendered speechless by the horror of not seeing "Gwennie" anymore. Cooper met with them after refereeing for the Kearnses who, once the shock of the attack on Bette had dissipated, were at it again. He had been called to their home because Eric Volker was making threats against Phil, and Phil, who'd been allowed back in the house, was threatening right back. As far as Cooper was concerned, the only good thing about this week was the anticipation of seeing Jamie again, and the loosening of the reins on Marissa; Laura had allowed the girl to spend the night at Cooper's. To say that was unusual was not giving enough weight by far to the rarity of the event, but then, David and Laura were also at it, over money, apparently, and promises broken. It wasn't that long ago that Cooper and Marissa were both saying how glad they were that David was there for Laura. Now that appeared to be over.

So, Cooper was in the process of setting aside everything on his plate when he met with Winkelmans. They deserved his full attention and he was bound and determined to give it to them.

"There is no way Gwennie would commit suicide," Myrna Winkelman now declared for about the twentieth time. Cooper had told them about the tetrahydrozoline and shown them the "Sorry" note, which had caused Myrna to keen with grief, while Al Winkelman put his arm around her bony shoulders.

"That's her handwriting?" Cooper asked.

Al nodded, but Myrna denied it, her voice muffled against her husband's shoulder. "She wouldn't do it. She loved life."

Al cleared his throat. "Gwen had high blood pressure and a slight arrhythmia. A valve in her heart that didn't work properly. She never told anybody, but she was always careful."

"She was very careful," Myrna agreed. "She just wouldn't do this. Not this way. Not ever."

"It had to have been an accident," Al said.

Cooper didn't respond. They'd been over the same territory several times. He didn't see how that much of the drug could have accidentally found its way into her cup. And if it wasn't an accident, and it wasn't suicide, it was a homicide.

As if divining his thoughts, Myrna pulled herself back from her husband, swiping at her red nose. "No one would want to kill Gwennie. She was too *good.* She helped people."

"She helped people who were disturbed," her husband reminded her.

"No . . ." Myrna wouldn't hear of it. "Mostly they were just people with some problems that she helped them with. They weren't disturbed. Oh, why do people live in cities anyway? It's not healthy. We told Gwennie to join us. We begged her."

"She had friends here." Al was clearly the voice of reason in the relationship.

"I know my Gwennie. I *know* her. She wouldn't do this." She gazed up at Cooper with conviction. "Someone hurt her. You need to find out who."

Jamie helped clean out the larger pumpkin and watched Harley somewhat nervously work a knife to carve out the jack-o'-lantern face. Harley had always had an artistic bent and had seen one on the internet that seemed to be throwing up the seeds and innards from its mouth. She was determined to copy the idea.

"Lovely," Jamie remarked.

"Greer has one where the knife is sticking out of its head and it's looking up at it in horror. He sent me a picture. See?" She stopped what she was doing to grab her phone. Jamie dutifully looked at the photo, though it surprised her that Harley had no qualms about the image based on what had happened to Marissa and Bette.

"Mmm," she said. She supposed she should be glad Harley, apparently, was suffering no ill effects.

But then, it didn't happen to her.

They heard Theo's van pull up, and Jamie said, "Maybe let's stop. Just until Emma gets inside and we're all on board."

"Sure." Harley set down the knife and wiped her hands on a paper towel. Sometimes she was obtuse, but sometimes she was totally in tune with other people.

Emma, as it turned out, was totally into the jack-o'-lanterns. "Mom said I can't use a knife," she told Jamie.

"I know. We'll let Harley do it."

"You can use a knife," Emma told Jamie.

"If she needs some help, I'll certainly jump in."

Harley managed to carve both pumpkins. The larger one was retching up its innards, but the smaller one just had a goofy smile on its face. Emma seemed to like them both.

Cooper called just as they were putting the jack-o'-lanterns on the porch. Harley wanted to light them, but Emma wouldn't let her. "They won't last," she warned.

Jamie let them bicker about pumpkin etiquette as she went back inside and took Cooper's call. "How's it going?" she asked.

"Gwen's mother won't believe it's suicide."

"What do you think?" Jamie asked. She heard some indecision in his voice.

"They're going through some of her personal items. Her client list is with her lawyer, as is her will. Maybe something will pop out. Forensics still hasn't found anything at the Kearns' to help identify the intruder."

"I was going to stop by to see Bette tomorrow. I'm glad she's home." Jamie hesitated. He'd been so busy, she hadn't been able to see him. "Can you come over for dinner?" she asked, certain he couldn't, still wanting him to. "Nothing fancy. Spaghetti."

"Emma still on her pasta kick?" She could hear him smiling.

"Never off it." She still hadn't been able to have an in-depth conversation with him about Emma's one-time boyfriend, though she had mentioned the pasta.

"I'll see what I can do. I just finished with the Winkelmans. I want to stop by Glen Gen to pick up a copy of a security tape from the night Dr. Metcalf was killed. We had a copy, but it was degraded. Hard to see. Luckily, the hospital saved the original. I want to go check it out."

"Come when you can," she said.

As soon as they were off the phone, she ran upstairs into her mom's bedroom and changed into a fresh shirt and pants, then hurried to the bathroom to check her appearance. When she returned downstairs, Emma said, "Is Cooper moving in with us?"

"No."

She looked scared. "You're moving in with him."

"No," Jamie stated more firmly. "We're dating. That's all."

"And having sex," she said seriously.

Jamie rolled her eyes.

Harley drawled, "That's more than dating. That's a relationship."

"And it's personal," Emma added.

"The two of you . . ." Jamie muttered.

"Three of us," Emma corrected. "Right, Duchess?"

The dog barked happily.

"Are you moving into Mom's room?" Emma asked.

"Maybe. I don't know. Yes, probably."

"Then Cooper can come and stay."

Jamie let that one go by. There was no arguing with Emma when she got on a subject. "Help me get this spaghetti ready," she said. "Emma, I'm putting you in charge of the garlic bread." She plucked a spreader from the knife caddy, but Emma shied away. "It's not a knife," Jamie said. "Not the same kind. It's rounded on the end."

Reluctantly, she took it up and began the task of buttering the slices that Jamie had already cut from the loaf of French bread.

Cooper checked his watch. He should've put Jamie off. He wasn't sure he had enough time to check out the tape and get to her house by the time she liked to serve dinner for Emma and Harley.

He'd parked in the hospital lot where Dr. Alain Metcalf had the last night of his life. From the file, Cooper knew that Metcalf had put in a late shift and headed out to his car at around one a.m. An unknown assailant had come up behind him as he was getting into his car and smashed what had been described by the detective who'd seen the video as a heavy concrete block of some kind in his head. The killer had then dashed into the line of trees behind the parking lot, taking the block with him, to an access road below, where it was assumed he'd left his own vehicle. A bottle of unlabeled painkillers was found in Metcalf's Mercedes, and it was theorized he'd been selling them and had run afoul of one of his clients. That theory hadn't held up, though. No other evidence of his being a so-called "pill doctor" had emerged.

Cooper mounted the concrete steps to the walkway that led to the hospital. He walked through an open breezeway to reach the front of the building from the back parking lot where Metcalf had preferred to leave his car.

Inside, he was directed to the security offices, where the man in charge, Kyle Johnson, was waiting for him. He set Cooper up in front of a screen and played the tape. Cooper watched as Metcalf walked to his car from the hospital, blithely unaware of what was in store for him as he hit the remote. The vehicle's lights flashed and he walked to the driver's side, reaching for the door handle. Suddenly, a person dressed all in black appeared. Before Metcalf could do more than make a half turn, the person hefted the heavy block and slammed it down on his head. He went down in a heap. The killer then bent over Metcalf, maybe checking his pulse. Satisfied, the killer headed through the trees, concrete block in hand, and disappeared.

Cooper watched the tape three times, looking for anything he might have missed, but though the tape was original, the grainy black-and-white of the security cameras made it difficult to see. The murder weapon looked like a cinder block in a kind of daisy pattern.

"Could you make me a copy? I'd like to try to refine it," he said to Kyle.

"That is a copy, sir. I made it before you came. You're welcome to it."

"Thank you. Were you here when Dr. Metcalf worked at the hospital?" Cooper asked, sizing Kyle up to be somewhere in his late fifties or early sixties.

"Yes, sir."

"Did you know him?"

Johnson hesitated. "I knew of him."

"What did you know?" Cooper asked curiously. It was clear the man was reluctant to say anything.

"He was considered an excellent orthopedic surgeon."

Cooper nodded. "I got that from the file. Anything else?"

"He was . . . always on the make. I never wanted to be-smirch the man's reputation after he was dead, but that's just a fact. Some of the younger women found it hard to keep him at arm's length. If he were around today, I don't think he'd be able to get away with half of what he did fifteen years ago. He flirted with my daughter when she was a teen. Made her and me uncomfortable. I didn't like him much."

"None of that was in the report."

He shrugged. "We all thought he crossed the wrong guy over drugs. It's not a crime to come on too strong."

Cooper rolled that around in his head as he drove to Jamie's. Metcalf had been at the charity function with William and Nadine Ryerson and had taken Nadine home. He had a penchant for young women, flirted with teenagers. What if he'd hooked up with one of those teenagers? A bright, attractive young woman who wasn't interested in high school boys?

Could he be Emma's older man? Irene Whelan had been a nurse at Glen Gen at the same time as Metcalf worked there. Might Emma and he have crossed paths during that time? The night of Emma's attack, there was an unaccounted for hour or so when Nadine Ryerson was asleep on Met-calf's couch and William Ryerson was still at the charity event. Had Metcalf been the man who'd attacked Emma?

Jamie greeted him at the door. He almost kissed her, but Emma and Harley and Duchess, wriggling between them as if she knew what he had in mind, were behind them. "Sorry I'm late. I have some things I want to talk about," he whispered.

"You're not late and I have things to tell you, too."

"After dinner, maybe we can sneak out for a little while?"

"Yes," she said simply.

* * *

I didn't want to kill Gwen, but she was too close. She was going to say something to Jamie. Maybe she already did. I didn't want to poison her, but she could sense things. She was teetering, ready to tell. She started to write the note and I realized how I could make it work for me. I had to do what I did. I had to. I knew she'd had some trouble with her heart and the tea was a perfect delivery system.

It worries me that Jamie might know.

I don't want to kill her. It's Emma who deserves to die. Yet, if I killed Emma now, would she even know why?

But Jamie . . .

I can't wait long.

Chapter Thirty-Two

Friday morning, and luckily, Jamie didn't have to substitute because she'd had so little sleep it was almost criminal. And she wouldn't trade it for the world.

She'd tiptoed back into the house at around two a.m. after spending the night in bed with Cooper, making love and talking and touching and loving. She felt like a teenager herself, reliving the past, indulging herself. But it was effing incredible.

In between lovemaking, they'd brought each other up-to-date on everything they'd learned over the past few days. Cooper took in everything Jamie said about Emma's boyfriend and came back with his own theory, that the man in question might be Alain Metcalf.

"It's a hunch," he told her. "I wasn't sure there was somebody, but hearing from the security guard that Metcalf favored teenagers made me think back to that night. Nadine Ryerson fell asleep on his couch. When you think about it, does that read right to you? She was that tired?"

"Or she was given something," Jamie said, jolted at the thought.

"Maybe he wanted her to sleep through everything. She was adamant that nothing happened between them, but that was just to prove that William was the cheater, not her. I don't think she really knows what happened."

"You think he went to see Emma."

"I think he had opportunity. I'm not sure about motive. He could easily have had something that put Nadine out."

"You think he attacked Emma. But why?"

"I don't know. Emma told Dug she was getting married. Practically threw it in his face. Was she even eighteen yet that fall?"

"No."

"Then she was underage. How does that look for a physician?"

That gave Jamie pause. She couldn't remember Emma being involved with anyone at all, but she hadn't been paying close attention either.

"What do you think about asking Emma?" Cooper asked.

"I might get a circular answer, but I could try. I wonder if he liked pasta. . . ."

In the light of day, Jamie wasn't so certain Cooper's hunch was correct. She watched Emma make herself some toast and carefully smear it with jam. Jamie had washed the dish towels and stacked them on the counter, and Emma had looked at them while she ate, growing ever twitchier until she had to quickly wash her hands and then line up the towels so they hung perfectly.

Jamie hadn't been able to pull the trigger on asking her about Metcalf. Recalling her reaction to Allen, the dishwasher repairman, she wondered if he resembled Metcalf.

Or maybe it wasn't Metcalf at all. He would have had to drug Nadine, drive to the Ryersons', confront and attack Emma, and head back and wake up Nadine so he could take her back to the scene of the crime. For all he knew, Emma could rise up, point a finger at him and reveal what he'd done.

Unless he thought he'd killed her.

Cooper had gone on to tell her about Metcalf's murder and the overarching theory that the reason he was killed had something to do with drugs. It was believed he was somehow making money on the side. Writing prescriptions under fake names and then selling the pills. He'd apparently had quite a healthy bank account when he died.

Jamie pretended to be up and at 'em when she took Harley to school, hoping to hide the effects of her late night, but she hadn't fooled her daughter.

"If we didn't have Duchess, I would be really pissed that you left us alone last night," she said as she was hauling her backpack out of the car.

Jamie hadn't even tried to refute her comment, though she was a bit embarrassed. "By the way, I'm babysitting the Ryerson twins at their house on Saturday."

Harley had been about to slam the door behind her, but now she peered in at Jamie. "I could do it. I'm not scared."

And you would tell Greer Douglas and God knows what would happen.

"No, I'm fine."

"Okay . . . I know I just said it's good to have Duchess, but do you think your friend Camryn would come over if you're not going to be home? It's almost Halloween. I don't really care. I just kind of want someone, maybe. Never mind." She slammed the door before Jamie could answer.

In any event, she called Camryn, who jumped at the chance, and Jamie realized she seemed to feel she'd let her down by being so unavailable. "Can I be honest with you? Nate and I are back on again, and that's why I've been hard to reach, and yes, this time I agreed to move to Seattle."

"When?" Jamie asked.

"The end of the school year, probably. I'm sorry. I was so happy you came back, and here I'm the one to leave."

Jamie tried to sound enthusiastic, but she already felt

bereft. If it weren't for Cooper, she knew she'd be thinking of leaving herself . . . but, of course, there was Emma.

Harley came home from school with Marissa, who was planning to spend the night. Jamie made a point of calling Laura to make sure they were really on the same page, but Cooper's ex was perfunctory, saying it was fine with her as long as Marissa felt safe and now she had to go.

Marissa overheard just enough of the conversation to offer an opinion. "She's really scared. David's gone. She kicked him out. We're both scared."

"What happened?" Jamie asked, knowing she was prying, but not caring.

Marissa shrugged. "I think he took some money and lied about it and got caught."

"From the law firm? You said he lost his job."

Harley, who'd been listening in silence up till then, chipped in. "He's an embezzler?"

"Nobody tells me anything. They're trying to protect me." Marissa made a face. "But that's what I'd guess."

Jamie sent a silent message to Teddy Ryerson, hoping he was doing as he'd said, fighting as her financial advocate.

The rest of the evening passed uneventfully. Jamie picked up Emma from work, giving Theo a break from driving, and brought her home. The two pumpkins on the porch had been lit and were glowing in the descending nightfall as Jamie pulled into the driveway. "Halloween is too far away," Emma complained.

"Not that far," Jamie said. She'd been trying to think of how to ask her about Alain Metcalf and finally decided to just come out with it. "Emma, I want to ask you a question, and I want an honest answer."

"All my answers are honest."

"Yes. Okay. That's true. But I want you to think hard before you answer this question. It might be a difficult one for you, but I think you can answer it. Just try not to get upset, okay?"

"Okay."

They were sitting in the car in the driveway. Beyond them was the backyard, already deeply shadowed. Emma turned to face the garden and said, "I had a dream about Mom. I was driving her car. And we were sailing in the clouds and she said, 'Emma. He's bad news.'"

Jamie seized on that. "Your boyfriend? The one Mom called bad news? Was that Dr. Alain Metcalf?"

Emma jerked as if stung. "You know him?"

"He was your boyfriend?" she pressed. "Alain Metcalf?"

Emma didn't speak for a moment, then finally said, "That repairman's name was Allen. Not spelled the same way."

Allen who'd replaced their dishwasher? "That's why you noticed him? Allen?" she asked quickly. "Because his name was the same as Dr. Metcalf's?"

"Not spelled the same," she repeated.

"But similar. Similar enough for you to remember?"

"Similar," said Emma.

"So, Alain Metcalf was your boyfriend when you were in high school?" Jamie tried again, seeking to pin Emma down. Maybe Cooper's hunch was paying off.

Emma started to breathe harder. Jamie recognized the signs that Emma's anxiety had been triggered and she was heading for another fit.

"You see his eyes," Jamie said quickly, hoping to intervene and stave off full-blown hysteria. "Where? Where, Emma? Where do you see his eyes?"

She blinked, and her breath quivered.

"Where, Emma? Where do you see his eyes?"

"I see his eyes . . ."

"Where, Emma? Where? Behind the mask? Emma! Behind the *mask*?"

"*Yes! I see his eyes! I see his eyes!*"

"Stop! Stop! Slow down, slow down. Stop. It's okay, Emma. It's okay. He's not here. He's not here. He can't hurt you."

"*I see his eyes.*"

"Take a breath. Stop. I'm here for you. *Right here!*"

Emma threw a wild glance Jamie's way. She was hyperventilating, but she was clearly trying to get a grip on herself.

"It's Metcalf's eyes behind the ski mask. That's who it is, right? Your boyfriend. Dr. Alain Metcalf. He came to the Ryersons to see you . . . ?"

Emma slowly lifted her hand near her ear, as if she were cradling a phone receiver. "I love you. Don't yell at me. I love you! Come over . . ."

Jamie stopped, aware this was more than she'd ever gotten from Emma before. "Did he attack you at the Ryersons'? Your boyfriend?"

"We were supposed to have sex, but he was mad. He came over . . . and I could see his eyes inside the mask. But I knew . . . I knew . . ." Her voice was a mere whisper.

Jamie leaned toward her to hear.

"*I know who you are!*" she suddenly yelled.

Jamie jumped and gasped at her loud voice.

"He said it was a pipe dream. He said he wouldn't marry me because it was a pipe dream."

Jamie looked at her sister, her own breath coming short and fast. "He's dead, Emma," she said gently. This was as close to an eyewitness account of the attack on her as anything Jamie was likely to get. "He can't hurt you anymore."

"He was bad news, but I loved him," she said gravely.

"I know you did." She wanted to grab Emma's hand and console her, but she knew Emma needed to make the first move.

Emma looked from the garden back to Jamie. "Are you going to have sex with Cooper again?"

Jamie wanted to brush that aside, but that rarely worked with Emma. "Probably," she admitted.

"It's very personal."

"*Very* personal," Jamie agreed.

Cooper's phone buzzed as he was leaving work. He'd stayed later than he'd intended, updating reports. He was just grabbing his coat when his cell rang, and he saw it was Bette Kearns. "Can you stop by?" she begged. "Phil's not here and I don't feel safe."

"Where are your kids?"

"With Phil. I just want you to come by . . . there's something I want to talk about."

Cooper sensed this could become an everyday event. "I can stop in tomorrow," he said.

"I don't want to be alone."

He couldn't tell for certain if she was really scared, or if she was just trying to get him to be with her. "I'll make sure one of the patrols keeps a watch on your house tonight."

"You're really not coming?" She sounded like she was about to cry.

"What about one of your girlfriends?"

"Oh, never mind. But I do have something to tell you, so be here tomorrow."

"Okay."

She certainly has a way of ordering you around, Cooper thought.

Almost immediately, his phone rang again. He looked at the screen suspiciously, but this time it was Jamie.

"It's Alain Metcalf," she told him. "You were right. Emma's lover was Dr. Alain Metcalf. She basically admitted it. . . ."

* * *

Saturday morning dawned gray and gloomy. It was after eight when Jamie staggered out of her sleeping alcove. She hadn't done anything the night before to speak of, but Emma's revelations had left an indelible mark on her brain, and her dreams had been bits of vivid moments that all seemed to be of a violent nature.

She took a long, hot shower, washed her hair, and then dressed in jogging gear. It had been so long since she'd been on an exercise regimen that her clothes were loose on her frame. She hadn't realized she'd lost weight. It was a product of worry.

She ran down the block and around the neighborhood. She thought about going up Stillwell Hill, but decided she needed to work up to that. She circled back on a route that took her past Deno's Pizzeria. Tonight, maybe she'd order in pizza for Harley, Emma, and Camryn because she would be babysitting at the Ryerson house.

One night, she told herself.

Her mind fretted about Elgin DeGuerre, David Musgrave, and her mother's supposed nest egg for Emma. Nothing to do there but wait. Teddy had emailed her and alluded to the fact that if DeGuerre and Musgrave didn't come up with the money—the *supposed* money, as Teddy was more convinced than Jamie that there was more—government regulators, the justice system, the SEC, and God knew who else would be called in.

The day passed excruciatingly slowly. Emma went to work around noon, putting in a half day, and Harley and Marissa seemed content to hang around in their pajamas and play on their phones. Harley raised the expectation of getting her permit, but the DMV was closed on Saturdays.

She spoke to Cooper twice. It felt anticlimactic somehow that Emma's boyfriend and attacker had been literally un-masked and yet no justice could be served upon a dead man. Cooper and the River Glen Police Department were actively trying to determine who'd gone after Marissa and Bette, and whether Gwen had chosen to commit suicide by poisoning herself with tetrahydrozoline, but Emma's story appeared disconnected from present-day issues.

Camryn showed up at six p.m. with a pizza in hand. "I stopped at Deno's," she said.

"That's what I was going to do!" Jamie exclaimed. "Great minds think alike."

"I wish you were joining us, but I guess that's why I'm here."

Theo dropped Emma off and came in for a few minutes to let Bartholomew and Duchess chase each other around. The two dogs had been careful of each other at first, but they seemed to be building a fast friendship after being introduced to each other a number of times.

"I can't stay," Theo said. "I've got to go buy Halloween candy. I have no decorations up and it's next week."

"Don't I know it," said Camryn. "I've been gone practically every weekend."

Marissa had left around noon, and Harley had been on her phone ever since, texting her friends. "Put that thing away," Emma said. "Bad things are on cell phones."

"Not always," Harley said, but she did stuff her phone in her pocket.

When Theo headed out, Jamie went to her car. She drove to the Ryersons', thinking how much the weather was the same as that last evening she'd babysat for them. Now that she knew who'd attacked her sister, she wondered how different things might have been if she hadn't convinced Emma to trade places with her. Maybe her toxic romance with Metcalf would have ended up the same way. Or, maybe things would have been vastly different.

She thought about Metcalf attacking her in a ski mask and wondered if he'd gotten the idea from the Vancouver home invasion, which had taken place earlier that year, or maybe he was influenced by Halloween, or maybe he just had the gear in his vehicle.

Teddy opened the front door in a skeleton costume and a Day of the Dead mask. Jamie was immediately taken aback, and he swiftly removed the mask. "Sorry. I was chasing the kids around." Then, "It's a costume party."

"No problem."

Her heart rate had momentarily hit the stratosphere. Behind him, Serena was sharing candy with the twins. Disturbingly, she was dressed in ski gear, although it was a woman's outfit, which molded against her long legs, and the jacket was pink. Her ski mask was on her head, not over her face, and topped by a pair of goggles. The twins said hi to Jamie by Anika shyly raising her hand while Oliver left the candy to come over and meet her with a hearty handshake.

Serena said, "I hate costume parties. I never have anything to wear, and I don't want to put on those smelly costumes from the rental stores."

"Parties are fun," Oliver objected, frowning at his aunt.

"Oh, come on." Teddy smiled at his sister. "You always have a good time."

"*You* always have a good time," she contradicted him. "I have an okay time."

The kids both went back to their candy until Serena shooed them away from her gift, saying they wouldn't sleep well if they kept loading up on sugar. They then raced each other to their bedroom to play.

"The women at this party keep changing," Teddy revealed, his gaze following after his children. "I've known the guys for a long time, but none of them have stayed married to their first wives. The only one Serena ever knew well was Kira, my wife."

"I liked Kira," Serena said. "Everybody did."

"I wish I'd known her," said Jamie.

"Me too." He sobered for a moment, then said, "I wanted you to come to this party with us. Next year," he promised.

If I'm still here . . .

They left a few moments later, and Jamie coaxed the twins to come out of their rooms and play some board games with her. Like his father before him, Oliver was very quick at the Memory Game, the same box game from twenty years earlier, Jamie was pretty sure. They spread out the cards on the coffee table. It was such a déjà vu experience that Jamie felt a cold frisson slide down her spine.

Her phone rang, and she saw it was Cooper.

"You're not going to talk on the phone, are you?" Oliver complained, throwing himself on the couch as if he couldn't bear the idea one more second.

"Just for a minute." She walked into the kitchen so the kids wouldn't overhear her and answered, "Hey there."

"How's it going?" he asked.

"Pretty good. The kids are about ready for bed and—"

"*No!*" Oliver yelled from the living room, and Anika giggled and called, "*No!*" as well.

"Well, maybe not just yet," Jamie allowed.

She and Cooper chatted for a few more minutes and then he said, "I'll call again later, maybe stop by."

"Good." They'd agreed earlier to keep in touch. Since the attack on Marissa, they'd both ramped up their efforts to make sure everything and everyone was safe and sound while babysitting at the Ryersons.

It took another hour and a half before the twins were ready for bed. When Jamie finally put them down in their separate bedrooms, Anika immediately ran to Oliver's, the room where they'd holed up with Marissa. Teddy had warned her that six nights out of seven, this was their preferred sleeping arrangement, before and after the attack, so she just let it happen.

Once the twins were down, Jamie turned on the television,

mindlessly flipping through the channels. There were a number of classic horror films available.

"Perfect," she muttered sarcastically.

Cooper called again at about nine o'clock to check in and told her he was on his way to see Bette Kearns. "She wanted me to come by yesterday. She says she has something she wants to talk about. When I'm done there I'll text you."

Remembering Bette's vow to date Cooper, Jamie said, "Hmmm," in a skeptical voice.

He laughed. "It's not like that."

"I wouldn't be so sure," she said, adding more seriously, "Let me know how she's doing."

"Will do."

Cooper clicked off with a smile on his face. Dumb as it was, it made him feel good that Jamie had shown the slightest blip of jealousy. However, the smile slowly disappeared as he neared the Kearns' house. The drama Phil and Bette seemed to thrive on made him tired. He didn't even know why he was here. Bette could as easily talk to him on the phone as in person.

Phil actually was the one who answered the door when Cooper knocked, and he braced himself for another go-round with the two of them. His eyes automatically traveled to where Bette's blood had stained the carpet. Now there was a hole through the carpet and pad where that section had been cut away.

"Bette's in here," Phil said, walking into the family room, where they watched TV. As soon as Bette saw Cooper, she switched off the set. There was a bandage down the side of her neck and over her shoulder.

"Cooper," she said, struggling up from her lounge chair.

"Don't get up," he said.

"No, I want to show you something."

She led him back toward the living room, with its missing piece of carpet. She went to stand in front of a mirror in the shape of a sun, its rays separate shards of reflective glass.

Bette said, "She stopped and looked at herself in the mirror. It gave me enough time to call for help."

"She?"

"Phil thinks it was Eric, and Eric thinks it was Phil, but I've thought about it and thought about it, and I think it was a woman who attacked me. She was big, but she had a lot of ski gear on. She looked in this mirror. That's what I wanted to tell you."

When Jamie heard a car pull into the driveway at the back of the house, she was immediately on alert. That wasn't Cooper's engine. She'd made a point to memorize the sound of it.

She immediately looked around for a weapon. Her heart raced, beating erratically.

The knife drawer.

She ran toward the kitchen, then stopped. No. She just couldn't do it.

She ran back to the living room and looked around for something else, just in case. She thought about yanking out the nearest lamp and using it as a bludgeon when she heard the key in the lock followed by Teddy's voice, then Serena's, announcing their return.

Relief made her weak.

When they entered the living room, Teddy had taken off his mask. He tossed it on the coffee table as Serena unbuttoned her coat. Jamie said a bit shakily, "You're both back early."

Teddy slid a look at his sister, who shrugged and said, "I wanted to come home."

"How was it?" Teddy asked Jamie, inclining his head toward the twins' bedrooms.

"Fine. They're sleeping in the same room, as you said they might."

He nodded deeply. "It's been a long time since you babysat for some Ryerson twins."

Jamie grimaced. "I've always felt kind of guilty for having Emma take my place."

Serena pulled off the goggles and said coolly, "So, it's really your fault."

Jamie was taken aback by that and Teddy whipped his head around. "Well, I didn't attack her," she said slowly.

"Oh, I know. Dad did," Serena said.

"Oh, for God's sake, Serena. That's not true. You know that's not true." Teddy turned to Jamie. "Serena always says that. She keeps thinking she saw Dad attack Emma, but it's not true."

"Well, it isn't public knowledge yet, but Cooper and I are pretty sure it was Alain Metcalf," Jamie said. To Serena, she added, "I thought you didn't wake up."

"We both woke up," Teddy admitted. "We just didn't tell anybody."

Jamie blinked at him. "Why not?"

Before Teddy could respond, Serena answered, "We didn't want anyone to know Dad did it."

Phil Kearns scoffed at his wife. "Fine. Go ahead. Make up stories. I'm putting my money on Eric Volker."

Bette glared daggers at him. "You always belittle me."

Cooper pointed out, "A man could look in a mirror, too."

"Yeah, but there was something about it," she said. "That's all I'm saying. You're the investigator. You figure it out. I just don't want *her* coming back to get me, so start looking for a woman."

* * *

"I saw Dad," Serena said. "He had on a ski mask. He stabbed at her and she fell and he ran away."

"I heard Serena scream," Teddy said, frowning at his sister. "I came out and she was standing there, white-faced, over Emma's body."

"And you never told . . . ?" Jamie asked.

"Serena bent down and came up with the knife. I yelled at her and she dropped it and ran back to the bedroom. She said Dad did it. Killed Emma. I believed her. Emma was different than you. I knew it even then. She was older, sexy, brash . . . I knew she was more Dad's type, and that was maybe why he killed her. I was sick with relief to hear she was okay. Only she wasn't. Not really."

Jamie just stared at him.

"I grabbed the knife and hid it inside the secret drawer of the coffee table," Teddy said.

Jamie's gaze moved to the coffee table.

Turning to look at Serena, Teddy said, "Only it *wasn't* Dad. He was still at the charity event. We just didn't know it. Serena wanted to tell, but I wouldn't let her."

Serena was looking off into space. "No, you wouldn't let me."

"Serena's had some trouble making serious attachments ever since. . . ." Teddy didn't take his eyes off her.

Serena's gaze dropped to the coffee table. "Do you think it's still there?"

Teddy glanced down, and Jamie's eyes followed as well. To Jamie's shock, he bent down to the table, slipped his hand underneath. After several seconds of him fumbling beneath it, a shallow drawer slid outward. Inside was a knife with rust-colored flecks of what looked like dried blood on the blade.

"My God," Jamie whispered.

"I've wanted to tell you so many times," Teddy said. "I

just didn't know if I should. But you say now that it was Dr. Metcalf?"

"We have to take that . . . we have to get it to the police . . ." Jamie stammered.

"They'll arrest Dad," Serena said.

"No, they won't." Teddy was adamant. "You know it wasn't Dad. It was Emma's lover!"

Serena's eyes slid toward the kitchen. "I heard her talking to him on the phone. I tiptoed to the hall door and looked out through the crack. She was pacing around. Upset. She was on the wall phone yelling at Dad, and he was yelling at her, too. I could hear his voice. They were having an affair. He was trying to get away from her, but Emma wouldn't let him go. She said she was going to tell. She said, 'What'll Nadine think of you then?' Then her other lover came in and wanted her to give him up, and she yelled at him, too. She screamed at him that she was going to marry Dad."

"It wasn't Dad!" Teddy moaned. "Jesus, Serena. Get a grip."

"That . . . that was Dug . . . Patrick Douglas . . ." Jamie said. "He wasn't Emma's lover."

Serena slowly wagged her head from side to side. "That's not true."

Teddy said quietly, "I stay close to Serena because reality is difficult for her sometimes."

Serena glared at him. Then she bent down and picked up the knife from its bed inside the secret drawer. Both Jamie and Teddy stared at her with real concern.

"Put that down," Jamie ordered.

"What are you doing?" Teddy asked, aghast as Serena lifted the knife above her head. Teddy thrust out his hands in front of himself. "Stop," he whispered, stepping toward her.

To Jamie's horror, Serena suddenly thrust downward, slicing into one of Teddy's outstretched hands.

* * *

Cooper left the Kearns' home and drove back into town, his head full of questions. Did he believe Bette? It was possible. But it was a hunch more than a fact. But it was also a hunch that had led him to Alain Metcalf.

His phone rang, and he saw it was Howie. "Did the Winkelmans connect with you again?" Howie asked. "They called the station. Said they needed to talk to you. I meant to tell you and forgot till now. You're probably out partying."

"I'm not partying and I haven't heard from the Winkelmans."

"They're convinced their daughter's suicide note is a fake. They say the 'S' is hers, but the body of the text is someone else's handwriting. I figured we'd send it to a handwriting expert and put the matter to rest. The Winkelmans wanted you to call them. Were pretty insistent about it. That's why I wondered if you'd talked to them."

"Okay, I'll call them tomorrow," he said, then clicked off.

An "s." A capital "S." Had Gwen been trying to write something other than "Sorry"?

"You're all lying to me!" Serena cried. "I know what I saw. Dad was there. He was mad at Emma. He chased her into the living room!"

"That was Dr. Metcalf," Jamie said again.

"No! *No!*" She violently shook her head. "I'm not crazy!"

Teddy held one hand with the other. Blood ran in rivulets down his arm. "No one thinks you're crazy."

"Gwen did. I went to her for help, but she looked at me in *that way*. And then that babysitter . . ." She stopped for a moment, fighting emotion. "She looked at you the same way Emma looked at Dad. . . ."

"For the last time, Serena. It wasn't Dad!" Teddy roared. Then he stopped himself. "That babysitter?" he repeated, as gooseflesh rose on Jamie's arms. "Is that why you left dinner early that night? To attack *Marissa*?"

"These women . . . I know you don't see it, but these women, these awful, evil women, are out to get you . . . that Bette person wouldn't leave you alone. I had to protect you. I needed to stop them. . . ." She swept the knife Jamie's way. "You won't succeed. All of you who are trying to break us up."

"I'm not trying to break you up," Jamie said. What time was it? If Cooper texted, could she get to her phone? It was inside her purse, and the purse was in the kitchen.

"Liar," Serena whispered. "You're all such liars."

"Serena, I—" Teddy began just as she leaped toward Jamie.

Jamie stumbled backward, but Serena was on her. They fell into the wall, and Teddy jumped forward. But Jamie was falling, falling, and Serena slammed the knife downward into Jamie's neck and shoulder. A sharp sting. Jamie slipped to the ground. As Serena pulled back the knife again, Jamie reached up and grabbed her wrist with both hands.

"Serena!" Teddy was behind his sister, grappling with her. She elbowed him in the ear and he fell backward.

Then Jamie heard the back door slam against the wall and Cooper was there, pulling Serena back by her hair. She slashed backward at him, but he caught the wrist Jamie had lost a grip on and slammed Serena's hand into the wall until the bloody knife slipped from her grasp and fell to the carpet.

"Let me go! Let me go!" Serena screamed.

"Serena," Teddy said brokenly.

Her gaze found him and the bloody mess of his left hand. Her face slackened in horror. "Dad . . ." she whimpered, and then her eyes rolled back and Cooper caught her in his arms before she fell to the ground.

Epilogue

Jamie looked critically at the ugly purple slash alongside her neck and shoulder in the bathroom mirror, aware of how lucky she was that the knife had hit her collarbone, saving her from more serious injury.

"Mom?" Harley's voice sounded from outside.

Jamie, who'd just stepped out of a sponge bath, pulled her robe back over her wound and opened the door.

Harley was in the hall and there was a thumping sound coming from Mom's bedroom. It was Emma, determined to move things around so Jamie would move into the room for good.

"Is she moving the vanity?" Jamie asked. "I made the mistake of saying I'd never use it. It's okay, Emma!" she called out.

"Mom," Harley said again. She'd pulled her hair back into a ponytail and was in jeans, sneakers, and a thin blue hoodie. "It's the last football game. I don't want to miss it."

Greer and Tyler had been allowed to play. Some kind of arrangement had been made between the families involved in the thefts and vandalism and Tyler, though not officially charged with a crime, was facing some kind of ongoing sanctions at school. Katie Timbolt was already attending her new school and Cathy had put her house up for sale. She had not used Vicky as her real estate agent.

"I'll get you over to Marissa's in time."

"I'll drive. She's at Mr. Haynes's."

"I know."

In the intervening weeks since Jamie had been injured, Harley had gotten her permit and was desperate for Jamie to let her drive anywhere and everywhere. Marissa was staying with Cooper more, because Laura had taken a job as a receptionist at one of the medical offices around Glen Gen, the job she'd held before marrying Cooper, while she worked out not living with David Musgrave any longer. Since irregularities with the law firm's books had been found out, she'd lost his financial support, and not only had the deal to buy in Staffordshire Estates fallen through, David had been unable to help with any household expenses. Laura was leaning on Marissa's father for child support, which he'd never been either willing or able to make. Cooper was helping her out through this rough time, and in return, she'd stopped fighting him for Marissa, at least temporarily.

Jamie finished getting dressed and climbed into the Camry with Harley at the wheel. Though her daughter was a conscientious driver, Jamie was still white-knuckling it everywhere they went. Through the rearview mirror she saw a black SUV cruise by on the road behind them, a near clone to the one Serena had used as she'd followed various women she considered threats around River Glen. An icy frisson slid down her spine.

"Is Emma sure she wants to go?" Harley asked as she tentatively backed out of the drive.

"She says she is."

"Yeah, but is she?"

Jamie had put Emma's name on the list for a one-bedroom apartment in Ridge Pointe. Though they were still working out the details of how much money David, and Elgin before him, who'd been the originator of playing fast and loose with clients' investment money, pooling it in an account that violated all kinds of legal rules, it appeared that Emma had been right all along: Mom had set aside funds for her.

"It's going to be a while until we get it all worked out," Jamie said.

Teddy Ryerson had put his parents' home up for sale. After everything that had happened, he didn't want the memories. He'd talked to Nadine and was planning a move up to Bellevue, so Anika and Oliver would be near their grandmother. Teddy was planning to bring his clients with him to a national investment firm that had offices in the area. In the meantime, he was still working to extricate the money Mom had set aside for Emma.

"Are you going to get the car going this weekend?" Harley asked as she climbed out of the Camry at Cooper's house. She was angling for Mom's Outback.

"Yes, yes. I said I would."

"Just checking." She gave Jamie a bright smile.

Cooper walked out the front door as Harley hurried inside. He came up to Jamie's window. "You look good," he said, smiling at her.

"So do you. Maybe I'll come over later . . ."

"Feeling up to it?"

"I think so."

Teddy had actually taken the worst of Serena's attack on the both of them. His right hand had required extensive surgery and there was more on the horizon. He'd been told he might never regain full use of his right hand. Luckily, he was left-handed.

Serena completely lost touch with reality after stabbing her brother and was currently checked into a mental facility in Salem, about an hour's drive down I-5 from River Glen. Teddy had explained that she'd always struggled with personal relationships. The events of the night of Emma's attack had been forever mixed up in her head and she'd resisted any other narrative than the one she'd made up for herself, especially now, in the throes of a full psychotic break upon seeing what she'd done to Teddy. She was still convinced that Emma had been trying to steal their father away, and her un-shakeable belief had morphed into possession and jealousy of Teddy, who she was convinced was being lured by evil, conniving women like Bette Kearns, whom he'd briefly dated, and the babysitter, Marissa, who was a stand-in for Emma. Her sessions with Gwen Winkelman, which no one had known of, not even Teddy, had devolved from Serena knowing there was something wrong with her and seeking clarity, to prolonged rants about those "women" who were out to steal Teddy's soul. Realizing Gwen was on to her, Serena devised the poisoning with tetrahydrozoline. She hadn't wanted to hurt Gwen, not like the other women, but she'd had to eliminate her to keep her from revealing Serena's descent into madness.

Now Jamie said, "Harley's really got a thing for Greer Douglas."

"I'm not going to hold pranking Marissa against him," Cooper said. "But Dug, holding out all these years . . . that's another story."

Jamie nodded. She'd met Teri, Greer's mother, a time or two, but had yet to reconnect with Dug. He was either on the road, checking in on his insurance agencies, or warming a seat at the Waystation.

"Vicky said Race and Deon have finally put their house in her hands. She has a buyer," Jamie said.

"Good. I'd hate to see it go into foreclosure."

"She's being very secretive about the buyer, but I get the feeling it might be someone we know."

"Huh." Cooper shook his head. "It's a big property, but to bring it back is going to be a helluva lot of work. You know who it is?"

"I've got a guess," she said. "Nate Farland. Camryn's boyfriend. She told me his job was 'something in tech,' but apparently, it's a pretty big something. He's going to move to River Glen instead of having her come to Seattle."

"Good," he said, meaning it.

"One more reason to stay."

"Just one more?" he asked.

"Give me a kiss and I'll see you later." She smiled.

He leaned in and laid a long one on her, then waved his hands in front of his face as if he were going to pass out from the heat of it. Jamie laughed.

She drove home, thinking how good it was they'd come this far. During her recovery, Cooper had been by her side nearly every minute. She'd been released fairly quickly after she was patched up, but Cooper had only recently relaxed his vigil over her.

Now that they knew who was behind the attacks on Marissa and Bette, Cooper had worked on the last pieces of the puzzle concerning Emma's attack. He'd interviewed more of the staff at Glen Gen who'd worked with Alain Metcalf and had uncovered the fact that Irene Whelan had suspected the doctor's affair with her daughter. Though there was no proof, it was likely that Irene had confronted Metcalf, which was what made him decide to cool things with Emma, which had led to the fight. Even though Metcalf was known for liking decidedly younger women, he'd begun cozying up to Nadine Ryerson, the trust fund baby. He'd seized the opportunity of the charity event to get closer to her. But then Emma kept calling him from the Ryersons'. Possibly, he'd hoped to keep that relationship going even while he was wooing Nadine away from her husband, but Emma had made that impossible. She really felt they were going to marry. He likely spiked Nadine's drink then raced over to the Ryersons' while she was unconscious. Had he intended to attack Emma all along? Was that why he brought the ski mask, or had it just been in his vehicle? Maybe he'd planned to try to reason with Emma, let her down easy, but she hadn't seen it that way and thereby had sealed her fate. Teenaged Emma had always been in control, and maybe that had frightened Metcalf. In the end, he'd grabbed a kitchen knife and stabbed her, likely in a fit of rage.

What he probably didn't know was that Serena had overheard Emma on the phone with him, though she thought it was her father. When the man in a ski mask rushed in and stabbed Emma with the knife, Serena shrank back, tiptoed to her bed, and pretended to be asleep. When she felt she was alone, she went back out and picked up the knife, certain it was her father who'd done the deed. She was almost sorry Emma was still alive. Even though she was only seven, she entertained thoughts of killing her. If Teddy hadn't come out and taken the knife from her, it was hard to know what she would've done.

Back at the house, Jamie hurried up the rear steps. She hesitated at the top and turned back toward the garden and garage. Now was as good a time as any to finally check out Mom's Outback, maybe take it out for a drive as it had been locked away for months.

She went inside the house and into the kitchen, rummaging through the junk drawer for the garage door remote. As she headed back outside, she looked up at the sliver of a moon, hanging low in the darkening sky. Maybe there would be no moon by Halloween, which was only a few days away. She shivered instinctively, her mind on all the masks people wore.

"Jamie."

Jamie gasped, nearly dropping the remote. She glanced back to see Emma standing on the back porch, closing the door behind her. Duchess began barking and scratching at the door. "Duchess, stop," Emma snapped, which caused Duchess to switch to a whine, but she quit scratching.

"You scared me," said Jamie as Emma came down the steps to join her outside the garage.

"What are you doing?" Emma asked.

"I was going to check on Mom's car. See how it's running."

"It's dark out."

"I know, but I didn't feel like waiting till tomorrow. I've barely looked inside the garage."

"I haven't seen it in a while," Emma said, making Jamie wonder if she meant the garage or the car.

She pressed the button and the garage door began humming upward, and the light attached to the roof automatically turned on. The Subaru's green hatchback was in front of Jamie and she tested it to see if it was locked. It opened easily on hydraulics to show the inside of the back cargo space, its carpet immaculately clean.

"Mom took care of her car," Jamie observed.

Emma didn't answer. Jamie looked around and saw that Emma was focused on some shelving cluttered with cans of weed killer, a spade, a rake, and other gardening items, all held up by concrete blocks.

Jamie recalled the light that had danced across the yard, ending at the garage at about the same spot as that shelving. She stared at the blocks. They were a daisy pattern. Just like Cooper had told her he'd seen in the security tape of Metcalf's murder.

"I stayed with the car," said Emma.

"What?" Jamie asked, her gaze riveted on the blocks, the hairs on her arms lifting in premonition.

"I stayed with the car while she did it."

Jamie slowly turned to Emma, who gave a full-body shudder. "She?" Jamie asked.

"She had to do it for justice."

Jamie's heart started beating in her ears. "You were in the car while our mother . . . murdered Dr. Metcalf . . . ?"

"Alain. She hit him with that one." Emma pointed to one of the concrete blocks. Jamie leaned forward, then took a step closer, bending to look at it closely. There were tiny traces of rust-colored flecks on the daisy pattern.

"Our mother killed Dr. Metcalf?" Jamie asked again faintly.

Emma patted Jamie on the shoulder. "Mom knew. That's why she called you home."